SERPENT BOY

"A thrilling adventure story that reveals a family's forbidden secrets. I couldn't put it down!"

—Barbara Weisberg, author of *Strong Passions*

"Serpent Boy is a remarkable story—intensely felt and beautifully written."

—David Black, award-winning novelist, journalist, and screenwriter

"Serpent Boy is a tremendous and eye-opening journey into a world of family secrets, heartbreak, and ancient traditions. If you want to be taken to lands magical and unknown, this is the book for you."

—Alex Johnson, freelance writer

"Powerful! Serpent Boy will provide an education for new generations to recognize that the ancestral beliefs described in this novel must be abandoned."

—Mamadu Lamarana Bari, PhD, associate professor at the Federal University of Mato Grosso, Mato Grosso, Brazil

"Serpent Boy reveals the unsettling realities of cultural ignorance that still thrive in our world, shedding light on the sad truths that persist today."

—Don Privett, chairman at Boys Hope Girls Hope of New York

SERPENT BOY

SERPENT BOY

SULEIMANE CAMARA

SONCATA PRESS

New York, New York

This edition first published in 2024 by Soncata Press LLC.
   340 West 57 Street, Suite 2C
   New York, NY 10019
   www.soncatapress.com

Hardback ISBN: 979-8-9898574-9-4
Paperback ISBN: 979-8-9898574-5-6
E-book ISBN: 979-8-9908510-4-7
Audiobook ISBN: 979-8-9908510-5-4

Library of Congress Control Number: 2024941389

Cover design by Howard Grossman

Attn: Educational Institutions and Businesses:
Soncata Press books are available at special quantity discounts with bulk purchase
for educational, business, or sales promotional use. For information, please write
to contact@soncatapress.com.

To my beloved wife, Mariama Balde, without whom this book would not exist. You believed in me when I doubted myself and provided invaluable feedback. Thank you for your unwavering dedication and love.

Throughout this book, you'll encounter terms in Fulani, Mandinka, and Guinea-Bissau Creole.
To enhance your reading experience, a glossary has been included at the back of the book, providing expanded definitions in addition to cultural and regional information.

PROLOGUE

The strong smell of fresh cow dung, used to smear the floors, filled the room. It was a smell Maladho knew well, but that night, it kept him from falling asleep quickly. As he finally neared sleep, in that groggy, half-awake phase, a faint sound reached his ears. It was the muffled sobs of his mother, then her frantic whispering. "Shouldn't we do something? They might kill the boy!"

"No need to panic," came his father's reply, his tone cool and calm. "They're just taking him back home. Hush, let's not disturb Maladho."

When he woke the next morning, he found his cousin Kamboda missing.

CHAPTER ONE

THE WHISPER

Maladho N'Gayou's footsteps crunched through the dry foliage and grass, a crisp, rustling soundtrack on his journey toward the compound where his life's story began. Now in his thirties, each step seemed to echo with the weight of years, drawing him deeper into the remnants of Kopiro, his childhood village, now just a shadow of its former self. He paused, eyes wide with a blend of disbelief and nostalgia, taking in the landmark of his once-vibrant home. With care, he pulled out his camera, the soft clicks of the shutter capturing the poignant scenes of a time that once was.

Nestled by the Koff Label River in the savanna of eastern Guinea-Bissau, Kopiro was the vibrant heart of the Mana province, known far and wide, connected to the brave Kopironkos tribe, and named after the legendary Queen Kopirondin Kumo. The stories and glory of Kopiro hung in the air, a quiet testament to a rich but fading past.

But as Maladho's camera clicked, capturing the stillness, it was apparent time had taken its toll, leaving only memories behind. Nature had claimed the town, with plants and trees standing where laughter and life once filled the air. Even the animals seemed to stay away, leaving the village in peaceful solitude.

This was the first time he returned to the land of his early years, the land he and his mom ran away from to stay alive. He hoped to see many differences but never expected the reality he faced. If he could bring back the past, undoubtedly, he would have done so.

Maladho walked around the landmarks, seeing signs of mud huts. Maladho approached the old water well, a place full of memories from his childhood, and as he leaned in closer, a mix of earthy scents filled the air. The water seemed to ripple, as if it recognized him after so many years. His shadow reflected and danced. He remembered when he and his friends used to stand there and yell so they could hear their voices echoing. They used to have so much fun, until one scary day, a little girl tried to imitate them and fell into the well. The whole village rushed to rescue her. Thankfully, she was okay, just a few scrapes on her head. After that, Maladho wasn't allowed to play near the well anymore. Some of the older folks in the village whispered that a restless spirit lived in the well who got upset and pushed the little girl just to scare the other children away.

Maladho turned to the stone where the women used to wash their clothes and scrub their heels. He used to sit naked on that stone to take a bath, where he spent most of the time singing and whistling. Grandmother N'naa-Sona used to tease him. "Shameless boy sitting here naked in broad daylight! No girl will want you, naughty boy!" she would say, joking.

Maladho left the well and went to the mango tree. The tree was still standing intact and in the same shape. The mango tree was a silent sentinel in the heart of the compound. He stood motionless as if he were talking to the tree about a serious business. It had some secrets he needed to know. If the mango tree could speak, Maladho would have asked it about the whereabouts of his cousin or what had happened the night they took him, the night when Kamboda mysteriously vanished when they were both eight years old. Standing in the exact spot where Kamboda used to sit brought forth the memories of that night.

Suddenly, a breeze rustled the tree's leaves, and small branches snapped and fell, bringing Maladho out of his reverie. It felt as if the tree was trying to speak to him, to share the secret of what happened the night Kamboda was taken. It was a mystery nobody talked about. Even his parents, whom he trusted, hadn't given him answers. They told him, "Kamboda was taken home," and nothing more. Those words left him wondering, trying to picture the place that was meant to be called "home." The more Maladho dug, the more afraid he became about Kamboda's tragic destiny. He wanted to tell his mind that everything was a lie, a fabrication like the one he used to hear as a child.

Maladho turned and walked back to the truck where the driver was waiting, cool and patient. He didn't look back at the town of his past. "Let's go," he said as he climbed into the truck. "I am sorry for taking so long."

The driver shrugged and started the vehicle. "Never mind, I like this place. I was enjoying nature. Isn't as bad as people describe it out there."

Maladho looked at him without saying a word. Kopiro had become bitter in people's mouths and memories over the years. What he heard in Koyang when he was a kid during the days before he ran away was surreal and scary. Most talk about it, but they don't know what really happened.

The car bounced and jolted on the rough road, swerving around large holes and fallen branches. After a bumpy ride, they finally arrived at Koff Label, the most beautiful river in

Mana, and got out to take in the scenery. It stretched out to other provinces and had continuously fed the villages around it by providing tasty fish and watering their crops. After what happened, most of the water was gone, leaving just a small stream trickling eastward. The rest was mud, except for the Woudou area, a spot even the bravest villagers avoided. Under huge trees and thick vines, it was always shadowy and eerie. Even now, Woudou was still full of water, looking darker and more frightening than ever. It was said that whatever ended up in Woudou rarely made it out.

People believed the river's spirit guardian lived there. In Kopiro, every person, locals and visitors, had at some point seen the giant snake, known as the master of the river, slithering through the waters. The creature would slither from its hiding place on Fridays at noon to sunbathe. It was possible to see the colossal turtle in that place as well, which the elders said was the worker that dug the river. Kids weren't sure what to believe, except that Woudou had something mystical in it.

After walking around the banks of the river, reliving the memories of his childhood, Maladho and the driver finally left. They drove off on the unpaved, bumpy road once again. Maladho put his sunglasses on and acted as if he were sleeping. After nearly two hours, he took them off and peeked in the rearview mirror. There was a cloud of thick, red dust billowing behind them as if chasing after the car, angry as though they'd taken something. The quicker they drove, the bigger and more dramatic the cloud of dust grew, swirling and dancing in the air like it had a mind of its own.

Maladho broke his long silence. "I spent my childhood in that abandoned village. I used to swim and play in that river."

The driver glanced at Maladho with a look on his face

that said he could sense Maladho's special bond with the village and the river. But he couldn't realize how much this connection had shaped Maladho's life, the way he saw the world and other people. The driver couldn't possibly know about the terrible thing that happened to Maladho's cousin, something so terrible it almost cost Maladho his own life. *What really happened there?* he thought to himself as he watched the dust storm behind them.

The driver pulled him from his thoughts by asking, "Sir, what happened to the village?"

Maladho thought for a minute before replying. "Only my grandpa knows the answer to that."

"Is he still alive?" the driver questioned, curiosity filling his voice.

Maladho chuckled. "I don't know."

The driver may have thought Maladho faked the answer, but he was honest. Karamoko's death was a mystery. He vanished and never came back. A hunter returned his clothes to the compound, which were found near the river. Maybe he drowned, or he killed himself. One thing was for sure, his body had not been recovered. People gossiped, saying different things depending on which side they supported. His followers would say that his forefathers took him to become the supreme sage like Kopirondin, the matriarch of Kopironkos, and he would return to conquer the world. His opposers believed the river took him as vengeance for the evil things he had committed.

After the journey, the truck rolled into the city as the evening began to settle in. Bissau was semi-dark, softly illuminated by the headlights of cars and the soft flicker of kerosene lanterns from street vendors. The streets were alive and bustling. Old Mercedes-Benz taxis filled the roads, moving like a swarm of ants, each one honking and rushing to grab passengers in a hurry. The air was heavy with the scent of diesel and the lingering heat from the day. In between all this hustle, there were the old vans, called toka-tokas, picking up folks who needed a cheaper ride. It was a busy mix of lights, sounds, and movement, everyone pushing forward in the dim glow of the city.

Street vendors zigzagged between cars and lined up along the sidewalks, each one eagerly showing off their goods. They called out their wares—homemade juice, cool water in squishy plastic bags, SIM cards, clothes, radios, and more—trying to get people to buy. Close to the curb, makeshift stalls of food and various goods added to the lively mix. The aroma of local dishes filled the air, mingling with the buzz of voices and laughter. It was a vibrant scene, each vendor adding their own color to the tapestry of Bissau at night.

When Maladho arrived at his home, his gatekeeper, M'bemba, went to turn on the generator since there wasn't any light. The city lights weren't reliable. If residents were lucky, they might have two hours of light after dusk. Most people had a generator, making the city noise nearly unbearable. With all those generators rumbling, the neighborhoods sounded like a construction site with heavy machines working all over the place.

After a shower, Maladho grabbed a quick snack and then dialed his mom's number. "Hey Mom, good evening. I wasn't sure if you'd be asleep already," he said when she picked up.

"Hello, my boy," Fenda answered, her voice groggy. "I was dozing off, but your call woke me. I was just thinking about you, wondering if you'd swing by for dinner."

Rather than answering, he said, "Mom, you won't believe it. Guess where I went today?" Too excited to wait for her guess, he said, "I visited Kopiro!" There was a pause on the other end. "Mom? Mom, you still there?" he asked, a bit worried.

Fenda was quiet, as if her mind was somewhere else.

"Hello, Mom? Can you hear me?" Maladho asked again.

"Yes, I'm here," she replied, her voice now a bit stern and wide awake.

"Oh, I thought the call dropped," he said, trying to lighten the mood.

"Maladho, I told you many times to avoid going to that place. You are so stubborn! This is the problem with you young folks who are educated in the white people's land. You think you can just ignore our ways. You defy everything! You underestimate our reality," his mom said, her tone full of concern, her frustration evident.

Maladho knew his mom had always been against him going back to Kopiro and understood she wouldn't be happy about him not listening to her advice. "Mom, I'm sorry. I didn't mean to upset you. I just really wanted to see, after all these years, where I was born. I'm sorry," he said gently.

"Maladho, my boy, you know I love you. But please, I can't go through that pain again. You were so little when we left. Maybe that's why you don't understand why I don't want you back there. But you must feel that Kopiro is still not a safe place," Fenda replied.

"Okay, Mom," Maladho said, hearing the concern in her voice. They talked for a bit more, and he promised to visit for lunch the next day.

After they hung up, he thought about his mom's words. Although it had been many years, he still remembered the day they fled from Kopiro. *Why can't she just leave the past behind?* he wondered. He turned on his laptop and plugged in his USB to transfer the photos he had taken in Kopiro. While looking through them, he noticed a blurry area in one of the pictures near the mango tree. He squinted and tried to zoom in for a closer look, but it remained too blurry to make out. Unsure what to make of it, he shut off his laptop and went to bed.

The generator's rumble kept Maladho awake most of the night. When he finally fell asleep around four in the morning, his dream was troubling. He was in Kopiro, near the compound. Standing underneath the mango tree was Kamboda with a gloomy look on his face. Maladho ran toward him, but Kamboda started walking away, so he called out, "Kamboda, don't you want to talk to me? I missed you, cousin! Where have you been all this time?" His cousin remained silent and kept walking, heading toward the river. Maladho ran after him. "Wait for me, cousin! I want to talk to you." Kamboda never looked back.

Just when Maladho caught up, reached out . . . the alarm on his phone blared. He jumped out of bed and almost fell to the ground as he reached for it, grabbing the phone as he had been about to grab his cousin's arm in his dream.

Maladho found himself breathing heavily. He wiped the sweat off his brow and headed to the bathroom. He wanted to go back to sleep and talk to Kamboda to understand why his best friend was avoiding him! Instead, he showered, ate breakfast, and got ready to visit his mother for lunch, as promised.

He hopped in his car and headed to the Bandim neighborhood where she lived. On weekdays, the Chapa di Bissau intersection was usually a wild scene with cars zipping and zooming as if each driver was trying to grab a trophy for the most daring stunt on the road. Maladho smiled, thinking of his mom whenever they drive through the busy spot. "Is this the way they drive in other countries too?" she'd ask, her eyes sparkling with amusement. Then she'd laugh and joke,

"If these cars had a choice, they'd probably drive themselves away from all this craziness!" She'd burst into laughter, which would fill the car, followed by her plea, "Oh gods, help us dodge this traffic madness!" To stay out of the traffic chaos, Maladho usually drove only at night or on the weekends, and since it was a Sunday morning, the streets were calm. There were just a few people going about their business, enjoying the peaceful morning.

When he arrived, his mom was outside, sipping on kinkeliba, a favorite hot drink. Kinkeliba is a West African sacred plant used for tea and herbal medicine. It is also known as the health tree or the plant of long life. Older folks often call it the drink of the gods because it can heal many sicknesses. Steam twirled up from her shiny silver cup, swirling and dancing in the soft breeze. The sweet smell filled the air, drawing in bees that buzzed around, almost like they wanted to take that yummy scent back to their hives.

As he walked up to the house, children ran toward him with greetings and asking if he had brought them presents. Maladho smiled as he greeted them with hugs, giving them candy and then joined his mom to take tea.

Fenda was in her fifties but still full of vibrant energy. Life hadn't been easy for her, especially after losing her husband, Demba, and fleeing Kopiro with her young son. She had worked as a cleaner at a mental hospital. But strikes and tough working conditions led her to start selling fish instead. Every morning, she headed to the Bandim port to buy fresh fish from the fishermen, known locally as Nyominkas, to sell at Bandim Market.

Through all this, she managed to support Maladho's studies in medicine in São Paulo, Brazil. Even when Maladho returned with a job at a big hospital, Fenda didn't stop selling fish. Mama Fenda, as everyone called her, was known for her hard work and honesty.

He sat next to her and took a sip of his tea. "Mom, I'm sorry about yesterday. I know you were upset. I promise I won't let you down again," he said. He always tried his best not to upset his mom, knowing all the sacrifices she'd made since his dad passed away.

Fenda gave Maladho a loving look and replied, "Yes, son, I forgive you. But you need to be careful and avoid risks. Remember the old saying, 'The blind man you bump into once will step aside the next time.' I just want to live peacefully and forget about Kopiro."

"I'm really sorry. It won't happen again," Maladho assured her.

"Come, sit on my lap," Fenda said with a smile.

"Mom, I'm a grown man now, and I weigh 209 pounds!"

They both burst into laughter, the mood lightening with their shared joy. Fenda's eyes stayed on Maladho, with a look he recognized as one she got when she was thinking of her late husband. Maladho's height and strength mirrored his father's, and his skin was a stunning deep brown, like the velvet night sky. His nose was long, his eyes wide and full of life, telling silent stories. His smile, effortless and bright, seemed to light up the space, much like Demba's used to.

She had told him once that she could see the essence of Demba living on in him, especially when Maladho smiled or stood with confidence. He wore his style casually but smartly, with his long sleeves neatly rolled up and his crisp white shirt tucked into a pair of stylish gray shorts. It was clear, even in the way he dressed, a part of Demba's spirit was woven into Maladho.

She sighed. "My son, when will you get married? I want to see your child before I die."

"No worries, Mom. Next year, by this time, you will be

happy. I will bring you a beautiful daughter-in-law," Maladho replied, smiling.

"Hurry up! I can't wait, my handsome doctor."

They chatted for a while before Maladho decided to ask his mother about his dream. It was bothering him, and he wanted her advice. "Mom, I had a dream this last night," he said.

"A dream about what?" Fenda asked.

"I saw Kamboda. He was upset and was avoiding me."

Fenda sighed. She closed her eyes for a few minutes as though deep in thought. She then replied, "Poor soul. He must be distraught wherever he might be. But remember, it was just a dream."

He wanted to ask more but decided not to pursue the topic any longer after seeing how talking about Kopiro upset her. He could tell that even though many years had passed, Fenda was still traumatized. Maladho, on the contrary, wanted to understand exactly what had happened to his cousin.

As he sipped the hot kinkeliba, he looked up at the sky. He felt nostalgic about the years he spent in São Paulo. The sky was the same shade of blue as at Praça do Relógio when studying at the university. He used to stare at it, lost in many thoughts to distract himself from thinking about Kamboda's disappearance. He was doing it again now. Although Fenda was talking to him, his eyes remained fixed on the sky as he watched birds fly in formation.

He was interrupted by the sound of girls passing by to fetch water at the nearby well. Two of them walked up and knelt as a sign of respect. They greeted Fenda and Maladho and shook their hands before walking away.

Fenda followed them with her eyes and asked, "Son, what do you think about Binta, the girl on the left? She is the older sister, and she is both beautiful and polite."

"Mom, again? I told you, I am in love with someone. You will meet her soon."

"Do you want to bring someone here from Brazil? Toubabou?" asked Fenda. "I heard white people don't let others play with their kids. I wouldn't get to play with my grandchild! She will never help me cook jamboo or braid my hair."

"Who told you that? It's not true!" Maladho chuckled.

"I like Binta," Fenda continued, as if she hadn't heard him. "She reminds me of your aunt Tombom when she was young. She is so pretty, and I am sure she will give us beautiful kids."

"By the way, where is Auntie Tombom now?" Maladho asked, changing the subject.

"I don't know her whereabouts." She paused. "Poor Tombom, she went through a lot."

Maladho didn't ask more questions, wanting to keep the mood light. He stayed with his mom until dark, leaving after dinner. As he turned the last corner to his house, Maladho's car lights shone on something strange in the darkness. Right in front of his home, there was a weird, shimmering shape. He hit the brakes hard, and his car screeched to a stop. He stared for a few seconds, but then the strange shape vanished into the shadows over his house.

Breathing fast and heart pounding, Maladho quickly tried to reach his mom on the phone, but the call wouldn't go through. "Ugh! Damn it! Why can't these stupid phone companies fix their networks?" he grumbled, slamming the phone against the car dashboard in frustration.

M'bemba swung the gate open as Maladho drove up. Leaning his head out the window, he asked, "M'bemba, have you seen anything weird around here tonight?"

M'bemba shook his head. "No, sir, just the usual wind. Is everything okay, sir? You seem a bit shaken."

Maladho tried to brush it off. "No, it's nothing. Just wondering. You know, sometimes the dark makes your mind think of weird things." He parked and quickly got out of his car before rushing into his apartment.

N'damesse, his girlfriend, was on the couch watching TV. Her petite frame was dressed casually in a snug gray skirt and crisp white blouse, always effortlessly stylish and captivating. Even lounging, her confident posture exuded youthfulness and determination. Her beauty was striking, with her chocolate-colored skin and sharp nose, yet it was her intelligent gaze that truly set her apart. She turned that gaze to him now, likely seeing the fear on his face. "Honey, why are you out of breath? What happened?"

"I am just tired, and I was running up the stairs," he replied. He was bothered by the image he saw outside. But he sat on the couch next to N'damesse and tried to put it out of his mind. *Maybe the wind raised the dust to form that weird shape.*

In the middle of the night, as he lay awake thinking, he put two and two together: the blur in the picture the night before looked like the shimmering image he saw outside that evening. He quickly got out of bed and headed to the living room. He turned on his laptop and searched for the picture. It was still there! Something unexplainable. He still couldn't tell what it was. However, the more he looked at it, the stranger the spot appeared. He zoomed in on the picture again.

This time, he put on his reading glasses and focused. "Strange," he mumbled. An undefinable image was standing right there when he shot the picture. He removed his glasses and rubbed his eyes. He put his glasses on again and stared at the image. It was the same thing he saw while driving. He put his face in his hands and tried to figure out what it was. He studied medicine, had seen corpses and other horrible things. But what he saw tonight was nothing like he had ever seen. It was mysterious, creepy, and terrifying.

N'damesse moved gracefully into the living room, like a sleek cat. "Baby, what's up? It's almost three in the morning, why are you still up?" she asked, concerned. "What's on your mind?"

"It's just work stuff. One of my patients is very ill. I'm not sure he'll make it through the night," Maladho said, not wanting to worry her about the strange thing he'd seen.

"Hey, it's okay, you can't fix everything. You need your rest too," N'damesse reassured him, giving him a comforting kiss on the forehead. She gently led him back to bed.

But Maladho barely slept that night, his mind stuck on the strange shadow. The wind kept howling, and a loose metal sheet clanged outside, making it even harder to rest.

In the morning, N'damesse gently shook him awake. "Maladho. Maladho, it's time to get up, baby."

"Ah, let me sleep a bit more. That noise outside kept me up. Can you ask M'bemba to fix that metal sheet later?" he groaned, still tired. He had planned to have the day off, knowing he'd be tired from his trip. He rolled over and got a little more sleep. Eventually, he got up for a shower.

When he came into the kitchen, he found N'damesse had made breakfast. As he sat down to eat, he came to a decision. "N'damesse, I know we planned to go out today, but something's come up. I need to see my mom."

"But you just got back from there yesterday! You promised today would be our day," N'damesse said, clearly upset.

"I'm really sorry I can't keep my promise. We'll go out

later, okay?"

She sighed in defeat. "I guess you've already made up your mind." But her tone made it clear she was suspicious.

"Please, don't think I'm lying. I just need to talk to my mom about something serious," Maladho tried to explain.

"Why can't you tell me what it is? I'm your girlfriend. Shouldn't you trust me?" N'damesse asked, half-joking, half-serious.

"It's just a mother-son thing, nothing to worry about," he said, hesitating to tell her the real reason. He still didn't want to worry her with what he saw last night. "I'll be back soon."

When he got to his mother's house, Fenda wasn't home. He tried calling her a bunch of times, but there was no signal. One of the neighborhood girls said Fenda might be at the market, so Maladho drove off, his car kicking up dust and gravel.

When he got to the market, his nose was greeted by a cacophony of smells. There was the strong smell of fresh fish, the clean scent of vegetables, and the many aromas and spices of other foods all mixing together in the busy, noisy market. He found Fenda, busy with her fish, getting ready for the day. "Mom, good morning." he said as he approached.

Fenda looked up, surprised. "Oh! What brings you here, Maladho?"

"I needed to see you."

"You look troubled. What's the matter?" she pressed.

"Mom, I really need to figure something out. You're the only one who can help," Maladho pleaded.

"Let's talk in your car then." She took his hand as they walked over.

Once seated in the car, Maladho shared the details about the weird image he saw.

Fenda held his hand, trying to make him feel better. "Relax, son. I'm here for you. Don't let fear get the best of you," she soothed him.

He opened his laptop and showed her the photo. "Look at this, Mom. Tell me I'm just seeing things. This can't be a mere coincidence. This image from Kopiro is the same as the shimmering figure I saw last night," Maladho insisted, zooming in on the picture.

Fenda studied the photo. "Maladho," she said gently, "what you're showing me is probably just a blur from moving the camera or a leaf drifting past just as you were about to snap the picture. It's nothing. As for the shimmering image, perhaps you were drunk last night, and you saw the dust raised by the wind and associated it with the figure in the picture. By the way, you should stop drinking," she added.

"Mom, I don't drink anymore." Maladho grew frustrated. "It feels like something's after me," he insisted.

"Maladho, please. I've told you so many times not to go to Kopiro. You went anyway, thinking you're all grown up. And now you are bothering me with this conversation," she scolded.

"Mom, I just need some information—" Maladho started, but before he could finish, Fenda opened the car door and went back to her fish stall, leaving him alone with his thoughts.

Maladho sped off, his car tires screeching on the tarred road. He drove so fast that he ran over some trash on the street and almost hit a person walking. "Why won't she trust me?" he muttered, hitting the dashboard and steering wheel in frustration. His car swerved a bit, almost hitting the curb. Other drivers saw him driving carelessly and honked at him.

Suddenly, his phone rang. It was N'damesse, but he

didn't answer. The phone rang again, and he was now very annoyed. He grabbed it to turn it off but saw it was his mom this time. He hesitated, not sure if he wanted to listen to more of her warnings. Finally, he answered.

She spoke first. "Hello! Maladho, are you there?"

"Yes, Mom," he said after a pause.

"I'm sorry you're upset. Please come back. We need to go somewhere."

Maladho made a quick U-turn and headed back to the market. His mom was waiting with a black plastic bag. "Let's go to Antula. We're going to see Uncle Ossanti," she told him.

"Mom, I don't think we need a sorcerer. I just need one little piece of information to solve this puzzle."

"Just drive, Maladho. You get into trouble because you don't listen," she said firmly.

They drove off the main road into Antula, bumping along a rough path toward big kapok trees. They parked under their shade. Beneath the trees, it was nice and cool, with little bits of sunlight coming through the leaves. The air smelled clean and a little like wet dirt and foliage. The soft whispering of the trees made it feel calm and mysterious, as though it were a secret place.

There, under the trees, sat an old man smoking his pipe, the smoke curling up into the air. He wore a red cloth wrapped around his head and another one covering his body. As they walked toward him, he spat out black tobacco.

"N'yu Ossanti, good morning," Fenda greeted, waving.

"Morning. Is that my daughter, Fenda?" the old man asked.

"Yes, it's me, Uncle," she replied.

"What brings you here so early?"

"We've come to see you. You know we can't face the world

without your guidance," Fenda said as she approached him for a hug.

"Oh, Fenda, you're truly blessed by the gods, a real Kopironko." They hugged, and then he hugged Maladho too. "Doctor, please don't let me die before the festival," Ossanti joked. They all laughed. "Is he still as stubborn as ever?" he asked Fenda, still chuckling.

"Yes, he's as hardheaded as they come," Fenda agreed. "Uncle Ossanti, I brought your favorite fish," she said, handing him the bag.

"Ah, you read my mind, Fenda. I was just wondering what to eat with my rice today. Thank you." Ossanti took the bag gratefully. They sat quietly for a bit. Uncle Ossanti didn't need to ask why they were there. He chatted away, arranging his little figurines and masks. Inside the bag with the fish, Fenda had also packed some brandy. He spotted the bottle, grinned, and took a sip. "This is a good day!" he declared.

After more casual conversation, Uncle Ossanti finally got down to business. "You are not here just to visit me." He nodded and turned to Maladho. "Come here, my hardheaded boy." Maladho approached him, and he laid his hand on Maladho's head, lifting his hand and placing it again, repeatedly, as he performed the ritual. Uncle Ossanti shook his head. "I smell fear and anxiety. Don't let the fear consume you, son. In addition, Kopironkos never fear. We do not want the past to repeat itself."

He must have seen the worry in Maladho's eyes because his voice softened as he said, "Don't worry, son. We occasionally face moments like this of fear and confusion, but it reminds us that we have battles to fight, gods to fear, and forefathers to honor. I will look it up carefully and diagnose it, then let you know."

Ossanti's words put Fenda and Maladho at ease and they

relaxed. The conversation turned casual again and a few minutes later, they left. But on the drive back to the market, Maladho's thoughts were still swirling.

As he dropped her off in front of the market, he tried to convince Fenda before she got out of the car. "Mom, regardless of what I saw last night or what happened back in Kopiro, we should talk about it because we all know what may have happened."

"What are you talking about?"

"I mean about Kamboda." He paused. "This can't be a permanent taboo."

"Son, please don't be as stubborn as your grandpa, who started this for no reason." She paused and wet her lips. "I told you to let it go, let it pass. We don't want more trouble. I know how hard it was to be able to bring you up and survive till now."

"Do you prefer to see other kids face the same thing? Let's fight this and end everything. It is the best we can do to bring our pride back. To some extent, I know what happened, but I need more information!"

"So, you know what happened when you were just a little boy?"

"I overheard the conversation in the Koyang when Grandpa was arguing with Jaigol."

"That means you do know what happened! Son, that was just the smoke. The fire had started years before you were born."

Chapter Two

THE OFFERING

Years ago, Bakar Kumo was the boy everyone in town knew. He was popular not just because he was the son of the Kopironkos leader, Karamoko, but also because he was extremely good-looking. Bakar was fit and strong, with a bright smile, and amazing in every way.

Kaawu-Garanké's daughter, Tombom, was considered the most beautiful girl in Mana, and everyone wanted her as their wife. Rich and powerful families asked him for her hand in marriage. Rumors flew that he had made a deal with the spirits or that he wanted her to marry someone from another world! Some even said spirits turned into princes to win her over. But Kaawu-Garanké had other plans, and everyone was buzzing with guesses until he finally said who he wanted Tombom to marry.

Kaawu-Garanké was from Guyankos, the infamous tribe known for stealing. A true Guyanko must steal, and that makes them proud; they show their bravery when they steal, not just anything, but something precious. Despite Kaawu-Garanké's origins in that tribe, he was a man of character, hardworking, and committed.

Tombom would tell her parents she was going to get water from the stream, but she was really meeting Bakar.

They would sneak off to the edges of Kankelifa, a place not too far from Kopiro, and sit under a tambakoumba tree, chatting and enjoying their secret time away from everyone else.

Once, under the tree, Tombom was resting her head on Bakar's lap and looking up at him with a smile. The sweet smell of tambakoumba fruit was in the air, insects buzzed around, checking out the yummy fruit, while the trees whispered and birds chirped as if they were gossiping about the couple. "My Bakar," Tombom called him. She sat up and leaned against him. "My father had a family meeting last night."

Bakar looked down at her, curious. "What was the meeting about?"

"My fate."

"Hmm! Who's the lucky guy?" He chuckled.

"Stop it, it's serious," she said. "My dad has gone crazy. I don't know who's filling his head with this stuff." She got quiet and looked down at her hands in her lap.

Bakar gently lifted her chin. "Hey, look at me. Don't worry, I love you, and I'll do anything to stay with you, no matter what."

Tombom smiled sweetly at him. "My dad said only the champ of the wrestling match can marry me. And you've never wrestled. How will you win that tough match?"

Bakar was stunned. "Are you serious? The Kopirondin Festival champ?" He paused then sat up a little straighter. "I've never wrestled, but I'll try for you," he said bravely.

Tombom leaned in closer. "I don't want anyone else but you. I want us to be together forever. But it seems impossible. Should we run away and start fresh somewhere else?" she suggested.

"Never. I'm a true Kopironko. We don't run. I'll fight and

win if that's what your dad wants," Bakar declared.

He went home that evening worn out, lying awake, his mind racing for a way to win Tombom's hand. He was up against a huge challenge. Wrestling wasn't his thing, and the competition was just three months away.

As the sun rose, Bakar eagerly got out of bed, ready to head to the farm. His adopted cousin, Demba, was also preparing to go. The two were around the same age and had a close relationship. Demba's past was a secret; he had been taken in by Karamoko when he was sick and seeking refuge. He was brought in on a donkey-pulled cart and has been welcomed under Karamoko's care ever since.

They walked to the farm in silence, and Demba kept glancing at Bakar with concern. When they arrived, Demba turned to his cousin and asked, "Brother, are you ok?"

Bakar seemed distracted when he answered, "I am fine, just tired."

"Hmm, you usually excitedly fill me in on your dates with Tombom as soon as you finish saying hello. Your date yesterday not as good as usual? Tell me," Demba said.

Bakar didn't respond.

"Don't mind women. They drive you sometimes. They make sure you love them, and a woman like Tombom loves you, and she doesn't want to share you. Beautiful women are greedy," Demba said. He chuckled and tapped his cousin on the shoulder.

That speech didn't move him at all, and Bakar barely reacted. Demba's laughter died away and he took on a more serious tone. "Bakar, tell me. I am your brother. I will help you if I can."

"I know, but you can't help me with this."

"What is that? Just tell me."

Bakar sighed and relayed the conversation he had with

Tombom and his plans to learn how to wrestle.

Demba grinned and clapped his cousin on the back. "Brother, we can try. It seems complicated, but it's not impossible. Don't worry! We will start training after work."

Bakar gave him a skeptical look, but there was a hint of a smile on his lips.

After work, they entered the bush and went straight to the kapok tree. Demba clapped his hands and shuffled his feet on the soft brown sand. "Bakar, this is our lesson number one. Always be prepared. Let's get to it." His tall, muscular form dropped into a fighting stance.

"Wow, wow, calm down!" Bakar held up his hands to calm his cousin. "Do you think a little knowledge will function in that competition? I need a real trainer, not an amateur, because winning the competition is my only chance to marry Tombom."

Demba just laughed and tackled his cousin to the sand without warning. "Lesson number two: Never underestimate an opponent," Demba said.

On the floor, Bakar groaned. "Hey, hey, hey, calm down; it hurts." He laughed and decided to give it a try.

Over the next three months, Demba taught him how to wrestle, and Bakar soon realized that Demba knew a lot more than he originally claimed. No one in Kopiro had seen Demba exhibit this level of skill, and he wondered how his cousin had mastered the sport and yet had never competed in the festival. Bakar set a training goal to best Demba in combat, a difficult task considering how tough his cousin was. Every day, Demba put him through heavy and skillful training. He was amazed by his own progress, but by the end of the second month, Bakar still couldn't pass the combat test. He was strong and fast but lacked the most important thing: concentration.

During one particular training session, Demba took Bakar down again. Demba held out a hand to help him up, but Bakar slammed his arms in the sand in frustration. "How am I supposed to do this? It has been two months, and I still haven't achieved my training goals. I can't pass!"

Demba replied calmly, "Brother, I know you can make it. Everything should be calculated, that's why your head is on top of your body. Clear your mind and focus. Don't think about anything else except winning." He held out his hand again.

This time Bakar took it. He brushed himself off and took a deep breath, centering his state of mind. Releasing the breath from his lungs, he squared off again with his cousin.

After an epic battle, Bakar took Demba down for the first time. After the fight, the two of them sat panting and sweating, but Demba had a bright grin on his face.

"You made it. Congratulations! You are a great pupil and a fast learner," Demba said.

"Thanks, master," Bakar said, still panting.

"Please, call me cousin, the way you always have."

"Demba, my beloved cousin, why have you never competed in the festival knowing you have all these skills?" Bakar asked.

"For no particular reason. I just don't want to do it," Demba replied.

"Where did you learn wrestling?"

After a long silence, Demba responded, "My father." Demba had never shared his past or talked about his father with anyone except Karamoko. Karamoko was the only one who knew it and kept it secret.

"May I know who your biological father is?" Bakar asked.

Demba looked at him, his face strained and eyes showing a glint of anger, and shook his head. "It is not that important.

I am just glad Karamoko accepted me and loved me, and I am grateful for that."

"Well, alright, as you said so, cousin."

Demba had been training Bakar nonstop for weeks, getting him ready for the big day. During the training, Demba taught him secret moves that only Demba's dad knew. Yet, to ensure Bakar was ready, there was a final test: Bakar needed to wrestle a wild giant hog. They set out early, heading to the swamp in search of giant Kopiro forest hogs, strong animals that could weigh as much as six hundred pounds. Bakar's task? To wrestle one to the ground using just his hands.

As they waited, hidden under leaves and grass, Demba warned him, "These hogs are like an unstoppable force, always ready to show off their power. It will be tough, but I believe you can prevail." He gave his cousin an encouraging slap on the back.

The sun rose, and they heard the beasts coming. Those Kopiro hogs didn't dodge anything; they always wanted to fight. A massive hog came close to where they lay, crashing through the bushes and sniffing around suspiciously.

Without hesitation, Bakar leaped out and grabbed the giant beast. Just like Demba said, the hog didn't back down. The others ran around, grunting and squealing. The fight was wild. Bakar and the hog, neither scared nor holding back, wrestled fiercely. The hog's tusks sliced Bakar's arms, but he didn't notice. It was like a noisy tank battle, the ground shaking and plants flattening under them.

Then, swiftly, Bakar flipped the beast over and pinned it down. The hog grunted, defeated on the ground and still making an effort to fight back, but Bakar held it down tightly. Moments later, he let the hog go; it ran away, squealing.

Bakar had passed his final test! Thanks to the adrenaline rush, he didn't even feel his wounds, but Demba quickly made a healing paste from herbs and applied it to his cuts. They left the swamp in high spirits. Demba felt Bakar was ready for the competition.

Bakar was all set to try to win Tombom's heart in the upcoming wrestling match. He had the moves, the strength, and even some secret techniques, but he felt something was still missing. He needed one more thing—his dad's blessing, so that the gods and ancestors could accompany him on his journey.

After his family finished their meal that evening, Bakar asked his dad to speak in private. They entered the hut, and Bakar sat on the floor while Karamoko settled on a goat-skin mat.

Karamoko looked at him, a look of worry on his face. "Tell me, son."

Bakar cleared his throat. "I want to make you proud, Dad," he started. His father's eyes lit up, sensing something big was coming. "I am considering joining the Kopirondin Festival wrestling match this year."

Karamoko was stunned, his eyes widened. "Bakar, you have never wrestled, yet you want to compete. Really? Is this what you want to tell me?" he asked.

"Yes. I've been practicing in secret. I'm ready, but I need your blessing," Bakar explained.

A war of emotions crossed his dad's face, a mix of confusion and excitement. He sighed. "If it is real that you want to join, that is fine." He paused. "I remember how great it felt when I won the contest three times as a young man." He paused again before continuing, "You may have been practicing, but you have no idea how tough it is! You know it's a tough competition, right?"

Bakar nodded confidently.

Karamoko looked at his son and made his decision. "I grant you my blessings, may the soul of Kopirondin accompany you, may the ancestors stand by your side, and may the gods choose you over the crowd," Karamoko prayed and blessed him. "Son, winning would make any family proud. But listen, if you won, there's a rumor about a special prize—a cherry on top of the victory cake. It is *tanaa*, forbidden. Stay away from that cherry. Enjoy your victory and the honor but leave that fruit alone. It's off-limits for us."

Bakar quickly agreed. His spirit felt lighter, and he was one step closer to fulfilling his dream. "Thank you, Baaba." He kneeled and kissed his father's feet, and Karamoko grabbed him, lifting him.

The Kopirondin Festival was the most exciting time of the year, happening between November and December just after the rainy season, when all the crops are harvested and there is plenty of food to go around. It was a celebration to show gratitude to their ancestors and the gods, and to remember Queen Kopirondin's bravery, for without her, their world wouldn't be the same. The festival would have games, fashion, art, magic, music, and storytelling. But the highlight was the wrestling match, a showcase of prowess and power. The best wrestler got the popularity and the opportunity to marry beautiful women.

This year, there was only one woman everyone was buzzing about, a girl whose beauty was like no other. They said when Tombom smiled, it was like the stars twinkling at night, and her skin shimmered like the sun's rays by day. Some even whispered she was a magical being, a jinni, because she was just too stunning. But with such beauty came danger. A long time ago, a wise sorcerer had warned her dad to keep her safe because her charm not only attracted admirers but also jealousy.

As the festival's eve arrived, a cloud of dust rose in the distance. People from every village were heading to Kankelifa, the host of this year's festival. Demba and Bakar were among the crowd, riding in on their horses. The village was like a rainbow that had touched the ground. Each hut was a splash of happy colors. Their walls—which were covered in clay and smoothed over with cow dung, making them strong and cool inside—were painted in blues and greens and reds and more, creating true pieces of art. The roofs were made of straw, snug and cozy. And everywhere you looked, fabrics of every color fluttered in the breeze. They hung from poles along the road and from the houses, waving as if saying "hello" to everyone who passed by. It felt like the whole village was throwing its arms wide open, ready to welcome the guests.

The festival was a celebration of colors and joy, a tribute to the gods. Drums beat tirelessly, creating a rhythm that pulsed through the crowd. The village overflowed with offerings of food and the finest palm wine, a generous display of gratitude to the gods of the land and rain. Women, looking like vibrant flowers in bloom, graced the streets. Their smiles, made unique by their bright teeth on dyed gums, were like rays of sunshine. Intricate braids, adorned with beads and shells, crowned their heads, and their skin, caressed by black soap and shea butter, glowed under the sun's gaze.

But the real expectation was for Tombom's appearance. When she finally arrived on the second day, the crowd was captivated, drawn to her like flowers to sunlight. She was so stunning that her beauty seemed almost unreal, like a masterpiece painted by the gods. Her elegance was the kind that made the sun pause in the sky and the breeze whisper more softly. Some men, completely mesmerized, forgot their manners and wrestled in the streets, hoping for a mere glance from her. If not for the vigilant guards, the admiration for her might have turned the festival into chaos. Indeed, even the sun seemed to bow in respect, hiding behind clouds to offer her a gentle shade, acknowledging that her beauty was the true highlight of the day.

Kaawu-Garanké may have been short and sturdy, but you could tell he was once a mighty wrestler. He stood tall among the village elders and Jargas, the village guardians, declaring his wish, "Only a champion wrestler can win my daughter's hand in marriage!"

With that announcement, it felt like even spirits and mysterious beings joined the competition, eager to prove their worth. Every wrestler would give it their all, even turning to magic tricks and visiting powerful wise men. People crowded sacred places and shrines, called jalangs, like Tamba Dibi of the Nyantchos and Gaika-Tchurki of the Kopironkos, seeking blessings, all dreaming of winning the match and marrying Tombom.

The village storytellers, the griots, still talk about how tough and intense the competition was that year. It was like nothing they'd ever seen before. It was wild and chaotic. The air was thick with dust, the sound of the crowd and drums could be heard for miles, and the excitement was electric. Every evening, when the drums rolled out, it was time for another face-off. Every evening, as the drums echoed a new challenge, the wrestlers readied themselves for battle.

The wrestling event was supposed to last just two weeks, but it stretched to almost a month because the wrestlers were so evenly matched. On the first day alone, there were seven ties! Each wrestler had a nickname, and Bakar was known as "the Snake." His style was sneaky, wrapping around his opponent until they stumbled. As time went on, the wrestlers grew fatigued, and some, heartbroken by defeat, took their lives, feeling as though they had lost everything. As the final day approached, only a few were left standing, and the excitement in the village reached its peak.

Karamoko was up all that night preparing a special amulet and praying—hoping—the next day would crown his son as the new champion. When he gave it to Bakar, he asked for a deal. "If you win, you must not marry Tombom. It is tanaa, our tribes are too different, and it would be wrong. I have another girl in mind for you, my friend's daughter, a beautiful woman in her own right."

Bakar reluctantly agreed and took the amulet from his father's hands.

When the big day arrived, the village was buzzing with excitement and nerves. A gentle breeze blew, but only the thunderous sound of drums and other instruments could be heard. It felt like the ground itself was dancing with the rhythm.

In one corner, Bakar was getting ready, his team rubbing his muscles. He wore his father's powerful amulet and vines wrapped around his waist, arms, and feet. Gari Baldy, his opponent, was doing the same on the other side. He was a huge man no one knew much about. Rumors flew that he might be a spirit because of his unbelievable strength and skilled moves.

When they finally faced off, their clash stirred up so much dust it was like a mini storm had hit the village. The fight had to pause until the dust settled down. Once they started again, it was intense. Bakar and Gari Baldy threw themselves into the battle, their bodies crashing against each other, muscles straining under the effort. Karamoko watched silently, his eyes fixed on the sky, not blinking once. When Bakar finally won, Karamoko was so overwhelmed that he fainted for a few minutes, coming to only to find Bakar embracing Tombom in joyful celebration.

CHAPTER THREE

PLOTTING

What was supposed to be a happy day for Karamoko turned sour when he saw Bakar choose Tombom. He felt betrayed, thinking about how his son had gone against their traditions, against his promise. He went home heavy-hearted and called for Sona. "Your son is defying me," he said to his wife. "He wants to mix our pure bloodline with another tribe. I won't allow it." Karamoko changed his clothes and walked into his shrine, determined to undo what had been done.

For a whole month, Karamoko kept to himself, not joining his friends or eating with his family. It wasn't just about Bakar marrying a girl from outside their tribe. Bakar had defied him. No one had ever stood up to Karamoko before, as he was known for his incredible power. Some said he could even make a bird fall from the sky by pointing his finger at it.

There was a time when Karamoko argued with his neighbor about an orange tree. He asked his neighbor to trim the branches hanging over his yard, but the neighbor said no. In anger, Karamoko pointed a finger at the tree, and suddenly, its leaves began to drop as if caught in a storm. In just minutes, the tree was completely bare. The occurrence left everyone shocked, and some bowed to Karamoko with respect. The neighbor quickly apologized and even gave Karamoko a goat to make peace.

Yet Bakar didn't let his father's mood stop him. Whether oblivious to his anger or caught up in the excitement of marrying Tombom, Bakar planned a big wedding. Some in the village whispered it was a risky move, like trying to put out a fire with more fire. Kopiro was a place full of mysteries and a dangerous playground for amateurs. Opposing Karamoko was a brave thing to do. And for it to be his son to do so surprised more than just himself.

Karamoko remembered that when Bakar was little, he was so sick and about to die that even the flies seemed to avoid him. Karamoko had even gone to buy white fabric at the Mauritanian shop across the street for what he thought would be his son's funeral. *Perhaps Bakar was meant to die, the gods wanted Bakar dead; maybe they wanted to get rid of him because they knew he would give me sadness*, Karamoko thought.

Every healer and magician they met had refused to take Karamoko's money, thinking Bakar wouldn't survive. They had almost given up hope, but Bakar held onto life much longer than anyone expected. Every morning, Karamoko had quietly walked over to his son's bed and gently touched him, just to feel the small rise and fall of his chest. He had often wondered if ending his son's struggle would be kinder—but he never could bring himself to do it.

One day back then, a ragged looking woman had appeared at their door. Despite her unkempt appearance, Sona welcomed her with water and a meal. Karamoko wasn't pleased and thought about sending the lady away, but Sona insisted, saying she was just passing through. She placed the meal on the small wooden table and went to check on Bakar before returning to sit with the woman as she ate in silence.

When the woman had finished her meal, she turned to

Sona, taking in her tired eyes slumped posture, and asked for her name.

"Sona, ma'am," she replied politely.

"I can see you have a kind heart, even though times are tough," the woman observed.

"Thank you, ma'am. It's just been a rough day. I didn't sleep well is all."

The woman smiled softly. "You know, our faces can't hide what our hearts feel. I see your worry and sadness, but hold on, things will get better."

Sona frowned in puzzlement, trying to figure out who this stranger was and why she seemed to know so much. Before she could respond, the woman suddenly asked, "Why do you cling to him if the gods are calling him to the ancestors?"

Her question had struck Sona deeply. She tried to recall if they had met before. The woman couldn't have known their situation just in the time it took to eat her meal. Had she heard of their plight from the healers? Or perhaps the woman had some type of hidden power.

Karamoko had been listening from just outside the hut. Upon hearing this, he stepped in and declared firmly, "He's our son. We want him to live."

"Oh, I didn't realize you were part of our conversation. Welcome," the lady said smoothly.

"Who might you be, and where do you come from?" Karamoko asked, his curiosity piqued.

"You can call me Balaba. I live nearby," she replied, her answer baffling Karamoko. "I must leave now," she said, standing up. "But if you're seeking help for your son, visit me tomorrow. I might know how to help."

Sona gasped.

Karamoko's eyes widened with hope. "Why not now? Please, I don't want him to suffer anymore," he pleaded.

"Because you won't find what's needed today," the lady responded calmly.

"I can offer anything," Karamoko said, a bit too proudly. "Money, gold, silver, fabric—"

"I don't need material things," the lady interrupted. "Just bring a live female porcupine and a strand of your son's hair when you come tomorrow." Turning to Sona, she said, "Thank you for your company and a warm meal." Then she left, shuffling past Karamoko and out of the hut.

Realizing he didn't know where to meet her, Karamoko rushed after her. "Where do I find you?" he called out, breathless.

The lady pointed to the enormous kapok tree at the northern edge of the village, a tree so old and sturdy that not even wildfires or storms could harm it. "Meet me there at noon. Don't forget the porcupine and the hair," she instructed, then turned and walked toward the cemetery in the south.

Karamoko was puzzled and a bit skeptical. He knew every face in Kopiro. Yet she was a stranger. Walking back to his hut, he couldn't stop scratching his head, wondering if this was some trick. He'd seen healers and wise folks, but this old lady? She seemed different, and not in a way he trusted. Even the respected jalangs hadn't cured Bakar, so why should he trust this mysterious woman?

Reaching home, he found Sona tending to their little garden, the green leaves of hibiscus and pepper plants glistening with water. He shared his doubts with her, saying he didn't want to go on this wild porcupine chase. But Sona, ever the hopeful one, urged him to take a chance, reminding him the lady didn't ask for money or gold.

Karamoko scoffed. "You can go if you like, but I won't let anyone make a fool of me. What will people think?"

"Don't worry about others," Sona replied gently. "This will be our secret."

Their conversation was cut short by a sudden noise from inside. They rushed to find Bakar shaking uncontrollably, his eyes wide with fear. It was a terrifying sight. After giving him some medicine, they watched as he slowly calmed down and weakly pointed toward the kapok tree Balaba mentioned. Karamoko and Sona exchanged a look of disbelief. Was this a sign? A hint to meet the old lady, or a warning of danger ahead? Bakar wasn't able to speak to explain.

At noon, Karamoko hesitantly made his way to the meeting spot, the porcupine carefully in his grasp. The old lady was already there, calm and composed. "Sorry I'm late," Karamoko said, his hands stained with blood from the porcupine's quills.

"No need to apologize. I've always loved it here," Balaba replied, her words stirring a distant memory in Karamoko of childhood days spent playing under the very same tree.

She instructed him to put down the porcupine and hand over Bakar's hair. Watching her, Karamoko marveled at how gently she handled the prickly creature and how she seemed to guide it with just a hair and a gesture. She sat among the tree's massive roots, starting a ritual unlike anything Karamoko had ever seen. She softly stroked the porcupine's quills and then directed it toward the river, where it vanished into the bushes. Karamoko watched in awe, his mind racing with questions.

The old lady then began drawing in the sand, spitting dark saliva onto her drawing, and circling it with more sand. She stayed like that, focused and still, for what felt like an eternity to Karamoko. When she finally looked up, her smile revealed a set of perfect teeth, leaving Karamoko wondering how someone her age could be so vibrant and full of life. "We've found a way to help. The gods have heard our prayers. Your son will be okay, but . . ." Balaba's voice trailed off into a sigh.

"But what? Please, can you tell me?" Karamoko leaned in, his heart racing with worry.

"It's nothing. Just remember, Bakar is special. He's got a unique purpose. He's a bridge to something important," she said. "Above all, he's your son. Care for him. He will be hardheaded, but whatever happens, forgive him. He's got a bit of you in him," she added.

Karamoko nodded, his mind swirling with questions. *Bakar, a bridge? To what?*

"When you get home, gather your charms. Dip them in water and use it to bathe Bakar, from his feet to his head. You got that?"

"Yes, I understand. And, um, if I need to find you again?" Karamoko asked, hoping for a clue.

"Don't worry. I'll be around. Now, go take care of your boy," she assured him.

Karamoko reached into his bag, pulling out some money. "Please, take this. It's not much, but it's a thank you."

"Thanks, but I don't need money," she gently refused.

Karamoko hurried home, his mind buzzing about who the old lady was. When he stepped into the hut, he found Bakar sitting up in bed, asking for food. Overwhelmed with joy, Karamoko raced to tell Sona. They quickly made Bakar porridge. They were both in disbelief. He hadn't eaten or spoken in so long, and now he was asking for more! After Bakar ate, Karamoko followed Balaba's instructions, bathing him with the charmed water.

When he was finished, Bakar turned to Sona. "Mom, can I go outside? I want to feel the sun."

Beaming with smiles, they helped him outside. Everyone was amazed to see him up and about, but the shock quickly changed to celebration after seeing the joy on Karamoko's face. Karamoko dashed back to the kapok tree, wanting to thank the old lady and apologize for doubting her. But she was nowhere to be found. He searched everywhere, asking everyone, but it was like she had vanished.

Decades passed, and Bakar grew up strong-willed and stubborn, just as the old lady had hinted. And Karamoko was forever grateful for that. But now, Bakar was testing Karamoko's patience to the extreme. As a proud Kopironko, he wouldn't allow himself to be overshadowed, not by anyone. He was a direct descendant of Kopirondin, the legendary queen who was revered by both people and jinn, the queen before whom lions bowed.

Kopirondin Kumo, the warrior lady, was raised by jinn. They adored her and granted her immortality, showering her with wealth, gold, and diamonds. Kopirondin had everything she could ever want, except for one thing—she couldn't have a family or children. At first, she was content with her endless riches and youth, but as time went on, she began to feel something was missing. Despite all her wealth, she longed for a family, a child of her own.

One day, noticing Kopirondin's sadness, the queen of the jinni approached her. "What's troubling you, my dear? You seem so different these days," she asked with concern.

Kopirondin hesitated, fearing the queen's reaction. "If I share my wish, will you be angry? I don't want to be sent away from your kingdom," she said.

The queen reassured her, "We jinn value honesty and respect others' wishes. Tell me, and I promise to consider it."

Kopirondin took a deep breath and confessed, "I want a family. I want children of my own."

The queen was surprised. "But aren't we your family? I've always treated you as my daughter."

"Yes, Your Majesty, and I'm grateful. But I long for children of my own."

The queen warned her, "If I grant this wish, you'll lose your immortality and all the privileges that come with it. You'll grow old and eventually die. Is that what you truly want?"

Kopirondin nodded, accepting the trade. "Yes, I'd rather live a mortal life and bring new life into the world."

"Getting old and dying shouldn't be enjoyable. I see humans grow and raise a family, then their kids die, or they die. But I will talk it over with the counsel if that is what you want," the queen said.

After consulting with her counsel, the queen agreed to Kopirondin's request. "You'll live as a human, but we will allow you to keep some of your powers. You'll be strong and wise, and your tribe will be respected and feared. But use your powers wisely, never to harm or exploit. If you or your descendants misuse them, there will be consequences."

Thus, Kopirondin returned to the human world, becoming a queen, the Lion Lady. She conquered lands, leaving a lasting legacy wherever she went. She founded a tribe called Kopironko and established the town of Kopiro, blessing it as a land of strength and wisdom. Her story inspired her descendants, including Karamoko, to live with courage and honor. The thought of Bakar's actions disgracing their family name filled him with a fierce resolve. Feeling both betrayed and humiliated, Karamoko decided it was time for revenge.

CHAPTER FOUR

THE PACT

Starting a fire is easy, but knowing when and how it will end is a mystery. Karamoko was caught in a storm of anger, ready to move mountains to keep his promise. He visited the jalang, not because he couldn't act on his own, but because he respected traditions and sought formal approval first.

Early one morning, while it was still dark, Karamoko hopped on his horse and rode to Gaika-Tchurki, the most sacred shrine in Kopironko land. He galloped down a narrow, winding path, arriving as the morning dew was still fresh on the grass. The shrine, nestled in a valley surrounded by trees that seemed to smoke, looked like it was always burning due to the thick fog rising from below. Villagers believed this was the breath of spirits rising to the sky.

The priest welcomed him warmly, offering him a hot cup of kinkeliba. After a bit of small talk, he presented the priest with some tobacco and drink. The priest thanked him with enthusiasm. "Why have you come to visit us today?" the priest asked, honoring Karamoko's presence.

Karamoko, his voice filled with authority, explained, "We Kopironkos never back down. Something terrible and disrespectful has happened. My son has defied me in the worst way. I'm here to teach him a lesson he'll never forget." His anger grew with each word. "I want to stop this relationship before it goes any further. I'm looking for a solution, just like my ancestors did when they faced problems."

The priest had listened quietly and now thoughtfully poured some liquid onto a cloth, then drank from a small gourd spoon. For a few minutes, they sat in silence, the priest nodding as he contemplated Karamoko's request. Finally, the priest said, "This place stands for justice and protection, especially for those who are weak or wronged. It's our duty to shield our people from harm. This marriage you speak of is already approved by the ancestors and gods. It's bound by our traditions. If we break it now, we risk angering them."

Karamoko's expression turned dark and ominous, like a dangerous snake. "There must be a way. Our bloodlines can't mix. Can't we just . . . end this by getting rid of the girl?" His voice was filled with desperation.

The priest firmly replied, "Remember our ways, Mister Karamoko. We don't strike first without a good reason. If we act without just cause, the gods will turn their backs on us, leaving us alone in our struggles."

Karamoko, growing increasingly frustrated, made one last plea. "Then do something to stop her from having children," he said, his voice tinged with urgency.

The priest shook his head. "We can't do that here. It goes against our principles. And don't try to handle this yourself. It'll only backfire."

Disappointed and angry, Karamoko left the shrine without another word. He rode his horse home, lost in his thoughts, not even stopping at his ancestors' tomb as he usually did after visiting the shrine. Arriving home around noon, he didn't speak to anyone and went straight to his hut.

He stayed there alone for the rest of the day, refusing to eat or talk to his family. Determined, he whispered to himself, "I won't back down. I'll fight this, no matter what happens."

Sona, sensing the turmoil in her husband, approached him gently. "What's bothering you, my dear?" she asked, noticing the unrest in his eyes.

"It's nothing. How many times must I say I'm fine?" Karamoko replied sharply.

"I know you're not okay. Ever since Bakar chose to marry that girl, you've been different. Can't you just accept it? Everyone in Kopiro adores her. She's kind and friendly," Sona pleaded.

Karamoko, feeling cornered, retorted, "So, you're against me too?"

She sighed, laying a gentle hand on his arm. "I'm not against you, Kotoo," she said, addressing him as elder brother out of respect. "We've been together for years, and I've always supported you. But this time, please, let it be."

"You should be on my side. You know our traditions. Bakar's decision could bring us misfortune," he insisted.

Sona was losing patience. "Let go of this obsession with royalty and tradition! Just let it be." She left the hut, leaving Karamoko alone with his thoughts.

The next day, Karamoko sought advice from another shrine, seeing an oracle in Wolloto, only to receive the same message: Let it be. His frustration grew as he felt isolated in his quest. He began to think the whole world was against him, especially when he saw or heard about Tombom or Bakar. To avoid his anger, he spent his days on his farm, away from the sight of his son. While munching on peanuts in the quiet of his farm, Karamoko plotted. He needed a discreet way to carry out his plan, someone from outside his tribe. Suddenly, he thought of Jaigol, an old friend from the village of Lenkerin in the province of Sama Yerondin. The man was a tricky choice for Karamoko. Jaigol was a powerful king of the Samanco tribe, wise, but a shady character, and their friendship had cooled over some recent disagreements. Years ago, he had wanted to marry Karamoko's teenage daughter, Fenda, but she had already been promised to Demba, the boy he raised, and Karamoko couldn't break his word. This decision strained their friendship, leading to years of silence. But Karamoko was convinced Jaigol was the right person to help him teach his son a lesson. Sometimes you have to mend fences. Determined, he planned to set aside his pride and reach out to Jaigol.

Karamoko would have to travel to Sama Yerondin quickly to strike a deal with his old ally. The night before he left, he called Demba, his trusted general and soon-to-be son-in-law. He explained he'd be away on an important mission and asked Demba to watch over the family in his absence.

Before the sun rose, while the stars still twinkled in the sky, Karamoko set off southeast, an old shotgun slung over his shoulder for protection. This gun, a legacy from his father, was a symbol of his commitment to act without angering the gods or his ancestors. He also packed some gifts for Jaigol and his family as a peace offering.

As Karamoko traveled to Sama Yerondin, he saw places that reminded him of his past. He thought about when he was younger and first met Sona in the town of Pitche. She looked beautiful in the crowd at the market day on a beautiful Monday. Karamoko had been a bit of a troublemaker back then. He had followed Sona home and almost got into a fight with her brothers. Sona's parents didn't like him at first, but Karamoko didn't give up. He kept trying, and eventually, Sona fell in love with him, and they got married.

After a long journey, Karamoko finally arrived in Lenkerin on his giant black horse. As he approached, a familiar voice called out.

"Sanaku! Is it really you?" Jaigol exclaimed with a wide smile, using the special term they had for each other, meaning "cousin."

At the nickname, Karamoko felt a wave of relief. "Yes, Sanaku, it's me," Karamoko replied. He had been nervous about how Jaigol would react, but his old friend welcomed him with open arms. They sat down and spent the evening like old times, laughing and sharing stories, their friendship warming up like a cozy fire.

The whole village buzzed with the news of Jaigol's special guest. A goat was prepared for a feast in Karamoko's honor. Even though he was exhausted from his long trip, the celebration was too good to miss. They lounged in hammocks, enjoyed roasted meat and tea, and puffed on fine tobacco—just like in the old days.

Karamoko was eager for the next day to start. Despite his tiredness, he was too anxious to sleep. He was up at the crack of dawn, and Jaigol was already up, paying his respects to the gods in his backyard shrine. They prayed together, just like they used to.

After their prayers, they walked to the bush, their usual spot for discussing important matters. Jaigol finally asked, "So, what brings you here after all this time?"

Karamoko took a deep breath and said, "You know, in tough times, it's great to have a trustworthy friend. Even though we've had our differences, I still see you as my closest ally." He spoke from the heart, hoping to rekindle their friendship and receive Jaigol's help.

Jaigol smiled. "I am honored to know our friendship is still in good standing, and I am still your friend."

"I have a delicate issue. It's like having a mosquito on your balls," Karamoko said.

Jaigol nodded, intrigued.

Karamoko continued. "My son, the stubborn one, Bakar, went mad. He defied me terribly. And I want to teach him a lesson, together with his little wife."

Jaigol laughed loud and long.

"It is not funny, Sanaku! They made me look like a fool and pathetic in Kopiro. Almost nobody respects me now due to this nonsense." But then Karamoko started laughing as well, as if his pain had vanished.

As the laughter slowly dissolved, Jaigol spoke with serenity and confidence. "That's what brought you here from Kopiro? I know you are old, yet you can still solve this issue alone. Or do you want to tell me you forgot the mad tricks we learned while young? I remember you used to be good and nasty."

"You know the tradition. There are some lines you can't cross," Karamoko said.

"Yes, I know." Jaigol paused thoughtfully. "They shouldn't exist, because sometimes they block our way. Don't tell me you want to make them sleep like we did to those boys in Koyang that year?"

"Yes, something like that. I was told I shouldn't harm the tribe, otherwise, it would backfire, and at the same time, we can't attack first," Karamoko said.

Jaigol nodded. "My friend, I do understand now. You want me to be the proxy? Hm?"

"Yes, if you can. Since you are from a different lineage, it won't hurt you or me."

"But why don't you want them to stay in that relationship?" Jaigol asked.

"You know we can't mix with low tribes. If they have a kid,

my grandchild won't be the pure blood of Kopironko," Karamoko replied. "She is from the Guyankos family."

"Guyankos? The thieves? Oh no. Our ancestors wouldn't have wanted this. Kids these days don't listen. The same thing was about to happen to me, but I cut it right in the root."

"Now you see my problem. Karamoko's firstborn son is married to a thief!? Hah! The embarrassment my son is causing me is unbearable," Karamoko said, almost in tears.

"For sure, I am in. I will help you no matter what." Jaigol reached out and embraced his friend. "You can't have a weak ally. Imagine these kids tomorrow; they won't be brave when my grandkids want a reliable ally like their grandfather. We must build our forces for tomorrow because you never know. Tomorrow is dark."

"Sanaku, *wallan mi hersi*, help me, I am embarrassed." Karamoko knelt, still wrapped in his friend's arms, and cried like a baby.

Jaigol assured him, "We are together in this friend. We will consult the oracles and see the best way to attack and eliminate this shame."

Karamoko was overjoyed by Jaigol's guaranteed support, but conflicting thoughts swirled in his mind. *Why was Jaigol so willing to support an old enemy? Will there be another request like the last time? A trap? Perhaps the old grudge was forgotten and Jaigol meant to truly help.* It would be difficult to trust Jaigol completely, but when a zebra is thirsty, it doesn't matter whether a crocodile is in the pond.

Afterward, they rode their horses to Kenné-Ba, the big jalang, to consult the oracles for their next battle. It was a beautiful place in flat lands with white and shining rocks. The tales say that a female jinni built it to meet a lover. It shines so bright, even at night, that you would think you were in Times Square. The two cantered on their horses. The ride had been calm, the birds chirping, the vegetation rustling, the wind blowing the trees and causing them to sway as if they were greeting the two royalties on their way, sometimes the horses neighing as if talking to nature. Karamoko spent the time brooding, his anger at Bakar beginning to fester. He wanted a solution. It didn't matter where it came from or what the outcome was from it.

As they approached the shrine, Baaba Mansali, the elder priest, was seated and covered in a red mantle, holding his stick. No one knew his age, only that he seemed to have lived an unnaturally long life, yet all his teeth were intact and white. They greeted him and gave him presents before relaying the reason for their visit.

After a long silence, Baaba Mansali said to Karamoko, "Your Highness, I am pleased to serve you as I did in the past for your fathers. Your request can be fulfilled, but first, let me ask you something."

Karamoko's face went pale, but Jaigol said, "Yes, Baaba, please ask."

"Can we avoid death? It brings so much suffering, especially inside our compound."

Karamoko's anger and hatred exploded in him. "Baaba, I am fed up with that boy! Let's eliminate him so the next person who wants to stand against me will fear."

"Son, don't take action when angry and hurt. Plus, he is your blood. You may end up regretting it, as the action is irreversible."

"I am sure I won't regret it; I have other children. I don't want him as a son. I disown him now."

"You may suffer any harm you do to him," Baaba Mansali warned.

Karamoko thought back to when Bakar was an ill kid,

near death. *If I could have predicted the future, I wouldn't have saved that bastard,* Karamoko thought.

After a long quiet moment, Baaba Mansali whispered something to Jaigol. Jaigol then smiled and whispered it to Karamoko, who also smiled. The plan was not good, so they spoke it quietly so as not to upset the spirits. However, they agreed to do it to make Karamoko happy.

Jaigol placed a hand on Karamoko's shoulder, and said, "You are doing the right thing, but be careful. Some of your tribe members might want you to fail."

They celebrated that night, and the next day, Karamoko returned to Kopiro. As he walked into his home, a spring in his step and a joyful tune on his lips, he hummed the Koyang song, feeling triumphant about his mission.

Sona noticed his bright mood. "Dear husband, you're in such good spirits today," she said with a smile.

Karamoko playfully replied, "When I'm down, you worry, and when I'm cheerful, you wonder why!"

"I'm not worrying, just glad to see you shake off the gloom that's been shadowing you."

Grasping her gently by the waist, Karamoko beamed. "This is when I'm truly content. Soon, another Koyang is approaching; you know it is my favorite season. Could you fetch me some water to take a bath? And maybe cook some cassava with palm oil, how I like it?"

Sona studied her husband. She knew him well enough to sense when his joy might be a prelude to trouble. This time, Karamoko had overlooked one crucial detail—he hadn't considered the cost of his request, a mistake that could lead to a whirlwind of consequences.

Chapter Five

THE SIGN

The air buzzed with excitement, the beat of drums filling the village with a lively rhythm that made everyone move. Tombom stepped out of her hut, dressed in white to symbolize purity and a new beginning. Her friends and sister trailed her in a swirl of colors. They made their way to the cool shade beneath a large tree. Batuli, renowned across the land for her skill with hair, sat ready to work her magic on the bride's hair. Tombom took her seat, and the crowd circled, eager to witness Batuli's artistry come to life. While Batuli plaited the bride, the women sang harmoniously, rhythmically clapping and dancing. At the same time, the men showed their appreciation by tossing bills onto Tombom's emerging braid. The ground itself seemed to pulse with the joy of the celebration.

On Kaawu-Garanké's porch, the elders gathered in the shade, some brewing tea, others tending to the roasting meat. The sweet melody of a kora filled the air. Emissaries from both families hustled about, ensuring every wedding detail was perfect. The air was rich with the aroma of various dishes, smoke curling up toward the sky. Children laughed and played, chasing after the juicy scraps while curious vultures circled overhead.

The hot wind whirled around, swaying the trees, and dropping their fruits. Eager kids scrambled around, trying to catch the tumbling fruits. But Batuli, still busy braiding the bride's hair, suddenly froze. She spotted a cloud of dust swirling in the distance.

The drumming stopped, and everyone just stared at the wind. It seemed to dance and twirl, growing into a mini tornado. Something strange seemed to be in the middle of it, but no one could figure out what it was. As it got closer, the hot wind turned into a wild twister, zooming straight toward the gathering.

It ripped the roofs off several huts as it passed and headed right for the crowd. There was chaos as everyone dashed to find shelter. Tombom scrambled with them, but Batuli remained in her seat, the twister spinning madly toward them, kicking up dust everywhere. After whirling around for what felt like forever, it finally moved on and vanished near a taba tree.

Once the dust settled, everyone came out to find Batuli still there, alone and dusty. She cried out in anger, "Who dares? What a disrespect!" She pointed at where the wind had gone, then stood and dusted herself off. "This is your issue to solve, not mine. Find someone else for the bride's hair. I am done," she said as she angrily walked away with her bag, shocking everyone.

People began whispering, wondering what had happened or what she had seen. Was it a message or a sign that the marriage would bring both sides sadness, grief, and tears?

Then Kaawu-Garanké stepped forward, stopping the gossip. "Nobody can stop this wedding. The gods and our ancestors are with us! We're here in peace, and the wedding will be peaceful too. Jali, let's keep the party going," he instructed, signaling the musicians to start playing again.

The drums kicked back in, playing like nothing unusual had happened. The rest of the wedding carried on without a hitch, and after a few weeks, the village forgot all about the strange occurrence.

Bakar and Tombom's love was like a story from a fairytale. "See, we made it through, my love. My dad's choices won't affect us," Bakar assured his new wife, holding her close and giving her a gentle kiss.

"I'm still scared, though. Your dad's looks give me the shivers," Tombom confessed, her voice tinged with worry.

"Don't worry. He'll come around when he sees there's no changing our minds."

"But why don't we just leave this place?"

"Not just yet. Let's follow the tradition of moving out. Let's plan it out properly. I need a blessing from my father. And we will have a baby soon. I can't wait!" Bakar smiled, wrapping his arms around her as they relaxed in the hammock.

Two years flew by, and the baby didn't appear. Though they had the usual ups and downs like any couple, their love remained strong. Tombom was especially excited about having a baby, not only because she wanted it but also because it was necessary to have children in Kopiro. It was part of her duty to the village and her husband.

One day, while washing dishes, a group of girls walked by, chatting on their way to fetch water. "What would you do with a fruitless tree?" one of the girls called out, carrying a basin on her head. "I'd chop it down and plant a new one," she laughed, and her friends giggled.

Tombom's heart sank as she listened. Their words stung like a slap. She realized people were calling her "a fruitless tree." Everywhere she went, she felt eyes on her, judging. It was all too much. The cruel game Karamoko had started was taking its toll, leaving her feeling alone and trapped. She ran inside, tears streaming down her face.

When Bakar got home that night, he found her curled up, trying to hide her tears. "What's wrong, Tombom?" he asked, concerned.

"I'm okay, just really tired," she said quietly, hiding her true feelings. Inside, her thoughts were racing. *This isn't right. If I'd known, maybe I wouldn't have chosen this path.* But she didn't share these worries with Bakar, holding back because her love for him was too strong. She clung to the hope that love would win in the end, not realizing this was just the start of her troubles. It was hard for her, especially since she had always been the beloved, cherished one back in Kankelifa. Sometimes, she'd just stay inside, crying, her mind a whirlwind of pain and confusion.

Tombom and Bakar tried to show everyone how happy they were together. But in Kopiro, that wasn't the way things worked. They believed a woman who couldn't have a baby wasn't doing her part. As a result, they visited many places looking for help, but nothing they heard or tried worked.

Three years went by without a baby. Rumors continued to fly around the village. Some folks said Tombom couldn't have a baby because she was secretly married to a spirit, and that's why she was so pretty and popular. Karamoko kept telling Bakar to leave her. "Son, stop wasting your seed," Karamoko would say.

But Bakar stood by Tombom. He always told her they'd stick together no matter what. On the other hand, she felt guilty. She even suggested to Bakar that they should break up so his family wouldn't be hurt.

One chilly evening, while they were sitting by a fire, roasting sweet potatoes, Tombom decided to speak her heart. "Bakar, you know I love you a lot, right?" He nodded and she continued. "I've got something to tell you."

"What's on your mind?" he asked, looking at her with concern.

"Well, what if you found another woman who could have a baby? I think that would be okay," Tombom said bravely.

Bakar was taken aback, surprised by her suggestion. "Hold on. Did you overhear me talking with my dad?"

Tombom sat quietly, tears rolling down her cheeks. She looked down, not saying anything. He stood up and walked over to the fence, standing there for a few minutes, lost in thought. He came back and gently held Tombom in his arms.

"Tombom, don't listen to what others say. My father, he's tricky, like a snake," Bakar said softly.

"But why can't we just leave this place? Why is it so hard?" Tombom asked, looking up at him with hopeful eyes.

"I need a bit more time. I can't leave without my father's blessing; whenever I ask him, he tells me to wait," he explained.

"Blessing? I'll get blessings from my parents; then we can leave."

"No, never leave without me," Bakar insisted, holding his forehead in frustration.

"I'm so tired. Your dad always picks on me, and the other women spread lies. You don't do anything about it," she said, her voice trembling.

"That's not true! I've stood up for you many times. I'm always on your side, and I'd do anything for you." His voice was firm.

"Then show it, Bakar! Act like you mean it," Tombom pleaded, wiping her tears away.

Bakar felt stuck between two hard choices. He didn't want to leave his home as Tombom wished, but staying meant no peace for his wife. He couldn't imagine letting her go. Puzzled about what to do, he went to his mother for advice.

"*N'naa*, mother, you've always helped me out. I need your advice again," Bakar said, looking worried.

"Is this about Tombom?" Sona asked, knowing her son well.

"Yes. She is struggling and wants to leave now, but Dad is making things tough. What should I do?"

Sona sighed. "Your father can be difficult, I know. But I think you both should be patient. It's important not to leave without his blessing."

Bakar nodded and left, feeling a bit better. But when he got back to his hut, Tombom wasn't there. He thought she might have gone to the well or Fenda's hut, but after waiting until well after the time she would normally return, he started to worry. He asked around, but no one had seen her.

Suddenly, a man on a bicycle stopped in front of the compound looking for Bakar, who was out searching for Tombom. The man walked over to where Karamoko was sitting then crouched down and whispered something in his ear. Karamoko burst into loud laughter, clapping his hands. The man joined in the laughter as he walked back to his bicycle and rode away. No one knew what they were laughing about, and nobody dared to ask.

When Bakar returned, he approached his father, still swiveling his head as if hoping to suddenly spot Tombom. He flopped onto the chair next to Karamoko, placing his head in his hands.

"Did you see her?" Karamoko asked.

"No, Baaba, she's just vanished. I'll go to Kankelifa tomorrow, maybe she's there with her family," Bakar replied, his voice full of worry.

Karamoko let out a small laugh.

Bakar's head snapped up to look at his father. "Baaba, how can you laugh at a time like this? Tombom is gone!" he said, his voice rising in anguish.

"That's exactly it, son. You don't pick a wife just because she's pretty. I warned you, but you wouldn't listen. Now, she's probably realized you're not the man she thought and left with someone else." Karamoko expressed his disdain with a sharp hiss of his teeth.

Bakar gazed at his father, his eyes wide with confusion and a hint of pain. "Baaba, what do you mean by that?" He moved closer, trying to understand the strange words coming from his father.

"Exactly what you heard. I've been told your wife ran off with another man," Karamoko said, a slight smirk on his face, a hint of satisfaction in his voice. It seemed like his wish was slowly becoming a reality.

The air around the compound grew heavy, like a sudden chill had swept through. Bakar felt lost, not knowing how to react. Tears brimmed in his eyes. His mother, sensing his pain, came over to offer some comfort, gently placing her arms around him and rubbing his back.

But Karamoko's voice rose, filled with disdain. "Crying over a barren woman? A true Kopironko stands tall, unshaken even by the sharpest spear!" he bellowed, then briskly rolled up his hammock and disappeared into his hut.

Bakar went to his own hut and lay on his bed, his mind racing with his father's harsh words. The thought that Tombom, the girl he loved and fought for, might have left him was too much to bear. He felt a deep, aching pain, like a dark cloud had settled over his heart.

In the stillness of the night, unable to sleep, Bakar got up and walked to the veranda, where his old box of belongings was stored. He rummaged through it, looking for a rope, his heart heavy with sadness. As he reached into the depths of the box, a sharp pain shot through his hand. Startled, he shone his flashlight inside and found a scorpion, its tail raised, ready to strike again.

The scorpion seemed to be sending him a message, a warning. In a rush of anger and frustration, Bakar grabbed his slipper to swat the scorpion. But he missed, and in his flustered state, he dropped his flashlight. When it hit the ground, the light flickered and went out, leaving him in darkness. He growled in frustration. "Damn it!" he yelled into the quiet night. "I'll find you and crush you, nasty creature!"

Bakar stumbled in the dark, his hand throbbing from the scorpion sting. He searched for his matchbox to light up the room, but it was nowhere to be found. Outside, the night was alive with sounds—dogs barking in the distance, cows mooing, and other night creatures making their presence known.

In pain and needing help, Bakar went to Demba's hut and knocked on his door. "Cousin, please can I borrow your flashlight?" he called out softly.

Demba came out, rubbing his eyes. "What's happening, cousin? It's late. Weren't you sleeping?" he asked.

"I need your flashlight. A scorpion stung me. I need to treat it and then find and get rid of it."

"Let me see that." Demba grabbed Bakar's swollen hand, examining it. Demba's face showed worry as he saw the extent of the swelling. He quickly went inside to prepare an herbal ointment. Gently, he applied it to Bakar's hand, hoping to ease the pain.

A few minutes later, Demba returned with Bakar to his hut. They searched the veranda with the flashlight, looking everywhere, but the scorpion was gone.

"It was right here when I was looking for my rope," Bakar said, pointing to the spot where he'd encountered the scorpion.

"Rope? Why are you looking for your rope at such a late hour?" Demba asked, his sharp mind quickly connecting the dots. He knew too well the heartache in the village, having seen the pain of those who chose a tragic escape and hanged themselves. The memory of a friend lost in such a way still lingered.

"Just prepping for tomorrow," Bakar said, his voice a bit too casual.

Demba's eyes narrowed, sensing something was off. "This isn't about Tombom, is it? You're not letting her troubles lead you to do something foolish, right?" His voice was firm, filled with both concern and a plea for reason.

Bakar didn't reply. He had his eyes closed.

"Listen, cousin, you will never lose something that truly belongs to you. Whatever you lost, know that the gods didn't grant you it," Demba said.

Bakar burst out crying. "You don't know how painful it is to be betrayed by someone you love. Tombom gave me no options. I need to end it all." He looked away, covering his face with his non-swollen hand.

"I wouldn't give up like that. Running away from a problem is what cowards do. Think about it. What would you say to our ancestors? 'I left this world because of a rumor that Tombom left with another guy.' Did you see it happen or talk to Tombom about it? Leaving this way isn't brave. Stand up, Bakar. Be strong," Demba said firmly.

"Cousin, it hurts a lot. It doesn't mean I'm a coward. You know that," Bakar replied, his voice shaky but determined.

Demba walked up to him, his voice gentle. "I'm here for you. We'll figure this out together. Tombom still cares about you, I'm sure of it. Wherever she is, she belongs with you. You need to rest to get over this sting. Sleep now. Tomorrow, we'll solve this mystery," Demba encouraged him, and then he headed off to bed, leaving Bakar alone in his hut.

As the first rooster crowed, Bakar was already up, his hand still aching. Demba checked in on him, asking about his hand.

"Much better, thanks. That ointment really helped, and I got some sleep," Bakar replied, sounding a bit more hopeful.

"That's great. Keep using it, and the pain will fade," Demba said reassuringly. "Ready to ride to Kankelifa to find Tombom?"

Bakar shook his head. "No, let's not. Tombom chose to leave, and she's not alone."

"Really? I talked to your dad. He mentioned someone saw her riding a bike with a stranger toward Kankelifa."

"He told you that?" Bakar asked, surprised.

"Yes, I just talked to him. Maybe the stranger was just helping her," Demba suggested. "But that doesn't clear things up. The stranger might have just given her a ride. We should go see what really happened. Remember, the snake says going back and forth won't break its back."

After a moment, Bakar nodded, agreeing to the plan. Together, they headed northwest on their horses, aiming for Kankelifa to uncover the truth about Tombom. They arrived around noon but didn't head straight to Tombom's family's house. Instead, they asked a friend who confirmed she was there. Following tradition, Bakar and Demba sought out elders to go with them to Tombom's family. Visiting in-laws wasn't simple; you couldn't just show up. It was important to bring respected elders along to speak on your behalf. In-laws were held in high regard, and there were strict rules about how to approach them. Talking directly to an in-law was often not allowed. The jalang chief, Bakar's uncle, and a friend of Tombom's dad agreed to come along.

When they arrived, the children were sent to play in the backyard. Kaawu-Garanké invited his own friends and allies to join then called for Tombom and her mom to come sit with them. Bakar and Tombom sat apart, but they kept glancing at each other. Once everyone was seated, Bakar offered a kola nut to Kaawu-Garanké, a sign of respect. Kaawu-Garanké did the same, presenting a kola nut to his guests. The talk went smoothly, with respect shown on both sides. Soon, everything was made clear. "I didn't leave with another man," Tombom said. "I was just walking when a kind stranger offered me a ride. At first, I said no, and he insisted, so eventually I agreed."

"So you see, the man was just helping her get to Kankelifa safely," Kaawu-Garanké assured Bakar. "Please talk to your dad. Ask him to be kinder to my daughter."

Bakar looked at his wife, the tension released from his shoulders. "You can come home, and I promise, things will be better from now on."

The elders in the village had a special piece of advice: "Head back to Kopiro as night falls. The cool night air is good for love and understanding. But if you move out in the hot sun, your tempers might flare just like the heat, and your love may be in crisis."

The mood in the hut relaxed and there was relief in the air. Lunch was served, and they all enjoyed the meal together, munching on kola nuts for dessert. Taking the elders' advice, when the sun began to say its goodbye, turning the sky into a painting of oranges and pinks, Bakar, Tombom, and Demba started their journey back to Kopiro. Their horses pranced proudly beneath them, moving in a rhythm that matched the calm of the approaching evening.

Demba led the way, with Bakar and Tombom close behind, sharing soft smiles and quiet words.

Around them, the villagers paused to watch. Their faces lit up with gentle grins, waving and sending good wishes as the trio passed by. The cool breeze whispered through the leaves, carrying with it a promise of peace and fresh starts, wrapping around the little group like a comforting blanket as they headed home under the softening sky.

Arriving back at the compound, they got off their horses, smiling and cheerful. The horse let out a soft nicker as they got down, almost as if it were happy, too. Everyone rushed to greet them. Karamoko just watched from a distance. He sat on his hammock, feeling a bit grumpy about how things had turned out.

Sona's voice floated through the darkness, filled with so much joy you could almost see her smile in the night. "Oh, how I prayed for you to come back, Tombom, my daughter!"

Karamoko suddenly stood up from his hammock. He quickly went into his hut, closing the door to all the cheer and noise outside. Meanwhile, the laughter and chatting outside mixed together, creating a happy melody that danced through the night air. But inside, Karamoko tried to block it all out, not ready to join the celebration of Tombom's return just yet.

Sona tiptoed to where Karamoko had shut himself, seeing the glow of a kerosene lantern flickering through the metal door, casting dancing shadows in tune with the wind. She tapped gently.

"Who's there? What do you want?" Karamoko's voice, heavy and tired, came from inside.

"It's me, Kotoo," she replied.

"Well, what do you want?" Karamoko's voice grew louder, tinged with annoyance.

"Please, open the door," Sona pleaded softly.

After what felt like an eternity, the door creaked open. "Well? Speak," he urged, his face tight with impatience.

"Why won't you talk to Tombom? She's just come back," Sona asked, her voice calm and steady.

Karamoko's anger flared, and his words came sharp like a knife. "Are you out of your mind? Have you been drinking or smoking something?"

Sona stood her ground, her voice still peaceful. "I'm just asking you to follow our traditions, our way. Just go and greet her. It's not going to hurt you, my husband."

Karamoko scoffed, his frustration evident. "Hurt me? It will! Can't you see? She's a cheater, a stain on our family name, Sona. You must be losing your senses. We shouldn't even keep her here. Mark my words; she'll never bear children, she's cursed, tied to a spirit."

Sona's eyes widened in shock. "Who filled your head with these macabre tales, Kotoo?"

"Oracles." He spat the word as if it were a curse, his voice booming in the hut's small space.

Sona had heard enough. Without another word, she turned and left the hut, shutting the door behind her as he continued to grumble and curse like a stormy sky. Outside, the night was perfect, starkly contrasting the dark cloud of Karamoko's mood.

For Bakar and Tombom, none of that mattered. They lay close that night, whispering sweet words and sharing soft laughter, their joy a melody harmonizing with the night's gentle symphony, celebrating their reunion.

The morning arrived in a rush, the early sun peeking over the horizon, bathing the waking world in its warm glow. The land, fresh with dew, sparkled as it welcomed the day. Birds chirped and fluttered about, busy with their morning tasks, their songs a lively chorus to start the day.

Under the mango tree, Tombom hummed a tune, a soft, happy sound that seemed to call forth the spirits of joy. Her short broom swept the ground rhythmically, leaves rustling in response, dust swirling up to meet the new day's sky. And as she worked, the village came to life, each person starting their day, their chores a dance of routine and harmony.

After lunch, Fenda, Bakar's sister, came by her door with a playful request. "Tombom, can you plait my hair?"

"Do you think I am Batuli the hairdresser?" Tombom replied with a teasing grin.

"Sure, my brother will pay you. Plus, don't forget, you're *our* wife! You married the whole family!" Fenda laughed, and both women shared a light, carefree moment.

They settled down under the mango tree, on a bamboo mat Tombom rolled out. The air was calm, the tree providing a cool shade. Tombom's fingers gently lifted Fenda's hair and began working them into a braid. They sat chatting while she worked, listening to the rustling of the leaves. "Tombom, I had a dream about you last night," Fenda suddenly shared, her tone shifting a bit.

"Was it a good dream or a bad one?" Tombom asked, her hands skillfully moving through Fenda's hair.

"I'm not sure. It's hard to interpret. We could ask Mother," Fenda suggested.

Tombom's curiosity was peaked. "What happened in it?"

"You and my brother were by the river, fishing. You both caught so many big fish and were laughing joyfully. The river was so clear. But then, Kankurangs appeared, waving their machetes fiercely, sparks flying as their blades met. They surrounded you, trying to snatch your fish. As you resisted, one of them struck your head with his machete, and you started bleeding. That's when I woke up, terrified,"

Fenda recounted, her voice a mix of awe and fear.

Tombom felt a chill run through her. "May the gods protect us," she murmured, her heart heavy with worry.

"It might mean something else, perhaps something positive," Fenda tried to reassure her, but the concern was evident in her tone.

"Let's not wait. You're right. We should talk to Mother," Tombom decided, her voice tinged with urgency.

Together, they walked to Sona's hut. There, in the narrow veranda's shade, they found her, silent and absorbed in her work. She held raw cotton in one hand and a wooden spindle in the other. Her hands moved quickly and skillfully, twisting the soft cotton into strong thread. They watched, mesmerized by her skilled hands working the spindle and cotton. The spindle twirled round and round, winding the thread tightly. Sona and her peers had been doing this for many years, just like their ancestors before them, keeping the tradition. Surrounded by the tranquil sounds of nature, the scene was so serene that the young women hesitated to break the silence.

Finally, Sona spoke without looking up. "What brings you here? Or are you here to learn spinning? You should," she said, her eyes twinkling with a mix of sternness and warmth.

"Yes, ma'am. I'd love to learn," Tombom replied eagerly, her respect for the tradition evident in her voice.

"And you, Fenda, will start learning too, especially with your marriage coming up," Sona added, her words carrying the weight of responsibility and heritage.

"Of course, Mother. But we did come here with a purpose. I had a dream last night, about Tombom and Bakar, and we need your help interpreting it."

The atmosphere shifted as Fenda began to recount her troubling dream, the details vivid and stirring. Sona listened intently, her expression turning contemplative, as if she were deciphering messages from another realm.

"Not everything in your dream spells doom. Water and fish are often symbols of prosperity and life. Fish can signify many things—fertility, fortune . . ." Sona mused, a faint smile gracing her lips. But her expression grew serious again as she probed further. "Did the Kankurangs take the fish?"

"I . . . I don't remember. I was too scared, and that's when I woke up," Fenda confessed, her voice shaky.

Sona sighed, a sound heavy with knowledge and understanding. "We'll uncover its meaning in time," she assured them, her confidence a solid ground in the midst of uncertainty. "And the blood? When the Kankurang struck Tombom, did you see it?" Her gaze was sharp.

"Yes, blood was flowing from her head," Fenda replied, her heart heavy with the memory.

"That might be a sign of cleansing, a good omen. Don't worry. I'll seek guidance and protection at the shrine later. For now, go. I must return to my work," Sona concluded, her words wrapping the young women in a blanket of reassurance.

Leaving Sona to her peaceful spinning, Tombom and Fenda stepped back into the flow of life outside, the weight of the dream a little lighter on their shoulders.

CHAPTER SIX

CANTAUDA

Tombom was tirelessly doing everything she could, hoping to have a child and proudly carry the title of a Kopironko mother. She often wandered into the bush, singing songs to the gods, praying to them for a child. But as days passed, she started to feel like the gods weren't hearing her prayers. *Why aren't the gods listening to me?* she wondered quietly.

One day, the sun was scorching, and Tombom went to the stream, like she always did, to bathe and get some water. The place was packed with women and kids. When they saw her, some started laughing. Tombom tried not to let it bother her.

An old lady appeared, shuffling to the stream. She reached the water, setting her pot down, and looked around. Leaning toward the women closest to her, she asked in a scratchy voice, "Could one of you young ladies help me fill my water pot, please?" The women ignored her. She kept asking politely, but they and others around them just laughed and told her to go away.

That's when Tombom stepped in. "Here, give me your pot, ma'am," she said kindly. She took the pot and bent down to let the water flow in before lifting it to hand back to the woman.

The lady smiled and asked, "Will you also carry it for

me?" Tombom nodded, and they walked together through the bush, reaching a small, isolated hut under a big tree after a short while. As Tombom set the water pot down, the old lady turned to her with gratitude. "Thank you for your help, dear. May I know your name?" she asked gently.

"I'm Tombom, ma'am," Tombom answered with a small, polite smile.

"What a lovely name."

"Thank you, ma'am," Tombom replied, feeling a bit more at ease.

The old lady studied her closely. "You seem troubled, Tombom. Is something wrong?"

"Oh, no, ma'am. It's just the heat getting to me," Tombom said, wiping the sweat from her brow, trying to hide her real worries.

The old lady leaned in. "Do you know how old I am?" she asked mysteriously.

Tombom shook her head, curious.

"I'm older than all the trees and rocks around us. I knew you even before you were born."

Tombom's eyes widened in shock at these baffling words. Her heart raced. She didn't know whether to run away or call for help. The old lady's words had left her completely stunned.

"Don't worry, I'm here to help, not to scare you. They call me Balaba, the mother of the motherless. I've seen you in the bush, crying to the gods for a child," Balaba said softly.

A gentle breeze rustled the leaves around them, and the tree crickets sang their loud chorus, celebrating the warmth of the sun. Tombom listened quietly, her fears slowly easing.

Balaba invited Tombom into the hut. Trusting her kind words, Tombom stepped inside.

"Please, have a seat." Balaba gestured to a stool near the

door. Once Tombom took her seat, Balaba inquired gently, "Why is having a child so important to you?"

"It's a blessing, a gift," Tombom replied sincerely.

"Yes, but remember, a child is also a big responsibility," Balaba reminded her.

Tombom nodded. "I understand. My mother taught me that."

"I hope your desire for a child isn't just because of what others say or because of your husband's family name. A child should be wanted for love, to be cherished as a true blessing," Balaba said seriously.

Tombom nodded, agreeing wholeheartedly.

"The challenge you face isn't simple. It's more complex than you think. I can't solve it for you, but I know of a special place in the land of Mandinkas, a Well of Fertility. They might offer the help you seek. But be cautious," Balaba warned.

Tombom barely noticed the warning. Her heart was set on one thing: having a child of her own. She believed she could handle anything else that came her way.

Balaba put her hand into the petite pochette under her cloth and pulled out a small item held in her fist. "Hold this. This is the key to our appointment." She took Tombom's hand in hers and gently placed the item into Tombom's open palm. It was a sword bean. "Whenever you want to see me, tie it somewhere in your cloth and come to this place, and you will see me. Please do not lose it. Now go and return with your husband tomorrow around this time. But keep this a secret," the old lady said.

The conversation ended abruptly as Balaba ushered her out of the hut. Tombom, lost in thought, made her way back to the stream to fetch water. The pot felt heavier than usual as she trudged back home, her mind clouded with worry.

Upon her return, Bakar paced anxiously, his face clouded with anger. "Where have you been, Tombom?" he demanded.

Before she could utter a word, Bakar's temper flared, and he slapped her. "You said you were going to get water, but everyone else returned except you. I looked for you at the stream, but you were nowhere to be found!" he yelled, his voice rising with each word.

Accusations poured out of him, fueled by suspicion and rage. "Were you with another man in the bush?" Another slap, and he shouted, not waiting for her reply. As Tombom tried to defend herself, tears streaming down her face, her cries for help were drowned out by his angry words.

Sona and some villagers hurried over, alarmed by the commotion, and intervened, pulling Bakar away from Tombom. The air was heavy with tension, making any attempt at conversation futile. Tombom, overwhelmed with emotions, continued to weep, her secret weighing heavily on her heart. She tried to reach out to Bakar that evening and throughout the night, but her efforts were in vain.

In the morning, Tombom attempted to persuade Bakar to visit the old lady, hoping it might help clear up the misunderstanding. However, Bakar was unyielding, his mind firmly entrenched in the belief that Tombom had been unfaithful, a rumor that had been whispered into his ears. His distrust and anger formed an impenetrable barrier, leaving Tombom feeling isolated and misunderstood.

In the midst of all the turmoil, Tombom decided to take a chance and meet the mysterious Balaba. Without a word to anyone, she picked up her pot, the sword bean in her cloth, and made her way to the stream. Passing the houses and venturing into the bush, she found the lady waiting for her under the giant tree, as if she knew Tombom would come.

"I was on my way to see you—" Tombom began, but the lady cut her short.

"There's no need for that. I had errands nearby, so I thought I'd meet you here instead, to save you the journey," Balaba explained with a gentle smile. As the lady's gaze fell upon Tombom's face, her expression changed. The sadness in Tombom's face and the redness in her eyes told a story of pain and suffering. "Tombom, my dear, I'm so sorry. Had I known, I wouldn't have kept you for so long yesterday," she said, her voice filled with regret.

Tombom looked down, her eyes closed, and her lips pressed tightly together. "It's alright, ma'am. I'm used to it. Sometimes, I feel like the gods have forgotten me," she murmured, a hint of despair in her voice.

The lady shook her head firmly. "Don't ever think that. Our gods never forsake us."

"Ma'am, about my husband, I couldn't bring him because . . ."

"I understand, my dear. You don't need to explain," Balaba said gently, her voice reassuring. She knew more than words could say, and her presence offered a silent promise of understanding and support.

The natural symphony around them—the chirping of birds in the tree above, the rustling of leaves in the gentle wind, the insistent chirping of a cricket, and the soft popping of grass in the heat—created a backdrop to their conversation. Squirrels darted up and down the tree trunks, adding to the lively atmosphere.

Now aware of Tombom's situation, Balaba spoke with urgency. "I won't keep you long today, unlike yesterday. You must go to the Well of Fertility, and quickly. The time is now. If you miss this chance, you'll have to wait another whole year. The ceremony is coming up soon—next week.

Remember, do this in secret."

Tombom's eyes widened with curiosity and confusion. "The Well of Fertility? You mentioned it yesterday, but I've never even heard of it."

"Yes, it's in the east, in the land of rocks and hills, where the wise Mandinkas live. The village is called Cantauda," Balaba said, her voice low but clear. "You must go there, and don't forget to bring a kola nut. I'll explain exactly what you need to do." She leaned in closer and began to instruct Tombom in a hushed tone, outlining each step she needed to take on this crucial and secretive journey to the Well of Fertility. "Be extra careful, Tombom. Your father-in-law isn't your biggest fan. If he finds out what you're planning, he might try to stop you," she warned, her voice serious but kind.

Tombom knew this all too well. Everyone in the village knew Karamoko was against her. She hoped the lady would tell her something more encouraging.

As if sensing Tombom's thoughts, the lady added, "And remember, you have to be cautious. Some people are jealous of your beauty and might cause trouble. But don't worry, everything will turn out okay."

With those words, the lady disappeared into the bushes, leaving Tombom to continue on her way to the stream. She felt a mix of nerves and excitement. She was determined to visit Cantauda, no matter what. Would this trip solve her problems, or was it just going to be another letdown? That was something only time could tell.

Traveling to Cantauda was no easy feat. Tombom began her journey on a bike, pedaling her way to Pitche. The sun blazed overhead, casting a relentless heat as she navigated the rugged, dusty road. With each turn of the bike's wheels, a puff of dust rose into the air, coating her clothes and skin.

The path was uneven and challenging, but Tombom pushed forward, determined to reach her destination.

Once in Pitche, she left the bike with a friend and hopped on a kandonga truck, notorious for its cramped and bustling interior. Inside the car, the air was a mix of chatter, laughter, and occasional complaints as passengers were packed tightly together. Tombom found herself wedged between strangers, her personal space limited to just the spot she occupied.

The truck's engine growled to life, and they were off, rumbling down the bumpy, uneven roads. Every pothole and bump sent a collective shudder through the truck, making passengers cling tighter to their seats or each other. Dust swirled in through the open windows, a gritty reminder of the rough path they traveled. It mingled with the sweat that beaded on everyone's skin, a testament to the sweltering heat that seemed to penetrate the very walls of the truck.

Conversations buzzed around Tombom, a tapestry of stories, laughter, and the shared experience of the journey. The close quarters fostered an unlikely camaraderie among them, each person a part of the collective adventure, bound by the dusty roads that led them toward their varied destinations. Despite the discomfort, there was a sense of unity in the air, each bump in the road a shared challenge they faced together on the way to Cantauda.

After what felt like an endless ride, Tombom arrived in Gabu. There, she transferred to another vehicle, which would take her to Bafata. Initially, she had her doubts about the trip. She wondered if Cantauda was just a hoax. But as she reached Gabu and saw the changing landscape and the increased number of pilgrims and travelers, her perception began to shift. She started to realize the significance of Cantauda. The air buzzed with a sense of purpose and anticipation, and Tombom could feel the importance of her journey growing with every mile she traveled.

People were everywhere, finding shade under the trees dotted around the red, dusty ground. The air was thick with the smell of car exhaust and dust, and loud noises bounced around the place. Getting a ride to Cantauda was tough. There weren't enough vehicles, and it felt like a battle to grab a spot on any transport heading that way. Even trucks meant for carrying goods and animals were packed with people all trying to get to the Well of Fertility.

Tombom couldn't believe the chaos at the terminal. She watched in shock as a woman with a baby strapped to her back struggled to board a moving van. The crowd pushed, and the woman nearly fell. Tombom, along with a few others, rushed to help, saving the woman and her baby from what could have been a terrible accident. Shaken, Tombom stepped back from the frenzy and found a quieter spot under a tree, where an older man stood watching the madness unfold.

Curious, Tombom approached the man and pretended she didn't know what was going on. "Excuse me, sir, can you tell me what all this is about?" she asked, gesturing toward the chaotic scene.

The man glanced at her and replied, "Today is the eve of the cleansing ceremony at the Well of Fertility in Cantauda."

Tombom's heart skipped a beat. Balaba had mentioned how important the next day would be. Trying to learn more, she asked, "Is it true that in Cantauda, the wise man can bless you with a child?"

The man's face lit up with a mix of excitement and reverence. "Not only a child, the grace of King Kamboda gives everything," he said before slowly walking away, leaving Tombom with more questions than answers.

Realizing the significance of the event, Tombom knew she

had to be part of it. She pushed her way through the crowd and managed to squeeze into an old, creaky van. The van's engine groaned and rattled, telling tales of its age and wear. The van was packed inside, with even more people crowded on top.

The journey was slow, the van moving through a sea of people on foot, bicycles, motorbikes, and even some on donkeys and horses. Everyone was heading in the same direction, drawn by the promise of the ceremony at the Well of Fertility.

Two hours later, Tombom and the others arrived at Cantauda. The place was packed beyond belief, mostly with women and children and merchants looking to sell their goods. Tombom had never seen anything like it—the crowd was even bigger than the bustling Pitche Market on Mondays.

Cantauda, with its quiet charm and sacred whispers, held the hopes and dreams of many, like a treasure chest waiting to be unlocked. It was a small, peaceful village in the Bafata region, famous for its sacred spots that people from all over the world came to see. A place where the air hummed with ancient magic. The Well of Fertility was one of those special places that people believed promised miracles. It was a quiet, beautiful spot away from all the hustle and bustle. People visited the well to ask for all kinds of things like good luck or better health.

From miles away, you could see a cloud of dust hovering over the area, stirred up by the countless footsteps of the gathering crowd. Before even reaching the heart of the village, the sound of drums and music welcomed Tombom from afar. The sounds of chatter filled the air, creating a constant, lively hum. The surrounding grass and vegetation were flattened under the weight of so many people. It was an overwhelming sight, a sea of people brought together for this special event.

As she approached, her worries seemed to fade away, replaced by a sense of renewal. The village was alive with activity. The sky was a blend of smoke and dust, rising from the many fires where people were busy preparing food for the guests, with the scent of cooking filling the air. Animals were being prepared for the feast, a generous offering to all who came. The food was freely shared, a gesture of gratitude from those who had returned to give thanks for blessings received—be it the joy of a child or the fulfillment of other heartfelt requests. The atmosphere was one of celebration and profound thanksgiving, a community united in their reverence for the blessings of King Kamboda.

Tombom was amazed to see how far people had traveled to be part of this special occasion. There were visitors not only from all over Guinea-Bissau but also from other countries. She even noticed Toubabous mingling with the crowd, all of them united in the spirit of the festival. The atmosphere was vibrant, with everyone dancing, enjoying the festivities, and eagerly anticipating the main event the next day.

A short distance from the bustling village, in a serene and sacred forest near a stream, the elders gathered at the well. This was no ordinary place; it was a space of reverence. The elders would spend the entire night there, away from their homes, performing their sacred duties. This was the time for them to commune with Kamboda, the revered spirit of fertility and benevolence believed to reside in the spring. It was a night of deep spiritual significance, a bridge between the people and the divine, where prayers and hopes were offered in exchange for blessings and guidance.

Tombom was relieved to see the lady she had helped

earlier now holding a plate of food and looking much more at ease.

"Have you eaten yet?" the lady asked kindly.

"Not yet," Tombom admitted.

"You should go get some food! It's free and delicious," the lady encouraged with a smile.

Following her advice, Tombom quickly found a spot under nearby shade where she was generously served a plate full of tasty food. She returned to sit with the lady, and they ate together, chatting comfortably.

"My name is Taibo, and this is my son Kamboda," the lady introduced, pointing to a lively little boy playing nearby.

"My name is Tombom. It is nice to meet you," Tombom said, her voice warm.

Taibo smiled, "What a lovely name! And it suits you well. You're as beautiful as your name."

Tombom blushed at the compliment. "Thank you," she replied, glancing affectionately at Kamboda, who walked to his mother, interrupting their conversation.

"Mommy, I want the candy."

"No, Kamboda, you have just eaten. Now you want candy? Say hello to Auntie Tombom."

"Hello, auntie," Kamboda said in a gentle and tiny voice. Taibo grabbed the candy and gave it to Kamboda, who left to play with other kids.

"How old is he?"

"He's almost three years old. Kamboda, our majestic king, blessed me with him when I had lost all hope," Taibo explained, her eyes reflecting a mix of past sorrow and present joy.

"That's truly a blessing," Tombom responded, her heart touched by the story.

Taibo seemed about to ask Tombom a question when she

noticed a shadow pass over Tombom's face. Tombom looked down, her expression changing. As someone who experienced the same sorrow, Taibo instantly understood the heavy thoughts burdening Tombom's heart. "Hey, look at me," Taibo said gently, placing a comforting hand on Tombom's shoulder. "Don't be downhearted. I've been where you are. Everyone in my village, even doctors from Bissau to Dakar, Banjul, and Conakry, told me I'd never have a child. But Kamboda changed that." She sighed deeply, the memories vivid in her mind. "My journey wasn't easy. People spread cruel rumors—that I was bewitched or cursed, that I had angered the spirits. It was endless gossip and hurtful talk. I was so close to giving up. But then, one night, I had a dream. A lady came to me, saying Kamboda was calling me. She showed me the way, told me when to go to Cantauda. And now, here I am, with my son, my miracle."

Tombom listened intently, Taibo's words resonating deep within her. In Taibo's story, she found a glimmer of hope, a shared understanding, and the possibility of her own miracle waiting just beyond the horizon. Hearing about the lady who guided Taibo in her dream, Tombom couldn't help but think of Balaba, the mysterious lady she had met by the stream. She listened intently to Taibo's captivating story, finding comfort and hope in her words.

"You see, all these children are Kamboda's blessings. That's why they all share his name." Taibo gestured toward the kids playing joyfully around them. "Tomorrow, it's your turn to receive Kamboda's gift, sister!" she said with a reassuring smile.

"Thank you, sister. May it be so," Tombom replied, her heart filled with anticipation. "Did you have to pay for this blessing?"

Taibo shook her head. "No, sister. Kamboda doesn't ask

for money or material things. His only wish is that we cherish and care for his gifts. Some people long for children to show off, but raising a child is a commitment, a true blessing. Look around—all this joy unites us. We're all family here, connected by Kamboda's kindness." Taibo's words were comforting and heartfelt.

As night fell, they were given mats to sleep on. The village buzzed with energy as more and more people arrived, filling the night and early morning with their presence. The beat of the drums picked up again, invigorating the air with excitement. Amidst the lively atmosphere, everyone waited eagerly for the day to come, knowing that the Well of Fertility would soon bestow its blessings upon them.

Back in Kopiro, the mood was starkly different. Rumors swirled that Tombom had run away again, causing a wave of speculation and gossip. Bakar, overwhelmed with frustration and betrayal, was on the edge of deciding to end their relationship once and for all.

Karamoko, sensing his opportunity, whispered in Bakar's ear, fueling his anger and doubt with every passing minute. They concocted stories, claiming that Tombom had been seen leaving with another man, weaving a web of lies to paint her in the worst light possible.

Little did they know, Tombom wasn't fleeing from her life in Kopiro; she was out there, seeking a sliver of happiness, a chance at a life she longed for but had been denied. She was on a journey not of escape, but of hope and healing, looking for the joy and fulfillment that had eluded her for so long. In her heart, she carried the burden of being misunderstood and maligned, all because some believed she didn't deserve the happiness she so desperately sought. Tombom was very anxious and couldn't calm down. She was thinking about the morning's ritual where she would finally receive a gift from

King Kamboda. All she could think about was bathing in and drinking from the spring. She couldn't sleep because she was so excited.

At the spring, the atmosphere was charged with a heightened sense of vigilance. The security had been intensified, with Kankurangs meticulously patrolling the area, their eyes sharp for any sign of evil spirits or disturbances. Their presence contrasted with the relentless rhythm of the drums, which filled the air with a pulsating energy. The elders made their announcement: the ritual was about to commence. Tombom felt her stomach twist into knots, her anxiety manifesting in trembling hands and bitten nails.

"You're feeling it, sister," Taibo observed, noting Tombom's anxious demeanor.

"What's happening to me? My stomach . . . I . . . I can't seem to calm down," Tombom stammered, her words laced with worry.

Taibo offered a comforting smile, her voice steady and reassuring. "It's him—Kamboda. He knows you're here. It's the same sensation I had years ago. Look around. You're not alone. Many women are feeling the tremors of anticipation."

"It's so strange. I feel like something is stirring inside me," Tombom whispered, her eyes wide with a mix of fear and awe.

"Hold on to your faith, sister. Kamboda is kind. Believe in his benevolence," Taibo encouraged, her hand finding Tombom's in a gesture of solidarity. Together, they waited, surrounded by the energy of the crowd and the promise of the ritual, ready to embrace whatever blessings Kamboda had in store for them.

After the deeply moving ritual at the spring, Tombom made the return trip to Kopiro on the same day. The village was quiet as she arrived late in the evening, her heart heavy but resolved.

Bakar's anger burst forth as she stepped into the hut, barely setting down her bag. "Where have you been?" he demanded, his voice thunderous.

Before Tombom could reply, Bakar's hand struck her with a force that sent a sharp crack through the air. Tombom's cry for help tore through the silence of the evening.

"Stop! What are you doing?" Demba's voice boomed as he burst into the hut, pulling Bakar away firmly. "Enough, Bakar! Violence isn't the way!" he shouted, his words cutting through the tension as he dragged Bakar outside.

The commotion drew the villagers, who quickly gathered around, their voices a chorus of concern and disapproval. "Bakar, this isn't the man we know you to be," one villager said sternly, stepping forward to mediate. Karamoko sat nearby, calmly smoking his pipe, seemingly indifferent to the turmoil unfolding around him.

Tombom, scared but strong, watched as her community came together to help her. Even though things were chaotic, she felt safe with the community's help. She lay on the floor, her tears flowing uncontrollably as the pain and shock overwhelmed her.

Amid her distress, Sona rushed in. With a gentle but firm hand, she helped Tombom up from the ground and guided her to a room away from the chaos. "Daughter, sorry, it is fine now. I will deal with Bakar later. He will stop these beatings." Sona pulled her daughter-in-law into an embrace. "Where have you been since yesterday?" she asked, concern etching her face as she tenderly wiped Tombom's tears. "We searched everywhere for you. I was worried. I thought something bad had happened to you. You just vanished."

Tombom, still caught in her emotions, couldn't find the words to respond. Her sobs continued, each one a testament to the pain she felt.

"Please, stop crying," Sona implored softly, her voice a mix of worry and compassion. "Everything will be alright."

Outside, Bakar continued screaming like a madman. His shouts, filled with swearing and ranting, echoed through the air, adding to the tense atmosphere. But inside, Sona's presence offered a brief peace, a moment of calm amidst the storm raging outside.

Karamoko, still reclining on his hammock with indifference, chimed in with his harsh opinion. "I told you, son. I've been saying it for a while now—get rid of this fruitless woman. She's nothing but trouble, frivolous, and a disgusting bad seed," he said, his voice dripping with disdain.

Overhearing Karamoko's harsh words, Sona walked over to him, her expression a mix of anger and disappointment. She stood firmly before him, her finger pointedly raised as she addressed him. "Kotoo, I've told you repeatedly to stay out of the children's affairs and stop insulting the girl. We don't know the full story. Remember, she is someone's daughter, just as our daughters and sons are ours," she rebuked him sternly.

Her words reminded Karamoko of the basic respect and empathy that were sorely missing in his judgment. Sona's protective stance for Tombom, in contrast to Karamoko's scorn, highlighted the divide in their approaches and the underlying tensions within the family.

Karamoko, his pride wounded, shot back at Sona, his face twisted with anger. "Mad old woman! You dare to curse me in front of everyone?" he exclaimed, his voice rising in fury. "When a monkey wants misfortune, it asks for roasted peanuts. I am Karamoko Kumo! No one speaks to me like that. Sona, this is my compound, and you have no right to tell me what to do." He stood abruptly, his hands on his hips, clearly displaying his defiance and authority.

Undeterred and with a fire in her eyes, Sona shouted back, something she rarely did. "Karamoko!" she yelled, calling him by his first name, another rarity. The crowd fell silent, taken aback by the intensity of the moment. The air around them seemed to pause, the tension palpable. "Listen, Karamoko the proud Kopironko! This compound is mine, too. We built it together, remember? I am your wife, and there are times you ought to listen to me," Sona declared, her voice firm and unwavering.

But the situation, already teetering on a razor's edge, erupted like fire in the dry Harmattan season. In a sudden burst of fury, Karamoko lashed out at Sona, striking her. The force of his blow sent her tumbling to the ground, and chaos erupted.

Bakar, witnessing his father's aggression toward his mother, acted instinctively. He rushed at Karamoko, tackling him in an attempt to protect her. The family conflict escalated beyond words, becoming a physical altercation that shocked everyone present. The air was thick with tension, fear, and disbelief as the family's internal strife spilled out for all to see.

The sight of Karamoko falling to the ground sent shockwaves through the gathered crowd. Open mouths and gasps filled the air. Karamoko, the respected and feared figure of Kopiro, lying on the ground was a sight few had ever imagined. His swift and unexpected fall marked a moment of disbelief and fear.

Karamoko, pridefully wounded, scrambled to his feet and dashed toward his hut. Sensing the escalation, the crowd began to disperse, afraid that something terrible might happen. They knew Karamoko retreating to his hut, especially in such a state, could only mean trouble.

Demba knew he had to intervene immediately to prevent a catastrophe. He sprinted after Karamoko, determined to stop him before he could act on his rage. Reaching the hut just as Karamoko loaded his shotgun, ready to unleash his fury, Demba faced a critical moment. He stood firmly in front of Karamoko, grabbing both him and the gun in a desperate attempt to thwart any further violence. Karamoko practically growled, "Demba, let me kill this bastard. Let me kill them both."

With a firm grip on the gun, Demba knew the gravity of the situation. He understood that the consequences would be disastrous if Karamoko got his way with the weapon. Demba's resolve was the only thing between Karamoko's wrath and a potential tragedy.

Amid their struggle, the gun went off. The loud blast reverberated through the air, causing instant chaos. People who had gathered around scattered in fear, birds took flight from the trees in a flurry, and dogs in the vicinity started barking frenetically. The gunshot echoed across the village, reaching even the distant cows in the bush, who responded with unsettled moos.

The tension that had been building in Kopiro had reached its peak in that single, deafening moment.

Panic swept through the village as someone cried out, "Oh, *warri-mo*, he killed him! oh no!" The words spread like wildfire, repeating from one person to the next, "He killed him! He killed him! Oh gods, oh spirits of Kopiro, what have you done?" The voices multiplied, each echoing the moment's dread and disbelief.

Karamoko stood frozen, his hands and entire body

trembling uncontrollably. The gun lay abandoned on the ground, a silent witness to the chaos it had caused. Demba was sprawled on the ground, unmoving.

In a moment of sheer panic, Karamoko's voice broke through the confusion, desperate and frantic. "Someone help!" he screamed, his plea cutting through the air.

"You killed him, Baaba!" Bakar shouted at Karamoko, his voice charged with disbelief and accusation.

Manga, Karamoko's shepherd, and Tamba, the village hunter and Demba's friend, rushed to the scene, their hearts pounding with fear and confusion. Demba lay on the ground, still alive but struggling to speak, his words lost in the tumult of noise and panic that gripped the village. His attempts to communicate went unheard, drowned out by the cries and commotion.

Amid the chaos, Fenda caught a glimpse of her husband on the ground. Overcome with fear and uncertainty, she turned and ran toward the river, "*Aduna an on lâní*, my world is over. The man I love, the man who promised to love me and give me happiness. Oh, forefathers, what have you done? I am going to die too and go with him! I will drown in the river so my father will never find or see my body again." Three boys ran after her, reaching her just as she was about to throw herself into the deep waters.

The moon hung high in the sky, its light casting an eerie glow on the unfolding drama as if the chaos below had fueled its brilliance. The clouds parted, leaving the sky as clear and white as a pristine fabric. The village of Kopiro, once a place of peace and community, was now a scene of distress and disarray under the watchful gaze of the moonlit sky. The fear of what had happened—and what might come next—held everyone in its grip, waiting for clarity amidst the chaos. They were engulfed in turmoil, reflecting the old saying that bad luck is unpredictable and far-reaching like a wet cow's tail.

The elders and villagers of Kopiro converged around Demba, their faces etched with shock and sorrow. Blood stained the ground, blooming underneath him. Yet their grief turned to surprise when Demba's lips moved, his voice finally heard among the tumult.

"Please, water," Demba gasped, his voice barely above a whisper, the effort to speak evident in his strained tone.

Karamoko, frantic and desperate to help, echoed the plea. "Water, water! Someone, please bring water! He's still breathing!"

But a man from the crowd intervened with a cautionary tone. "No, don't give him water, it could be dangerous right now."

Karamoko took charge in the midst of the chaos, directing the others. "Let's move him inside, quickly." His tone was firm yet laced with worry, but the villagers scrambled to obey.

Carefully, they removed Demba's clothes to assess the injury. The bullet had gone through his abdomen and exited through his right leg—a grave wound, no doubt, but not immediately fatal if they acted quickly and correctly. The village healers set to work, carefully cleaning the wound, washing away the blood with gentle, precise movements. Then, drawing on their knowledge of traditional medicine, they applied herbs known for their healing properties.

The night stretched on, the moon bearing witness to their vigil. No one slept. The air was thick with tension and silent prayers, everyone united in their hope for Demba's recovery and the restoration of peace in Kopiro.

The incident sent ripples through the community, its impact far-reaching and profound. The clash between father and son, ignited by a domestic dispute, had escalated into a crisis that had nearly cost Demba his life. His brave intervention had been nothing short of heroic, a testament to his courage and his commitment to protect what was dear to him. Yet the consequences of that night loomed large over Kopiro, a village where Karamoko's influence and stature were undeniable.

In response to the crisis, the elders of the region convened an urgent meeting at Banta, a place where community matters were traditionally discussed and resolved. The gravity of the situation demanded wisdom and swift action to mend the fractures within the community and restore peace.

After much deliberation, the elders made their plea for harmony and understanding. They instructed Bakar to offer a gesture of reconciliation by kneeling before his father, a symbolic act meant to heal the rift between them. Sona, too, was asked to apologize, to bury the hatchet and move past the conflict.

Karamoko's shooting of Demba was deemed an accident caused by the devil's work. Nobody dared ask Karamoko to apologize; that was not how things were in Kopiro. Karamoko was the chief, the supreme chief. He only said to Demba, "You know I wouldn't shoot you; you are my son. It is the work of the devil." At least he acknowledged shooting Demba and told the elders there wouldn't be problems again.

The proceedings went smoothly, at least on the surface. However, beneath the veneer of resolution, uncertainty lingered. Karamoko's reaction remained an enigma, his next move shrouded in secrecy, known only to the heavens. The community held its breath, aware that Karamoko was not a man accustomed to accepting what he perceived as humiliation. The elders' decision may have calmed the immediate storm, but the undercurrents of tension suggested that the battle was far from over. Kopiro waited, watchful and wary, for what the future might hold.

Chapter Seven

THE BIRTH

Demba's recovery brought much joy to the village. Preparations were made, and as soon as he was up and walking, Karamoko decided that the wedding between Demba and Fenda should take place. Kopiro celebrated. The air was filled with the scent of spice and the sounds of music. Demba took Fenda in his arms, moving cautiously at first, but soon moving in time with the beat of the drums as they danced together, smiling and radiant. Others joined in, and the festivities continued long into the night.

Tombom danced among them, her thoughts a swirl of happiness at Demba's recovery and the beautiful wedding. She tried to lose herself in the music, when suddenly, her world seemed to tilt. The joyous atmosphere couldn't keep her steady and she stopped dancing, putting a hand to her head. She felt a sudden dizziness and her surroundings began to spin. With unsteady steps, she zigzagged her way to the edge of her hut and succumbed to nausea, vomiting.

"Are you okay?" Bakar's voice cut through her discomfort, concern lacing his words.

"Yes, I'm just a little dizzy, maybe tired, that's all," Tombom replied, trying to dismiss her unease, not wanting to cause any worry. "I'm going to go lie down, but you should go back to the celebration." She smiled at him reassuringly. He frowned but nodded and left.

As Tombom assisted with the cooking the following day, adding onions to hot oil triggered another wave of nausea. She hurried away, finding relief near the fence as she threw up once again.

"Are you okay, daughter?" Sona's voice reached her, filled with maternal worry.

"I'm okay. It's just that recently, smells, especially of food, make me feel nauseous," Tombom explained, trying to make sense of her body's reactions.

Without hesitating, Sona declared, "You're pregnant." The words hung in the air, a mix of statement and celebration.

"What? Really?" Tombom felt both skeptical and excited at the same time.

"Yes, you are. I can see it on your face. Congratulations to us!" Sona expressed her happiness with certainty, making it clear that she was delighted.

Tombom was awash with a whirlwind of emotions. The possibility of pregnancy, the thought that her visit to Cantauda and her prayers to Kamboda might have been answered, filled her with a profound sense of astonishment and gratitude. "Cantauda is real! Finally, Kamboda answered me," she whispered, the realization dawning on her that her life was about to change most beautifully.

The news of Tombom's pregnancy spread like wildfire. Initially met with skepticism, people visited her, curious to see if the incredible story was true. As weeks passed and Tombom's belly began to show, disbelief turned into belief. Her pregnancy became the talk of the village.

Tombom thought of Balaba amidst all the emotions and gossip. The wise old lady had directed her to Cantauda.

Feeling deeply grateful, she decided to visit and express her thanks. One morning, with the excuse of fetching water from the stream, Tombom set out to find Balaba, where she had seen her last. However, to her disappointment, Balaba was nowhere to be found. After a lengthy wait, Tombom recalled that Balaba had given her the sword bean. Realizing she had forgotten to bring it, Tombom hurried home to fetch it. But, to her disappointment, the bean had disappeared. She looked everywhere, but it vanished without a trace.

Over the following weeks, Tombom made several attempts to meet Balaba, hoping to reconnect and share her news. But each visit ended in vain; Balaba was never there. Eventually, Tombom accepted that their paths might not cross again and ceased her attempts, carrying on with her life, now filled with the tension and joy of her upcoming motherhood.

Most in the village celebrated Tombom's joyful news, but not everyone was happy. Karamoko was among the latter; he was distraught by the truth about Tombom, and his emotions were in turmoil. He felt a surge of anger, making his heart beat faster, and his body broke out in cold sweat. He needed counsel, and Jaigol was the only one he could turn to.

Karamoko's sudden arrival, with dust billowing behind his galloping horse, seemed unusual. Jaigol felt a knot of concern form in his stomach. This was different from the Karamoko he knew, his demeanor somehow off, an urgency to his arrival. "Is that you, Sanaku?" Jaigol called out as Karamoko arrived.

"Yes, it's me," Karamoko replied, his voice quivering, a clear sign of the storm raging within him.

Jaigol's eyes narrowed with concern as he observed his friend's chaotic appearance and the wild look in his eyes.

Karamoko looked upset, and his clothes were a mess. His face was full of madness and disappointment. "What's wrong? You seem deeply troubled. Let's go inside," Jaigol suggested, worried.

The mood in the room was tense. "What happened?" Jaigol asked, his voice steady yet filled with concern. He was ready to listen and offer the support that Karamoko so clearly needed in this moment of crisis.

"She's pregnant, Jaigol. Tombom is pregnant," Karamoko uttered the words as if they were coming hot from his mouth. His voice was heavy with grief, and his breathing was erratic.

"Your daughter-in-law? Pregnant? But that's impossible after what we did," Jaigol responded in disbelief.

Karamoko's voice broke as he replied, "It's true, Jaigol. My heart is shattering. I am about to have a thief's blood within my compound! The whole village of Kopiro is talking about it."

Jaigol, still struggling to accept the news, pressed on. "Are you sure, Karamoko? It seems absurd. Could it be just a misunderstanding?"

Karamoko shook his head firmly, a sense of resignation in his eyes. "No, it's the truth. Everyone in Kopiro knows."

Jaigol's expression turned solemn. "Karamoko, I swear by our gods and ancestors, I've never seen such a thing happen. Our jalang has never failed before. We need to go to the shrine. We must find out how this could have happened," he said, the weight of the situation pressing down on them both.

Karamoko and Jaigol made their way to Kenné-Ba, their hearts heavy with questions and the hope for clarity. Baaba Mansali was there as they expected, his presence was constant in the sacred space of the shrine. He greeted them with surprise and curiosity. "Your Highness, it must be urgent for you to visit now. I wasn't expecting you."

"Yes, it is urgent," Jaigol confirmed, his tone grave. "The girl, Tombom, she's pregnant."

Baaba Mansali's eyebrows furrowed in disbelief. He turned to Karamoko. "No, that can't be. Not from your son. Perhaps she's involved with another man in secret. However, we mustn't jump to conclusions. Rush could lead us to a grave mistake. The gods would not forgive such recklessness. Let's consult the oracles."

Baaba Mansali moved swiftly, gathering and preparing the necessary ingredients for the divination. His movements were precise, and his experience was evident in every gesture. The air in the shrine grew thick with uncertainty as Baaba Mansali consulted; each passing second seemed to be an eternity. Finally, Baaba Mansali looked up, his face solemn with the gravity of his discovery. "Yes, she is pregnant," he confirmed.

"And the father? Who is it?" Karamoko pressed, his voice tense with anxiety.

"Karamoko, that is exactly what we have to see next. But I am almost sure the kid doesn't belong to Bakar." Baaba Mansali's hands shook, and his voice quivered as he continued the ritual.

Karamoko pressed his fingers to his temples. "I knew it! I knew this girl was not just a thief but evil. The kid is a bastard. Perhaps the pregnancy was from the evil spirits that she visited in the bush." Karamoko spat the words like hot lava.

"I agree. There is no way she could get pregnant after what we did. The kid is an evil bastard, that is the only answer." Jaigol's words sliced the air like a hot blade.

"Wait, wait," Baaba Mansali cautioned, his hand raised

for patience. After a brief, tense pause, he continued, "The baby carries your blood, Karamoko." His voice was trembling.

The truth hit like a thunderbolt, sending shockwaves through the air and leaving Karamoko and Jaigol stunned and speechless. The certainty in Baaba Mansali's voice left no room for doubt, unveiling a reality that would change everything they thought they knew.

In the stillness of the shrine, the weight of the revelation hung heavy in the air. Baaba Mansali, the conduit of the oracles' wisdom, was visibly affected by the gravity of the situation. His hands trembled slightly, and beads of sweat gathered on his forehead, a testament to the intense focus and energy he was channeling to seek the truth.

Beside him, Jaigol stood frozen, his right hand pressed against his mouth, a silent gesture urging himself to listen and absorb before reacting. The news struck him deeply, leaving him with shock and disbelief.

Around them, the bush seemed to hold its breath, the usual rustle of leaves and chatter of wildlife momentarily hushed. In this moment of quietness, a yellow-headed lizard perched on a nearby tree, its head tilting and flexing as if it, too, focused on the scene, a contrast between human emotions and the calm of nature.

Karamoko's voice was thick with a tumult of emotions as he grappled with the news. "My blood? But Baaba, you mentioned the kid almost certainly doesn't belong to Bakar. Does it mean one of his siblings impregnated her?" he asked.

Baaba Mansali nodded solemnly. "That is one of the possibilities. It couldn't be your son, for I know well what I did, and it was effective. It's been nearly four years since they married, without a child," he stated uncertainly.

Jaigol sat quietly, deep in thought.

"One more reason I don't want that child to be born is because all this doesn't make sense. Let's say it turns out to be one of Bakar's brothers who impregnated her. I know Bakar, he won't tolerate it. It would rip our family apart," Karamoko said.

The air in the shrine was thick with tension as Baaba Mansali continued his rituals, seeking more profound insights. As he poured liquids over the figurines, a sense of presentiment grew. Karamoko and Jaigol, driven by anger and desperation, contemplated drastic measures. "Sanaku, you are right. I suggest we should get rid of her and the baby to end this for once," Jaigol whispered his proposal with a determined tone.

"Yes, now is the time. Everybody will assume it was the pregnancy that killed her. This might be the best course of action. It will be easier now than after the baby is born," Karamoko agreed.

Amidst their plotting, a sudden noise pierced the heavy atmosphere. The heavy buffalo horn hanging in the shrine inexplicably fell to the ground. The sound made Baaba Mansali jump, his eyes widening in alarm. He shifted his position on the stool, his gaze fixed on the fallen horn. "This is a bad omen! This baby isn't normal. There's something very powerful behind this pregnancy," he warned, his voice tinged with fear.

Jaigol's arrogant words transformed into a defiant statement. "Baaba, aren't we powerful too? The falling of the horns can be a mere coincidence. Things usually fall, and I don't see anything ominous in that."

But Baaba Mansali, deeply rooted in his wisdom and understanding of the spiritual world, resisted. "Your Highness, killing them can be dangerous. We don't know why the gods denied our requests before. To defy this now could invite disaster upon us all."

Jaigol, fueled by desperation and resolve, retorted, "Are you scared at a simple thing like smashing a filthy cockroach? I'll take care of it myself," he said with a sinister chuckle, revealing his dark red teeth. His eyes flickered like a mad devil.

Baaba Mansali, trembling with the weight of his words, responded, "My Highness, never in my life, nor in the time of your forefathers, have I defied a royal command. You are our king, the symbol of our people's strength and honor. Please listen to my warning and do not continue with this."

For the first time, Jaigol saw genuine fear in Baaba Mansali's eyes. The trembling of his hands was a clear testament to his fear. Baaba Mansali, the keeper of traditions and wisdom, was visibly shaken. "Not here, not in this way," he insisted. "This path you're considering is fraught with danger. It's a reckless gamble against forces we do not fully comprehend."

However, Jaigol refused to be convinced by Baaba Mansali's words. "I'll take responsibility for this act. Do it," Jaigol declared, beating his chest.

Karamoko said, "Baaba, just do it. It's nothing more than we can't handle."

"Alright, I will do as you asked. I am sorry if I offended you, my Highness," Baaba Mansali said in a humble voice.

With solemn expertise, Baaba Mansali gathered the necessary ingredients known for their potential damage. He prepared the mixture with care. Once ready, he handed the ominous package to Karamoko. "You can mix it into her water or food. She and the baby won't survive if she consumes it," Baaba Mansali instructed with a heavy heart, the words feeling like stones in his mouth.

Karamoko took the package, and his mind was set on

carrying out the plan. They departed the shrine with joy. Dark clouds amassed swiftly, and torrential rain poured like the heavens were weeping. Lightning flashed across the sky, followed by the deep, resonant rumble of thunder, each crack a reminder of the potential wrath of the gods. It was as if nature was protesting their decision.

Karamoko returned to Kopiro with a clear goal to execute his plan. He waited patiently for the right chance to carry it out. He started fiddling with the fence, whistling, and humming, pretending that he was working. He observed the people in the compound, looking for a moment when they were not paying attention.

Like a serpent stealthily moving toward its prey, Karamoko seized the moment when he was sure no one was paying attention. He slipped quietly into Tombom and Bakar's hut, his movements deliberate and silent. Once inside, he found Tombom's clay water pot. With a steady hand, Karamoko poured the herbal mixture into the pot, ensuring it mixed well with the water.

After completing the deed, he left as quietly as he had entered, careful not to leave any trace of his presence. His heart might have been racing, but his face showed no sign of inner turmoil. The bottle still held some of the mixture, holding enough for a potential second round, should it be necessary. His plot was set in motion, and he returned to his hut, waiting and watching.

The following day, the village was bustling as usual, but Tombom was still in bed, something very odd. Bakar noticed that he did not see his wife outside, and an eerie silence came from their hut. He went to check on her and grew increasingly worried when he found Tombom in agony, clutching her stomach and unable to stand. He called out for help urgently. "Mother, come quickly! Something's wrong with Tombom!"

Sona rushed in, deeply concerned. She saw Tombom writhing on the bed. "Oh, my child, what's going on with you?" she asked, her voice full of worry.

They tried to soothe her pain with some medicine, but it brought no relief. Tombom's condition only seemed to worsen, her cries piercing the hearts of those around her.

Panicked and desperate, Sona made her way to find Karamoko. Bursting into his hut, she exclaimed, "Karamoko, something terrible is happening to Tombom! She's in unbearable pain, and nothing we do helps. You need to see this!" The concern in Sona's eyes was unmistakable as she implored Karamoko to take action. "Kotoo, you must do something. Regardless of how you feel about her, she's in agony. She might need medicine for her stomach, and I fear she could lose the baby— your grandchild."

Karamoko feigned ignorance. "Oh? I wasn't aware," he said, his voice carefully neutral. He followed Sona to where Tombom lay in pain. Once he saw her condition, he exclaimed, "Oh my goodness! Since when did this start, and why didn't you tell me? Her pain is real!" On the inside, he was beaming with joy at the success of his plan.

"Baaba, I just found out," Bakar explained.

Karamoko excused himself. "Let me see if I can prepare something that might help," he said, heading to his hut with another plan in mind.

In the privacy of his hut, Karamoko retrieved the remaining herbal mixture. With a calculated calmness, he diluted the concoction, creating another dose of the harmful brew. Returning to Sona, he handed her the calabash bowl, masking his betrayal with a guise of helpfulness. "Give this to her. It should help ease her pain," he instructed with a confident voice.

Sona, seated on the edge of Tombom's bed, took the bowl gratefully, relieved to have something that might alleviate Tombom's suffering. Unknowingly aware of the danger of the liquid, she gave it to Tombom, who drank it and closed her eyes as she swallowed.

As the night wore on, Tombom's agony intensified, her cries of pain piercing the silence of the night. Despite their best efforts and traditional remedies, nothing seemed to alleviate her suffering. With each passing moment, her condition worsened, she began bleeding, her face growing pale and her body weak, a clear sign that something must be done urgently.

Bakar and Sona, driven by desperation and love, made the difficult decision to seek help beyond the confines of their traditional practices. They decided to take Tombom to the community health center, hoping that modern medicine might offer the relief that their remedies could not.

Karamoko, witnessing their preparations, couldn't hide his disdain. "Are you dismissing our ways, turning to the white man's medicine?" he questioned, his voice full of skepticism and a hint of scorn.

Sona, her resolve unshaken by Karamoko's words, responded with a determined tone. "Kotoo, we have to try everything. Our ways haven't brought relief. Let's also give the Toubabou's medicine a chance."

Karamoko was conflicted but knew he had better let them go, as they might suspect something was wrong. He resignedly muttered, "Okay, if you think that's best, go ahead."

The center was a small house with decaying walls. Dr. Sukai, as he was known in Kopiro and beyond, was the only health center staff member. He was absent most of the time.

In case of emergency, someone needed to go look for him. Upon arriving at the health center, the doors were closed. Bakar went to retrieve the doctor.

As Sukai arrived, he threw his old bicycle on the decaying veranda and greeted, "Good evening." He opened the door and lit the kerosene lamp, revealing the poorly equipped center with an old and rusty hospital bed and rusty furniture as if frozen in time. Sukai was tall and slender. He wore eyeglasses strapped to the back of his head with a black elastic band. His bald head gleamed under the dim lighting of the lamp on the wall. "Come in," he commanded with a lazy voice.

Sukai carefully examined Tombom, and he sighed. "I'm afraid there isn't much I can do in this situation. I recommend you take her to Gabu tomorrow," he said in a concerned voice. He grabbed his bag and reached for a pain reliever tablet. "Here, take this. It is the only medicine I have here, and it may help ease the pain."

Tombom spent the night at the center, but the pain didn't abate. She groaned and moaned at times, and when the pain got terrible, she dug her nails into the old mattress. In the morning, Bakar was exhausted from the previous night. He slept, snoring, on the bench at the health center veranda, and Sona went to make Tombom breakfast. As she lay in that strange place, Tombom remembered Balaba, who she believed could help her. The pain was unbearable. Nothing was working.

She summoned some strength and walked out of the center. She ventured into the bush, taking the narrow, winding path. Her thoughts were a turbulent combination of agony and supplication. Despite her suffering, Tombom sang and pleaded with the gods and spirits of the ancestors, her voice breaking with sobs. An intense cramp overwhelmed her, and she stumbled, cradling her belly. She couldn't hold on. The pain was becoming too much. Tombom decided to walk and die in the bush with her baby in her stomach because she knew her chances were slim. She wanted the gods and forefathers to see her suffering. Her head was pounding, and she was bleeding. She finally collapsed on the damp grass, unconscious.

She woke with a light headache. Smoke-like steam filled the air around her and she felt a damp pad on her forehead. At first, Tombom thought she was dreaming or in the ancestor's realm.

"Are you back?" a voice asked.

Tombom tried to sit on her elbows but couldn't muster the strength.

"If I were you, I wouldn't do that," the voice said again from behind.

Tombom thought she recognized the voice but couldn't be sure. She turned her head but couldn't see who was talking due to the thick smoke. "Who are you?" she asked.

The person didn't answer.

"Please, tell me what happened to my babe? Oh, my babe, I am sorry!" Tombom was heavily panting. She was weak from blood loss, her eyesight was blurry, and the hut spun like she was on a roller coaster. She felt exhausted deep in her bones, and it did not take long for her to fall back asleep.

When she woke again, she felt much better. She sat up slowly, testing the limits of her body.

"You must be so hungry. You need to eat. It will return some of your strength." A figure appeared out of the smoke. It was Balaba. She handed Tombom a bowl of hot liquid like porridge. "Eat, daughter, while it is hot."

Tombom took the bowl gratefully. "Thank you, Mother."

"I am glad you are getting better. It was so tough!" Balaba

said. Tombom took slow, steady sips of the porridge. After a while, she set down the bowl. "Eat more! You need to finish it while it is still hot," Balaba demanded.

"I am full. I will eat later. How did you find me? Last I remember, I left the health center to seek help."

Balaba nodded. "You didn't make it. I found you almost lifeless. You had passed away, and it took me a lot of effort to bring you back. Now, you need to rest," Balaba said.

Tombom's hands slowly moved to her belly, caressing it hesitantly. Her voice came out in a desperate whisper. "Did I lose my baby? Please, say no. Otherwise, I prefer to kill myself." Tombom started crying.

"Relax, Tombom. You haven't lost your baby. Whoever did this to you wanted that to happen, but you and your baby were lucky the gods called me on time," Balaba said.

Tombom sighed, tears still rolling down her face. Her hands continued to rub her belly. The fetus kicked smoothly, and Tombom smiled. "He is moving. Oh, my poor baby. I love you."

"Your baby is strong and resilient! I wonder how he survived this attack! You need to eat again because he might be hungry." Balaba took the bowl and returned with more of the porridge.

Tombom ate. "How long have I been here?" she asked between bites.

"It has been nearly a full day since yesterday morning. They are likely looking for you. You are out of danger, but you must still be careful. Take this root, chew it, and swallow the liquid at least three times a day." Balaba gave her the root, which Tombom tied on the edge of her wrapper.

"Thank you. I tried in the past to see you, but I couldn't find you. I lost the bean."

"I was busy, and as it was urgent, I didn't mind." Balaba

walked to a small leather bag and brought another bean. "Here, take this one. This time don't lose it because I am a busy old lady. And don't bother looking for me if it isn't an emergency."

"Thank you again for saving me. You have always been there for me. How can I pay you?"

"I help you because you are a good kid. I don't want your payment. Please care for yourself and your baby. Now you must leave before they grow too frantic."

The pain had vanished, but her body was weak, so Tombom moved slowly. She arrived to find everyone sick with worry and they bombarded her with questions about her whereabouts. "I must have been delirious with pain. I ran into the bush and fainted, only just now coming to. The rest must have helped, for I am feeling better," Tombom told them.

"But we looked everywhere for you!" Karamoko said.

Sona shushed him. "It doesn't matter now. She came back safe and much healthier. It is my fault! I shouldn't have left her alone in that filthy center. I am sorry."

"It is okay, Mother. It wasn't your fault," Tombom answered.

Sona began ushering her toward her hut. "I am going to make some soup for you. You should go and get some rest."

"Where is my husband?"

"They are still out looking for you in the bush. We will play drums to let them know you are safe," Sona said.

The drums carried the news of Tombom's return, and Bakar was overjoyed to see her safe and healthy—and still with child—but he couldn't help but wonder. *Could Tombom have faked her pain as an excuse to disappear and fulfill her fantasy of sleeping with another man?* His thoughts swirled with suspicion and jealousy, but they were overshadowed with the joy of impending fatherhood.

One evening, Tombom and Bakar were cuddled on the bed together, his hand touching her stomach. "What will we name the baby?" he asked.

Tombom was quiet, trying to find words to answer.

"Obviously, not after my father, as he has always opposed our bond," he continued. When she still didn't respond, he sat up on his elbow to look at her. "Tombom? What will we call the child?"

"Kamboda," she said.

"Huh. Cool name. I know some people with this mighty name. May I know why you call the baby Kamboda?"

Tombom decided to tell the truth. "Because I went to plead with King Kamboda, and he answered me."

"You went without telling me?"

"I tried, but you didn't listen, Bakar."

Bakar looked thoughtful for a moment and then said, "Well, if it is so, let it be. But one more question. Is it mandatory to name the child after him?"

"No, but it's right to honor him because he's benevolent. I thought I would never have a kid until I asked him, and he blessed me."

"Right! It makes sense. Kamboda, my bebe!" Bakar said it happily, wrapping his arms around her and holding her close. "I am sorry. I should have done more to help the situation, but I was under pressure, and my head got utterly lost in the middle of all this trouble my father created."

Tombom leaned into him. She didn't give forgiveness, but she finally felt at peace. Despite several attempts on his life, Kamboda showed determination and perseverance, resisting as a real Kopironko warrior would.

CHAPTER EIGHT

CHILDHOOD

Tombom gave birth at noon on a very hot Friday—the powerful combination of the spirits' meeting time and a sacred day. Kamboda's arrival into the world was as unique as his name. Unlike most newborns, he didn't cry at birth, perhaps a sign of the resilience he had already developed. He was a healthy, handsome boy, his eyes shining with the determination of a true Kopironko. Kamboda was a joyful child, his face often breaking into a happy giggle that seemed to light up the room.

The compound was filled with joy and celebration again three months later with the birth of his cousin, Maladho, to Fenda and Demba. Two beautiful babies in just ninety days was a rarity, a double blessing that brought immense happiness to their families.

However, as Kamboda grew, it became clear that he was not like other children his age. By the time he was two years old, signs of developmental delays began to emerge. He hadn't started talking, and he couldn't walk. Most of his days were spent in bed or sitting quietly, contrasting the lively, giggling baby he once was.

Tombom's heart ached with worry and confusion. The child she had longed for and struggled to bring into the world was facing challenges she couldn't comprehend. In a community where superstitions and rumors ran rampant, her situation became the subject of speculation and gossip.

"Forefather, why me? Why must I endure this endless torment?" Tombom would lament in silence.

Karamoko once again became the driving force behind the dark whispers that circulated. The village's judgment and the growing narrative of unfounded tales that Tombom had committed adultery by sleeping with another man in the forest, which is why the gods punished her, made life increasingly difficult for Tombom.

Each day brought new challenges, and the once joyous occasion of Kamboda's birth now seemed a distant memory. Tombom found herself navigating a world that was quick to judge and slow to understand, her journey as a mother marked by both profound love and unexpected hardship. Often, curious people came to see the child, pretending they were visiting out of courtesy. However, upon leaving, they began to whisper that the child was not normal; they claimed the child was a spirit.

Jaigol paid a visit to his friend and ally, and they sat in front of Karamoko's hut, each seated on their goat-skin mat, chewing a kola nut as they finished having lunch. "Have you seen the child, Sanaku?" Karamoko asked in a whispering but heavy voice.

"Yes, I did, Sanaku." Jaigol shook his head. "Huh! *Mi hulii*, I am afraid, Sanaku. The kid didn't die despite all the attempts! He doesn't belong here in this world of humans," he whispered.

"The kid is a bastard spirit; maybe that's why he didn't die. *Djineé mayata*, spirit doesn't die! But Bakar doesn't want to admit it. Now that you are here, I will call him, and we will talk to him," Karamoko suggested.

He summoned Bakar to his hut for a serious talk. The atmosphere was tense as the three faced each other. Karamoko turned to Jaigol and cleared his throat. "Sanaku, my brother, my friend. I want you to tell Bakar not to measure the depth of the river with his foot. He must see the truth. The child is not ordinary. Everyone knows."

Jaigol shifted to adjust his posture on the mat. "Bakar, our beloved child, you must listen to your father. I am the witness, and I can burn my hand in a fire for this. This kid is a spirit—a cursed spirit. You can see he is not human." He spat the words with assertiveness, wagging his finger in disapproval.

Bakar cautiously listened to the two elders. He bit his lower lip and weighed his answer. "Baaba, Uncle Jaigol, I have heard you. But I would like to ask you something. How is that possible? The kid has my face, our face, our features!"

"Bakar, you are naive! The spirits get this kind of power to resemble themselves to whoever they want. It is not a big deal to them. They trick foolish humans like you into dragging and trapping them to the abyss! You are asking how that is possible!? Your wife committed adultery with a man in the forest, period."

Torn between his love and the growing rumors, Bakar responded, "Father, I confronted Tombom several times about this issue. She swore in the name of the most sacred that she has been loyal, and Kamboda is my son, my blood."

Karamoko fixed a firm gaze on his son and shook his head in disbelief. Jaigol jumped in, "Bakar, you can clearly see the child is different, and it's clear why. Listen to your father; don't let love cloud your senses. Tombom has been unfaithful, and the kid bears the consequences. The spirits of the jungle have claimed the kid. Even the oracles have spoken."

Bakar felt a rush of emotions, his faith in Tombom clashing with his father's and Jaigol's words. "How can you accuse Tombom of such things? And Kamboda is just a child," he countered, his voice filled with disbelief and pain.

Karamoko's stance was unyielding. "I won't accept a grandchild marked by betrayal and cursed by the spirits. I'm disowning him. And you, Bakar, need to decide where your loyalty lies—with your family or with a woman who has dishonored us." Karamoko pounded his chest with his fist.

Silence enveloped the hut, the gravity of Karamoko's ultimatum leaving Bakar at a painful crossroads. His next choice would redefine his life, a struggle between his deepest affections and the harsh judgments of those around him.

Bakar was crestfallen when he returned to their hut. Tombom was sitting on the bed, Kamboda on her lap, making childish sounds and drooling. He sat on the edge of the bed. His voice was low, strained with doubt and pain, as he said, "Tombom, I know we spoke about this in the past. Just be honest with me; I will forgive you. I swear on the blood of Kopirondin. Did you betray our love?"

Tombom turned to him in surprise. "My love, as I have said in the past and will repeat it, I would never break your trust. I could have done that on several occasions, but I love you. I remember you gave it all for me in that wrestling match; you stood up to your father for our love."

Bakar didn't respond.

Tombom's eyes were brimming with tears. "You know this child is yours. Just look at him," she pleaded, her voice a blend of anguish and conviction.

Bakar, troubled, pressed on. "But why is he so different from Maladho and the others?"

Her tears flowed freely now, her heart aching under the weight of the unfair accusations. "I don't have all the answers. Maybe he's been through too much. We almost lost him, remember?"

Bakar nodded but remained silent, contemplating. In the quiet of their home, the couple faced a storm of doubts and fears, their love and trust tested by whispers and shadows.

As the seasons changed, so did the atmosphere around Tombom. She felt increasingly isolated, a stranger in her own community. In both Kopiro and her home village of Kankelifa, whispers of betrayal followed her. She only found solace in the company of Sona, Demba, Fenda, and a few others who showed her kindness in a sea of judgment.

There was a deep-seated belief among the different tribes that children like Kamboda, those with disabilities, were more than just mere mortals; they were spirits in human form. These children were often labeled snakes or serpent kids, a tag imbued with superstition and fear. "A snake can't live with humans," they would say. Kamboda, with his unique characteristics, soon found himself at the heart of these beliefs. The villagers began calling him "Bôdi-Serpent," a name that set him apart and marked him and his mother as different and unwelcome.

Tombom and Kamboda faced daily challenges. Their existence was clouded by the harsh treatment of those who believed they were a curse inside the community. The way people looked at them, the sharp words and cold shoulders, constantly reminded them of their isolation. This harsh landscape of suspicion and folklore only strengthened the bond between mother and child. But over time, the whispers of Karamoko and the rumors of the villagers seeped into Bakar's mind. Bakar, Tombom's pillar of strength, began to drift away from the woman he had said he loved.

One evening, Tombom sat alone, her eyes red and swollen from days of tears. Bakar approached and informed her that Kamboda would start to sleep in a hut in the far corner of the compound rather than in their hut. "He is too dangerous. A snake can't coexist with humans," he murmured, the judgment of the villagers echoing through his strained voice. His words stung like venom.

Tombom felt the sting of his words deep in her soul, yet her spirit did not falter. "He's not a snake, Bakar. He's our child, born of our love, our flesh and blood." Her voice remained calm despite her husband's aberration.

Caught in a tempest of confusion and suspicion, Bakar countered with a heavy heart, "Tombom, you kept hiding and playing dirty games, but you can't hide from the gods. The truth has been revealed. You did something, not realizing the consequences. Look at Maladho, my nephew. Look at the other children! They're all thriving because their mothers were true. But you, you chose betrayal."

Tombom wiped her nose as tears rolled down her cheeks. "Believe in our bond and the love that brought our child into this world. Don't let their whispers taint the purity of what we share. It's all lies, Bakar, all lies," she implored, her voice carrying pain. Tears streamed down her face as she sniffled.

That night, under Karamoko's lead, they took Kamboda to a distant, isolated hut. Inside, they chained him like an animal, securing him because they believed spirits of that kind were too dangerous to be loose at night. Every morning, his parents unshackled him and led him to the shade of the mango tree, binding his leg with another shackle to the trunk, as Karamoko instructed. There Kamboda sat, bathed in dirt. There, in his quiet solitude, he whistled softly to himself. Whistling was his passion. But even this tiny, innocent act stirred unrest in Karamoko and some of the elders. They believed whistling was an invitation to evil spirits, especially at night. They would silence Kamboda as night fell, covering his mouth to mute his gentle tunes and lead him back to his hut.

Every day brought pain and suffering for Kamboda, creating a gloomy atmosphere in the compound. The clank of the chain and the quiet night whispers painted the sorrow and misunderstanding that filled Kamboda's life. At night, the silence was filled by the sound of Kamboda's chains rattling softly as he shifted in the small, secluded hut. Sleep rarely came to him, his nights long and restless.

Tombom usually made her way to the hut under the cloak of darkness, her visits a secret act of love and care. She would clean him gently, her presence a quiet comfort in the loneliness of his confinement. In the dim light of the hut, Tombom would sit beside Kamboda, her voice a soft murmur of comfort. "My dear Kamboda, my warrior, you are the light of my life. No chain or darkness can ever dim the love I have for you. You are strong, my child, stronger than they know. One day, the world will see the beauty and joy you carry within you. One day, they will apologize for the mistakes they committed against you, me, and all others out there in similar situations. Until then, remember, I am here, always by your side. You are never alone, my precious one."

Her words wove a tapestry of hope and love as she spoke, a tender lullaby to soothe her son's troubled heart.

Every night, Tombom would lie beside him, singing for him. She'd hold him close, offering her warmth and love. In those quiet moments, mother and son shared an unspoken bond, their connection a quiet rebellion against the harsh judgment of the world outside.

Tombom was stuck between the sword and the wall, with nowhere to move. She was brutalized by society, suffering attacks because of Kamboda. At the same time, her family members disowned her, saying she dishonored her clan. Such a betrayal was unforgivable. But what kind of betrayal? Nobody could prove it, and even though Tombom cried many times, pleading that she had never been disloyal, nobody listened to her—and that hurt her even more.

Kamboda was segregated. He couldn't talk, couldn't go to school, couldn't play with other kids. Despite all this, Kamboda was always happy, smiling and whistling often. Other kids were forbidden to play with him. They were told to stay away because he was a snake, a serpent, a horrific creature of the dark world. His cousin Maladho was the only one who dared to approach him.

Chapter Nine

JATIGUI

Whispers began about Kamboda's mysterious powers, which were said to be visible only to those with a special sight, the third eye. People claimed Kamboda could scale walls effortlessly, transforming into a fearsome creature of the night. They said he roamed the wilds, not just hunting for food but also seeking the souls of the unwary. That's why Kamboda hardly ever ate like ordinary people. They murmured that his appetite was for something far more chilling.

One bright morning, Massibo, a well-known cattle owner from the village across the Koff Label River, came storming in, dragging the remains of his cow. Known for his pride in his cattle, he was visibly upset as he approached Karamoko. "The oracles said this is the work of evil spirits," he claimed, pointing to the cow, which looked as if a pack of lions had mauled it. The cow's feet were chewed beyond recognition, and its head was gruesomely damaged. The sight shocked everyone who gathered around. "This is the seventh incident since you chose to harbor a dangerous spirit in your compound," Massibo grunted.

Seeing the condition of the cow, Karamoko felt a wave of sorrow and quickly responded, "I'm deeply sorry to see this,

Massibo. I'll address this situation as soon as possible." Despite this promise, Massibo was still upset and stomped off, grumbling loudly, like a dog that lost its bone.

The night enveloped the village, a deep silence punctuated only by the occasional jangle of chains from Kamboda's hut. Maladho lay in his bed, the events of the day turning over in his mind, leaving him in a state of confusion. The smoke from the lantern wove through the oval hut, its fumes performing a slow dance upward toward the roof, casting flickering shadows across the walls. How was it possible for his cousin, who couldn't even move on his own, to cause damage? It seemed absurd. Struggling with these conflicting images, he found sleep elusive.

His bed, built simply of sacks stuffed with straws, rustled and creaked with every turn he made, echoing his restless thoughts. The more Maladho pondered the situation, the deeper he sank into a maze of doubts and questions. The idea of Kamboda, whom he knew as gentle and incapable of harm, being cast in such a sinister role by their own people was something he couldn't reconcile. As the night stretched on, Maladho remained awake, alone with his thoughts in the dimly lit hut, the smell of kerosene smoke lingering in the air. The disparity between the cousin he knew and the creature of the night described by the villagers left him troubled.

No matter what anyone said, Maladho wasn't bothered. Each morning, before heading off to school or starting his day, he made it a point to visit his cousin, whether in his hut or sitting under the mango tree. Karamoko often yelled at him, "I've told you to stay away from him several times! You and your parents keep ignoring my warnings, but a day will come when the dark spirits act."

But Maladho just grinned and dashed off, not taking

Karamoko's words to heart. "Kamboda, I'm off to school. Be ready! I'll bring back the lesson for you," Maladho cheerfully announced each day.

At these words, Kamboda's face would light up with joy, his laughter filling the air as he clapped his hands, which didn't always move the way he wanted them to. Sometimes, he'd even drool a bit in his excitement. Kamboda eagerly gestured for Maladho to come closer. Without hesitation, Maladho ran over and hugged him, the two cousins sharing a moment of warmth and laughter, staying locked in their embrace for a few precious minutes.

"Oh, the shoes!" Maladho remembered aloud. "I'll bring them back, like always," he added with a smile.

Maladho adored his old white jelly sandals, fixed with bits of melted rubber. They weren't just shoes to him; they were his companions for school, soccer games, celebrations, and baths. Demba had bought them on market day, making them the most extraordinary pair Maladho had ever owned.

Kamboda never had shoes of his own, so Maladho made sure to share his. Every time Maladho came home from school or didn't need the sandals, he'd slip them onto Kamboda's feet, saying, "Here, cousin, it's your turn," with a big grin. Kamboda would burst into joyful laughter, thrilled to share in something simple yet meaningful. Whenever Maladho got a new pair of shoes, which wasn't very often, he made sure Kamboda got to share them, too. Their bond was more than just family; it was about sharing every little joy, including a worn but cherished pair of sandals.

After school, Maladho didn't waste any time. He grabbed his food and hurried over to Kamboda, saying with a smile, "Let's eat, cousin." He sat down close to Kamboda, eagerly digging into his meal while Kamboda watched him eat.

Kamboda usually had porridge or torri, which was his favorite. Maladho pulled out his notebook and textbook. "Time for today's lesson, Kamboda. I've got homework to do," he said, handing the book over.

Kamboda took the book, carefully turning the pages, his eyes scanning each picture with interest. He was quiet, absorbed in the book until he came across a picture of a pig. Seeing it made him laugh out loud, shaking his head with joy. The image reminded him of Bruto, the mischievous pig in the village. Bruto belonged to John Nyanki, a former war veteran left behind in Kopiro like a drift boat. Bruto loved palm wine, and when drunk, he acted a bit wild and crazy. He loved causing trouble by chasing kids, especially if they had food.

"Do you remember Bruto, that crazy drunk pig, hah?" Maladho chuckled, sparking laughter between him and Kamboda. Their giggles filled the air.

After finishing their studies, Maladho brought out a bit of fun. He took a mango leaf and cleverly cut it into the shape of a cross. He inserted a stick in the middle of the cross, making a simple wind-fan toy. He handed one to Kamboda, who watched in astonishment as the leaf spun around and around without stopping, a smile spreading across his face.

Fueled by a burst of energy, Maladho ran into the wind, making his own leaf spinner whirl even faster. "*Avion, avion,* vroom vroom!" he shouted joyfully, his voice a melody of pure delight that echoed through the compound. The other kids joined in, running around with their leaf spinners, laughing and watching the spinning leaves. It was a simple but magical moment of childhood joy.

When they grew tired, Maladho sat in the shade again and pulled out his coloring book, eager to color the animals inside. He laid out his colored pencils, ready for action. He placed them in front of Kamboda, who adored the color blue. Kamboda eagerly flipped through the pages, hunting for the perfect picture to color. "What are you searching for, cousin?" Maladho asked, neatly arranging his pencils. Kamboda's search ended with a picture of a pig. "Alright, let's color the pig," Maladho declared, remembering Bruto's gray hide and black spots. "Pick one," Maladho said, offering Kamboda a gray pencil and a black pencil. But Kamboda had other ideas. Shaking his head, he reached past the offered pencils and grabbed a blue one instead.

"Hey, Kamboda, you are crazy! Bruto isn't blue. He's black and gray," Maladho burst out laughing. But Kamboda was unfazed, clutching the blue pencil with determination. "Okay, okay, it is up to you, cousin. I'll start with my gray, then you add your blue," Maladho said, still chuckling. Together, they colored the pig sky blue and gray.

The next day at school, Maladho became the center of a friendly joke when his classmates saw the picture. "A blue pig? That's a new one!" they laughed. But Maladho just smiled and didn't blame Kamboda. After all, pigs could be of any color in their world.

Maladho spent much of his time playing with Kamboda under the mango tree. Often, in the evenings, he went to Kamboda's hut. Sometimes, he would play there until it got late, and when he fell asleep, his parents would go and carry him back to their hut.

One morning, after a late night playing with Kamboda, Fenda tried her best to wake Maladho up for school. "Maladho, come on, get up! Do I need to wake you up for school every day?"

Rubbing his eyes, he struggled to stand, still half asleep. He stumbled around the room, looking for the plastic kettle to clean himself and get ready. He finally found it outside the back door, empty. "Ugh, I can't stand this! I'm the only one who fills it with water. Then everyone else uses it all and doesn't bother refilling it," he grumbled.

Fenda's voice carried from inside, a bit sharper this time. "You better hurry up. You know what happens when you are late, your teacher will flog you mercilessly again!"

Fenda was right to worry. Maladho's teacher, Mr. Tunkan, was very strict about being on time. He had a rule: students would be flogged one lash for every minute they were late. This strict rule scared some kids, like Maladho's friend Saiko Banna, away from school. Everyone in the village had nicknamed him Tonso, which meant "bat," because of his love for mangoes. They were his favorite thing to eat. He would munch on them every day before heading to school.

Saiko had a habit of picking mangoes in the early morning. He often arrived five minutes late and would end up receiving five lashes as a consequence. One day, he didn't realize that his mango picking had made him thirty minutes late for class. Mr. Tunkan was especially stern that morning. He flogged Saiko more harshly than usual and then made him kneel on the sharp gravel outside. The punishment was so severe that Saiko couldn't even walk home by himself. In the end, they had to get Nyartanka to carry him back on the back of his bicycle. After that day, Saiko never returned to school.

Maladho was nearly late. Quickly, he cupped his hand over his mouth and breathed out to check his breath. *Yuck!* It smelled like locust beans. There was no time to properly clean his teeth with charcoal powder. He rushed to rinse his mouth and gargled in a hurry. He wasn't too bothered about getting it perfectly clean. Grabbing his crumpled notebook and stuffing a pen and a bent pencil into his back pocket, he dashed off to school. He had to keep one hand on his pants to ensure they didn't fall as he ran.

Maladho's school was in an old, empty barracks near the village. The buildings used to be bustling when Portuguese soldiers occupied them, but after they left in the 1970s, the entire place was abandoned and fell into disrepair. The government didn't bother fixing it up, so it turned into ruins. It was a bit risky to hang around because there were still dangerous things like live bullets, grenades, and other explosives lying around. Once, two boys were out there with their cows, and a grenade went off by accident, killing them both. Even though it was dangerous, people kept going back to the old barracks, digging around, hoping to find cool stuff the soldiers might have left behind, like old artifacts or maybe even something valuable.

Maladho was in a full sprint to school. His sandals were so worn out they flapped against the ground, scooping up sand with each step. It sounded almost like they were clapping, urging him, "Faster, Maladho, faster!" Now and then, he'd stumble, feeling like he might faceplant into the sand, but he couldn't slow down. Being late was not an option.

Just as he neared the school gate, a strange sound made him glance back. Behind him, Bruto was on a mission, charging after him. He was not on a leash, as usual. "Seriously, Bruto? Not today! I don't have time for games. Back off, stay away from me, you filthy pig!" Maladho yelled.

The more Maladho sprinted, the more Bruto charged, chasing him with even more energy. Maladho looked everywhere for help, but he couldn't see anyone. There was no way Maladho could stop at the school's entrance with Bruto hot on his heels. Instead, he zoomed off like a rocket into the nearby orchard full of mango and cashew trees, and without a second thought, he climbed a cashew tree. "Go, go away, Bruto. Can't you see I am already late!"

Down below, Bruto kept grunting and poking around the base of the tree, mad as if Maladho had done something to him. Maladho yelled for help, but his voice got lost among the leaves. No one heard him screaming.

Just when Maladho thought he'd be stuck up there forever, Bruto's owner gave a sharp whistle. Bruto paused, gave Maladho a look that seemed to say, "You got lucky this time," and ran toward John.

After ensuring he was gone, Maladho climbed down, his face worried and his arms covered in scratches from the tree branches. It was a morning he definitely wouldn't forget anytime soon. "Ugh, bad luck! Stupid pig. I want him dead and rotten. Ugh!" Maladho muttered under his breath, wiping his body.

He wished he had a watch to check how late he was for school. The thought of facing his teacher made his stomach twist. Maladho made his way to the school door, dragging his feet as if carrying something heavy on his back. He paused at the classroom door. Inside, everyone was already seated. Half the class couldn't help but laugh as soon as they saw him, while a few shook their heads in sympathy.

"Quiet!" roared Teacher Tunkan, and the room fell instantly silent.

Maladho was so scared that he felt like he was about to pee his pants.

"What time is it? Is this the time class starts, you little rat?" Tunkan shouted madly, looking at Maladho with his fiery red eyes, like lava, and his dirty and uneven mustache. His T-shirt was so wrinkled it seemed like it had just been taken out of a bottle. "What happened, Maladho? Tell me."

"It is . . . it is Bruto who chased me . . ."

"Bruto? Liar, shut up." Tunkan turned to the room. "What time is it?" When no one responded, Tunkan pointed directly at Baabagalle, who had a watch. Baabagalle started to tremble like a leaf in the wind, fumbling with his watch, unable to spit out the time.

Maladho watched, thinking to himself, *Come on, tell him the damn time*.

Tunkan, growing impatient, yelled at Baabagalle, "Are you kidding me? If you can't even tell the time, why wear a watch? Do you wear it like some kind of decoration? What, are you trying to be a monkey showing off a new trick?" he scolded, his words sharp as knives. He sucked his teeth in disapproval. "Pah! I'll deal with you later. By the end of it, you'll learn to tell the time just by looking at the sun," he threatened, leaving Baabagalle to wonder about his fate. At the same time, the rest of the class was quietly amused by the turn of events.

Teacher Tunkan glanced at his old watch and announced, "It's 8:25." His smile was more mischievous than kind. He seemed to find a strange joy in disciplining his students. Sometimes, he'd even play a guessing game with them, asking them to figure out what he was thinking. Guessing wrong meant punishment.

This might just be the longest and most painful twenty-five minutes of my life, Maladho thought, his body shaking in anticipation.

"Come, stand over there," Tunkan directed.

With heavy steps, Maladho moved and stood in front of him, feeling his classmates' eyes on him, all wrapped in silence and tension.

Tunkan picked up a paddle, holes drilled through it for extra sting, and alternated his gaze between the paddle and Maladho, preparing for what was to come. "Stay still, or it'll be worse for you," he warned with an evil smile. He raised the paddle so high that everyone got a glimpse of his ugly armpit. Maladho squeezed his eyes shut, bracing for the first strike he knew would hurt the most. Around him, classmates gawked with eyes wide open, while others couldn't bear to look, fearing how harsh it would be.

Teacher Tunkan let out a laugh that sent shivers down everyone's spines. Then, suddenly, his tone changed. "You're lucky today. I just remembered it's my mother's birthday today," he announced. Maladho opened his eyes, hardly believing his ears. "Go take your seat. It seems the stars have aligned for you today. But remember, these twenty-five minutes you've saved yourself? They'll carry over. Be late again, and it'll be double trouble. Got it, you little rascal?"

Maladho let out a breath, feeling like he'd just dodged the biggest bullet. Relief washed over him as he returned to his seat. He was grateful for the unexpected birthday mercy that saved him from punishment that day.

"That was weird, super weird. Tunkan never lets anyone off the hook," Maladho mumbled to himself on his way home. While the rest of the kids teased Baabagalle for not knowing how to tell time, Maladho's mind was elsewhere. It was Friday, after all—hunting day in the bush.

As the kids went their separate ways for lunch, his friend Yero said, "Okay, team, let's not mess around. Be on time and get the dogs ready. Today's hunt is going to be epic!"

The sun was shining just right, not too hot, and a gentle breeze was blowing. Before eating his lunch, Maladho heard his friends whistling, the signal that it was time to gather for their hunting adventure. But first, he took his meal to share a moment under the mango tree with Kamboda.

 Before sitting down to eat, he removed his shoes and placed them on Kamboda's feet. Kamboda looked at him with understanding and gratitude. Then Kamboda gently touched the scratch on Maladho's arm, a silent way of acknowledging that he saw the hurt his cousin had experienced and showing how much he cared and paid attention.

"Oh yes! Bruto and I had a bit of misunderstanding this morning. I kicked his ass and showed him who's boss," Maladho declared with a straight face.

Kamboda burst out laughing so hard he ended up rolling on the ground. He probably guessed Maladho was spinning a tall tale.

"You don't think I could whoop Bruto's ass, huh?" Maladho said, this time joining in the laughter. Bits of rice stuck to his lips, and his mouth was shiny with oil from his meal. He dug into the cabbage for another bite, but Kamboda kept laughing, shaking his head in disbelief.

"Okay, okay, you got me, cousin. Here's what really happened. That walking disaster of a pig chased me like it was out for blood. Seriously, I can't stand Bruto. He nearly got me into so much trouble today," Maladho confessed.

Hearing the real story, Kamboda found it even funnier. He laughed so hard he had to hold his head, thoroughly entertained by Maladho's misadventure with the notorious village pig.

The other kids began gathering around, all set for their hunting adventure, calling out to their dogs with whistles. They waited a bit for Maladho but eventually decided to leave, calling out, "Maladho, we're going! You'll catch up."

Maladho quickly washed his hands in a basin near the well and dried them on his clothes. "Kamboda, I'm heading out for the hunt. Please let me have the shoes. I'll return soon," he said, hoping for the usual quick exchange. But Kamboda didn't want to give the shoes back. He held onto the shoes, making no move to give them back. "Come on,

Kamboda, give me the shoes. Everyone's already left," Maladho begged, but Kamboda still wouldn't budge.

Tombom was nearby and had to step in. "Kamboda, please, let him have the shoes," she urged. Finally, Kamboda handed over the shoes, but then he grabbed Maladho's shirt, unwilling to let go.

"Let go of me, Kamboda! I promise, we'll play again later. I have to go now," Maladho yelled, trying to break free from Kamboda's grip. His patience was running thin with the unexpected delay. As Maladho tried to wiggle free, Kamboda clung to him tighter, like an anaconda wrapping around its prey. It could have been a funny scene, like something out of a comedy, except Kamboda wasn't laughing, and Maladho couldn't escape.

"Kamboda, let Maladho go this instant," Tombom called out, her voice firm.

Fenda came out of her hut, drawn by the commotion. "Oh Tombom, let them play," she said with a gentle laugh, thinking it was all in good fun.

"Mom, seriously, I'm already late! My friends are going to start hunting without me. Please, tell him to let go," Maladho said, his frustration boiling. "Kamboda, why are you doing this?" he pleaded, baffled by his cousin's unusual behavior. Yet he still refused to let go.

"Oh, Maladho, just stay and play with him. You have been at school since morning; he missed you. Stay. You can go hunting tomorrow," Fenda pleaded.

Suddenly, there was a huge explosion. It was so loud and powerful that it knocked the two cousins off their feet and sent them flying a few feet away. The dogs in the village went crazy, barking and darting every which way, not knowing where to run. Birds sitting quietly in the trees tumbled down, and the mango tree shuddered, dropping its leaves like rain. For a moment, they could only hear the ringing in their ears. In the distance, toward the barracks, a great plume of black smoke started to curl up into the sky, marking the spot of the explosion.

Everyone stood stunned, staring at the smoke with hearts racing and minds buzzing with questions.

Maladho quickly got back on his feet, a bit shaky, and brushed the dirt off himself. He stared down the path to the barracks, where the smoke was thickest. Kamboda had a small cut above his eyebrow but seemed unfazed, gazing intently in the same direction. Maladho couldn't help but tremble, worried about his friends who had headed in that direction. With a determined step, Maladho started to move, driven by concern for his friends. But his dad reached out and firmly held him back, preventing him from going any further.

"Hey, hey! Maladho, get back here now! It's too dangerous out there, and we have no idea what's going on," his mom exclaimed, her voice filled with worry.

Maladho watched as the village elders hurried toward the site of the explosion. His heart raced, and he breathed hard like a horse after a long run. Something caught his eye from a nearby tree—a blackened object still smoking. It took him a moment to realize it was a human limb. The sight made him shake in horror.

Cries and wails began to fill the air from the direction of the barracks. "Oh, gods of Kopiro, oh forefathers, what have we done to deserve this?" voices echoed in despair.

Among the chaos, Maladho spotted a man wandering, his hands clasped over his head, overcome with grief. "They're gone, oh! All of them are gone!" the man sobbed.

Maladho realized all at once that he had lost all his friends. This made him feel numb. The day brought unprecedented sadness across the country, a tragedy that Kopiro and its neighboring regions had never witnessed before. Eighteen young lives were lost in an instant—a blast caused by the children accidentally igniting a bomb in the barracks—leaving a void that could never be filled. Among those who should have been with them, Maladho was the sole survivor, spared by a twist of fate.

Kamboda, in his own way, had become Maladho's guardian angel. If it weren't for him, Maladho realized, he would have been among those lost to the blast. Clutching his mother in a tearful embrace, Maladho sobbed, "He saved my life, Mom." Tears flowed freely among everyone present, united in their grief. He was hailed as Maladho's hero.

After the funerals and traditional ceremonies were done, a hush fell over the village. But whispers started to spread. Villagers said they'd sought advice from the oracles, who warned that Kopiro was now home to evil spirits. They insisted the village needed a cleansing soon, or else they'd face even greater calamities. They were sure that this was the work of evil spirits, and they pointed fingers directly at Kamboda.

This belief put Kamboda in a precarious situation, as the call for action against him grew louder. Tension was thick in Kopiro, as dilemmas about how to protect the village transformed into a heated debate.

The air in Kopiro grew heavy with blame and fear. "Kamboda must have known. Why else would he have held Maladho like that? He's responsible," voices began to accuse, pointing fingers at the innocent boy who couldn't defend himself. "Why can't we act quickly to remove him like we did with other kids in the past? Why, because he is Karamoko's grandchild!"

The grief of the tragedy turned into anger, and some

parents, hearts broken by the loss of their children, stormed Karamoko's home. Their cries filled the compound, "Remove this child! Remove the curse you've brought upon us. This is your fault!" Murmurs spread like wildfire. "We need to act now, send him away from Kopiro. He doesn't belong here. We can't suffer more because of him," voices echoed, pushing for Kamboda to be cast out and sent to a place they deemed he belonged. The community's pain and loss were transforming into a dire ultimatum for Kamboda, marking him a scapegoat for a tragedy he had no hand in.

Maladho couldn't wrap his head around the accusations flying at his cousin. To him, Kamboda was just a harmless person, incapable of causing the disaster that had unfolded. He knew, just like everyone else, that the barracks were a ticking time bomb filled with explosives. Yet people had always wandered in and out of there, ignoring the danger. How could they pin the blame on Kamboda for their own recklessness? *Stupid people*, he thought, frustrated and saddened by the unfairness of it all. *How could they not see the truth?*

Even though people whispered and plotted, Maladho didn't care. He continued to spend time with Kamboda, their laughter and games a small oasis of joy in an increasingly hostile world. They played and giggled. But that happiness was short-lived.

Karamoko had long wanted to distance himself from his grandson, and now it seemed everything aligned for him to do just that. In the afternoon, the village elders called Tombom and Bakar to a meeting in Karamoko's hut. "We've gathered here after much thought and discussion," began the announcer, glancing between Tombom and Bakar. "Our leader will soon share the decision regarding Kamboda's future."

Tombom's face showed tiredness and fear. Her eyes were filled with silent pleas, begging for mercy for her son. The weight of the moment was crushing. She braced for the words she feared most, yet leaving the gathering was out of the question. To walk away would be seen as a grave insult to the elders, a choice she couldn't afford to make, no matter how much she wished to avoid those words.

"Thank you, everyone, for gathering once more," Karamoko began, his voice echoing a sense of community spirit that Kopiro prided itself on. "This village has always thrived on unity and togetherness. Unfortunately, we find ourselves discussing such matters today, which could have been avoided if not for the stubbornness of some."

A few elders coughed softly, a subtle hint for Karamoko to be careful in his words and avoid confrontation. Understanding the warning, Karamoko shifted his tone slightly, "Sorry. Kamboda is my grandson and part of my family. But the elders and oracles suggested that he must return to his real home. If we don't do it urgently, the gods will punish us. Therefore, we have to run the test, which should enlighten us further. However, it's clear to me that for our village to return to its peaceful state and to avoid the wrath of dark spirits that seem to have already begun their torment, Kamboda cannot stay among us."

Tombom lightly shook her head and looked down. Tears streaming down her eyes, but she dared not object. She didn't have the power to stop what was to happen.

The announcer started again. "The ritual must be held tomorrow night. It must be conducted secretly, as the rules mandate, and only some chosen individuals will take part."

Later when the sun was disappearing, Tombom quietly sought out the wisdom of Balaba. The sword bean tied in her wrapper, she sought out the old lady who had helped her so many times before, hoping for a way to protect Kamboda. When she arrived, she was surprised to find Balaba waiting. They exchanged quick greetings, then Tombom fell to her knees, grabbing Balaba's feet. "Please, ma'am, they're planning to take my son away," she pleaded, tears streaming down her face.

Moved by Tombom's plea, Balaba helped her to her feet and guided her to sit on a nearby stool. "I can feel the depth of your sorrow and the torment in your heart. I wish there were something I could do. However, there are limits to what I'm permitted to intervene in. Destiny has charted its course, and sadly, it's not within my power to change it," she said, her voice heavy with regret.

Uncertainty lingered in the air. Which destiny was Balaba referring to? Was it the path laid out for Kamboda or her lack of action to run to save her kid? Tombom felt confused and defeated. She returned to the village, where she spent the night with her son.

Before sunrise, Kamboda was awake. His father brought him to the mango tree, and he was happy and playful. Maladho, who was on vacation from school, joined him early, and they began to play. Kamboda showed an energy and happiness he had never shown before, perhaps sensing it would be his last day at the compound and Kopiro, his last time playing with his cousin. Maybe he felt alleviated that he was leaving, and he was ready. Perhaps he foresaw that his new home would offer him peace, dignity, and respect.

Maladho didn't suspect anything. He built toy cars from bamboo and gave one to Kamboda. They built sand houses. They clapped and played games. Sometimes, Kamboda whistled his melodic tunes.

It was all fun until almost dusk when Tombom came for her son. She prepared Kamboda for the evening, bathing him for the last time. She covered him with his wrapper and gave him his favorite food, *gossi-gerte,* a peanut rice porridge. After his meal, he drank a lot of water and burped. Then he smiled at his mother, who smiled back at him. A smile of pure love and heartbreak. Tombom carried him back to his hut.

That evening, Fenda told Maladho that he needed to rest and go to sleep early because they would be leaving before sunrise to go to Buruntuma and buy him something at Lumo. She knew Maladho loved going to market day and used it as a way to prevent him from visiting Kamboda's hut.

CHAPTER TEN

THE NIGHT

Sometimes Kamboda wondered what set him apart from others, what made his life so different. His life had been like that for the past eight years. He would sit innocently under the tree, looking down at his floppy legs, the chains biting into his skin, and bathed with dirt, hopelessly surrounded by misery and agony. All he had was his tune and the certainty that this world wasn't for him and that humans were unfair. He would sit the entire day whistling as if communicating with a different world. Kamboda's incredible whistling melody amused the birds perched calmly on the mango tree, and they listened carefully to him. Even the air seemed to pause and listen, and the sun lingered a bit longer in the sky, reluctant to move on as his melodies filled the air.

That night, for what she feared would be the last time, Tombom entered her beloved son's hut. Kamboda looked up at her. Tombom sat close to him, gently placing her hand on his head, and there was a silent exchange of love and sorrow between them. Kamboda reached out and wiped her tears with his small hand. If he could speak, there were so many things he might have said to her at that moment, but his actions were enough.

Tombom wrapped her arms around him, holding him as

tightly as she could. "Kamboda, my son, forgive me. If only I had known the life you'd have. I wouldn't have fought to bring you into this scary world! I'm so sorry I couldn't protect you," she sobbed, her heart breaking with each word. "No matter where they take you, always remember I love you. I did everything I could to save you," she whispered, looking into his eyes, searching for understanding.

"Mama, Mama," Kamboda uttered softly, nodding.

Tombom's heart skipped a beat. "You can talk? Please, Kamboda, say something more. Tell me, say something, Kamboda." she urged, her voice trembling with hope.

But Kamboda fell silent again, returning to his usual state. Yet, those two simple words were a precious gift that Tombom would hold in her heart forever.

Bakar stood outside the hut listening, his heart softening with each word he overheard. He wanted to go and join them, but he was motionless, as if he felt pinned to the ground. He realized perhaps he should have listened to Tombom's plea to flee with Kamboda, to protect him at all costs. But fear held him back. Fear of punishment from the gods, as elders told him. *I am a coward*, he thought. With resolve stirring within him, he rushed to confront his father.

Bursting into Karamoko's house, Bakar pleaded, "Baaba, please, we have to stop this! He's just a boy! He's human. Please, do not go through with it." In a desperate move, he knelt, clutching at his father's legs, hoping to appeal to his better nature.

Karamoko looked down at his son with disdain. "Are you mad? Do you want to disgrace the tribe and everybody in our community? Don't be greedy. You are the future leader of this community. Don't fail. Don't be a coward."

"Baaba, I am not a coward, but I feel this isn't right."

Karamoko was unmoved. "Look at me, son. You'll have plenty of chances to have other children. Don't jeopardize the future. Now get up and go!"

The haunting melody of Kamboda's whistle echoed for the last time that day.

Maladho was unable to fall asleep. He assumed it was due to his excitement over the visit to Lumo in the morning, but something in the air felt off. His mother's muffled sobs reached his ears, and he craned his neck to hear. He could just make out her whispering. "Shouldn't we do something? They might kill the boy!"

"No need to panic. They're just taking him back home. Hush, let's not disturb Maladho," his father replied.

A kid being taken home? The whisper made him wide awake, his mind filled with questions and worries. He wondered who the child could be. *It couldn't be me*, he thought. Then he realized it must be Kamboda, his best friend, the only child who faced so much dislike from everyone. Maladho wished he could forget what he had heard, wished the night was a dream. But in their small hut, where no wall separated him from his parents, secrets were hard to keep. Every sound traveled quickly inside their round room.

Maladho knew the rules. Asking questions or being too curious about adult matters was forbidden and disrespectful. He promised himself he wouldn't fall asleep. If the whispers were about Kamboda, he wouldn't just ignore them. He wouldn't let his friend down. He would find out where they were taking his cousin. The night was unusually quiet. Even Kamboda, who often made noise with his chains, was silent. The wind whispered through the night.

But later, after hours of lying awake, new night sounds penetrated the dark: the barking of Kulanjan, their loyal dog, and other village dogs, creating a restless chorus. It was different from the usual bark. To Maladho, it sounded like Kulanjan was sad, as if he sensed something was about to happen. Maladho suspected that something was going on in their compound beyond their usual routines. Visits from village elders and his aunt Tombom's tears after they left were signs. Despite his determination, Maladho eventually fell asleep.

Under the cover of night, while Maladho was sleeping, Kamboda was taken, torn from his mother's grasp as harshly as an unripe mango is plucked from its branch. The elders and the village guardians, despite their belief that Kamboda was a spirit, agreed to a daring test. They would seat him at the riverbank in the dead of night. If he remained there until sunrise, he would be proven human. But if he were a spirit, he would vanish, slipping into the river's depths.

The night was alive with a chorus of protest. Dogs barked in defiance, their howls echoing through the darkness. Kulanjan seemed agitated, his barks piercing the night. He ran side to side, barking and howling, then was joined by other dogs. Crickets chirped, frogs croaked, and owls hooted from the margins of the river. Even the river seemed restless. They left Kamboda alone on the banks and returned without looking back, because if they looked back, they would spoil the ritual. After the ritual, all the sounds of the night faded away, and silence returned, a deafening silence. Perhaps nature felt the pain.

Eager to find out their test's outcome, the elders rushed to the river at dawn, but Kamboda wasn't there; he had vanished. Only the river knew what happened and how. Koff Label was the last to see Kamboda. The river was his witness.

"We were right. He is a spirit, that's why he left. Now it is clear," Karamoko said and sighed.

In the morning, Maladho awoke to a sight that cut deep into his heart. His mother was sitting, tears streaming down her face.

At that moment, Maladho remembered the promise he had made to himself—to always be there for Kamboda—a promise he now felt he had broken. Maladho jumped up and, wearing only his brown khaki shorts, ran to the door, realizing he had failed his cousin.

He ran to Kamboda's hut only to find a scene that confirmed his worst fears. The chain that had once restrained his cousin lay discarded on the ground, and adult footprints were scattered throughout the hut. It was too late. His cousin was gone.

Kamboda hadn't escaped on his own, he couldn't have. Someone had taken him away. The moment Maladho understood, it felt like a punch in the gut. He felt guilty for not being able to help his friend when he needed him. It marked the end of Maladho's childhood innocence, thrusting him into a premature maturity despite his young age.

He didn't waste another moment. He dashed straight to his aunt Tombom's place. Her face was etched with sadness, but she managed a warm smile and hugged Maladho as soon as she saw him. This morning, he skipped the usual greetings. "Where's my cousin?" he asked, his voice heavy with concern.

"Kamboda's okay," she assured him, her gaze not meeting his. She gently placed her left hand on his head as she spoke, lightly scratching his ringworm.

"But if he's okay, then where is he?" Maladho pressed, needing to know more.

His mother had followed him and stepped in before he could ask anything else. "Son, let's give your aunt some space, dear. Let's go. You need to brush your teeth. I've got the charcoal ready," she said, gently pulling him away.

Back inside their hut, Fenda looked serious as she spoke to Maladho. "I need you to listen carefully. You shouldn't be running around asking questions," she cautioned him firmly.

"But, Mom, I just need to know where Kamboda is."

Fenda bowed her head sadly. "Kamboda went home."

"Where? Where is his home? I thought here is his home."

"Maladho, you will understand later. Right now, keep your mouth shut. Now go and wash your mouth and get your breakfast," Fenda ordered.

It was a different morning. Everything seemed gloomy to Maladho. Walking under the mango tree toward the kitchen, he noticed birds patiently sitting on the branches as if they were waiting for Kamboda, too. The tree itself appeared somber. The usual gentle breeze was absent, leaving the air still and heavy. Maladho's mind wandered, and as he looked down at his powerless and skinny body, he felt a deep sense of helplessness.

The whispers he heard the previous night lingered in his mind, haunting him over and over. He hoped Kamboda would appear one day, or they might meet one day somewhere. He was certain that one day he would know what had happened.

Waking up to the reality of Kamboda's absence, Maladho had to face the harsh truth that sometimes, no matter how hard we try, we can't control what happens. This realization was hard to accept, marking the loss of his friend and the end of his childhood all at once. That night changed Maladho, making him see the cruelty and darkness in people. It left him feeling guilty for not being able to protect his friend, for not standing by him when he needed it most.

This guilt would stay with him for years to come.

As days turned into weeks and weeks turned into months, the sharp pain of Kamboda's absence started to fade. The constant hope of seeing his friend again slowly disappeared, washed away by time. Life continued. Maladho made new friends, and encounters with his Auntie Tombom no longer brought the same sadness. What had once filled his thoughts and feelings gradually became another part of his past.

CHAPTER ELEVEN

DREAM

A year after Kamboda's disappearance, Maladho's life took a strange turn. Once peaceful nights became filled with disturbing dreams and visions he couldn't explain. In one vivid dream, Kamboda returned, walking slowly back into Maladho's life. He looked worn out, with a deep sadness in his eyes and a thoughtful frown on his face.

Maladho didn't hesitate, running up to his cousin and wrapping him tightly, overwhelmed with relief and happiness. But when he looked around, he realized they were alone, surrounded by a thick fog that made everything else invisible. "Kamboda, my friend! I'm so happy to see you again. Wow, you can walk! That's awesome, cousin," he said happily.

"Yes, my new mother taught me how to walk and talk," he said, his voice surprising Maladho.

Maladho's heart swelled with joy at this new development. "Wow, that's cool! I have missed you a lot. Where have you been all this time? They said you went 'home,' but I always thought this was your home. We're supposed to be friends forever. Why didn't you come back or tell me where you were going?"

Kamboda looked at him and offered a gentle smile. "May

I have some food? I'm starving." Wasting no time, Maladho dashed inside and quickly returned with some food for Kamboda. He watched silently as his friend ate and then drank some water with quiet gratitude.

"Thanks, Maladho, my buddy, for the food. I am so happy to see you. I missed you too. It is hot here. Let's walk to the river, it is much cooler there."

"Hot?" Maladho was puzzled. It was the middle of Harmattan, the air crisp with the season's characteristic cool winds. "Aren't you going to visit your parents?"

Kamboda shook his head. "No, that doesn't matter now. I specifically came to see you," he replied.

Maladho nodded in excitement. "Let's hang out under the mango tree like we used to. We could build sand houses, look at our books, do homework—remember dealing with Bruto?"

Kamboda offered a soft smile. "Next time. This visit is just for you. But come with me. There's something I want to show you." He gently wrapped his left arm over Maladho's shoulders, a gesture of friendship that Maladho warmly returned.

Together, they made their way to the river, the cool air brushing against their faces. Arriving at the riverbank, Kamboda turned to Maladho with a smile. "I'm going to show you my home and my mother. But first, let's have some fun and I'll teach you a new song," he said, leading the way to a nearby taba tree. Under the shade of the tree, they happily played. "Now let's sing. Are you ready?" he asked, excitement in his voice. When Maladho nodded, Kamboda began to sing, his voice carrying a beautiful and melancholic melody.

"Kamboda the denied Kopironko, it's going to be okay. They can't take your spirit. You're a true Kopironko, strong as steel yet gentle

as cotton. Ayoo Kopironko, denied freedom, Kopironko Kumo. Though men have taken you, your essence remains untouched, your lineage powerful. No matter where you find yourself, your legacy will endure. Shame on them, shame on them. One day, the truth will prevail."

With its poignant lyrics, the song resonated deeply, echoing around them, a sad yet beautiful tribute to the resilience and the indomitable spirit of Kamboda.

"Wow, I had no idea you could sing, but I love it!" Maladho exclaimed, genuinely surprised.

Kamboda patiently repeated it until Maladho could join in. Together, they sang, their laughter mingling with the melody as they danced around the taba tree. After some time, Kamboda looked toward the river, his playful attitude becoming gentle and serious. "Maladho, it's time for me to return home now," he announced.

"But you said you'd show me your home," Maladho reminded him, not ready for their reunion to end.

Kamboda smiled gently, looking at the calm water. "This river, this is my home now. You're always welcome to visit me here. I'm sorry I couldn't return to see you or tell you where I was. Just remember, we're friends, and we should always look out for each other," he explained with wisdom beyond his years.

Standing at the edge of the river, surrounded by wilderness, Maladho scanned the area, expecting to see some sort of home. But there was nothing—no house, no structure in sight. "Kamboda, come on. You said this is your home, but where's the house? You must be joking."

Kamboda replied calmly, "You might not see it, but I promise you, this is where I belong."

Maladho shivered slightly, noticing the chill in the air. "It's cold out here. Let's head back to the village, to your real home. Plus, your parents are there," he suggested, hoping to convince Kamboda.

Kamboda shook his head and looked down at the ground. "No, Maladho, I don't fit in there."

"It doesn't matter if they love you or not. I love you."

Kamboda stepped closer to Maladho, placing his arms gently on his friend's shoulders, and tenderly wiping away the tears that had started to form. "Maladho, my brother, there's no need to cry. My new mother says that tears drain good energy and fill you with sadness. Try to keep smiling because you have a kind heart. Remember, that's all they can offer those who aren't nice to us. They don't know any better," he explained, his voice soft.

"You have a new mother?"

"Yes, I do. She's not around now, but I'll introduce you to her one day. I promise you'll get to come inside and meet my new brothers and sisters, too. You'll like it there," Kamboda assured him with a smile. But then, glancing at the sky as it darkened, he added, "It's getting late. You should head back to the village. I need to leave now."

Maladho felt proud and sad at the same time. He smiled in response, yet when he hugged Kamboda goodbye, he sensed how cold and ghostly Kamboda's body felt—soft as cotton and insubstantial as the mist above the river. Goodbye was hard. As Kamboda turned to leave, Maladho felt an urge to follow him, to not let his friend disappear again. But despite his desire, his feet wouldn't move, as if they were glued to the ground on the riverbank. Helpless, he could only watch as Kamboda walked away. Kamboda started to sing and cry, and Maladho joined him in singing. Kamboda walked and entered the mud, then to the river, singing until he disappeared into the water. Maladho couldn't stop crying and singing, tears streaming down his face.

Chapter Twelve

CONSEQUENCES

Returning from the well, Fenda heard something unusual—Maladho was singing in his sleep. Terrified, she rushed to his side, finding him with tears on his cheeks and a song on his lips. Frightened and confused, she shook him, trying to wake him up.

"Maladho. Maladho, my son, what is wrong?" She was becoming terrified. "Maladho, Maladho, my son, why are you crying? What song is that?"

He opened his eyes, but before he could reply, she grabbed and held him in her arms, cuddling him as if she were protecting him from an invisible force.

Maladho struggled to talk. His lips were quivering, and he felt a lump in his throat. "Mom, I saw Kamboda. He came to visit me, and we went together to the river. He is the one who taught me the song. He has a new mom." Maladho tried to tell his mother about his encounter with Kamboda in his dreams in a hurry.

Fenda's heart raced with a mix of fear and confusion. She panicked, picking Maladho up into her arms, she rushed outside, tears streaming down their faces. She took him to Karamoko's hut. Everybody panicked in the compound, and some outsiders even ran to see what was happening.

Karamoko, busy at the back of his hut, heard the commotion and hurried to see what was causing such distress. He rushed and met his daughter and his grandchild at the door.

"Please, Baaba, help me, my son . . . my son . . . I believe the demons of the river have possessed him," she kept repeating the words. She handed Maladho over to his grandpa.

Karamoko took a deep breath, trying to calm the situation. "Fenda, calm down, my daughter, and tell me what is happening," he urged her gently.

Fenda told him what she had witnessed, and then Karamoko asked Maladho to describe his dream.

Karamoko's concern quickly turned to frustration. He turned to Fenda. "It is your fault. You and your husband didn't want to listen to me when I warned you in the past. You thought I was crazy," Karamoko shouted. "I told you to keep him away! No one's kid is possessed or haunted by demons because they did as they were told to do. You and your husband confronted me when I told you to halt your kid playing with Kamboda. You denied me, knowing he was a product of evil spirits, a serpent from the dark world. Now the time has come when the dark will engulf you. Get ready to pay the price." He groaned. "Now here you run to me, 'Baaba, Baaba, help!'" Karamoko mocked her.

Fenda was overwhelmed by his words, fear gripping her heart. Maladho was indifferent because he didn't care and didn't think it made sense. He didn't share his grandfather's beliefs and wasn't frightened by the talk of spirits and curses. Instead, he cherished the dream about Kamboda, treating it more like a precious memory than a mere figment of his imagination. He wished to have dreamed more often about his cousin.

Karamoko took his cowries and consulted them, seeking

insight from the spirits and gods. After a long silence, he said, "The dark spirits have plagued your son. Something needs to be done before it is too late." Later, he wrote mysterious symbols on his wooden board and washed them into the calabash bowl. He bathed Maladho with the mixture and said it was for protection against dark forces.

Maladho stayed at Karamoko's hut for a few hours, which was his first time entering Karamoko's hut. It was forbidden for non-initiated kids to enter there, and only a few people had that privilege. While he was alone, he browsed the items inside the hut. Some uncanny objects, such as sculptures, figurines, and cowries glued into red cloth, people's hair, bones, animal heads, carcasses, skin . . . he felt goosebumps. Still, it didn't stop him from browsing. When he heard steps, he lay down and pretended to be asleep. What he saw in that hut was so scary and powerful, maybe that's why everybody feared Karamoko.

Maladho remembered the day a fire swept through their compound, devouring everything in its path—except for Karamoko's hut. It was as if the flames themselves were afraid to come near it. That's how everyone knew just how strong Karamoko was. Rumors swirled around the village about what secrets Karamoko kept. Some whispered he shared his back room with a serpent, while others claimed he had nightly visits from jinn. The stories about his mystical abilities were endless, and his reputation as a descendant of the mighty Kopirondin only added to the mystery surrounding him.

From that day, Maladho had never fully recovered his mind. It was as if someone was watching him the whole time. When the dark came, he saw shadows everywhere, shadows that seemed to come alive, flickering and dancing around him, making him jump at even his own silhouette, which left him trapped in a world where reality and shadows blurred. He had never before been like that. Even when Manga, Karamoko's shepherd, told him scary tales of terrifying creatures, he had never felt so moved as now.

Maladho's dreams about Kamboda didn't stop; they kept coming, night after night. Then, when he was wide awake, he started to hear voices. It was late one night when the first whispers reached him, sounds that seemed to float on the wind from the direction of the river. They carried the melody of the song he had sung in his dreams, followed by a giggle, distant but unmistakably clear. A voice calling his name, "Maladho, come, come, let's play."

He sat on his bed, listening carefully. The voices seemed so natural, as if Kamboda was right there. The boundary between his dreams and reality began to blur, making him wonder if the voice was reaching out to him, trying to tell him something from beyond.

His parents were worried about his recent behavior and what Karamoko told them about dark spirits possessing him. Fenda started taking him to her bed and told Demba to sleep on the mat. His parents knew something mysterious, bigger than Kamboda's departure, was messing with his head. Whenever he woke and sat up in bed, his parents woke too, worried. No one got a full night's sleep, these habits draining each of them thoroughly in their own way.

Sometimes, Maladho would run to his parents with a frantic look in his eyes. "Dad, Mom, can you hear that? It's Kamboda! He's calling me. Maybe he is hungry or cold. We must go help him," he'd insist, his voice filled with concern and a desperate need to act. Upon hearing those words, Fenda would burst into tears, hugging her son tight. Demba, meanwhile, would sit quietly, a hand pressed against his forehead, lost in worry.

One night, Maladho didn't eat his food, but instead placed it under his bed, hidden from Fenda and Demba. He pretended to fall asleep, waiting for his parents to go to bed, listening in the darkness until he heard the sound again. Then he slowly took his food, held his shoes, and snuck slowly and quietly from the hut, like a chameleon. The moon was bright and full, lighting everything with a soft glow that made it easy to see. The night was alive. Animals roamed freely, enjoying the moonlight.

Guided by the sound, Maladho made his way toward the river. With each step, the whistling and giggling grew louder, pulling him closer. As he ventured deeper into the night, the bushes around him seemed to come alive, rustling and moving as though something was darting through them. But Maladho wasn't afraid. His mind was set on one thing only: finding Kamboda.

When he was a safe distance from the village, he called out. "Kamboda, Kamboda where are you? Let's play jarnakoli under the mango tree. I know you are probably hungry, so I brought you some food." He was screaming, and his voice echoed in the bush and the riverbank. Maladho stood there, alone but determined, the moon casting long shadows around him.

Suddenly, everything stopped moving. The wind died. The mangroves and the forest froze. The animals seemed to quiet. It seemed everything was calmly listening to Maladho. "Kamboda, come on. I know you are here. Please, I miss you." He felt a fresh breeze, the cool wind feeling different against his skin. The river before him began to stir, sending small waves rippling toward him as if answering his call. Maladho watched, his heart pounding with excitement and bravery, as the water seemed to dance toward him. He was fearlessly staring, mesmerized by that movement, and waiting for what might come next. But then he heard distant voices coming from the direction of the village, calling his name. When he turned, he saw the flickering of lanterns. The voices echoed into the night. "Maladho! Maladho, where are you?"

He recognized his mom's voice, crying and calling his name in the middle of all those voices. The sound of drums joined the chorus, signaling a search was underway. He realized they were looking for him. He was annoyed. *They are interrupting my chance to see Kamboda again, just when something was about to happen,* he thought angrily. He looked around and hid under the vast taba tree near the riverbank. Facing the river, he called out to Kamboda in a soft voice, urging him to come forth.

The river responded. The waves grew more extensive. Maladho felt excitement and nervousness build, sure something extraordinary was about to happen. His eyes were fixed on the moving water, waiting for Kamboda to appear from the depths. As he was concentrating, something grabbed the back of his neck, and he screamed.

Fenda heard it, and she panicked. Maladho could hear her voice calling out, "It's him. He is by the river!"

The hand on his neck loosened. "Shush, it is ok. It's just me, your uncle. Calm down." It was Uncle Tamba. He patted Maladho's shoulder and pulled a horn to his lips, blowing a warning signal to the others, indicating Maladho had been found.

At that moment, something large plunged into the water nearby, sending a spray of cold droplets over them. The shape and details were obscured, only the rippling of the water indicated where it had landed. Even the fearless Tamba was astonished and shaking, scared and unsure of what he had witnessed.

The crowd apprehensively arrived, Karamoko leading the group. "There he is, there he is, thank ancestors and our gods!"

Fenda rushed forward, followed more stoically by Demba, and they embraced Maladho. His mother was sobbing uncontrollably, pulling him close. The other villagers began praying to invoke the gods for protecting him. Maladho recognized people from the neighboring village, who it seemed had joined in the search.

"Are you crazy, naughty boy? You scared us half to death," Karamoko grumbled. "Stubborn boy. The demons of the dark are after you."

They took him home, and people murmured on the way. "He was kidnapped by Fenkatos, the foolish jinn," some whispered. Others said, a little more harshly, "It was that Kamboda. His serpent spirit lured the boy." Uncle Tamba remained quiet as if something locked his tongue. He seemed shocked by the shape in the water. He knew something wasn't right.

The next day, it was a trending topic. Everybody now believed Maladho was possessed by the same spirits that embodied Kamboda. His parents didn't let him go out for several days other than to visit Karamoko, who cleansed him with his magic water and herbs. As he tied a protecting charm around Maladho's waist, he said to Fenda and Demba, "He was lucky. The spirits of our ancestors stood up for him that night. Otherwise, it would have been a tragic ending."

But that event didn't cease Maladho's willingness to return to Kamboda.

Repeatedly, he woke up in the middle of the night to listen to the song, the whistle, the giggles, and other incomprehensible words. He stopped eating and never went out to play again as he used to. His parents were worried and feared the worst, rapidly connecting him with Kamboda. It continued to worsen, and Maladho was ruled mad and possessed by the spirits of the river and forest, the same ones that embodied Kamboda.

Chapter Thirteen

THE MANICOMIO

Karamoko's friend Giovanni came to visit, seeking advice of his own. He was tall and thin, with a bald head, big eyes, and a gray mustache. He liked wearing short-sleeved shirts and blue jeans. He worked at a psychiatric hospital in Bissau, and even though Giovanni was a skilled doctor from Italy, he realized that being in a new country meant learning traditional medicine from locals like Karamoko.

During his visit, Giovanni noticed something was off with Maladho and decided to gently address the issue with Karamoko. After hearing the story, Giovanni offered his help. "Karamoko, you're excellent in your field, but let me take Maladho under my care for a bit," he suggested.

Karamoko shook his head, "Thank you, Doctor, but this disease isn't something the white people's medicine can fix. I've got it under control."

Giovanni nodded thoughtfully. He shifted his strategy. "What if I study Maladho's condition for a few days? It'll help me learn about illnesses of this variety and understand his particular case. I'll bring him back in two weeks, and I'll even use the remedies you've been trying," he proposed.

This time, Karamoko agreed, and Maladho found himself in the city, with Fenda accompanying him for support, under the care of Dr. Giovanni. The hospital was nestled among many cashew trees, a bit away from the main hustle of Bissau. It was a quiet place by day, but at night, it changed. The sounds of patients crying out filled the darkness. The scariest moments came when the hospital lost power for a few minutes. The darkness deepened, and the air filled with the sounds of patients screaming and pounding on the walls, heightening the fear and confusion of the night.

The doctor asked him many questions about Kamboda, and Maladho shared all he knew. Giovanni gave him pills that made him sleep deeply all day, leaving him dizzy when he was awake. Maladho dreamt but couldn't remember anything once he woke.

Peering out his window, where the light from the hospital faded into the shadows cast by the cashew trees, Maladho saw figures beckoning to him, their forms barely distinguishable in the dim light. "Mom!" Maladho's shout pierced the quiet night.

Fenda looked at him from where she sat in the chair next to his bed. She rubbed her tired eyes. "Maladho, what's wrong now?"

"Mom, he's calling me. Open the door, please!"

"Who's calling?" Fenda asked, her concern growing.

"Look under the cashew tree. He's there. It's Kamboda. I need to go to him," Maladho insisted.

Fenda glanced outside, seeing nothing but the surrounding darkness. Sighing, she gave Maladho the pills, like every other night, watching as he drifted back to sleep, escaping the shadows for a while.

One day, Fenda went to the market, so Maladho was left under the care of Famata, a short, dark-skinned woman. She wore a green gown and kept her gray-streaked hair tied back, revealing a scar on her forehead. She approached

Maladho with a smile, which made him tense up, expecting the dreaded pills. "Why the long face? Don't like me much?" Famata teased gently.

Maladho just stared quietly, his distrust evident.

"I'm not here with medicine today. You are looking much better," Famata reassured him, trying to lighten his mood. She sat down beside him.

His expression softened.

Famata placed her hands gently on his. "You'll get through this. I've been where you are. As a teen," she shared.

"Was your best friend taken too?"

"No, my struggle was losing my mom," Famata replied, her voice tinged with sadness.

"Oh. I'm sorry."

She smiled warmly. "It's okay. Thank you. You're a nice kid."

"Do you think I'm crazy, too?"

"Not at all. You've just got to fight through what's bothering you."

Maladho gave her an exasperated look. "They won't listen to me. It's frustrating and makes me mad and sad at the same time."

Famata nodded and patted his hand. "Keep your faith in yourself. Your mom shared your story with me. *She* doesn't think you're crazy."

Maladho suddenly looked interested, with a glimmer of hope in his eyes. "Really?"

"Yes. But she's cautious around your grandpa. So let's keep this chat between us, okay? Your mom wouldn't want to upset him." He nodded in agreement, and she paused for a moment before asking, "Maladho, would you like to have a little brother or sister?"

Maladho hesitated. "I'm not sure. I'd be worried they might be taken away like Kamboda was."

Famata didn't press further, and they sat in silence together until Fenda returned from the market, looking worried and empty-handed again. Famata left them alone.

Maladho said, "Mom, why go to the market if you're not buying anything? Take a break. I'll get you nice things one day."

His mom smiled gently, patting his head. "Just focus on getting better. That's the best gift for me. When you are better, we'll return to Kopiro." This declaration made Maladho swell with joy and excitement. He wanted to go home. He didn't want to stay in the hospital with its boring pills that made him sleepy.

On a day when Maladho was left in Famata's care, they sat together by the cashew tree outside. Over time, they had grown closer. He had confided in her about not wanting the medicine, and she understood the strange way it made a person feel. She had been pretending to give it to him since. He had also taken to leaving Karamoko's charm on the table by his bed.

When Fenda returned, she noticed something was different about him and immediately knew he wasn't taking the pills. "Maladho, you haven't been taking your pills, have you?" When Maladho looked away, she ushered him over. "Head here and take the pills right now. People are helping you, and you are not helping yourself." She moved to give him a pill. She paused, glancing at his waist. "Maladho, where's the protective charm from your grandpa?"

Famata gave him a sympathetic look, but the slippers in Fenda's hand made him worried. He knew what might happen next, so he ran inside to put the charm back on and took the pill his mother handed him. He was soon asleep.

Maladho blinked. He wasn't sure if he was awake or dreaming. Bright lights blurred his vision, and he heard someone crying, the noise swirling around him. He felt nauseous and weak as if the world itself was spinning. When he tried to sit up, dizziness overtook him. He turned his head instead and saw his mother crying. Famata and Uncle Tamba stood beside her, consoling her. *Why is Uncle Tamba here?* he thought. *Why is Mom crying?* He attempted to speak, but all that came out was incoherent mumbling. Overwhelmed, he closed his eyes and slept again.

Maladho woke up feeling incredibly weak. The medication had hit him hard, leaving him barely able to stand. He staggered toward the bathroom, but someone was already inside, singing. He knocked.

"What?!" the man yelled out. "Go away!"

Unable to hold it any longer, he peed in the corner. The area had a strong smell of urine, and he remembered Doctor Giovanni's warnings about not peeing there. However, he couldn't wait, as he urgently needed to relieve himself. Maladho finished and felt relieved, thankful nobody had caught him. But as he turned to return to his room, his heart almost fell out as he saw Doctor Giovanni watching him. He froze, staring at him fearfully. Memories flashed in Maladho's mind when he remembered he'd once seen him disciplining someone by pulling their ears.

But to his surprise, Dr. Giovanni approached calmly, placing a reassuring hand on his shoulder. Instead of scolding, he gently said, "Don't worry, Maladho. Come with me."

As they made their way down the hallway to the doctor's office, Maladho felt the weight of many eyes on him. Sad, curious faces glanced his way, making him wonder if they thought something terrible was about to happen to him or if they simply saw him as the crazy kid.

Entering the office, Maladho observed the chaos: papers and medical journals littered every surface, and the air was thick with the scent of medicines. An old, dusty typewriter was shoved in one corner, and a kerosene fridge hummed in another, the smell of its smoke mingling with the drugs. Bulletin boards crowded with notes and reminders covered the walls.

Dr. Giovanni gestured to a chair, brushing off the dust. "Please, sit down. I want to have a conversation with you," he said, moving to a row of papers on one of the boards and beginning to cross things out with a red pen.

Conversation?! Maladho silently exclaimed. No adult ever asked him to have a conversation. He considered countless things the doctor could want to say. He hoped it was about his return to Kopiro to see his father. He missed Demba a lot. A glimpse of his dream—or vision—came to his mind, his mom crying with Famata and Uncle Tamba. He shrugged it off, blaming the heavy pills for messing with his memory.

"These people are killing me with work. They must think I never get tired," Dr. Giovanni sighed, reviewing his paperwork. "I can't even find time for a vacation back home," he said.

Maladho, growing impatient, asked, "Mister Giovanni, if you are busy, can I leave? I'd like to see my mom. I haven't seen her since this morning."

Dr. Giovanni paused and glanced at him. "Your mom's out at the market, and Famata's tied up with other work. I thought I'd keep you company in my office for a bit. She'll be back shortly," he reassured Maladho. Getting up, he opened the fridge packed with various items and pulled out a bag of juice. He offered it to Maladho with a smile. "Here, drink up. There's plenty more inside if you want more. I know this particular drink is a favorite with the kids."

Maladho took it gratefully, sucking down a large gulp.

The doctor smiled and asked, "So, what do you want to be when you grow up?"

Maladho's face lit up with a smile as he pondered the question. "I want to be like my dad. Hunt, ride horses, farm well, and win the harvest competition," he said with a laugh, taking another gulp of the juice. Suddenly, he clutched his forehead, feeling the sharp sting of a brain freeze.

"Easy there, that can really hurt," Dr. Giovanni chuckled, watching Maladho pause his enthusiastic drinking. "I'm sure you'll grow up to be very responsible," he encouraged.

Maladho, curious, took his turn to inquire, "Doctor, where's your home?"

"It's far away, in Italy."

"So, is that your real home, or were you taken there like Kamboda was taken?" Maladho asked innocently.

Dr. Giovanni paused, offering a gentle smile. "It's my homeland," he answered softly.

"Do you know anyone who lives in a river?"

Leaning forward, Dr. Giovanni propped his elbows on the desk. "Yes, where I come from in Venice, people live with water all around."

"Are there houses, or is it just bush and water like where Kamboda lives?"

Dr. Giovanni scratched his mustache, taken aback by the question, then shrugged. "There are houses, of course. Venice is a beautiful city built entirely on water."

Maladho looked unsure. "Doctor, do you think Kamboda's mad at me?"

"Why would he be mad at you?" Giovanni questioned, curious about the boy's concern.

"I have promised to visit him by the river."

Giovanni nodded. "And have you gone?"

"Yes, but I couldn't see him. They didn't let me in. Maybe it's because of this charm my grandfather gave me." Maladho lifted his shirt, revealing the charm around his waist. "Karamoko said it would protect me as long as I wear it." Dr. Giovanni remained silent.

Maladho paused his questions and looked around. He couldn't believe he was sitting in the doctor's office, drinking juice, and having such an adult conversation. He had finished the juice bag, and Giovanni brought another one. His heart warmed at the gesture, and a smile spread across his face. "Thanks, Mister Giovanni," he said, feeling grateful and happy. He hesitated, then said, "Do you think I'm crazy?"

"Not at all," the doctor reassured him.

"Then why the pills if you know I'm sane?"

"They're just to protect you. Maladho, listen. If Karamoko feels threatened, he won't hesitate to act. You're nine now, soon to be ten, and your mother told me you are going to Koyang soon. It's time to grow up, to prepare to be brave like your ancestors. Your mother comes from a line of warriors. You have that courage in your blood."

Pausing to take a sip of water, he looked at Maladho intently. "Being brave means making tough choices. If you truly care for Kamboda, now's the time to show it. Remember, a snake carries its venom from birth." With that, he sipped his water, hoping his words would inspire Maladho to face whatever lay ahead. "Now, remember, loving Kamboda means controlling your thoughts, your emotions. Life's tough, but it's all in how you handle it. Be ready to change things."

"Can you help me find Kamboda? You believe me, don't you? Maybe Grandpa would listen if you spoke up,"

Maladho pleaded, looking hopeful.

Dr. Giovanni sighed deeply, running his hand over his face. "Maladho," he began, his mix of Crioulo and Italian accents making his words sound musical yet serious, "this situation is more complex than you know. I wish I could say yes, but I can't help you directly."

"Why not? Because you're friends with Grandpa?" Maladho asked, a hint of disappointment in his voice.

"It's not about your grandpa. I'm here on an assignment from my government, which limits my ability to do anything. There are rules I must follow. But remember, knowledge is your weapon. Study hard. You'll find a way to make a difference, not just for Kamboda but for others like him."

Maladho listened closely, his head full of thoughts. He stayed quiet, trying to understand all he'd heard. He thought the session was over, but then the doctor left and told him to wait. Maladho was surprised by Dr. Giovanni's kindness and wisdom. It made him question if what people said about the doctor being unkind to patients was true.

Dr. Giovanni walked through the door and checked that it was locked before returning to his chair. "Maladho, it's time for you to head home," Dr. Giovanni said, his voice gentle yet firm. "You've made excellent progress. Your mom needs you now. It's time to be there for your mom like a man."

A smile broke across Maladho's face. His heart swelled with relief and joy at the news, although the last words caused him some confusion.

"But there's more I need to discuss with you," Giovanni said. This made Maladho feel very excited and eager, but the doctor seemed hesitant, his usual confidence replaced with a noticeable nervousness. "You're growing up, Maladho. You've talked about becoming a man filled with courage and determination. Now's the time to start." Maladho listened intently, hanging on every word. "I'm sorry to tell you, but your father passed away last night."

After a second of shock, Maladho screamed in anguish, rushing to the door in a panic. It was locked, so he began banging on it, feeling more and more overwhelmed with emotions. He began calling out for his father, the words turning to jumbled sounds barely comprehensible through his tears. The last thing he remembered was Dr. Giovanni holding him tightly, trying to calm down his strong feelings, and then he passed out.

When he woke, his mother was there to comfort him, saying she too had become so overwhelmed from the news that she passed out. Maladho started to understand what had happened: his vision wasn't just a dream; it was real. Uncle Tamba's visit and Dr. Giovanni's kindness now made heartbreaking sense.

CHAPTER FOURTEEN

JANFAA

It was sweltering, as if the sun, too, raged over Demba's passing. Wails and chants could be heard far down the road to Kopiro. When Maladho arrived with his mother, the crowd gathered around them, crying and calling out in sorrow. As they walked through the crowd, some people collapsed, rolling on the ground and hitting their chests.

Fenda held Maladho tightly as they approached the hut where Demba's body lay. The crowd was even thicker here as they pushed through. Maladho felt people's hands on his head, touching him gently and calling out his father's name.

"Fenda, what a sad day! What will you do with Maladho without his father?" a lady shouted over him, and her tears dropped on his shoulders. Maladho felt suffocated within the large crowd, and he felt like a fish out of water. The humidity, odors, and sweat bathed him. He felt confused and overwhelmed. He couldn't even look up. His mind was wandering, trying to process everything all at once.

Fenda, still holding him tightly, finally pushed their way into the hut's center. There, his father was lying quietly and serenely as if sleeping. He lay on a bamboo mat covered with traditional woven fabric. Fenda knelt beside her husband's body and uncovered his face. Demba's skin had become pale and soft, his mouth slightly open, his hands folded across his chest. His face was serene, yet he looked angry as if maybe he didn't want to die, or his time hadn't arrived. It was the first time Maladho had seen a dead body. It didn't look like he had imagined.

Maladho fearlessly touched his father, studying the body, maybe to make sure he was dead. Demba's hands were open and relaxed as if he was expecting to receive something, and his mouth was open as if he had a last word stuck in his throat. Maybe he would tell Maladho what happened to him and why he left this world too early.

Maladho couldn't hold it in any longer, his tears finally spilling onto the mantle on top of the mat. He raised his head and saw Uncle Tamba carefully looking at him. Karamoko was at his side, his head bowed as if crying.

Maladho got up and pushed his way outside to breathe some fresh air. Everyone stared at him as he passed. Once outside, he walked slowly toward the backyard where the women were seated. He stood near the fence where they slaughtered the cow to give the guests food. The remains were still untouched. It seemed strange to him because the vultures and dogs would have usually devoured the animal bowels. The sky was empty, as were the surrounding trees. Swallows used to cross and parade the skies of Kopiro, flapping their wings and diving. But that day, they were also absent. The sky remained lonely. Even the voracious black, red-eyed crows didn't appear. The dogs had disappeared, too, and he checked everywhere. It seemed as if the animals boycotted the funeral, or they also were upset at what appeared to have been an unfair death.

The villagers whispered that a snake killed Demba because he had made a mistake in letting Maladho play with Kamboda. The elders said it was the gods' punishment since

Demba had crossed the line by allowing his son to be in such danger. This didn't make sense to Maladho, not only because his father had told him snakes were their cousins, and they rarely attacked their lineage, but also because Demba was a kind and caring man. It was the main reason Maladho had admired his father.

He remembered when Demba used to carry him on his white horse, and they rode the fields together. His father was the one who taught him how to ride a horse and shoot an arrow. His first time hunting, Maladho and his father were lying completely hidden, ready to ambush gazelles that wandered grazing in the meadows. When the herd approached, Demba told Maladho to get prepared. Maladho aimed the arrow and stretched the bow. But then, Demba whispered, "Don't move. Stay still. Don't be afraid; they are one of us."

A giant black snake was dangling from the branch. It descended slowly and slithered in front of them. It lifted its head, staring at them, flicking its tongue as if communicating. Demba softly whistled, and the snake waved its head, dancing with the tune. Soon, it slithered away.

It had been a daunting spectacle for the novice hunter. Letting out a breath, he asked, "Dad, why didn't you kill it?"

His dad looked at him and smiled. "Why would you kill it?"

"Because they are dangerous, and they kill people."

"Son, what if a stranger entered our property and threatened you? Would you stand there and do nothing?"

"No, of course not. I would be mad. And in the case of a threat, you always told me to get ready to stand my ground."

"Exactly, son, that snake is where it belongs. We came here disturbing him. We have to be reasonable. It is common sense. Plus, you don't kill animals just because you want to.

They are part of us. They don't attack unless they are under stress or threat. Snakes, in particular, are our cousins. They will never bite us. It's as rare as a blue moon for a snake to bite one of the Kopironkos. And there's a belief, deep as the roots of our oldest tree, that if you harm one, it's like tipping over a domino, setting off a chain reaction of sorrow right back into your own life. That's why if you kill a snake, legend says your newborn kid will die. It's all about balance, respect, and the ties that connect all living things."

Demba paused, looking deeply into Maladho's eyes, "Snakes only attack us if there's *janfaa*, betrayal. Remember, there are two kinds of janfaa: good and bad."

Maladho raised his eyebrows in surprise. "Baaba, there's good janfaa?"

"Yes, my son. Good janfaa is when the gods and our ancestors see that you have a special mission in another realm. It means you might leave this world early to fulfill your duties there. It's still called janfaa because it happens beyond your control and desire, often when you're full of life and dreams. People might wonder why the gods chose you so soon. But in reality, to tackle some tough problems, you need powers that ordinary humans don't have. Once you join our ancestors, you gain those powers. Do you get it?" Demba asked.

"Yes, Baaba." Maladho nodded.

"On the other hand," Demba went on, "bad janfaa is the common betrayal. For example, evil spirits using a snake to do their wishes, which is also rare." He paused for a moment. "Imagine if a snake bites you and you die. That could be considered good janfaa or bad janfaa. But, as I mentioned, it's quite rare for us."

Demba always shared his wisdom with Maladho, blending caution with knowledge of their traditions and beliefs. They had returned to their hunt, Maladho following Demba's instructions and hitting a male gazelle. It ran off, injured, and Demba led the way to their prey, cutting off branches to mark their trail. They finally found the gazelle on the ground, near death and in agony. Maladho felt the pain and thought this was a double standard. His father had said not to kill animals, but there was one he shot, slowly dying.

His father ordered him to kneel beside the animal and repeat this prayer: "Creator, uncreated, the gods, and ancestors, I hereby apologize for this tremendous violation. As your kids, we are just fetching food. Blood by blood to ask for forgiveness."

Demba turned to Maladho. "The kill is yours; you must pay it with your blood. Don't be afraid, the pain passes quickly."

Maladho was shaking, imagining the pain about to strike him, but he cut his left palm, and the blood flooded to the floor. Afterward, Demba gave him a cloth to tie the wound. He helped Maladho remove the arrow and asked him to cut the gazelle in the neck to purify the hunt. That event signaled that Maladho was ready to be initialized—the moment every parent waits for, the moment of the turning point and becoming an adult.

Unfortunately, his father had now departed without witnessing his initiation, Koyang. Maladho grappled with unanswered questions following his father's death. Was it a case of good janfaa or bad janfaa? The uncertainty weighed heavily on him. *If it was good janfaa, why would the gods take my father just as I'm about to be initiated?* he pondered. *And if it was bad janfaa, it makes even less sense, as he was cherished by all in the village and beyond.* The absence of clarity left Maladho in a state of deep contemplation.

CHAPTER FIFTEEN

KOYANG

The Koyang ceremony was on the horizon, and Maladho had finally been getting ready to participate. The initiation was considered the transition to adulthood, a moment of joy, even though delicate. There was no announcement, but everyone knew the time was near. There was a feeling in the air. Every young boy was eager to attend the event. The expectation filled them with excitement, knowing they'd no longer have to flee from the Kankurang masquerades after the rite of passage. Until now, their wild chases had sent those who hadn't been through the initiation ceremony into frenzies of fear.

Kankurangs did more than chase boys or dance; they had a unique ability to find witches and evil spirits. They could sniff them out as accurately as hunting dogs. Witches, for their part, always tried to disrupt Koyang, much like mold spoils food. In the world of witchcraft, the head of every initiate at Koyang was seen as a treasure, and claiming one was akin to striking gold, a prize worth a fortune. And witches don't go for the cheap or insignificant trophy. They don't like an easy target. Getting someone from a Kopironko tribe or family was like winning ten golden trophies in one competition. This is why ensuring the security of Koyang was of utmost importance.

In the past, a Koyang was organized in the village of Buruntuma, where hundreds of kids between the ages of ten and fifteen were initiated. The Kankurangs raided surrounding villages for twenty-six days, nonstop, because witches were wreaking havoc. Women had to cook inside, kids weren't allowed to go out, and the streets were empty. Even the birds stopped flying. Kankurangs combed the entire area until they dismantled the predator's network. Most of the kids came out alive, though some unfortunate ones passed away. It was a dark moment for Buruntuma.

Kaawu-Ansu led the operation. He was a remarkable figure known for his bravery and fairness but very secretive. No one could recall ever meeting his family or claiming to be his close friend. Despite his old age, he stood tall and slender, with a forehead that constantly glistened with sweat. A straight nose marked his smooth, unlined face. His long legs meant his pants never quite reached his ankles, and he was rarely seen without his long kaftan and a traditional red Sumbia hat adorned with white cowries. There were rumors about a secret hidden beneath that hat. He bathed and slept without ever removing it. Kaawu-Ansu was a specialist in finding witches.

But it wasn't just the Kankurangs that made Koyang appealing. Boys wanted to be initiated because it meant freedom. You could start dating beautiful young girls, go out with fewer restrictions, and enter the shrines. It was like having an easy pass, or *laisse passé*.

But for Maladho, Koyang held no meaning now. His dreams had been decimated by the loss of his cousin and the death of his father, who would no longer be there to witness his initiation. The only thing Maladho looked forward to was not having to sleep with his mother in the same oval room. He couldn't care less about other dangers that unfolded on the dark days of Koyang.

Karamoko summoned his grandchild, patting the goat skin on which he sat and saying, "Come here, naughty kid."

Maladho was playing with goats but approached his grandfather and sat beside him.

"You know, this year, you will attend the Koyang! I can see you are all excited." Karamoko smiled at Maladho, who returned a small smile. "Can you handle it, naughty boy?"

"Yes, Grandpa, I am a big and tough boy."

"Oh, I can see. But did you know after we cut everything this year, we'll use some salt and pepper?" Karamoko laughed.

"What?! No way. I am going to ask Uncle Bakar." Maladho ran to his uncle, who was apprehensively watching them, thinking about his son Kamboda, who, if he were present, would have attended Koyang as well. "Uncle, is that true what Grandpa said?"

"No, son. Grandpa is just messing you up," Bakar said, pulling him into his lap.

This year, Kopiro was ready to host the biggest Koyang ever seen. Everything under Karamoko's umbrella seemed safe. Elders and those responsible for the event scanned the area and shielded it against any threat, external or internal. The N'Ghamanós needed to do the same, guarding their circumcision knives in a safe place. Only the N'Ghamanós, chosen at birth, could handle the sacred knives. The easiest way for the dark spirits or witches to compromise a Koyang was if they got access to the holy knife, a disastrous happening that occurred on a few occasions.

The arrangements were made, and the last meeting of the elders occurred at Banta under the huge kapok tree.

They gathered information about which boys would be taken, and each family chose the N'Ghamanó they wanted to circumcise their kid. Karamoko announced that his best friend, Jaigol, would circumcise his favorite grandkid. It was an honor to be given such a responsibility, a way of saying thank you for their friendship. Many parents wished for Karamoko to be their son's N'Ghamanó, or if not, someone with the same status as Jaigol. The dates were scheduled, and the ceremony was to begin on Thursday. On Friday, each boy would be sent to the bush for the ritual.

Wednesday evening, Fenda had a strange dream about her late husband. Demba appeared and sat in front of the hut. When he sat, she whispered, "I am sorry for being absent."

"I missed you, darling," he said to her.

"I miss you, too, my husband."

"You are so beautiful!" He looked around. "By the way, where is Maladho?"

"He is sleeping inside."

"Let me see him." He stepped inside the hut and laid eyes on his son. Without taking his eyes off Maladho, he said to Fenda, "I know the Koyang is about to start. But please don't let him go."

"But Demba, you were excited about it. Why don't you want him to go?"

"I am worried, Fenda." He turned to her. "Look at me." Fenda looked at him and saw the worry written on his face. "There is a trap," he whispered. He began silently crying, the tears running down his face.

"Trap?!"

"Yes. Listen carefully . . ."

Kulanjan's barking jolted Fenda awake. She rubbed her eyes. Even though it was just a dream, it felt so real. She felt her husband's presence. She touched, smelled, and felt his breath. She tried to fall back asleep but felt restless. When the sun came up, she went to tell her father.

Karamoko didn't bother to look up when he responded, "Daughter, I know this is a crucial moment, and for you who lost your husband and have a kid that is finally reaching this stage—it causes anxiety and pressure simultaneously."

"Dad, I saw him and talked to him. When I looked into his eyes, he was worried. For that reason, I am worried."

"I know. Just relax. I am Karamoko, the one who carries the Kopironko's flag. I guarantee you nothing will happen to your kid. This dream is normal because you are thinking about the ceremony. Just watch and enjoy this as a great achievement for your son."

Fenda relaxed, assured everything was well. But the Koyang brought mixed feelings for her. She was happy her son would attend, but Demba could no longer witness it. The dream reminded her how much she missed her late husband. When she returned to her hut, she began to cry.

Maladho looked up, concern flooding his face when he saw the tears. "Mom, what is happening?"

"Nothing, Maladho."

"Tell me, Mom. Is it Grandpa again?"

"No. I am just emotional."

"It is okay, Mom. I love you, and soon I will become a man."

"Son, I am proud of you. I wish your dad were here to witness how grown you are." Fenda smiled, but tears still welled in her eyes. She gently touched Maladho's face.

He reached out and wiped away her tears. "Tomorrow, I will make you proud. I love you. Just don't let them take me as they did Kamboda."

"Nobody will ever take you or harm you. I will fight for

you because you are the only thing left, a product of love and suffering."

For Fenda and other parents, the Koyang was much more than a simple coming-of-age ritual. It was a gateway to their children's future, possibly setting them on a path to leadership within the village. The event wasn't just a test of physical strength or endurance; it was a fierce competition mirroring the challenges of leadership itself.

Decades ago, Karamoko emerged victorious in this contest, his win cementing his place as a key figure in the village. His example lingered in the air, a reminder that the Koyang was an opportunity for every young participant to prove their value. In this contest, every move was critical, and the wild, unwritten rules of the game encouraged each kid to show how brave and strong they were.

The game was challenging, a test of speed, bravery, and resilience. Each boy stood on a hill covered with bushes. They looked down at the riverbank where their N'Ghamanós were waiting. The race to the bottom was more than just a sprint; it was full of dangers. A boy had to navigate through a thick bush, dodge hidden traps, and avoid tripping over the uneven ground to win. The hill, with its treacherous trail, was a silent challenge. The first to reach the bottom wasn't just quick; he was agile and smart, earning the right to be the first to undergo the circumcision ritual and become the "Head of the Koyang."

In the past, the race had caused many casualties. Recently, a boy from Dunani met a tragic end when he tumbled into a hidden pit. But Maladho and his colleagues didn't worry too much because it was the terrain where they used to hunt and play. But sometimes, underestimating things can get you in trouble.

On Thursday at noon, Kopiro came alive with the start of

the ceremony. It was as if the whole land was shaking with excitement. Dust danced in the air, and a buzz of happiness filled the skies as guests from over a hundred and fifty towns and villages arrived, each group bringing along their own musicians and dancers. The air was rich with the aroma of feasts being prepared, as animals were cooked to welcome everyone with a grand meal. Gourds were filled with drinks, ready to refresh the joyful crowd. People danced everywhere, moving to the powerful beats of drums and melodies of instruments, sharing in the day's happiness.

Jaigol, with his elegant yet peculiar style, sipped from his gourd, his left hand pointing to the sky, signaling pleasure and thanking the gods. With his eyes closed, he shook his head, biting his lips. He liked to be in the spotlight wherever he went. At his back was his favorite jali, playing the kora, but he waved to the musician to stop. He approached Fenda, who was busy stirring some leaves for a special jamboo recipe, a tasty dish with cassava leaves, peanuts, and palm oil mixed with dry fish. They said if you go to Kopiro, you should taste jamboo; otherwise, it is like going to the beach without swimming.

"Fenda, the princess of Kopiro, long time? I hope they are not giving you too much work to do," he said, looking straight into her eyes. They both smiled, and Fenda knelt to greet him, a sign of respect toward a most respected man of Sama Yerondin. "No need, dear, please." He indicated for her to stand. "By the way, how is the boy?"

"Thank you, Baaba. I am fine. I hope the journey wasn't too harsh," Fenda said, still holding a bowl of vegetables. "Maladho is doing well, and he has been excited and nervous ever since the announcement of the Koyang."

"I know, every kid is feeling the same way. But I will take good care of him tomorrow and the rest of Koyang."

"Thank you, Baaba. I am so glad to know that." Fenda smiled and returned to her cooking.

The celebration lasted all day, full of food, music, and company. Some kept the celebration going, though others took a nap to await the dawn when the boys would be taken to the bush for forty-five days and nights.

On the way back to her home, Fenda walked past her brother's hut. From inside could be heard silent weeping. She entered her room and saw Tombom sitting on her bed. Fenda approached, sitting beside her sister-in-law and placing an arm around her shoulder. "It is okay, Tombom. We all wish it were different and that Kamboda had been here to attend the Koyang with Maladho. But we can't change destiny," she said.

Tombom didn't say a word, only wept. Fenda wiped her tears and held her close.

After a few minutes, Tombom broke the silence. Sniffling, she said, "We can't change destiny, but I could have avoided it. Anyway, thanks, Fenda, for always supporting me. But what happened to my Kamboda is unforgivable." She began to cry again.

Fenda comforted Tombom for a few more minutes, then left her to grieve, opting to return to her hut for a short nap. She was lying on her back with her eyes closed, the noises of the lingering celebration echoing in her ears, the flames of the lantern dancing to the rhythm of the wind against the back of her eyelids, when suddenly, the lantern went out. She opened her eyes to the darkness inside her hut. She thought it was the wind or maybe a swallow flying by, putting out the flames. A fresh breeze blew, and then the hut became warmer and heavier. When she looked toward the slightly open door, she saw a dark silhouette standing, and she bolted upright.

"Don't let him go," the shadow whispered.

Fenda screamed. "Who are you? What do you want?"

The door pushed open, and the silhouette disappeared. Fenda jumped out of her bed and, panicking, ran toward the door. She bumped into brother right outside.

"What is happening, sister?"

Fenda was panting and sweating, scared to death. Her wrapper had fallen. "The shadow, I saw it, and I heard it," she whispered.

"Sister, calm down, calm down! It is me, Bakar." He went inside and checked the hut with his flashlight and saw no one. He grabbed her wrapper and covered her. Still, Fenda had her eyes wide open and her heart beating fast. "Calm down, relax, sit. What happened, little sister?"

"I saw it, Bakar," Fenda whispered again.

"Okay, okay. Go sleep at Mother's hut. Tomorrow, we will do something about it." He led her to Sona's hut and gave her some water before returning to the celebration.

Fenda sat confused. She knew the whisper was real, and someone or something had been standing there before Bakar entered. It told her the same thing Demba had: not to let Maladho go to Koyang. But why? Afraid, she went to tell her mother what she had seen.

Sona told her to relax. "Maybe you are too thoughtful, or some foolish spirits are trying to scare you."

Fenda wasn't so sure and slept fitfully before being awoken before dawn to prepare for the boys, elders, and custodians. Koyang was a place for men only. Women were strictly forbidden. So Fenda wouldn't see her son for forty-five long days.

The stars lit the dark sky, celebrating the impending rite. Before dawn, a cool breeze carried the scent of the Koff Label River, adding a mystical touch to the atmosphere.

Birds sang melodies as if serenading the boys, while in the distance, an owl's call sent shivers down their spines. The hum of the gathering crowd blended with footsteps, creating a backdrop of anticipation.

At that time, the group of men who had gone to the forest the previous night to fetch the spirit guardians had returned with fifty Kankurangs. They were dressed in red fiber bark cords, uttering piercing sounds while striking their machetes, creating sparks in the dark.

Wrapped in white gowns, five hundred boys stood together, each anointed with protective herbs and sacred water. They shared a meal, part of which was offered to the gods' and ancestors' spirits by throwing the food onto the roof. Then, led by the beat of drums, they entered the bush. Mothers watched with mixed emotions. Some wept joyfully, others fretted with worry. Tombom, silent among them, shed tears for Kamboda's unfair judgment.

Each boy was lifted onto an adult's shoulders, moving through a landscape shrouded in thick mist. As they ventured deeper into the bush, darkness seemed to swallow them. Elders cleansed the way with horse tails and various instruments, chasing away the evil spirits and scanning the path for possible threats.

Upon reaching the hill, each boy was surrounded by family, friends, and mentors, all ensuring the participants were instructed and aware of the risks involved in the upcoming challenge. Karamoko, overseeing many boys, kept a watchful eye on Maladho in particular. Perhaps it was because Maladho was fatherless, or maybe Karamoko saw in him the potential to win and become the Head.

Under Karamoko's gaze, Maladho felt a surge of apprehension and fear. Karamoko encouraged him, "I know you can make it. I'll be waiting on the other side. Reach there first, and I promise you something good." Maladho remained silent, burdened by the weight of expectation. Feeling both excited and nervous, they proceeded to the event location.

A gunshot echoed, signaling the start of the contest, and the boys launched into action. They raced downhill through a veil of darkness, adult guides trailing behind them. It was hard to recognize anybody as they plunged through the thick haze. The noise of trampling grass and snapping twigs was amplified in the silence. Birds, startled by the commotion, took flight, their silhouettes flickering through the mist. It was as if the hill itself was whispering, alive with the vibrations of the race unfolding upon its slopes.

The race turned chaotic when a sharp yelp broke through the dark. "Ohh! I'm hurt! Please help!" a boy cried out, panic in his voice. He might have stepped on something sharp, or something more serious. Moments later, another shout of pain echoed, adding to the confusion. It was hard to tell where the cries were coming from in the darkness. Fear spread quickly, and the sounds of distress bounced around in the shadowy woods.

The forest became darker and diabolical. Maladho looked on both sides. He couldn't see a soul. He looked back carefully as he continued to run, and fear gripped him, his heart racing wildly. Sweat drenched his skin as he panted for air, trying to make sense of the shadows flickering toward him. Suddenly, something struck him hard. He flew through the air before crashing down onto the damp grass, his petite and skinny body hitting the earth with a thud.

Maladho raised his head. There was a sharp pain in his legs. He heard the fierce growls and snarls of what seemed like two powerful beasts locked in battle. The ground shook. Then the noise ceased, leaving only silence. Wincing in pain, Maladho curled up, feeling as vulnerable as a wounded centipede. A voice pierced the quiet atmosphere saying, "Maladho, Maladho."

Confused, he struggled to locate where the sound was coming from. With his legs numb and his hopes of winning dashed, he closed his eyes and blacked out.

Back in the compound, Fenda was doing her chores with stoicism. Tombom noticed her sister-in-law's quiet demeanor. "It is clear something is bothering you, Fenda. You may tell me, go ahead. Is it good or bad?"

"Bad or something like that, I am not sure," Fenda said. "I am scared for Maladho. I had a dream about his late father." She repeated what Demba had told her in the dream.

"Balaba," Tombom whispered, almost to herself.

"What?" Fenda asked.

"The lady in the bush, maybe she can help us."

"What makes you think so? How do you know this old woman?"

Tombom sighed. "It's a long story, but she saved my life a few times."

Fenda seemed unsure, but Tombom reassured her it was worth trying. She ran to her hut for the sword bean, and they took the buckets to the spring, entering the secret path to the bush.

They found Balaba waiting. "Tombom, it has been a long time!" she said. "It seems you are in trouble. What can I do for you today?"

"Hello, Mother. Yes, we were looking for you. My sister-in-law seeks help. Her name is—" Balaba interrupted before she could finish.

"Fenda. I have known her since she was a baby." She turned to Fenda. "You are lovely."

Fenda smiled but looked at the old lady with confusion. "Thank you, ma'am. I didn't know you knew me. I don't think we have ever met."

"Oh, come on. You are the prominent, powerful man's daughter. Even the plants know you because you are from a notable tribe," Balaba said. "Now, come. Tell me what troubles you."

Balaba listened intently as Fenda explained her dream and her worries about Maladho. She nodded before responding. "Sometimes, when we're in trouble, our ancestors come to help us. This might mean he is in danger, or it could just be a sign that you're scared, as any mom would be." Balaba started gathering sticks, stones, and cowries and laid them out before her. She studied them in silence, her eyes moving from one piece to another, searching for signs. After a moment, she spoke. "He seems alright to me," said Balaba softly.

Fenda, full of worry, begged, "Please if anything bad happens, use your powers to protect him."

Tombom, watching the scene, had a look of deep concern on her face.

Balaba sighed. "I'm sorry, but that's beyond my abilities. I serve as a guide, not an intervener. My role is to alert you to danger. Then, it's up to you to ask your father to look after him. Karamoko has the means, given his reputation and strength. But this time . . ." Her voice trailed off, leaving an uneasy silence.

The old lady dug into her bag and pulled out white, black, and red cotton threads. Closing her eyes, she murmured some words and spat on them. She then dipped them into water mixed with special ointments. Pouring the mixture into a small, clear bottle, she handed it over. "Hang this bottle on your room's wall and watch it closely. If it ever breaks, know that your boy is in danger," Balaba instructed. Hearing those words, Fenda felt a chill run down her spine.

Back in the bush, a mysterious call stirred Maladho awake. "Get up, let's go." The voice was unfamiliar, and though he tried to make out the figure standing over him, it was too dark to see clearly. He could only discern a shadowy shape as if mounted on a shimmering horse. "Get up. You don't have time."

"Who are you?" Maladho asked in a tiny voice.

"You don't have much time. Come on, let's go."

"But my legs, I don't know if I can walk," Maladho said.

The mysterious individual ignored his complaint. "I said, let's go. We don't have time."

Maladho stood up cautiously, readying for the bite of pain from his legs, but to his surprise, he found that his pain had vanished. Heartened, he took off, feeling as light as a feather, speeding through the air as if carried by an unseen force. It was like floating on the breeze, swift and weightless. The fog around him began to clear, and he zoomed past his peers with incredible speed. Down the hill, through the savanna, Maladho glimmered like a bright star against the dark. Onlookers could only catch a blur whizzing by, unable to identify it or how it moved so fast. He reached the bottom ahead of everyone else, leaving Karamoko and the crowd astonished. No one had ever seen him—or anyone—move with such incredible speed, shining brightly as he dashed to the finish.

Karamoko waved a white flag, guiding Maladho to where his N'Ghamanó awaited. Reaching his spot, Maladho bravely lifted his gown. Jaigol, with his shiny, sharp knife with a distinctive white handle, cut and carefully stored the chunk in his small, secretive pouch. While others cried during their circumcision, Maladho stood firm, not shedding a single tear, showcasing a bravery that left everyone, including Jaigol, in awe. Maladho, now bleeding, boldly raised a finger, challenging Jaigol, "Cut it too, I'm ready!" He felt strong, overjoyed at his spectacular win.

Karamoko fired his shotgun twice into the sky, signaling not just a victory but something remarkable. Maladho, the winner, danced despite his bleeding wound, pushing away the man who came to treat him and leaping into the salty water. At that moment, all eyes were on him. Maladho, now known as Kopiro's Brave Kid, carried the legacy of his late father, Demba, his mother, Fenda, and his grandfather, Karamoko. His act of bravery echoed far beyond the village, trending across the province and beyond.

Karamoko realized the victory wasn't just a triumph; it was a beacon that could ignite envy and conflict. He braced for the challenges ahead, knowing the Koyang had found its leader in Maladho, the boy who clinched the title "Head of the Koyang." Any harm coming to Maladho would spell disaster for the tribe and tarnish the honor of all the children. The community understood the gravity of their duty. The Head was sacred and safeguarding him was paramount. Now, it was up to the Kopironkos to protect him, for what's a body without its head?

At the break of dawn, the world was gently waking under a blanket of dew. Around smoldering fires, the boys and their guardians gathered for warmth. Sweet potatoes, cassava, and peanuts slowly roasted in the ashes of each fire, filling the air with their comforting aromas. Karamoko walked through the camp, cleaning his teeth with a *gossordu*, a chewing stick. "Morning, you naughty boy," Karamoko said to Maladho, affectionately ruffling his hair.

"Good morning, Grandpa," Maladho responded with a smile.

"Sleep well?"

"Yeah, except the kid next to me peed again, and now I'm all itchy from sleeping in it," Maladho complained.

Karamoko couldn't help but chuckle. "That's a shame. Maybe we should find you a different spot to sleep."

"It's fine, Grandpa. He's pretty funny. And his name's Demba, just like my dad's."

"Really? Then he's like a little dad to you," Karamoko joked. As they laughed together, Karamoko applied healing herbs to Maladho's leg wound. "Let's take a walk," he suggested, and they strolled around the camp, feeling the warmth of the fire on their faces and absorbing the tranquil morning vibes. "Your mom said hi. She's been worried, but I told her you're doing just fine."

Maladho nodded. Now that the immediate rush of his win had worn off, he was left puzzled about the voice and mysterious horse. Maladho knew this was now a secret he had to keep about how he really won.

CHAPTER SIXTEEN

KURIKOO

Great news came from Koyang. The kids were healing and making much progress in learning. Soon they would return, and everybody was eager for *jambadong*, the feast. So far, no incidents had been reported except for minor occurrences, such as someone taking food that didn't belong to them or a few boys getting in trouble for lying. However, there was concern when they caught an owl around the barracks. The boys were frightened because owls are believed to be messengers and spying birds used by witches or evil spirits. Since the incident, security had doubled in perimeters and the surrounding areas.

Despite apparent calmness, Fenda kept thinking about her son. She knew Maladho was the target, not only being Karamoko's grandchild but winning the race and becoming the Head of Koyang. As the temperature cooled down, she went to grind maize to prepare dinner. Soon after, drums could be heard approaching the village, along with Kankurangs banging machetes and uttering piercing cries, followed by the custodians in a harmonious chorus, raising clouds of dust, signaling their routine patrol through the community to check and comb the communities for threats.

The women and children scattered, leaving behind their stuff, no matter what they were doing. The top priority was to find a place to hide. Kopiro became deserted. It is forbidden to face the Kankurangs because they are holy spirits, the guardians of Koyang. Sometimes they demanded the custodians kneel down as a sign of obedience, and bad boys got beaten. Women and children watched the spectacle through the door and window holes.

That day, the Kankurangs visited with a clear goal: to warn certain mothers. They pointed out that some of the meals sent to the boys needed to be better. These meals were not nutritious and could harm the boys' health. Not only were they late with delivery, but they were consistently tardy. With their message delivered, they returned to the bush. The village returned to their duties, with some collecting the red threads dropped by the Kankurangs to tie around their wrists for protection.

Fenda and the other women quickly finished cooking, and the custodians were set to transport the food. The meals were always carried uncovered, with a long straw placed in the middle of the bowl. The custodians would then march to the woods, sometimes singing Koyang songs and whistling, a ritual performed twice daily.

Feeling a sense of relief after the day's duties, Fenda bathed and chose to retire early that night, exhausted from the day's work. Her eyes closed gently, and she drifted into sleep. Her dreams took her to a vivid scene of a Kankurang dance. In the dream, a single Kankurang danced before her, its movements wild and fierce, waving machetes in the air with threatening grace. On the ground in front of the masquerade, a boy knelt on all fours with a black cloth over his face. His white gown showed he was a newly initiated boy. The Kankurang's screams filled the air, a sharp, haunting sound as it scratched the ground with its machete, menacingly close to the boy.

Suddenly, the boy's scream pierced through the dream, "Mom, help me!" he cried out. "He's going to kill me. Please, Mom, hurry!"

"Maladho, is that you?" Fenda called out, panic gripping her voice.

"Yes, Mommy, please hurry!" the boy's voice urged.

Fenda raced toward the Kankurang, determined to save her son. But the Kankurang struck her across the throat with its machete. She stumbled, blood spilling. Just as the Kankurang lifted its machete for a final blow on the boy, a figure on a white, dazzling horse appeared from nowhere, striking the Kankurang down. Its head tumbled away, and its body staggered before collapsing at Karamoko's doorstep.

Fenda rushed to Maladho, pulling him close. When she looked up to see their savior, she couldn't recognize him. "Who are you?"

The masked rider turned to her and warned, "Run, or it'll be too late." With that, he galloped away.

Fenda called to him, "Wait!" The savior didn't look back as he followed the path to the river. Her neck wound continued to bleed, and she fell onto her back and passed away.

She woke frightened, sitting upright in bed and clutching her neck, looking for blood. "Oh my god, oh forefathers, what happened?!" In the morning, she told Tombom about her vision. "I am scared, my sister-in-law."

Tombom gestured to the bottle hanging on the wall. "Look at the bottle. It's still intact, which means Maladho is fine."

"The bottle? Can we really trust that old lady completely? She might be wrong."

"I trust her."

Fenda nodded. "Should we consult her again? This worry is growing within me. This feels ominous. I sense a dark presence hovering, eyeing my son, desiring his blood. It aims to rip my only child from me as it did his father. But I will fight with every breath to protect him."

"Let's not leap to conclusions just yet. Let's try to understand the situation first, but perhaps we can leave Balaba alone this time. How about we seek Mother Sona's insight?"

"You don't grasp the depth of my fear, Tombom. I am petrified. I am afraid this thing will take him," Fenda confessed, her voice trembling.

"Let's not summon misfortune with our words. Remember, as the elders advise, the mouth that tastes salt should not speak recklessly, for it might invite the very shadows we seek to evade," Tombom cautioned, her voice a blend of wisdom and warning.

Sona was busy nurturing her small food garden, her hands working the soil. Spotting her daughters approaching, she called out teasingly, "Good morning! Are you here to help me with the garden? Perhaps spread some ashes or give these plants a drink?" Her smile was as warm as the morning sun.

Their laughter mingled with the morning air, but it was tight, and it quickly faded from Fenda's lips. "Actually, Mother, something is troubling me."

"Ah, life is full of troubles, my child. May I know what it is this time? Tell me everything."

Fenda took a deep breath, gathering her thoughts before revealing the disturbing dream that had haunted her sleep. Sona listened intently, her face showing concern as Fenda spoke.

"Your dreams," Sona started, looking thoughtful, her eyes focused despite the morning haze, "they could be showing your worries. But they might also be a warning, a message from somewhere beyond. The good part, though, is the arrival of a guardian in your dream. It signifies protection. I'll make sure to offer prayers to the gods on behalf of Maladho," she said reassuringly. Then she asked, "Have you, by any chance, left anything outside these past nights? Something personal, perhaps?"

Fenda was puzzled at first. "Something like what?" she prompted.

"Any clothing? A turban, or maybe your underwear?"

"Oh, yes! Just yesterday, after my bath, I left my underwear out to dry. It was still hanging on the fence near the toilet when I went to bed."

Sona's expression turned cold. "I've repeatedly told you not to leave your belongings unattended at night, especially not your undergarments. And I've warned you about the dangers of nighttime baths. Yet, you seem to ignore my advice," she scolded. "You've made two big mistakes. These are open invitations to trouble, especially when evil spirits wander around, looking for ways to cause damage."

Fenda remembered Karamoko also cautioning her about the dangers of bathing late and leaving personal items out in the open. Despite his warnings, she hadn't paid much attention. As Fenda thought about Sona's words, she couldn't shake off the feeling of being targeted by these nighttime dangers. Following Sona's warnings, she stopped bathing at night and made sure to bring her clothing inside, and the rest of Koyang passed with no further nightmares plaguing Fenda.

For safety, the boys weren't allowed to take their laundry home. If a witch got hold of their clothes, it could lead to trouble. They usually washed their clothes together at the river in a group. The Kurikoo day is the laundry day. On the eve of Kurikoo, they are allowed to visit the village to ask for money to buy soap and other items before going to wash their clothes a final time.

The full moon lit up the sky over Kopiro and the neighboring villages, casting a glow that seemed to sprinkle joy everywhere. The children played happily, clapping, dancing, and laughing as they chased each other. The grown-ups sat around fires, chatting in the evening. Some relaxed on mats, drinking tea and sharing peanuts, while others told stories passed down through generations.

It was a lively night, with everyone in the community coming together. Sometimes, they stopped talking to listen to the faraway sounds of singing carried by the wind from the woods. Then they went back to chatting and laughing.

When Fenda asked if she could spend the night in Tombom's hut, Sona laughed. "You are only going there because you want to spy on Kankurangs to see if you can see your son." At Tombom's hut, there was a big hole in the door. That's why it was their favorite hideout.

The sound increased from the woods. They needed to stay put because there were no drums, only Kankurangs. A song echoed from the distance, a lone voice calling out and a chorus answering.

"Mother, come and welcome me."

"Mother! Oh, yes!"

"Come and welcome me because I miss you. Welcome me, Mother."

"Mother, come and welcome me. Oh, yes!"

"Show me the path, the path our elders follow; guide me to the right path."

"Show me the right path to follow. Oh, yes!"

"This is the path I am following, guided by my elders. It's not easy being the custodians of the circumcised boys."

"Oh, yes!"

"Everyday beatings of the Kankurangs make it difficult to be the custodians of the circumcised boys."

As the melodies grew louder, it was a signal for the women and children of Kopiro to head indoors. Soon, the village streets were alive with the vibrant procession of Kankurangs, their machetes clashing in the air, sending sparks flying, and their distinct, piercing cries cutting through the night. Alongside them, another group tapped rhythmically on the ground with sticks, adding to the symphony of the night.

Leading the parade was the Head of Koyang, constantly bowing and holding onto Kaawu-Ansu, their revered guardian, with other initiates linked arm in arm behind him. They walked from one house to another with a purpose, singing songs that bounced off the walls. It was a tradition that connected them to each home. In exchange for their songs and company, families gave them donations—coins, sacks of rice, corn, vegetables, and sometimes chickens—as a way to show thanks and help with the next day's activities.

They arrived at Karamoko's place. The compound was alive with energy as the group made its grand entrance, their movements stirring up clouds of dust into the evening sky. The intensity of the dance grew, and the custodians were urged to sing louder, their sticks beating the rhythm into the air with enthusiasm.

From her hidden vantage point, Fenda watched eagerly, her gaze fixed on the procession with a mixture of joy and longing. It had been weeks since the boys were taken to the woods for their initiation, and she ached to see her son among them. "Tombom, look, there he is—my son!" Fenda whispered.

"Yes, I see him. Oh, he looks strong, my nephew," Tombom said joyfully.

"Oh, how I wish I could run out there and wrap him in my arms. I miss him so dearly."

"You are crazy! If you go outside right now with all these Kankurangs around, they are going to beat you to death."

"I know, that's why I said, 'wish I could.'" They laughed softly.

The ceremony continued with vibrant energy until Karamoko presented them with a goat, which ignited even more joy among the group. Cheers and shouts filled the air as they jumped and danced with renewed energy, celebrating the generous gift. Joyous and sated, they eventually left, leaving behind dust and happiness. The fading sounds of the Kankurangs and their entourage lingered in the air, a distant melody carried away by the night breeze.

The following day, as Fenda was sweeping the yard, a glance over her shoulder revealed visitors stepping into the compound. Jaigol and his entourage were coming for the ceremonial laundry event by the river. Quickly, Fenda motioned to Tombom, who was washing dishes, and they hurried to fetch mats for their guests to sit on. Handing Jaigol a cup of water, Fenda greeted him warmly. "Some water for you, Uncle Jaigol." Other family members scrambled to serve water to the rest of the group.

Taking the cup, Jaigol poked Fenda's palm with his finger. He kept looking at her, almost leering. After a refreshing sip, he inquired, "Where's your father?"

"He's gone back to the Koyang,"

Jaigol nodded appreciatively. "Ah, we've come a bit late then. Thank you, kind Fenda. We should make our way to the river now." With that, he and his companions made their exit, leaving Fenda and Tombom to resume their chores.

"I don't like the way he looks at me," Fenda said.

"What do you mean?" Tombom asked.

"That old man is a *pukala*, a pervert! When I gave him the water, he poked my palm. And the way he looks at me! I don't like it," Fenda growled.

"He did that? He is a nasty old man. Your father should cut him off."

Fenda sucked her teeth and spat. "Let him dream. I don't know what he wants, but he better quit. Ugh, his teeth are all red and nasty."

Tombom chuckled. "Imagine seeing you kissing that mouth!"

"Stop it, you crazy woman!" Fenda hit her with the broom. Tombom ran laughing, and Fenda chased her, laughing as well.

Back at the river, everything was ready. The place was full of people, and the drums were beating nonstop. The perimeter was secured with maximum security to halt intruders. The boys were playing and screaming. It was their day off. While some were washing the clothes, others were fetching logs to prepare food. Some elders were preparing the meat while others chatted under the adjacent trees, sharing kola nuts and tobacco.

When they had finished their laundry, they laid clothing on the grass and small trees to let it dry. Some boys went swimming to refresh themselves a little bit. When the food was ready, they ate, and the party continued, laughing and joking and drinking natural juice made of orange, ginger, and mango. With full bellies, they took naps under the trees.

Maladho, lying next to his friend Demba, felt his stomach ache, making it hard for him to sleep. Annoyed by the sudden discomfort, he hurried to the bushes to find some relief. "Crazy stomach! Why don't you let me enjoy this day?" he grumbled.

When he had finished relieving himself, Maladho spotted a bird struggling on the ground. The bird couldn't fly. He ran to help it. He gently tried to assist, following its every attempt to take off. But the bird kept falling. He followed the bird, but he didn't realize he had already gone so far into the bush. When the bird finally managed to fly away, Maladho chuckled, "Sly little thing."

As he walked through the bushes, he heard voices. They sounded like they were arguing. Interested, he moved closer. When he recognized one of the voices, he got even more curious. *What are they doing here?* he thought. He crouched to watch without being seen, excited to discover what was happening. Staying silent and unseen was crucial. Being discovered eavesdropping on such a heated exchange would surely spell trouble for him.

Hidden among the bushes, he watched as Karamoko and Jaigol faced off, their voices raised in anger. Karamoko's hand sliced through the air as he spoke with visible frustration, "What do you expect me to do?"

Jaigol, equally agitated, shot back, "You know exactly what I want. Just handle it!"

The intensity of their argument was clear, yet the details eluded Maladho, leaving him puzzled and anxious.

Jaigol's frustration boiled over. "I expected some kindness, Karamoko, repayment for the favor I once did for you. I thought our friendship meant something!" he shouted.

Karamoko's face tightened with anger. "You know who I am, Jaigol. I've always been a man of honor. Had I known you'd come back expecting a favor in return, I might not have asked you a favor. I told you I tried."

"You didn't try hard enough. You and I both know it would happen if you truly wanted it." Jaigol pointed his finger. "Karamoko, I'm done with this conversation. It's clear now to me that you're nothing but selfish and heartless. You came to me when your pants were on fire. And now, you want to be ungrateful, trying to fool me like a child."

"I came to you thinking we were friends, never expecting you to ask for something so ridiculous," he replied angrily.

"Ah, ridiculous? So, my need is now ridiculous to you? Karamoko, you are as greedy as a worm! Now, I demand repayment."

"Repayment? We had no deal. You offered your help without any conditions, and frankly, your solution achieved nothing. Enough with your baseless claims."

Jaigol jabbed his finger at Karamoko again. "You are very arrogant and egocentric! You are an ungrateful motherfucker!" he yelled.

Maladho shook where he was hiding and nearly screamed in fear. Jaigol looked terrifying, and his words were filled with anger.

"Jaigol, *A-Féti*, are you crazy? Are you insulting me in my territory?"

"Of course. You insulted me in my territory first when you brought your macabre plot to be done in my grandparents' jalang. At that time, you ran to me like a small girl. 'Oh please, Sanaku, help me!' Now, you are telling me that this is your territory! Why didn't you do it here then, in this powerful territory?"

Karamoko laughed angrily and shook his head. "You are out of your mind. If I had known, I would not have asked you for help. You are a charlatan and deranged person. A decent man with integrity and character would never do what you are doing right now. Please think, and stop being

191

stupid." Both men were outrageous. Maladho noted the knives at their waists and grew afraid the anger would spill to violence.

Jaigol's laughter echoed. "Decency? Honor? You've trampled those words into the dirt with your actions, Karamoko. Dragging your family through the mud for the sake of tribal pride!" He smirked, his voice dripping with sarcasm.

Karamoko's face turned a shade darker, his hand instinctively moving toward the knife at his waist. "Dare to denigrate my family name again, and you'll regret it, Jaigol. My patience has its limits. If you insist, I will make your life miserable."

Maladho's fear increased as he saw the intense hatred and problems between the two men he thought were friends. He realized how dangerous their fight was, not just physically but also because of the harm it could cause to their families and the community.

"You are going to make my life miserable?! Karamoko, your life is the one that's miserable. The gods know what you've done. You'll be punished before you die because of your ego, thinking you're some pure-blooded Kopironko. You think you're untouchable, ahh?" Jaigol's words were sharp and bitter.

"Yes, I am a proud Kopironko. That's precisely why you envy me."

"Remember, Karamoko, you have blood on your hands. Do you want me to tell everybody in Kopiro? Ahh?"

"You can say whatever you want. It doesn't matter to me." Karamoko dismissed him, waving his hand flippantly toward Jaigol, trying to maintain his composure despite the gravity of the words.

"Alright, but it should matter to you. Remember, I am

your grandson's N'Ghamanó . . . I can destroy him, destroy you and your Koyang in the blink of an eye."

"Stop, Jaigol. Stop right there. You're going too far!" Karamoko finally exploded, his patience running out.

"Karamoko, you have a choice to make. Either I marry Fenda, or I ensure your grandson joins his father. And let me remind you, Maladho is the Head of your Koyang. I possess the knife and the chunk. Guess what? Your reign, your family, your Koyang, and your reputation could all crumble. Decide." Jaigol issued his ultimatum, punctuated with menacing, calm, and diabolical laughter.

A chill ran through Maladho. True fear over the threats he overheard. He wanted to scream for help, but fear choked his voice, leaving him silent, his legs too numb to run. Karamoko, feeling the weight of threat, looked upset. He pressed his temples.

Jaigol gave one final warning. "Karamoko, my patience is over. You have three days to consent to my marrying Fenda. If I don't get a 'yes' from her, be prepared for the consequences. You know what I'm capable of."

Karamoko, with his hands clasped over his face, suddenly looked up, his eyes burning with defiance. "Don't you dare lay a finger on Maladho. No one threatens my blood. Do you understand?" he shouted.

"Oh, but wasn't Kamboda your blood too?" Jaigol replied sarcastically, laughing mockingly.

From a distance, calls of "Maladho, Maladho, where are you?" echoed, signaling that his absence had been noticed. Karamoko and Jaigol, halting their heated exchange, moved back to join the group.

Maladho gathered his courage and quietly moved from where he was hiding to meet the people who were looking for him, running into Kaawu-Ansu on his way back to camp.

"Where have you been? We've been searching all over for you," Kaawu-Ansu asked with relief.

"I needed to . . . My stomach was upset after eating the meat," Maladho explained, trying to mask the true reason for his distress. The weight of the words he overheard left a heavy burden on his young shoulders.

"Come on, let's head back," Kaawu-Ansu said, guiding him toward the riverbank. Noticing Maladho shivering, he said, "Don't worry, I'll give you some medicine to help."

Karamoko and Jaigol had returned to the riverside before him, acting as if all was well. Jaigol moved toward Maladho, but Karamoko got to him first, wrapping the boy in a reassuring hug. "Where have you been, naughty boy? Is everything okay with you, my champion?" Karamoko inquired gently.

"It's just my stomach," Maladho replied in soft and tiny voice. He felt like a frightened dog caught between two monsters he once trusted.

Jaigol reached into his pocket, pulling out some leaves. "Take this, Maladho. It'll help you feel better."

As Maladho extended his hand to take the herbs, Karamoko intercepted them, snatching them from Jaigol's hand. Their eyes met briefly before Jaigol walked away.

"Don't worry, I'll take care of you," Karamoko assured him.

Despite the comforting words, Maladho felt anything but comforted. Maladho was beginning to feel increasingly isolated. Everyone else appeared as a potential threat, and he felt alarmingly vulnerable. He urgently needed to find Tamba and have someone he could trust to forward his alarming situation to his mother. "Grandpa, where's Uncle Tamba?"

"I haven't seen him today. Naughty boy, they say he went

hunting. It's been three days now, but don't worry, he'll return soon. In the meantime, I'm here for you. I'm your grandpa, your family. And unlike Tamba, I'm your blood, here to protect you," he said, offering a comforting smile. To Maladho, it felt fake.

They soon made their way back to the barracks, and Maladho's mind raced. He felt trapped, unable to communicate with his mother, and with Tamba gone for an extended hunt, he feared time was not on his side. Mentioning anything about the Koyang back in the village was forbidden, a rule so strict that breaking it meant facing harsh punishments. With Jaigol's ultimatum approaching, he was torn between hope for Tamba's return and the looming threat of his own uncertain fate.

CHAPTER SEVENTEEN

THE DECISION

Karamoko felt the pressure. He had to protect his grandson, the Koyang, and his reputation. Understanding how serious the situation was, he knew he had to put aside his pride and act quickly. The balance of power had changed; he wasn't in control anymore. He asked Fenda to come to his hut, hoping to persuade her. Karamoko sat on a goat-skin mat in front of his bed. "My dear daughter. Please, have a seat." He gestured for her to sit on a stool near the door.

"Good evening, Baaba. Mother said you wanted to see me," Fenda said. She took her seat, facing her father.

He cleared his throat, "Yes, we need to talk about something important. Please, my dear daughter. I love you very much and only want what's best for you. I hope you can trust that any decision I make for you is because I care about you and want to keep you safe." Fenda nodded, so he continued. "It's been some time since your husband's passing, and it's important for you to remarry. Our culture holds marriage in high regard, and as a chief, my actions and those of my family are closely watched. It doesn't sit well with our customs for my daughter to be without a husband."

"Baaba, I understand."

"Now, tell me, would you follow someone who doesn't

follow our community's rules?" When she slowly shook her head, Karamoko responded, "Yoo! You see, daughter, this is what I am talking about. May the gods bless you."

"Baaba, I do wish to marry again, but I've yet to meet the right partner. Rest assured, I'll inform you when I do."

They both smiled, and Karamoko broke a piece of kola nut, putting one in his mouth and offering the other to Fenda. She politely declined.

"I'm glad to hear that," Karamoko said warmly. "I want you and your child to be blessed and to bring good luck to the Kopironko community. Therefore, I've found a good match for you. He's a kind and important man. What do you say now, daughter?"

"I want to marry and bring you more grandchildren."

"Yoo! *A-djaráma*, thank you. May the gods hear you, Fenda, my blood."

Fenda leaned forward, eager. *Could it be someone important in the community?* she wondered. *Or perhaps it is the prince of Ganadu who has feelings for me.* She listened closely, excited to discover the identity of this honorable gentleman.

"The man I have in mind is my longtime friend, Jaigol," Karamoko revealed.

Fenda's heart sank as soon as she heard the name, a chill running down her spine. It felt like an arrow had pierced her throat, causing her body to go numb. She struggled to regain her breath and senses. After a moment of shock, she said, "Baaba, with all due respect, I do not want to marry Jaigol."

"Please, do not defy me, daughter. You have never done so before."

"I am not defying you, Baaba. But Jaigol is an old man. He could be my father or grandfather," Fenda replied, her tone firm yet respectful.

"You do not understand, daughter. There are many things at stake. Just accept the offer."

"What things, Baaba? Am I your ransom?" Fenda's voice cracked as she spoke, her frustration evident.

Karamoko threw up his hands. "For gods' sake, it's not about what you think! It's about our family, your son, and our people. Please, just trust me on this. We'll sort everything out."

"No, Baaba. No deals involving me or my son. He's out there, vulnerable, without his father, without protection," her voice rose in defiance.

Karamoko was visibly shaken. "Raising your voice to your father? Have you lost your mind, Fenda?" Karamoko's voice thundered. He stormed toward her, his hand raised in anger, but he stopped abruptly, remembering the sacred silence of the Koyang period.

Fenda noticed his restraint. "Hit me if you must. But know this: I will not marry Jaigol—not now, not ever. Come hit me, kill me if that's what you desire!" she cried out. Then, overwhelmed by emotion, her voice softened. "Baaba, just bring back my son." She let out a sob and dropped to the ground.

Alarmed by the commotion, Sona and Tombom rushed into the hut. They found Fenda on the ground, in tears, her wrapper in disarray.

"It's okay, baby, don't cry," Sona comforted her. Tombom helped her stand, wrapped her again, and guided Fenda outside to her hut. Sona turned to confront Karamoko, who sat silently, visibly shaken and avoiding eye contact. "Kotoo! What's this all about? Our home is supposed to welcome guests, not host conflicts."

Karamoko sighed deeply, frustration evident in his voice. "Fenda is opposing me. I won't stand for such defiance. This is my compound here; what I say will prevail."

Knowing exactly what he was referring to, Sona shook her head. "Kotoo, I've warned you. Let Jaigol rot in hell. He's too old for Fenda, and you know it. Please tell me you haven't promised her to him in one of your shady deals again."

"Enough!" Karamoko barked. "Get out and leave me alone, you mad old woman! I knew it was you brainwashing Fenda. Her behavior is the result of your influence. And it's gone too far. Leave now, or I'll lose my patience," he warned, his temper rising again.

The tables had turned, transforming the hunter into the prey. Were the gods out for revenge or seeking justice? Karamoko and Maladho were both painfully aware that their time was diminishing. Without a way to communicate, Fenda had no idea of the threat her son faced. Though reports claimed Maladho was in good health, the reality was far from it.

That evening, Fenda finished grinding corn for the next day's meal. Tired, she went to bed right away. Just as she was falling asleep, she heard a strange sound. She grabbed her flashlight and looked around the hut, but everything seemed okay. Shrugging it off as something outside, she went back to sleep.

When morning came, Fenda woke up and started her usual routine. As she dressed, she looked at the bottle from Balaba, which she had done every day since she got it.

She gasped. The bottle lay shattered on the floor. The broken bottle, a sinister warning of upcoming danger, left her paralyzed with fear. She couldn't move or scream, feeling overwhelmed by fear as she stared at the broken pieces.

Finally, she managed to break free and frantically

ran out of the hut, calling for her sister-in-law. "Tombom! Tombom!"

Her voice echoed through the compound until Tombom replied from the backyard toilet. "Yes, Fenda, what is it?"

Fenda called urgently, "Quick, come!" They rushed to Fenda's hut. "Look at the bottle!" Her voice trembled with fear, her finger shaking as she pointed to the shattered bottle.

"*Éwuu!*" Tombom said in surprise. "This means Maladho is in danger." She covered her mouth.

"What can we do now? Please, help me," Fenda implored.

"Tamba. He is the only one we can trust," Tombom said with determination. Together, they dashed toward his house. They breathed heavily, scared and desperate, as they hurried along the path. Upon reaching his house, they were met with silence. The door was firmly shut, and there were no signs of life within. Feeling defeated, they went back home, planning to return later. Hope was slim, but it was all they had left.

At dusk, Tombom and Fenda returned to his house. Fenda knocked on the door, praying for a quick answer.

A voice responded, "Who's there?"

"It's me, Fenda," she said, her voice tense.

After a moment, the door creaked open, and a figure emerged, silhouetted against the dim light inside. It was Konko, Tamba's brother, looking surprised but cautious with his T-shirt on his shoulder.

"Is Tamba here?" Fenda asked.

"No, he's gone hunting." Konko sensed her unease. "What's the matter?"

Fenda and Tombom exchanged glances, their anxiety mounting. "We need to find him. It's urgent. Do you know when he'll be back?"

Konko hesitated before answering. "He was supposed to be here by now, but I don't know why he hasn't arrived yet."

"*Woy, woy!*" Fenda whimpered and held her hands up to her head.

Tombom comforted her, then turned to Konko. "Please, we need help. I know you can help us. We need someone to go to Koyang tonight. A kid is in danger. Your brother would have done it for us, and we know you will keep the secret as your brother would."

"I'm sorry, ma'am. It's risky. I can't go there," Konko said, his voice heavy with concern.

"Why risky? Aren't you an initiated man?"

"Yes, I am," Konko admitted, "but I am quarantined because some obscure spirits followed me the other day to Koyang. A few kids got sick upon my arrival. If I return, I will be in trouble."

"Do you have anybody you trust that can do it for us? Please, Konko," Tombom implored.

He shook his head, his expression somber. "No, unfortunately, and please don't let anybody hear what you are planning," he warned them.

Fenda and Tombom walked home in silence, feeling worried. The spooky sounds of the night surrounded them, making them even more afraid with every rustle and hoot. The distant cries of the Kankurangs echoing through the air put them more on edge.

Fenda remembered her dream, thinking about the mysterious figure on the dazzling horse who had told her to run. It felt like a message. Still, she felt powerless thinking about reaching Maladho, who was well-guarded and far away in the Koyang, the ground forbidden for women. Even though it seemed impossible, she knew she had to find a way to keep her son safe.

As they sat in the dimly lit hut, Fenda felt increasingly desperate. She even considered talking to her father or asking Bakar for help, but Tombom's words stopped her. "Your father? Do you really think he's unaware of what's happening? And as for marrying Jaigol, it's clear there's more at play here than we know," Tombom said, her voice tinged with skepticism. "And Bakar. If he had the power or will to intervene, wouldn't Kamboda still be with us?"

"Then what should I do?" Fenda's voice was barely a whisper. "We're seemingly out of options, and every moment we waste, Maladho's danger grows." She sighed and shook her head. "I wish Demba were here, but death betrayed me. Death failed my life. All I want now is to kill myself and end my suffering."

"Killing yourself will not save your child in the bush! Only weak and cowardly people kill themselves. Aren't you a Kopironko? I want Kopirondin to revive herself in you and save your kid. You have it in your blood. I know the spirit of Queen Kopirondin won't abandon you in battle," Tombom said.

Her sister-in-law's words gave her courage. "You are right. Thank you," Fenda said. They sat close together on Fenda's bed, wrapped in the silence of the night. Suddenly, Tombom leaned in, whispering a bold secret plan that made Fenda gasp in disbelief. "What? Are you crazy, Tombom?" Fenda's eyes widened in shock, her head shaking in disbelief. "That's way too risky!"

Tombom gave a nervous smile. Her eyes gleamed with fear and hope. "Sometimes, the craziest plans are the only ones to save us. We have to consider everything for Maladho. Think about it carefully."

Fenda wasn't convinced. She shook her head. "No, not that plan. There has to be another way."

Seeing Fenda's distress, Tombom stood to leave. "Let us rest. We need all the strength we can get for tomorrow. Let's hope for a brighter day where we find a safer solution," she said softly.

But the night was long and sleeping seemed impossible. What Tombom had said stayed in their minds, making them fretful and anxious. As the night went on, they wondered what would happen next, worried about what the new day would bring.

Chapter Eighteen

THE ESCAPE

As dawn broke, Fenda had hardly slept, aware that time was slipping away without a clear solution in sight. She approached the well where Tombom was busily washing clothes, glancing around to ensure their conversation remained private. "Sister-in-law, I've been thinking about the plan you mentioned last night. It might be our only chance," Fenda began.

Tombom looked up with a hopeful smile. "Are you still hesitant?"

"No, it's not that. I just want to be sure it's the right move. It's a big risk."

Tombom's smile grew determined. "I've made up my mind. I don't care whether you are afraid or not. I'm doing it for Maladho, even if it will cost my life."

Fenda bit her lip. "I appreciate your courage, Tombom. But I've got another idea. How about we get Manga involved? He might help us rescue Maladho."

"Manga? That filthy rat!" Tombom raised an eyebrow, skeptical. "You do realize Manga's first loyalty is to your father, right? He's likely to blab everything to him, given the chance. His big dirty mouth is infamous for not keeping secrets."

"True. But perhaps we could get some crucial details from him without putting our plan at risk. We need to know more about Koyang's security and layout. Manga's feelings for me might be the key to getting that information without raising his suspicions."

Tombom conceded with a thoughtful frown. "Just be careful, I am warning you! I don't trust Manga."

Manga worked for her father, Karamoko, looking after the cattle. Fenda spotted him under the mango tree, like always, busy with his kola nut. Manga was in his thirties, from Boé. He wore a long brown kaftan that looked like it had never been washed since Karamoko gave it to him, and stains from the kola nut marked it. His old sandals had been patched up many times; his toes poked out, showing his dark nails. He was sturdy, with light skin and short, curly brown hair that never seemed to grow straight, no matter how much he tried to comb it.

She approached him and said in a serious voice, "Manga, I need to talk to you."

"What do you want? If it's to fetch wood for you, forget it because I'm dead tired," Manga said in a deep voice, chewing his kola nut, bits stuck in the side of his mouth. His loud and deep voice matched his broad nose and big mouth, and his teeth were reddish-brown from being kola-stained.

"I don't need wood. I just want to talk to you," Fenda whispered, glancing around to ensure no one was eavesdropping.

Manga's eyes widened with curiosity. "Tell me here."

"It is a secret; you have to come with me, where we can't be overheard."

"Woman, don't make me leave this cool shade for futile talk. If you're not serious, don't make me get up." This time, his deep voice grew louder.

"Alright, don't come then if you want."

Manga sighed. "Okay, I am coming, but it better be serious."

He followed her to her hut. Inside, she sat on her bed, her wrapper tied to her chest. "Sit here, next to me," she directed him.

He hesitated, puzzled, then shrugged. "Hmm. This is a good day, I guess," Manga said, chuckling under his breath.

Fenda was about to play her biggest card yet. "You know about the situation with my father, right? He's trying to force me into marrying Jaigol, but that's not what I want." Manga nodded, and she continued. "Yes, I need a partner, but Jaigol is old. Do you think Jaigol can handle me?" She gave him a sly smile.

"Oh, hell no. You need a new blood like me to take you to the skies." He laughed hysterically and clapped his hands.

"Well, it may all depend on you because I need someone who can be there for my son and me," Fenda said, locking eyes with Manga.

He stopped laughing and looked at the situation with more interest. "Depend on me, how?"

"First, you should show me you want me not just to take me to the sky, but you will love and treat me well."

"Of course, if you give me a chance, I will provide you with love you have never seen in your life before. We Boé men are romantic! I will also give you the three cows your father gave me during these years. "

"Alright," she said with an enchanting smile on her face. "First, I have to talk to my father. I know he will accept because he likes you. That is it, but we still have a lot to talk about," Fenda said. "Are you going to Koyang today?" He nodded. "It must feel good to be able to enter. I have always wondered what it is like."

Manga seemed startled at the change of topic, but his elation at the possibility of finally being with Fenda loosened his lips. He began describing the area and his part in Koyang. The more attention Fenda paid him, the more he told. When they eventually parted, with Fenda promising again to speak to her father, Manga returned to his shade, pondering the conversation with Fenda.

While they prepared lunch, Fenda told Tombom what she had learned, and they discussed their plans to infiltrate Koyang. "It's tough to enter, Manga said there is a massive pile of straw south of where the barracks are built. I think we can use it to distract them. If we make it there, one of us can light it. The fire will alert them, and they'll rush to extinguish it. In the confusion, we can get Maladho."

Tombom nodded, impressed with Fenda's plan. "That's a wise move."

The two women understood the gravity of their mission. The plan was nothing short of daring, bordering on reckless. Koyang wasn't just any place—it was sacred ground, off-limits to those without the right to be there, especially women. The security around Koyang was notoriously strict, with guards always on high alert, ready to protect its secrets at any cost. Getting caught meant facing severe consequences, and no amount of pleading would change their fate. Yet, driven by desperation and love for Maladho, they were willing to risk it all.

After seeking blessings and protection at the shrine, they gathered at Tombom's hut for what could be their final meeting. "This journey we're embarking on is surrounded by uncertainty. We may return, or we may not. But let's remember, our fate rests in the hands of the gods and our ancestors. What we're doing is more than a mere task; it's a quest for life itself," Tombom prayed, her voice showing determination and sadness. "Now, give me your hand, Fenda," she continued, extending her arm. "We are united in this. You are more than my sister-in-law; you are my sister in spirit and in heart. I love you."

Fenda, moved by Tombom's words, said, "I love you, too. Together, we'll face whatever comes our way. If something happens to me, take care of Maladho."

As the sun went down and the evening got darker, Kopiro and nearby villages were excited for the upcoming jambadong. In just a few days Koyang would end. Kankurangs and custodians came to the village for their routine checking. While everyone was busy with the celebration and the Kankurangs led the dances, two brave women started a daring mission in the dark.

Disguised as men, Fenda and Tombom blended into a group heading toward Koyang, their only chance to slip into the highly secured and sacred site. Their disguise was their ticket in, but they were worried about how they would get away later. The Koyang site was bustling, the air filled with the noise of the crowd and the crackle of fires dotted around the area.

Focusing on their mission, Fenda recalled the crucial detail Manga had shared: Maladho could be identified by his red Sumbia, signifying his role as the Head of Koyang. They scanned the sea of hundreds of people, the dim light from the fires casting moving shadows and making their task more challenging. Finally, she spotted Maladho by the fire, but they couldn't get through the crowd to him.

"Keep an eye on him. I'll create the distraction," Tombom whispered. She pointed at the straw pile. "I'll light it up. Once it catches, grab Maladho and head to the entrance," she instructed before disappearing.

Fenda moved closer to Maladho and whispered his name.

"Maladho, it is me, don't make a noise. Don't worry, son. Mommy's here now. We're getting out of here. But quickly, follow me."

"Mom?" Maladho turned in surprise.

"Shush, just follow me," Fenda whispered. Fenda's heart was pounding with fear, waiting for the signal.

Soon, flames shot up, causing chaos. People ran to extinguish the fire, fearing it might reach their shelters. The Koyang erupted into chaos and pandemonium as the fire spread wildly, burning everything in its way. People were screaming, and the fire roared loudly, making it hard to think straight.

Fenda grabbed Maladho's hand in the chaos and pulled him toward the bush. Tombom wasn't where they had planned to meet. Fenda waited a moment, anxious for her sister-in-law, but she dared not wait long. Not wasting another moment, Fenda and Maladho ran into the dark night, unsure of where they were going, driven by the urgent need to escape. They felt terrified as they ran fast down the small path in total darkness. They could hear their own loud, rough breathing echoing around them.

Suddenly, a blinding beam of light pierced through the darkness, forcing them to shield their eyes. "Stop right there! Where do you think you're taking the boy?" a familiar voice growled in the dark.

Unable to see, Fenda and Maladho shielded their eyes and didn't see the kicks coming. Fenda fell back, hitting her head on the tree behind her, knocking her unconscious. The man bound and gagged them both before dragging them off the path. He then proceeded to remove Fenda's clothes, heavily breathing as he did so. The movement woke her, and she realized she was being stripped. Weakened, she tried to resist, but her head swam and the ropes restricted her movement. Her heart pounded in terror. Beside her, Maladho moaned in pain as he lay on the damp grass, unable to help his mother.

"You think you are smart? Ahh!" The voice boomed over Fenda, his panting breaths punctuating each word as he savagely tore away Fenda's clothes. "Ah, this was your plan, lying to me. But I am smarter than you." Manga, hatred burning in his voice as he finished taking off her clothes, began to undress, ready to carry out his sick plan. "When I am done with you here, I'll take you back to Koyang for your execution for trespassing the sacred place."

Trembling with fear and anger, Fenda knew this would be her final moments alive. She tried to shake him off, kicking and pushing, but Manga held her and pinned her tight to the ground.

Suddenly, Tombom's furious voice rang out, "You nasty pervert!" There was a loud crack as Tombom hit Manga in the back of his head with a piece of wood, followed by a thud as Manga's body hit the damp ground. Tombom untied Fenda and Maladho, their breaths coming in ragged gasps. "I'm so sorry for being late. Get your clothes quickly and let's go. We don't have much time." They grabbed Manga's flashlight and bicycle, leaving the injured shepherd behind, snorting like an injured buffalo, and made their way to the crossroads.

Tombom, her voice heavy with emotion, turned to Fenda. "Run, sister-in-law. Take Maladho and head for the road. Make it to Bissau as fast as you can. There, you can find help," she encouraged. After a heartfelt hug, tears streaming down all of their faces, Tombom said, "Here, this is five thousand francs. It is all I have saved. Go now. We'll reunite later."

Fenda tied the money on the edge of her wrapper.

"Thank you, sister. Stay safe." Without wasting time, she lifted Maladho onto the bicycle and began pedaling hard down the road toward safety, leaving Tombom to make her way back alone to the village. In Kopiro, flames flickered from the Koyang bushes, lighting up the night while shouts echoed. Smoke climbed high, sending ashes drifting over the village. Tombom slipped back unnoticed.

Fenda, pedaling the bike hard on the rough road through the dark, breathed heavily, the night sounds mingling with the hum of wheels. Bugs flew into their faces. "Maladho, my son, are you okay?" she checked.

Maladho, tears in his eyes, nodded. "Yes, Mommy."

They hit a bump, and Fenda cursed under her breath.

"What's wrong, Mom?" Maladho's concern grew.

"The bike's got a flat tire," she sighed. They were already a good distance from the Koyang, but Fenda knew they needed to push further. With no other choice, they left the bike behind to continue on foot, determined to escape the danger. The night covered Fenda and Maladho like a heavy blanket, silent and dark. They hurried on, hearts pounding, knowing that being discovered was only a matter of time. The road was deserted, with no lights, no movement, just them and the vast, silent darkness. Up in the sky, stars sparkled, watching quietly as Fenda and Maladho ran desperately. Fenda wished they could fly away to safety like birds. The fireflies glowed as if they were lighting up the darkness to guide them on their path to escape.

Back in the village, Tombom went to the shrine seeking safety. She spoke quietly but sincerely as she prayed. She begged the gods for forgiveness for entering Koyang, the sacred place, and asked them to protect Fenda and Maladho. By the flickering fire, she hoped her prayers would keep them safe and help them find their way in the dark.

Meanwhile, back in Koyang, Manga woke up but was seriously injured. He managed to crawl, and he arrived and collapsed right in the middle of the place, which was smoky and gloomy. It was a moment before the others saw him lying there with a deep wound on the back of his head, barely able to whisper. They rushed to his side, cleaning his wound with water and pressing healing herbs against the injury to stop the bleeding.

He delivered a shocking message with a voice as frail as a whisper. "Maladho is gone," he barely managed to say, pointing weakly toward the path, leaving a wave of confusion. They couldn't get more words out of him. He had passed out again.

"The Head of Koyang has been kidnapped!" At first, the words were swallowed by the noise. They blew the horn. "The Head of Koyang is missing! The Head of Koyang has been kidnapped!" a man shouted again, his voice ringing clearer this time. They started searching frantically for Maladho, confirming Manga's worrying news. The sound of the horn pierced the night, spreading a severe warning that echoed across the land. Something unthinkable had occurred—Maladho had disappeared into thin air, plunging everyone into a state of shock and fear. This was a tragedy like no other.

Fenda and Maladho quickened their pace under the cloak of night, Koyang almost an hour behind them. With every passing minute, their slim chances of getting a ride to the city diminished, and the next village seemed an eternity away. Fenda's breaths came in heavy pants, the flip-flop of her slippers echoing ominously in the darkness. Anxiously, she removed them, deciding barefoot was better, and tied them on her back with her wrapper. "Mom, I'm tired. Can we stop for a bit?" Maladho's request broke through the silence.

She considered pausing, but the distant sound of a horn sliced through the air, quickly followed by three gunshots. It was a warning from Koyang that trouble was coming. The distant barking of dogs signaled the start of a search, intensifying their fear. "We can't stop now, they've found out," Fenda whispered. Realizing the path was no longer safe, they entered the bush, disappearing into the dense forest to evade the search squads now combing the area for them.

Karamoko immediately ordered every exit and entrance to be sealed tight. With Maladho missing, the surrounding lands and every corner of Kopiro had to be combed meticulously. A red alert echoed through Kopiro, calling upon the village elders to summon Fambondin, the solitary spirit. This spirit, known for its fearsome reputation, could leap through the air with the agility of a grasshopper, striking terror in the hearts of even the bravest men. Unlike the usual Kankurangs, Fambondin was an agent of emergency, called upon only in times of grave danger. It had the unique ability to sniff out trouble like a hound. Fambondin could dance across the treetops and rooftops and glide through the air with a ghostly presence. When Fambondin shows up, it doesn't need companions like other Kankurangs. To summon it, the elders needed to go to the sacred forest. Usually, the ritual takes a long time, and it takes even more time for the spirit to appear. The search for Maladho was not just urgent; it was critical, and Fambondin's release into the night meant that the stakes were higher than ever.

Fenda and Maladho walked faster, feeling the tension rising. The forest around them was very dark, with the sounds of animals seeming too loud for the stealth they sought. Every step they took stirred up the smells of the forest—a damp, earthy smell mixed with the fresh, cool feeling of dew. The plants and grass were wet, giving off a strong scent as they walked quickly.

Far away, they could hear the loud shouts of the Kankurangs in the night. Maladho's feet hurt with every step, and he was very thirsty. But whenever they thought about stopping, they heard the sounds in the distance, fear urging them on.

Maladho abruptly halted. "Mom, listen. Something is coming, Mom," he whispered, terrified. He cocked his head, tuning into the distant, creepy, unfamiliar sound.

"We need to keep moving. They're after us."

"Just listen, Mommy. It's getting closer," he insisted.

Fenda stopped moving and listened carefully. Then, she heard it, too. "What the hell is that?"

From the direction they had come from, there was a loud, heavy sound like tanks charging toward them. Realizing the ground was unsafe, they hurried to a tall tree and climbed high into its branches to escape the danger. In just a few moments, the forest echoed with a thunderous sound. Dark shapes dashed through the underbrush—giant forest hogs, charging with incredible speed as if fleeing from an unseen threat. The beasts crushed the vegetation underfoot, sending dust clouds into the air, and the forest grew even darker.

From the top of the tree, Maladho clung to his mother, his heart beating fast and his breath coming in sharp gasps as the ground shook and the tree trembled. After the chaos, when the thick dust settled, he noticed a flickering, distant light among the trees. "Mom, look over there. It looks like fire. Maybe someone's there. I'm so thirsty. Can we go there and ask for some water?" he suggested, hope in his voice.

Fenda hesitated, knowing the dangers, but nodded. "You

are right. It is a fire, but it's risky. But we don't have a choice. We need water. Let's go, just be careful."

Climbing down from the tree, they cautiously made their way toward the glow of the fire. It wasn't as close as they thought it was. They walked carefully to avoid making noise, but it was difficult in the dark. With snapping twigs and rustling leaves they neared the fire.

Suddenly, a flashlight beam shone through the darkness, making their eyes gleam like those of a wild animal. "Stop right there!" A voice called out. A man approached, a flashlight strapped to his forehead.

It was difficult to see with the light in their eyes, but Fenda spotted a gun pointed straight at their faces. "Please don't shoot! I'm begging you. We're harmless! We just need water."

The man lowered his shotgun and removed the flashlight to reveal himself as Tamba. He ran to them. "Oh my goodness, Fenda? I almost shot you. I thought you were robbers or the Guyankos after my horse." He gestured to the animal grazing nearby. The trio hugged, their bodies trembling and tears mingling with relief and fear. "Tell me I am dreaming!" Pulling away, he took in their ragged appearance, the desperate look in their eyes. "What happened?" Tamba exclaimed. "What's going on?"

"They're after us, Tamba. I went to Koyang to rescue Maladho. We need your help," Fenda pleaded, her voice thick with desperation.

"You mean you went to Koyang? Oh my goodness! Fenda, do you understand the gravity of your violation?" Tamba placed his hands on his head.

"Yes, I know, but I had no other way to save him. His life was in danger. I looked for you to help me, but they told me you had been gone for days."

At this, Tamba understood the gravity of their trouble. "Then we can't spend another minute here." He gave them water to quench their thirst before they hurriedly prepared to leave. In order for this horse to carry all of them Tamba removed some of his cargo, mostly fresh and dry meat. Mounting his horse, he helped Fenda and Maladho up with him. As they galloped away, the distant sounds of barking dogs and haunting cries echoed behind them.

Tamba, who knew every inch of the forest like the back of his hand, guided them through the trail under the giant trees and vines. As they passed, branches whipped them, and their bodies became wet from the dew. The air was thick and humid. The horse's galloping echoed loudly in the dark. Far behind them, the piercing sounds of Kankurangs and Fambondin still lingered.

Tamba was worried and didn't talk. He was focused on running away with them. Later, little by little, the sounds behind them faded away. Tamba didn't want to stop at any village, fearful of being seen by those loyal to Karamoko. He went straight to Gabu with few breaks to rest and give the horse some food and water. They arrived in Gabu around three in the morning. Leaving the horse with a friend, they caught a truck that was carrying charcoal to Bissau. The driver asked for fifteen thousand francs, but Tamba pleaded with him and gave him ten thousand.

Tamba, Fenda, and Maladho hopped in the back of the truck as they left for Bissau. The cold wind blew, and the dust from the charcoal entered their eyes. They had to cover themselves with sheets Tamba had for camping.

Maladho was tired, scared and hypervigilant. He jumped at the slightest noise and sometimes yelled out in fear, "No, Jaigol, don't kill me." Fenda would hold him close to calm him down.

The old truck stopped several times along the way. The driver and his assistant poured water into its thirsty engine, waiting a while before continuing their journey. During a quiet moment in the night, Fenda confided in Tamba all the details about what had happened with Maladho and their entry into Koyang.

Tamba looked puzzled and then confessed, "I had a feeling something strange was going on. You know, I've been familiar with that forest for years from hunting in it, but since yesterday, I've been getting lost. It's like something unusual was leading me toward the creek and then to the ridge. I couldn't find my way back home. Even my horse was acting strangely, as if it sensed something. When I reached the spot where you found me, I was already exhausted and decided to wait until morning to see if I could find my way. Now I realize whatever spirit was guiding me, it wanted me to find you and save you. I don't think it was just a coincidence."

Finally, after an arduous journey, they reached Bissau around ten in the morning. They looked like they'd been rolling in charcoal and dust. Tamba hailed an old, beat-up taxi, a Mercedez painted blue and white, and they headed to a neighborhood called Antula, north of the city. There, they would go see a wise man named Nyu Ossanti, a well-known *djambakus*, healer and diviner. Tamba and Mr. Ossanti had known each other for a long time, ever since Tamba used to sell him meat. They'd become good friends over the years. He would know what to do.

CHAPTER NINETEEN

THE CITY

Inside the taxi, they remained silent. Tamba sat in the front seat while Maladho and his mother sat behind. Maladho rested his face on the window, but despite his exhaustion, he could not fall asleep. He observed the city's chaotic life, which was so different from the village. Cars honked, crowds filled the sidewalks, and dust and fumes mixed. It was an endless spectacle Maladho didn't like, but he wasn't sure when they would go back to Kopiro—if ever.

The taxi pulled over near some large trees surrounded by vegetation. It was shaded and quiet, with sunlight filtering through the leaves. "Wait here. I will be back soon," Tamba said at the shrine's entrance. A few minutes later, he reappeared with a man in his midfifties, tall, wrapped in a red mantle, and wearing a red turban.

Nyu Ossanti held a short broom and a calabash bowl with liquid and herbs. He swept Fenda and Maladho's bodies from top to bottom and vice versa to cleanse them in case any spirits followed. After that, they entered the grand Baloba. Inside, clay pots hung in the trees, and they sat in the round thatched hut that was the main shrine.

"This is serious," Ossanti said with a worried tone. As he arranged and talked, he shook his head. Fenda's face grew concerned. "Tamba, my brother, as you said, this is trouble. I know Karamoko and Jaigol. They're both wicked. We have to take care of this kid right away."

Ossanti summoned his associates. "The first thing to do is shave your hair. We will take the cut hair, wrap it with an amulet, and bury it under a termite mound. This is necessary because the spirit is out there searching for you. By camouflaging you this way, the spirit wouldn't be able to recognize you. And you must cast off your real names until everything is done. Until then, you must not be Fenda and Maladho, but rather woman and boy. Your identity must be hidden."

Tamba had to go to the market, buy a red hen, and bring it as soon as possible. When he returned, Ossanti started the ritual, pouring sugar cane rum into a figurine. He drank some and sprayed the liquid on the wooden figurines. Then he cut the hen's head with one blow. The fowl staggered, flapped its wings uncontrollably, and stumbled around in circles until it lay quiet at Maladho's feet. "The gods have answered." Ossanti closed his eyes and shivered as if bathed in cold water. Then, his aide grabbed the animal and poured the blood on the figurines. The whole ritual was something of another realm neither Fenda nor Maladho had seen.

After the ritual, Ossanti gave them food and led them to his compound, where he gave them a room. They were told to stay quarantined for ninety days without leaving the compound. Tamba went to the city to take care of some business. Everything seemed quiet. They slept a lot, spending most of their time confined to the small room. Tamba came and went, bringing them meat and other provisions they needed.

Maladho often stood by the window, watching other kids

play, or he listened to the noise beyond the compound, eager to join them. For Maladho, that was a long confinement. Every day, he watched people passing by and managed to make a friend, Ossanti's son Keba, a boy his age. Keba regularly visited him to talk and play. After the second month, Maladho was already tired of the confinement.

Keba noticed. "Let's play outside," he suggested.

"I can't."

Keba kept insisting. "Let's play. You won't be out long."

Tired of being cooped up, it didn't take much to convince him. Without a second thought, Maladho jumped out of the window and left with Keba to play. They played soccer, and Maladho met other boys his age.

When Fenda woke up to find Maladho missing, she panicked. Unable to leave the room herself, she asked for help from the window. Ossanti's second wife, Dalanda, ran out searching for Maladho and found him playing among the other kids. She took him back home.

"Maladho, where have you been?" Fenda asked, her voice filled with both anger and worry.

"Mom, I just went to play with Keba," Maladho admitted.

"Didn't I tell you to stay here as Uncle Ossanti instructed? Do you want trouble? You know the spirits are searching for us, right?" Fenda scolded. "I won't mention this to him, but you must stay inside from now on."

That night, Maladho started to mumble in his sleep, experiencing troubling dreams and hallucinations. When Fenda touched him, his body was hot, as if he had been roasted. By the morning, Maladho was mumbling, his mouth full of foam, and he lay unconscious on the mat. Fenda screamed when she saw him this way, and Ossanti ran to their room. He performed a ritual and prepared an amulet, which helped Maladho fall asleep and begin to recover. Turning to Fenda, he asked, "Did he leave this place, daughter?"

Fenda hesitated. "Yes, yesterday he left while I was sleeping. I didn't know, I swear."

"Ah, that's why. The wind found him. It was here searching. I have to take you both to the shrine because you have been compromised."

"I am sorry, uncle. I am so sorry. This kid doesn't listen, and I have warned him," Fenda apologized tearfully.

"Don't cry, daughter. I understand kids. You see how this place is full of them. They are all the same. And I know that hardheaded boy Keba is the one who took him out." Ossanti said gently.

They walked to the shrine where Ossanti performed another ritual and covered their bodies with sacred oil after the prayer and sacrifice to the gods. Maladho's health improved, and he recovered from the fever, but he continued to do strange things, like sleepwalk around the room. It was as if he was talking and singing to other people from beyond, sometimes in a language Fenda couldn't understand.

After the ninety days, Ossanti went to their room early in the morning. "Daughter, now you can go out, you and the kid. I believe whatever spirit that was behind you is gone. I checked, and you are fine," he declared.

From that day, Fenda and Maladho were freed. They never discussed what happened and tried to move on. They lived within the compound, and Ossanti loved them and treated them well. He even found Maladho a school. Maladho was good at school, but he was constantly distracted, as if he were living in another world.

Fenda, growing more and more concerned with this behavior, brought Maladho to Ossanti.

"He has the third eye," Ossanti said. "He is able to see what an ordinary human can't see. That's why he behaves in this way, possibly it is why he is distracted at school as well."

"Can you close his third eye?" Fenda asked.

"Yes, it can be done, but if he could control it, it would be good for him. It may be of use to him," Ossanti replied.

"Please, just close it. This thing brings more problems," she said. Ossanti nodded and performed the ritual.

It seemed to work, as Maladho started focusing on school. He became more social. Every Wednesday, he would get excited when his Uncle Tamba arrived, bringing them meat and other items from the city. Maladho was fascinated by the city, so Tamba took him out often. They visited the carousel at Alto Krim square, and sometimes they went to watch soccer.

One day, Tamba arrived on a Monday, looking somber. Fenda invited him in for tea while they waited for Maladho to get home from school. They sat in silence for a bit before Fenda asked, "Tell me, how is my family? Are they doing well?"

Tamba hesitated. Then in a quiet voice, he said, "Fenda, Kopiro is gone." He sighed deeply. "I didn't want to tell you, but since the day you left, things became ugly. First, the village burned completely, and as everybody was trying to recover, the Koff Label River flooded the crops, and everything was lost." Fenda gasped softly, covering her mouth. With deep grief in his voice, Tamba continued, "I am sorry, but your father also is dead. He drowned in the river, and another man from the village of Sagoya brought his clothes to the compound."

Fenda shook her head and closed her eyes, tears rolling down her cheeks. "Please," she pleaded, "tell me, my mother is fine."

"I am sorry, she passed away. They say it was too much at once, yours and Maladho's disappearance, your father's passing. She couldn't bear it all. It tormented her. She was buried at the compound. Everyone else fled Kopiro. Your brother and Tombom included. I don't know their whereabouts. I have moved to Ganadu because Kopiro and the entire province are plagued. It's haunted. The spirits of our ancestors and the gods aren't happy," Tamba said.

Fenda wept uncontrollably, feeling the guilt on her shoulders. "It is all my fault. Maybe I wasn't supposed to do what I did," Fenda cried.

"No, it isn't your fault. It was destined to happen, and you saved Maladho. It was your dad's fault," Tamba comforted her. "That was the end of the reign of Kopiro. Everything succumbed."

As time passed, Tamba and Fenda started developing a deep affection for each other. They had been through much together. Maladho was delighted to see them together. To him, Tamba had been like a second dad.

Tamba often left town for work, but one Wednesday, Tamba didn't come home. And the second Wednesday as well, Tamba didn't appear. Fenda and Maladho were worried. Nobody had news, and as more time passed, they became more and more concerned.

Once again, Fenda called upon Ossanti. He was grave when he told her, "Tamba is at risk. I warned him to cleanse himself because he saved you, and because he was involved directly in crossing the land of your ancestors with you. It is written."

Yet Fenda still awaited Tamba, or at least news of what had happened. Amidst this anguish, without Tamba to support them, Fenda knew she now needed a job to properly care for Maladho. She did not want to rely on Ossanti's kindness. She wanted a home of her own.

She went to the mental health hospital to see if Dr. Giovanni could find her a job, but she was told Dr. Giovanni had returned to Italy and was replaced by Dr. Lorenzo. But he was a kind man and gave her a job with the cleaning staff. She did the job for six months, but the conditions weren't good, and there were constant strikes. Luckily, she was able to save up enough money to start selling fish at the Bandim Market. There, she made a decent profit and could ask travelers for news of Tamba. Her new endeavor also enabled her to rent a room with Maladho in the Bandim neighborhood.

One day, Fenda came home crying.

Concerned, Maladho moved to comfort her. "Mom, what is happening? What's wrong?"

"I met a woman from Sagoya, who escaped due to the constant flooding. She knew of Tamba. She told me that Tamba passed away while on a short trip to Sagoya. He had been washing his horse by the river and was swallowed by the mud. He sank together with the horse. His body couldn't be recovered," Fenda said, sobbing.

The news broke Maladho's heart. Once again, they experienced a terrible loss, their world slowly crumbling at their feet. But life continued, and eventually, they moved on. Fenda's business continued to thrive, and Maladho excelled in school, finishing high school with great grades. The Brazilian government was offering scholarships to students from developing countries to study in Brazil. Maladho applied and was accepted, but it was a half scholarship. The government would cover tuition, but the rest—like rent, food, transportation, and other expenses—would be on him.

Fenda promised to pay for everything, so Maladho embarked on a trip to São Paulo to study medicine at The

University of São Paulo. During his studies, Fenda supported him in every way. Maladho chose medicine for a reason. For him, he had a mission to fulfill, the mission he had had since the disappearance of his cousin. Dr. Giovanni had told him that education and knowledge were the key to fulfilling his mission.

So when he finished his degree, he returned to Bissau and found a job at the biggest hospital, Simão Mendes. And now was the time to find out the truth about what happened to Kamboda.

Chapter Twenty

THE RIVER

In the past, Ossanti saved them from what could have been their extermination. In the present, however, the saga of Kopiro still lingered, and its shadows appeared to follow them. Since returning to his home village, Maladho's state of mind brought Fenda cause for concern. These visions and dreams reminded her of his behavior when he was a child, after Kamboda went missing. They had called upon Uncle Ossanti for cleansing and protection, and he asked them to return.

"I've spoken with our ancestors, who guide us between the world of the living and the spirits," Ossanti began, his voice calm but serious. "What you've encountered, the visions and the presence at your home, they're tied to Kopiro." Ossanti's gaze met theirs, causing Fenda's eyes to widen with worry. He paused, his finger lingering over a small figurine as if sharing a silent conversation with it. "According to what's been revealed to me," Ossanti continued with emphasis, turning his full attention to Maladho, "Dr. Maladho, when you were younger, you made a promise to someone or something. Do you recall any of that?" he asked.

Maladho shook his head, confusion and denial in his

gesture. "No," he whispered.

Ossanti looked at him in disbelief. "I doubt that. Indeed, you might not remember, but I know what I have done," Ossanti said.

"What did you do, Uncle Ossanti?" Maladho asked, his voice tinged with concern.

"Let it be, Maladho," Fenda interjected quickly, hoping to shield her son from the shadows of their past.

"Mom, why are you always keeping secrets from me?" His question hung in the air.

Ossanti, with a gentle smile, sought to ease the tension. "Maladho, your mom's just looking out for you. Your childhood was filled with mysteries. You had a unique gift, a third eye, which let you see and talk about things beyond our normal sight. You used to share stories about Kamboda and the river that none of us could understand. For your own good, I had to seal that gift away. It was distracting you from your studies." As he spoke, Ossanti gently waved a lion tail over the small figurine, symbolizing the protective measures he took long ago.

"Our next step is to uncover the truth. It might be connected to Kamboda, like you talked about when you were younger. You used to say Kamboda lived in the river and that you visited him there. Maybe the river itself holds the clues we're after. You can head home for now. Once I figure out our next move, I'll let you know what we need to do."

Maladho returned home from dropping off his mom, ready for another workday. Walking in, he saw his girlfriend buried in papers on the living room sofa, a heavy book on her lap. "Hey, didn't expect you so soon," he greeted.

"I came over early to study for my exam tomorrow," N'damesse explained.

"Keep at it, future lawyer," he encouraged.

"Thanks. How'd your meeting go?"

"Pretty good, we're making progress," Maladho replied, sitting on the sofa beside her.

She put away her book and cleaned up the papers. Snuggling up to Maladho, she gave him a soft kiss. "Can I ask you something? Will you be honest?" she asked.

Maladho let out a small laugh. "It depends. I know lawyers can be a bit tricky."

N'damesse smiled, then her face turned curious. "Who's Kamboda?"

The question caught Maladho off guard. He leaned in closer, looking surprised and cautious. "How did you hear about Kamboda?" he questioned.

"You're the one who mentioned him," she revealed with a gentle smile.

Maladho pretended to be confused, playing it off. "Me? No idea what you're talking about."

But N'damesse could tell there was more beneath the surface, that Maladho was holding something back. "Please, Maladho," she urged, "don't keep secrets from me."

"Keeping secrets from you? What do you mean?" Maladho asked, a perplexed expression on his face.

N'damesse looked into his eyes and spoke softly. "Maladho, when you're sleeping, you talk to Kamboda in your dreams every night. The things you say to him, the hope and friendship you express toward him, are astonishing."

Maladho looked down, and she could see the sadness and confusion in his eyes. "What did you hear?" he asked.

"You always promise to release him. You promise to go back for him."

"Kamboda is . . . well, he's my cousin," he started, his voice trembling slightly. "He was different, born with a unique condition that made him stand out. People cruelly called him 'Serpent Boy.' And then, one day, he just vanished without a trace." He paused, gathering his thoughts before sharing more about Kamboda's story with her.

He could feel the weight of his secrets lifting as he finally opened up to N'damesse. She listened intently, her heart going out to him. When he finished, she wrapped her arms around him in a comforting hug. "We'll figure this out together," she assured him. "Your cousin, your friend, he needs you. And I'm here with you every step of the way."

Maladho nodded, a look of both relief and determination in his eyes. His cell phone interrupted the moment, the sound of its ringtone breaking the silence. "Yes?" He listened, a frown forming on his face. "Tomorrow? But that's impossible. I have work." Another pause to listen. "Okay, I'll make it happen," he said before ending the call, a new determination in his voice. "That was my mother."

"What happened?"

"Ossanti needs us to go to Kopiro tomorrow," he responded.

"To the river?" she questioned.

"Yes," Maladho sighed.

"I think it's a good idea. But be careful."

Maladho contacted one of his colleagues to cover him, and the next day, as the sun cast a gentle glow and a cool breeze whispered through the air, they arrived in Kopiro. The world around the Koff Label River seemed to come alive with their presence. The leaves rustled, and distant birdcalls echoed, mingling with the distant cries of monkeys from the depths of the bush. It was as if nature itself was sending them a message.

Fenda gazed in disbelief at the river before them. The once vibrant and bustling Koff Label was now a mere shadow of its former self; the riverbanks were covered in dry mud, with only a small trickle of water flowing sadly. It was nothing like how she remembered the river, always full of life. Turning her gaze toward the village, she found nothing but silence and abandonment. The lively community that once thrived there was no more, leaving behind an aura of solitude.

Undeterred, Ossanti led the way toward Woudou, a place where the greenery was thicker, as if entering another world. The journey was not just a physical trek but a passage through memories and time, seeking answers hidden within the landscape that once cradled their past.

"No, no, don't go there, Uncle. It's creepy," Fenda called out, trying to stop Ossanti. But he didn't respond, moving forward as if he hadn't heard her.

Maladho, sensing his mother's fear, suggested, "Mom, maybe you should stay back in the truck?" Her face lined with apprehension, she nodded and returned to the truck, watching from a distance.

Ossanti, followed by his two aides and Maladho, led the way, cutting through the thick underbrush and making a path for them to follow.

When they reached a certain spot, Ossanti held up his hand, signaling for everyone to stop. He began murmuring under his breath, his lips moving in silent prayer or incantation. Then, clearly and confidently, he spoke to the unseen forces of the place, "We come in peace. Just passing through. We mean no harm. We're here on a mission with one of your own." He paused, lowering his hands as if waiting for an unseen gate to open or for someone to welcome them forward.

After moments of suspense, something darted into the water, creating a loud commotion. Maladho shuddered and took a few steps back while Ossanti continued into the dark, dense vegetation. The sun was barely visible, obscured by the thick foliage. The water bubbled, and small waves formed. "We apologize if we are intruding, but our mission is not to cause any harm," Ossanti said repeatedly.

Suddenly, a massive black snake emerged from the water, causing Maladho to nearly bolt, but one of the aides held him back. The serpent floated in the water, its size impressive. Ossanti gripped his lion's tail and gazed at the snake. After nearly a minute, the creature slithered out of the water and disappeared. Ossanti performed a ritual, talking and waving the tail, which bore an amulet. After a few minutes, he walked around and then ordered everyone to leave.

When they got in the car and drove away, Fenda asked, "What did you see?"

Ossanti took a deep breath, wiping sweat from his brow. "There were dark shadows, something beyond our understanding, lurking in the river. Whatever you've seen before, it was there, watching us intently. And let me be clear, it's not pleased with our presence," he explained, his voice serious.

No sooner had he finished than a massive tree crashed down right behind them, narrowly missing their truck. Ossanti glanced back at the close call and sighed. "Seems like Maladho's guardian angel is looking out for us once more. That tree could have ended our journey right here. But we came with peaceful intentions, and peacefully we'll leave," he concluded.

Upon hearing those words, Fenda nearly fainted. "Please drive fast. I don't want to die here," she pleaded.

"Don't worry. Your time hasn't come yet," Ossanti reassured her.

"It's both disappointing and frustrating," Maladho grumbled. "Uncle Ossanti, maybe I can't recall the pledge I made, but I know I'm meant to fight a big battle. I chose to study medicine to grasp things better and help others," he said, pausing to glance in the rearview mirror. "As a kid, I saw stuff that didn't add up. Those kids being called spirits? That's just made up. In other places, they're going to school and getting jobs. Why not here? It's my mission to open our people's eyes, to help them understand and protect kids with disabilities instead of hurting them."

Ossanti responded with a serious tone, "Maladho, in our country, there's a mix of spiritual leaders. While many guide us with genuine wisdom, a few misuse their powers for evil. These individuals exploit their influence for harmful practices. Stopping them isn't simple."

"Can you explain more?"

Ossanti continued, shifting in his seat. "Some of these so-called spiritual guides manipulate their followers, using fear and superstition. They claim to solve problems through dark rituals, but they're often just consolidating their power and wealth. It's a tricky situation because they're deeply entrenched in our society."

"But fighting for Kamboda and other kids is necessary," Maladho said.

"Maladho, forget it, it is in the past. What will it do to fight for something forgotten? It won't help Kamboda. Why fight?" Fenda said.

"Justice may help. I need justice for Kamboda, even if I won't see him again. And there are others like him who need protecting," Maladho said.

Ossanti lightly smiled as he adjusted his mantle. "Yes, maybe whatever is trying to contact you wants justice and awareness. But I am afraid. The corrupt politicians and government members rely on witchcraft and juju to get elected, maintain power, and remain in power. So let me ask you this. Do you think those in power will allow you to destroy their allies?"

Maladho shook his head. "I understand what you're saying. This won't be an easy task, but someone needs to do something to put a stop to it." Maladho recognized the truth in Ossanti's observations. His own return to his homeland had brought him face-to-face with the rampant issue of juju practices, especially at work. Each morning, he'd find mysterious charms placed before his office door, a clear attempt by someone to unsettle him and perhaps take his position. But Maladho wasn't easily intimidated; after all, he hailed from the resilient Kopironko lineage. The pervasive use of juju, once confined to hidden corners, had now spread across workplaces and the broader society like wildfire, yet it went largely unchallenged.

The topic of disabled children was particularly sensitive, shrouded in silence and stigma. Despite advancements in education and awareness, deep-seated superstitions and prejudices persisted, even among the well-informed. These children, instead of being seen through a lens of compassion and support, were often subjected to unfounded fears and misconceptions, leaving a gap in societal acceptance and understanding.

After dropping everyone off at their homes, Maladho returned home to rest after a long day.

N'damesse was reading her law book, as usual. "Hey, baby, I'm glad you're back. How was it? Did you make any progress?"

"Ossanti said the river is dark. I know it. That is the place where they take those kids as they did to Kamboda," Maladho confidently said.

N'damesse nodded, understanding the gravity of the situation. "It's almost as if ignorance has become a widespread disease, infecting nearly everyone in society," she reflected. "The reality that even hospitals, places meant for healing and care, turn away from disabled children due to societal pressures and prejudices deeply troubles me."

"It's not just ignorance; it's fear and superstition dictating actions. It's horrifying how backward thinking can be, even among those supposed to protect and heal," Maladho lamented. He recalled an incident where parents vanished with their child rather than seeking medical help, and the dismissive response from his superior highlighted the dire state of affairs. "We have a duty, though," he continued, his voice firm with conviction. "We must stand against this tide of ignorance and superstition. We must fight to bring awareness and change to ensure justice for these children. It's a daunting task, but it's necessary. We can't let fear win."

"Maladho, the problem is there is no justice in this country!" N'damesse said, placing her chin in her hand. "But as you said, we need to take steps."

"Where should we start? Because the time is ticking for these kids," Maladho asked.

"I have a friend, Mamasaidou, who is also my professor. He works in the judiciary police as chief of criminal investigation. We can talk to him. Maybe he can help us."

Her suggestion left Maladho slightly relaxed. His doubt was whether the authorities would take care of it or not. The judicial system was slow and inefficient. Combined with corruption, crooked politicians, and unprepared policymakers, the case probably would never take off, and this kind of crime would continue. His duty was to fight for those kids who were abandoned because they were different.

He needed to be their voice to honor the pledge and friendship with his cousin Kamboda, who was unjustly called a snake boy and mistreated by society.

N'damesse arranged for Maladho to meet the investigator the next day. When he arrived at the main office of the judiciary police, right in front of Bandim Market, he found it nearly impossible to find a parking spot. He had to squeeze right next to a store to park his car. While climbing the stairs to the overpass, the number of people begging and standing in the place was overwhelming. It was hot and humid. The air was thick with fragrances, food, sweat, and a putrefied smell. *Bandim Market never changes*, he thought. It was so noisy and effervescent.

He arrived at the gate, which was crowded with people angrily shouting about various occurrences. Maladho saw a man secretively handing some cash to a police officer, who quickly put it in his pocket. He shook his head at the corruption. Entering the police station wasn't an easy task. Maladho weaved his way through the crowd and managed to approach the gate and remove his badge from his pocket. "Good morning. I am a doctor, and I am here to see somebody."

The guard yanked his badge, looked at it, looked at him, then looked back to the badge several times and then asked, "What is your name, sir?"

"Dr. Maladho."

"Which hospital do you work in?"

"Simão Mendes."

"Oh. Okay, you can enter." The officer handed him back the badge. Smiling, he asked, "Doctor, may I have kola nut?"

Knowing the officer didn't mean an actual kola nut, but rather a cash bribe, Maladho said, "Next time. I left my wallet in the car."

Inside was complete chaos. The office was so hot, and flies were buzzing around. People were seated everywhere, some standing along the wall. Guards were armed with AK-47 rifles, looking madly at the crowd. He saw a man next to the cell, bleeding from machete wounds, clearly needing urgent medical attention. The medical staff treated him under the hot sun. Right next to him, another woman was screaming that her neighbor had stolen her husband.

He tried to reach Mamasaidou from his cell phone, but the call didn't go through. He walked to the reception desk, where a lady was playing with an old phone. "Good morning," he said.

"Yes, sir, how may I help you?" She continued to play on the phone, not bothering to look up at him.

"Yes, I am here to see Mamasaidou."

"Who are you?"

He removed his badge again. "I am Dr. Maladho."

This got her to stop playing, and she looked at him carefully. "Mamasaidou just stepped out like five minutes ago."

"Do you know when he is coming back?"

"Not sure when, but he is going a little bit far. He went to the border with Senegal because there were some issues."

Maladho was frustrated because that meant Mamasaidou wouldn't return anytime soon. "Is there anybody I can talk to?"

"His deputy is here but he is a little busy with a case. If you want to wait, you can sit over there. I will let him know you are waiting." She walked to the chief's room, and Maladho sat in the sweltering waiting room.

After a while, Maladho, seeking a break from the stuffiness, stepped into the open for some air. Outside, the precinct buzzed with life. There, amidst the hustle, a fair-skinned woman caught his eye. Dressed in tattered clothes, she begged for coins, her black hair slicked back, revealing her striking round eyes. Her presence at the precinct puzzled Maladho, so he returned indoors.

Back in the lobby, after another long fifteen minutes, his name was finally called. He navigated through the hallway to the back, noting the dilapidated state of the building. The walls had small holes, with patches of paint peeling off, and the floor showed signs of wear. The air was heavy, a blend of mold and lingering cigarette smoke filling the stale atmosphere.

He entered the room. It had a morbid smell and smoke. A greasy-looking officer greeted him. "Hello, Doctor. I am glad to have you here. I am Officer Klusseh. What can I do for you today?"

Maladho kindly explained his concerns and how he sought help to pursue a case to put a stop to the mistreatment of disabled children.

After carefully listening to him, the officer lit another cigarette. "Would you mind? Do you want one, Doctor?"

"No, thanks. I don't smoke."

"Lucky you. I have been trying to stop this addiction for years but can't. Isn't it funny how people burn their money and yet end up dying of lung cancer?" They both laughed, Maladho a little hollowly. He wasn't interested in this man's tobacco addiction.

Klusseh put down the cigarette and said, "It is disturbing the story you described here. But do you have proof or any evidence to sustain your argument?"

"I don't have any specifics, but I am sure you may find something if you do a proper investigation."

"Hmm, this is not the way it works. In addition, no one has called to denounce this kind of activity yet. And we cannot just start an investigation without the proper background or specific accusations."

"Please, trust me. I know what I am talking about. Something strange happens with those kids because they believe they are spirits or snakes—"

Klusseh interrupted him. "We can only help if we have something to follow. Otherwise, I am afraid to tell you there is nothing we can do in this case. Another thing, Doctor, in this country, sometimes you need to be quiet. Otherwise . . ." he trailed off, shaking his head. "Have you heard the phrase 'when a snake wants to grow big, it must hide'?" He chuckled.

Maladho had heard that phrase before, even from his mother. He was determined to defy that concept. Because what some people don't know is that snakes are born with venom in them. They don't need to be big to do damage. He was young, yet people needed to understand he was Kopironko. He was born with bravery and audacity already in his veins and bones. But he just said, "I see. Thanks, Officer, for your service and advice."

"Anytime, Doctor, please contact us if you find anything solid." He handed his card to Maladho and then accompanied him to the door.

Maladho walked hurriedly to the gate. At the exit, he saw the beggar woman again. This time, the lady smiled at him, and he did the same.

"Hi, handsome. Can I have your name?" she asked.

Maladho frowned. "Why do you want to know my name?"

"Nothing, you seem friendly, maybe that's why."

Maladho chuckled. He told himself that these people in the streets have many strategies for getting money. "Well, thank you. You are kind. My name is Maladho. What about yours?" he said as he walked to the overpass.

The woman followed him. "Call me Nené-Funé," she said. Maladho knew that was not her real name because Nené-Funé just meant "mother of twins" in Fulani. He kept walking, picking up his pace. All he wanted was to go to work and figure this thing out. He thought it would be easy, but the way things were going, it wasn't looking good.

"I can help you, Maladho."

Maladho froze, one leg on the stairs. He stopped and turned back to face the woman. "Help me with what?"

"The serpent kids. They will never help you, but I can help you." She laughed.

"Are you kidding me? Is this what you do, listen to people and then stalk them?" Maladho said it lightly, but he was annoyed.

"Look, I don't mean no trouble. I never did this before. It just happened. I was at the door when I heard you talking about the issue," Nené-Funé said.

"Okay, here." Maladho gave her a note of two thousand francs. "Now you have what you wanted."

"Thanks, Maladho, but wait," she said.

"I have to go. I am in a hurry." Maladho quickly climbed the stairs and didn't look back. He rushed to his car, starting it and lowering the windows because it was so hot. He put on his sunglasses and started checking his mirrors. He saw Nené-Funé standing by his passenger-side door. "What do you want? I have already given you money."

"I told you I can help you. I can take you to the river where they do it."

Maladho removed his sunglasses and looked at her. He hesitated, cautious, but curiosity won. "How can you help me?"

"I will take you there. You can take pictures or get the

proof you need."

"Good. Is it far?"

"No, it isn't. It is close."

"Can we go there now?" Excitement and determination bloomed in his stomach.

Nené-Funé chuckled. "Calm down, Doctor. Can you buy me food first? I like the goat's roasted meat with onions and some pepper."

"Seriously? But I gave you money already. Now you are asking me to buy you food as well. Foolish! Here, take this since it is what you really want." Maladho threw another note to her, shook his head, and closed his car windows. "Waste of time." Maladho put his sunglasses back on and drove away, leaving Nené-Funé standing there, the note at her feet.

CHAPTER TWENTY-ONE

THE BREAKDOWN

Over time, he realized that no matter how much effort he put in, more was needed to accomplish his mission. He analyzed numerous medical records in the hospital but couldn't find anything. Compounding his problems was the fact that the entire country's healthcare system lacked a comprehensive database or any reference material about what he was searching for. Despite his best efforts to talk to people, everyone guarded it as a secret. Some even advised him to give up and forget about it altogether.

He contemplated going on the radio and discussing the issue, hoping that someone would step forward and assist him in uncovering the truth. One day, after finishing work early, he drove straight to the national radio station. He spoke to the director and explained his intentions.

"You mean you want to talk about the serpent kids?" the director asked.

"First of all, they are not serpents. They are human beings with disabilities. I want to discuss them because it is a concerning issue, and we need to help them," Maladho clarified.

Maladho's response didn't sit well with the director, who became visibly agitated. "I don't care what you say, Doctor. I can't risk my job or my family's well-being by getting involved in something that could harm us. And as far as I'm concerned, those kids are dangerous. I've heard stories of them using supernatural powers to attack and kill people!"

Maladho's eyes narrowed, and his tone became stern. "That's just a rumor, and you know it. Those kids are vulnerable and need our help. You have a platform to spread awareness and mobilize support. How can you turn your back on them?"

The director leaned in, his face turning red with anger. "I'll tell you how, Doctor. It's called self-preservation. And if you know what's good for you, you'll keep your mouth shut and stay out of this. Or else, you'll regret it."

Maladho refused to back down. "I won't be intimidated by you or anyone else. These kids deserve a chance at a better life, and I won't rest until they get it. You can either help me or stand in my way, but I won't stop fighting for what's right."

The director scoffed. "You're a fool, Doctor. You'll see soon enough that serpent kids are not to be messed with."

Maladho left the radio station, feeling more determined than ever to uncover the truth. As he drove home, he racked his brain, trying to devise a new approach to finding the answers he sought. Suddenly, an idea dawned on him.

Mankoni was an older man who had worked at a morgue for many years. He knew the hospital inside and out and was known to keep many secrets. Perhaps Mankoni could provide some information about the serpent kids. He turned his car around and headed back to the hospital.

Maladho knocked on the door of the morgue, and after a few moments, it opened to reveal the wizened older man. He had a shiny, bald head, white eyebrows, and eyelashes that looked like soft cotton. Mankoni lived in a small room behind the morgue, earning him the nickname "Death's Neighbor." Although old, he was still strong, his muscles apparent under his curly gray arm hair.

"Come in," Mankoni said. He motioned Maladho to come inside and have a seat. "I'm just preparing another friend for their journey, my boy," he said, gesturing toward the body on the table.

Maladho couldn't help but feel a bit uneasy. Death was always a touchy subject, and being in a morgue only added to the somber atmosphere. But Mankoni seemed tranquil at the table, where he was preparing the body. Maladho winced slightly but tried to keep the conversation light. "So Uncle, how many friends have you sent on their way?"

Mankoni chuckled but softly answered, "Oh, more than I can count. I've been doing this since the colonial era. My father was a morgue man, too, and when he retired, I took over. I'll keep going until the gods decide it's my turn to go."

Maladho couldn't help but laugh. "Well, let's hope they're not in too much of a rush to take you away, Uncle. We still need you around."

Mankoni smiled, a glint of mischief in his eyes. "Ah, my boy. You know I've already lived longer than I ever expected. Every day is a blessing, even when surrounded by death."

Maladho nodded, feeling a newfound respect for the old morgue man. Despite his grim surroundings, Mankoni had a lighthearted and wise perspective on life. He leaned in closer, his eyes wide with curiosity. "Uncle, maybe death is scared of you," he joked.

Mankoni chuckled, the wrinkles on his face deepening. "Maybe, my boy. Or maybe it still has some use for an old morgue man like me."

Maladho took a deep breath, steeling himself for the

question he had come to ask. "Uncle, have you ever seen children with a disability brought here?"

Mankoni's expression shifted, his eyes darting around the morgue. "The serpent kids? No, not really," he stammered, shaking slightly.

Maladho pressed on. "Yes or no, Uncle?"

"I said no, son."

Maladho's heart sank. "You mean to say you've never buried any of them here?"

Mankoni shook his head. "No, they don't bring them here. The ones born here, their parents take them away for a cleansing ritual."

Maladho frowned, feeling his hopes fading. "So where could they be? What kind of treatment are they receiving?"

Mankoni shrugged, his expression solemn. "I couldn't say for sure, my boy. But I do know that there are many things in this world that we don't understand. Maybe the serpent kids are one of them."

"Why don't they bring them here, do you think?"

Mankoni's face grew somber as he responded. "There are rumors that they are spirits. And not just any spirits, but ones with a thirst for blood. There are whispers that they're cursed souls, condemned to wander the earth for eternity."

"Uncle, they are people like us, harmless. Why are people scared of harmless kids?"

Mankoni's eyes darted nervously around the room before leaning close to Maladho. "People fear what they don't understand, boy. And these spirits are beyond comprehension. I heard they prey on the living, draining their life force until there's nothing left but an empty shell. But I trust you, my boy. Maybe we do not understand them. Thanks for enlightening my mind."

"Uncle, I want people to know they are kids with

disabilities; they are not dangerous. I need to bring to justice whosoever is behind this."

"My boy, may the gods bless you. I see you have a good heart."

"I need to bring light to people's hearts." Maladho paused. "Can you tell me where they frequently perform this macabre practice?"

"I don't know. But if I find out, I will let you know. They often said it was in the river." Mankoni sighed deeply before responding. "I mean, things in this world are beyond our understanding. Things that we cannot comprehend or control. The more you dig, the more you might unearth something that should have been left buried." His expression grew somber. "Sometimes, there's nothing we can do. Sometimes, we must accept that there are things we cannot change. And sometimes, the price of trying to change them is too high. Be careful, Dr. Maladho. Sometimes, the cost of seeking the truth is more than we can bear. The more you dig, the deeper you'll descend into the darkness. May the gods and the spirits of our ancestors protect you," he said, his voice quivering. "You're a good man, and I'm proud of you. We Kopironkos have to stick together, you know?"

Maladho smiled warmly at the older man and handed him some cash. "Thanks for your time, Uncle," he said.

Mankoni's eyes lit up with joy. "Oh, my boy! You've made my day! I'm going to buy some tobacco and smoked fish right now," he exclaimed, chuckling heartily.

Maladho couldn't help but laugh at Mankoni's infectious energy. "You enjoy that smoked fish, Uncle," he said, patting him on the shoulder.

As Maladho left, Mankoni called after him, "Remember, Doctor, may God bless you. When you need some company, come and visit me. I will find the information for you!"

Maladho's friends had noticed how consumed he was with finding answers. So, one Friday evening, they surprised him by stopping by his house, and they went out together. They danced, drank, and had a great time all night long. They didn't get home until almost four in the morning.

As Maladho stumbled into his house, still feeling the buzz of the night's excitement, he checked his phone to find many missed calls from his mom. He tried calling back, but the phone was out of service. He felt a wave of panic wash over him, wondering what was happening and why his mother had been trying to reach him so desperately. Without hesitation, he knew he needed to go to his mother's place to ensure everything was okay. He grabbed his keys. "Let's go to my mom's," Maladho told N'damesse.

"Are you crazy? You're drunk and haven't slept the whole night," N'damesse replied, her voice tinged with frustration.

"I'm worried, and I don't know why she's been calling me," Maladho said, struggling to put on his shoes.

"Maladho, we'll go later. Let's rest a little bit. If it were serious, the guard would have told us. You need to sleep this off. It's not safe for you to drive in this condition," she reasoned.

"Alright, you're right," he relented. But Maladho couldn't shake the feeling of unease. As they lay down to rest, his mind raced with thoughts of his mother and what could be wrong. He knew he couldn't sleep until he had seen her. When he was sure that N'damesse had fallen asleep, Maladho quietly slipped out of bed and headed to his car. He knew driving in his current state was risky, but he couldn't wait any longer. He had to see his mother.

He was driving for two minutes when he saw a man waving at him. At first, Maladho assumed it was just a hitchhiker, but as he drove closer, the man reminded him of someone, although he couldn't place who. He came to a full stop and could see the person through the car's window. His eyes widened in surprise. It was his father, just as he looked on the last day Maladho saw him. "Baaba, is that you?"

Demba said, "Yes, my beloved son, it's me."

Maladho couldn't believe it. "I thought you had died a long time ago?"

Demba shook his head. "I faked my death and have been on a secret mission ever since. Won't you invite me into your car?"

Maladho quickly unlocked the vehicle's door and allowed him in. He took a deep breath, still in shock from seeing his father after all these years. Once his father was seated in the passenger seat, Maladho said, "You went on a mission and abandoned us. You couldn't even attend my Koyang. All the other kids had their fathers there."

"You know, son, you're right," Demba replied, sadness in his voice. "But I needed to be on that mission. Otherwise, you and your mother could have died long ago. But we can discuss this later. Right now, the priority is to get the job done. We need to save Kamboda in the river." Maladho seemed unconvinced, and a part of him believed he was in a dream. His father, whom he had mourned and grieved for so long, sat beside him in the car, talking about saving Kamboda in the river. It was all too much to take in. Demba noticed Maladho's hesitation. "I saw you are trying to save him and others like him. You can still save Kamboda. That's why I am here. Let's go to the river before it is too late."

"It would be better to take you to Mother's place first. She misses you."

Demba shook his head. "We don't have time. Let's go. If we don't do it right now, it will be too late to save your cousin."

This statement stirred something deep within Maladho. It was the thing he had wanted most throughout his life. To save Kamboda or know his whereabouts, to solve the mystery in the river. His father's urgency sent chills down his spine, and he knew they couldn't waste another moment. Without further hesitation, he turned the car around and drove toward the river.

They sped down the road, Maladho's heart racing as his mind swirled with thoughts of what could happen if they didn't make it in time. Demba was speaking, but Maladho's mind was completely consumed by the thought of saving his cousin. They passed Jugudul, and suddenly, a figure appeared in front of the car, like a specter in the night. Maladho slammed on the brakes and swerved to the left, but Demba grabbed the steering wheel and yanked it to the right, shouting, "Maladho, just go! We don't have time!"

He saw the figure more clearly now, and his blood ran cold. It was a child, no more than six or seven years old. Maladho tried to protest and swerve back to the left, but his father's grip on the wheel was unyielding. He closed his eyes, bracing for impact.

But it never came. The car careened off the road, tumbling into the swamp. As the world spun around them, Maladho felt a sense of dread wash over him, wondering what else awaited them on this dark and ominous journey.

The car was upside down, the headlights still on, diffused by the fog, creating an eerie glow. Through the dense mist, Maladho saw Demba dissolving like smoke in the wind. His heart raced with fear as he struggled to get out of the car. He was full of adrenaline and could feel injuries throbbing with pain. He reached up and felt blood pouring out of his head. He shouted for help, but his voice was barely audible over his heartbeat. Soon after, he blacked out.

When he awoke, he was in a different realm. Kamboda was standing outside the car, beckoning Maladho to follow him. "Come on," he said, waving his hand. Maladho's body suddenly felt weightless, like a feather, and he levitated out of the car to stand next to his cousin, who said, "I am glad you came. Remember, I promised to show you my home. Let's go. I will show you my new friends as well." He held Maladho in his arms, like cotton in the air, floating in the sky until it disappeared.

They arrived at a big house with no walls, the space infinite and white. Maladho noticed he was a little boy again, the same age as Kamboda. He looked around, his eyes meeting the countless other kids his age, all crowded in the hall. A lady, the only adult, was seated on a black stone. She had long black dreads, red eyes, and long nails. "This is my mother—our mother," Kamboda told him.

"Welcome, Maladho," she said. "Kamboda has told me about you." Her expression darkened. "Do you see all these kids here? They count on you. You are the chosen one, the one to break the trap that binds them. You are going back to fight for them, bring them justice. This is your mission. That's why some forces want to eliminate you. But you aren't going to succumb until you fulfill the mission to rescue their respect, their dignity, and end the centuries of suffering." She looked to both sides and sighed.

"But how can I do it?" Maladho asked.

"Their way. Use the right tools. Remember, wood doesn't cut iron; you have to use iron to cut iron." She paused then pointed at a little girl in the far corner, her nose and eyes wet from crying. "You see, she has just arrived, thrown here like a discarded object." She pointed to the door they had come in. "Now go back and fight for your brothers and sisters trapped in this melancholy place."

Maladho hugged Kamboda. "Cousin, I will be back for you, I promise." Both boys had tears in their eyes. Maladho pulled away and departed. He opened his eyes to find himself surrounded by people, with a beam of light on top of him. He felt the intense pain from his injuries and passed out.

Around midday, N'damesse's phone rang. She jolted awake to answer it. "Hello? Yes, Mama Fenda, how are you? Maladho?" She looked at the empty spot next to her in bed. "I think he went to the bathroom. Let me give him the phone," she said, her voice groggy from sleep. She went to the bathroom to find it empty. She wandered around, looking for him, no longer groggy. With each passing moment she couldn't find him, panic began to creep into her chest. She went outside to ask the guard if he had seen him.

"M'bemba, have you seen Maladho?" N'damesse asked, desperation lacing her words.

"Yes, he left here after you two arrived last night. He told me he was going to see his mother," the guard replied.

N'damesse's heart sank as she realized Maladho had driven drunk. She put the phone back to her ear. "Mama," she said anxiously, "the guard said he went to your house not long after we came back from the party!"

"But Maladho isn't here," Fenda said, her voice filling with concern. "I've been calling him, but his phone is off. Your tone worries me."

"The thing is, Maladho never listens. We got back from the party very late, almost morning. Maladho saw your missed calls and wanted to leave right away. I told him to wait and get some rest, but I think he snuck out after I fell asleep," N'damesse said, her voice trembling with anxiety. "It's been five hours. I can't believe he just disappeared like this. I'm afraid something might have happened to him because he was too drunk."

Fenda let out a loud wail on the other side of the line, her heart heavy with worry. "I fear something awful may have happened to him."

They continued reaching out to friends, searching for news, but no one had seen him. Fearing the worst, they informed the police but could do nothing else but wait. Their hopes were lifted when they received a call from the police after midnight, informing them that an unidentified individual had been found at the hospital in Mansôa.

N'damesse and Fenda were shocked when they heard the news, as they had assumed Maladho was still in Bissau. Despite the poor road conditions, they made the long journey to Mansôa, arriving at the hospital two hours later. A nurse showed them to the room where the unidentified man lay inside a mosquito net, his head completely wrapped and intubated.

As the police officer focused his flashlight on the person lying in bed, N'damesse and Fenda stepped closer, their faces filled with worry. From the depths of her mind, Fenda feared the worst. As the police officer's flashlight flickered over the injured man on the bed, she struggled to recognize him. Suddenly, Fenda's heart skipped a beat as she caught sight of something on the man's leg. "Wait, go back to his leg," she commanded, her voice shaky.

The officer complied, and Fenda saw what she had feared most—the scar from the Koyang, a gruesome reminder of deadly competition. Tears streamed down her face as she screamed, "It is him! It is him!"

N'damesse, who had been approaching the bed, stopped in her tracks. "Impossible, Mama," she muttered in disbelief.

But Fenda was resolute. "Look at the scar on his right leg!"

Seeing the scar, N'damesse collapsed, crying uncontrollably.

The hospital staff told them that Maladho had crashed a few miles away as he was going east. His car had been found in a swamp by some cow herders. They didn't understand how Maladho had ended up so far from his mother's house in the city, or what had caused the accident. The mystery would remain unsolved until Maladho woke, but the family's priority was clear—get him to Bissau as soon as possible for better treatment.

Twenty-four hours after the accident, Maladho finally opened his eyes. Confusion filled his mind as he tried to figure out where he was. N'damesse was sitting next to him, holding his hand. Fenda and Ossanti were in the room. His mother noticed his movements first.

"Oh, the spirit of Kopirondin heard me," Fenda exclaimed, tears of joy streaming down her face.

Ossanti walked over to the bed and spoke sternly to Maladho. "Stubborn boy, you scared us," he said, shaking his head, but a hint of a smile played on his lips.

Maladho tried to sit up. "Hi, Uncle Ossanti. Hi, Mother," he said.

"No, baby, stay still. Don't move too much. They said you should stay calm," N'damesse cautioned him.

Fenda sat down next to him, weeping with relief. "What happened, my boy? You almost killed me with worry," she said, her voice trembling with emotion.

Maladho shook his head, closed his eyes, and sighed deeply. "I'm still confused about whether I was dreaming or if what happened was real," he said.

"Everyone is confused, but please tell us what you remember," Ossanti urged.

Maladho took a sip of water and launched into his story

about seeing his father and his promise to Kamboda. "After this shocking vision, I can't shake the feeling I stumbled upon something larger than myself. And I know that, somehow, I have to make a difference."

The room fell silent, and a sense of dread hung heavily. Fenda and N'damesse wept uncontrollably while Ossanti tightly shut his eyes, muttering incantations under his breath and making arcane hand gestures. "Dark spirits," Ossanti muttered, his voice low and ominous. "That was not your father, Maladho. That evil entity was sent to lure you to the river and drown you. They're not happy we went to Kopiro. Your concerns about Kamboda's disappearance have made them aware of your presence. That's why I warned your mother to be vigilant."

Fenda clung to Maladho, her tears staining his shirt. "Please, my son, I beg you to let this go. You'll end up like your father. You're all I have left, and I can't bear to lose you."

N'damesse joined Fenda, taking Maladho's other hand. "Listen to your mother, my love. You've grown into a strong and courageous man, but there's no shame in walking away from this. We need you alive."

Maladho gazed upward, lost in thought. The room was silent except for the old ceiling fan above him. It whirred gently, a soft hum that filled the space with a somber mood. Each rotation seemed to echo his racing thoughts. He felt a deep sense of duty, a pull toward action that he couldn't ignore. This wasn't just about him; it was about honoring his father, finding Kamboda, and fulfilling a promise to himself.

"I hear you, Mama," Maladho said, his voice unwavering. "But I can't turn a blind eye to what's happening. I won't let these dark spirits take any more lives. I'll find a way to end this, no matter the cost."

Three weeks later, Maladho was sitting in his office when his mind drifted back to the past. He shook his head, trying to clear his thoughts. "Focus, Maladho," he muttered to himself. His injuries from the accident had healed, but the memories of what he had seen still haunted him. He had promised his mother never to talk about it again, but it was easier said than done. A nurse walked in, interrupting his reverie. "Dr. Maladho, there is a lady who has come here several times asking for you."

Maladho raised an eyebrow. "A lady? What is her name?"

The nurse hesitated. "I forgot, she told me, but I forgot."

Maladho sighed. "Do you have any other information about her?"

The nurse thought for a moment. "She wasn't that old, but she looked like a beggar. However, she spoke very well."

Maladho leaned back in his chair, deep in thought. "I don't know who that could be. Thanks for telling me, though." But as the nurse left, Maladho couldn't shake the unease over him. Who was this mysterious woman, and why was she looking for him? He was suspicious about who, especially after recent events.

Maladho had a busy day at the hospital due to the high number of malaria cases during the season. With a shortage of staff, he had to work double shifts. After finishing work late, he went to the market before heading home. As he loaded the bags into his car, he felt a tap on his back. He turned around and saw the woman he met at the judiciary police. "Nené-Funé?"

She smiled. "Yes, it is me, Doctor. I went to your office several times, but I wasn't fortunate enough to meet you," she said.

Maladho chuckled. "Do you still want some goat meat?" he joked.

Nené-Funé smiled, but it didn't reach her eyes. "No, thank you, Dr. Maladho. I'm not hungry for food. I'm hungry for justice."

Her sudden, serious tone took Maladho aback. "What do you mean?"

"My twins were taken from me and unjustly sacrificed because people believed they were spirits."

"I'm sorry to hear that," he said, his voice filled with empathy. "But I don't know how I can help you. I'm just a doctor, not a detective." Maladho felt a mix of emotions. He didn't know what to believe since the accident. However, hearing about the tragic fate of Nené-Funé's children stirred something in him.

Nené-Funé's expression turned dark. "I didn't expect you to be a coward and a hypocrite, Dr. Maladho. You went to school to save lives, but here you are, paying no heed to injustice."

Maladho's temper flared. "Excuse me? You don't know anything about me or my life. I demand respect from you, lady."

Nené-Funé scoffed. "You're not the hero you think you are, Doctor. You're just a mere lamb." She turned and walked away.

Maladho was frozen in disbelief. How could a stranger call him a hypocrite and a lamb? He got into the car, but his hands shook on the steering wheel. His nerves were on edge. Despite having the A/C on, he started sweating. He opened the window, but the hot wind was insolently blowing, so he had to close it again. He turned on the radio and continued driving. His hands were still shaking, and he felt an irregular heartbeat. "This is not good," he said to himself.

Maladho felt torn between his promise to his mother and his burning desire to solve the puzzle about his cousin

Kamboda. For weeks, he had been pondering over it. He realized that if nothing was done, many disabled children would succumb to their circumstances. This shouldn't be normal in society. Every life has value, and every person should be able to live freely, regardless of appearance.

After a few weeks, Maladho finally decided to ask around about Nené-Funé. He approached anyone he could find, but no one seemed to know who she was or where she might live. It wasn't until he arrived at the entrance of the judiciary police that he finally got some answers. The guard knew her, but when asked her whereabouts, his expression turned somber.

"Her situation has worsened. She became violent and upset, and it was difficult to restrain her that day. She was taken to a center and confined there."

Without wasting any time, Maladho got into his car and drove to the center, about seven miles northeast of Bissau. Upon arriving, he asked the staff about Nené-Funé and, because of his doctor status, was taken to her room.

As he approached, he could hear her talking. When he peered through the grated window, he saw her pretending to breastfeed two bones, referring to them as Assana and Ussainatou. Maladho assumed these were the names of her twins, which made him feel sorry for her. Clearly, Nené-Funé suffered from a severe mental illness and needed help.

As Nené-Funé slowly lifted her head and saw Maladho, she clutched the two bones tightly to her chest. "Doctor, did you come to see my babies? You aren't taking them away from me, are you?" she said, her voice shaking with fear.

Maladho looked at her with sadness in his eyes. "No, I am not going to do that," he reassured her.

"Thank you," she said, her lucidity surprising him. She smiled and asked, "What brought you here today?"

"To visit and talk about our last encounter," Maladho replied, his voice heavy with regret.

She giggled. "Our last encounter wasn't that good."

"I know, and I am sorry about it," Maladho said, his voice barely above a whisper.

"Never mind that." She shrugged. "Do you believe me now? Do you want me to take you to the river?"

Maladho walked halfway to the wall and stopped. "Yes, I do. That is why I am here," he said, his voice barely audible.

"It is too late now," she said, her voice filled with sadness. "They won't let me go out of this place. Even if they do, it's late. But if you want to go, I will tell you. It is tied to the moon's phase." She detailed the journey he needed to follow, then they chatted for a while, laughing a lot.

"Thank you, Nené-Funé. I am glad I had the chance to talk to you. I will be back again, and I won't forget your goat meat this time," he said, trying to lighten the mood.

She laughed. "Okay, Doctor. But please don't give up your mission."

As Maladho left the room, he couldn't help but feel a sense of sadness and despair. It was clear that Nené-Funé was a victim of her circumstances, and he felt powerless to help her.

CHAPTER TWENTY-TWO

THE RESURRECTION

None could change fate, and Maladho couldn't shake off the apprehension that had been creeping up on him. He had postponed his visit to the center to see Nené-Funé for weeks, and the guilt had weighed heavily on him. His mind raced with worries and doubts as he packed the goat meat. What if she had gotten worse? What if she no longer remembered him? The questions kept piling up in his mind, but he pushed them aside and got into his car.

As he walked up to the door at the center, he couldn't help but notice a man who kept staring at him. It made him feel uneasy, but he shrugged it off and continued. Inside, the surroundings were dusty and the smell of despair hung in the air. Maladho identified himself to the receptionist, stating he was there for Nené-Funé. The receptionist looked at him with bored eyes then went through the logs. She found the record in the corner bottom drawer of a dusty black cabinet. Maladho's heart sank as he realized how long it had been since his last visit. He felt someone's gaze on his back. When he turned around, it was the man who had been staring at him outside. He couldn't shake off the unease deep in his gut.

The walls seemed to close in on him as he walked through

the hallway. The screams and cries filled the air, and he felt a sense of dread wash over him. When he finally reached Nené-Funé's room, his apprehension turned into horror. Her eyes were empty, and she didn't seem to recognize him. Maladho felt a lump form in his throat as he realized the extent of her deterioration. She was no longer the same person he had known. He tried to talk to her, but she didn't respond, even when he showed her the goat meat he brought for her. He looked for a nurse to ask about her condition and spotted the man from earlier standing outside the door. Maladho began to worry that he was in danger. He quickly said his goodbyes despite not knowing if she understood and rushed out of the center, feeling like he was being watched every step of the way. The guilt of neglecting his friend and the fear of the unknown weighed heavily on him as he drove home.

Forty hours after his visit, Maladho found the courage to go back to the center, clinging to a sliver of hope. Walking in, he noticed the receptionist's usual calm demeanor had shifted to something more somber, mirroring the heavy feeling in his own heart. A tightness formed in his throat, and words seemed distant.

The receptionist, after a brief exchange, excused herself, disappearing behind the doors. The waiting felt endless, each second stretching out before her return, this time not alone but with a doctor beside her. "Dr. Maladho," the doctor began, an air of solemnity in his voice, "I'm Dr. Manjuba. We've been expecting you. I regret to inform you, Nené-Funé passed away last night."

The words fell like a weight, confirming his deepest fears. Maladho's world seemed to pause, his heart dropping to his stomach.

"She was calling for you, wondering where you were,"

Dr. Manjuba's words echoed with sadness. "We tried reaching you."

The news hit Maladho like a ton of bricks—his friend was gone, and he felt like he had let her down. His heart plummeted.

Dr. Manjuba then extended a bag toward him. "She wanted you to have this. Said it was important for you to bury them once you've uncovered the truth and fulfilled your purpose," he explained. Inside, Maladho found the two bones Nené-Funé had cherished as if they were her children. Tears blurred his vision as he grasped the gravity of her loneliness and the trust she placed in him. Nené-Funé suffered from stress and depression, and Maladho couldn't help but feel guilty for not doing more.

He left the center feeling dispirited, unsure of his next steps. He couldn't shake off the thought of his cousin and now the lady he had promised to help. He knew he had to find a way to fulfill his promise to both Kamboda and Nené-Funé, even if it meant going against his mother's wishes. The weight of his decision clouded his mind like a dense fog. Determined, he resolved to press on with his quest alone, keeping his plans hidden from his mother and everyone else.

He remembered Nené-Funé's words about the right moment to act, tied to the moon's cycle. When the night came, marked by that specific lunar phase, Maladho slipped away into the darkness toward the river she had mentioned.

Under the cloak of night, he moved silently toward the river, drawn by the distant sound of a ritual unknown to him. Caught up in the thrill of the moment, Maladho crept closer, his heart pounding in his chest. Her advice had led him here, to the edge of discovery. The air vibrated with their chants, a mysterious call pulling him closer to the unknown.

As he neared, the drumbeats intensified, beckoning him closer to the mysterious ceremony.

Peering through the shadows, Maladho spotted a group encircled by the soft glow of lanterns. Their faces, adorned with vibrant paints, flickered in the light, creating a mesmerizing spectacle. Maladho found a hidden spot behind a bush, hoping to catch a glimpse of the ritual's heart. Yet darkness veiled the scene, leaving him straining for a clearer view. The mystery of what lay within the circle filled him with excitement and apprehension. Maladho's heart pounded as he crept through the dark, unknown terrain. He hid behind a tree and readied his camera to capture the scene.

But his presence did not go unnoticed. An owl hooted several times, flying around the tree. Suddenly, the drums and chorus stopped. A man's voice boomed through the silence, "I believe we have a visitor. But whoever you are, we know you don't belong here. Show yourself before it's too late."

Fear crept into Maladho's mind as he realized he had been discovered. He started to run, his heart racing as he heard footsteps following him through the bush. Despite his efforts to escape, he was eventually captured.

The night was deep and dark, shrouded in a thick mist that added to the mystery and terror of the moment. The flickering torches cast eerie shadows on the faces of the fierce warriors, their eyes glinting like those of predators ready to pounce on their prey. One of the men, with intricate markings on his face, spoke to him mystically, "What brings you to this sacred place, young one? You have trespassed on hallowed ground."

"Who are you to come here and disturb our sacred ritual? You think you can waltz in here and not face the consequences?" the chief bellowed, his face twisted with anger.

Maladho trembled with fear, his heart pounding as he faced the armed men. "I swear, I got lost in the dark. I wasn't spying on anything!" he protested.

But the chief was having none of it. "Lost, my foot! You're a liar and a spy, and you'll pay for your insolence with your life!" he snarled, raising his spear.

Maladho's blood ran cold at the sight of the menacing weapon. He knew he was in deep trouble and might never see his family again. Instead, he was bound and dragged back to a village, where he was kept under lock and key for the rest of the night. The eerie silence was broken only by the distant howls of wild animals and the whispers of the villagers, who talked in hushed tones about the stranger who had trespassed on their sacred ground.

The following day, Maladho stood before the chief, who looked very serious on his throne. Maladho's future was up to the king, and he knew he had to explain himself well to get out of this safely. After Maladho finished telling his story, the chief looked around at everyone there. "Does anyone here believe this man?" he asked. The answer was a loud "No!" from the crowd, with people raising their spears and shouting together.

Maladho's fate seemed sealed as the chief declared, "He's been spying, and his story doesn't add up. We can't waste time on this. If we all agree he is spying, he deserves to be sentenced to death. Does anyone object?"

Suddenly, a voice rose from the crowd. "Yes, Chief, I speak. I know this man. He's not bad, so maybe he really did get lost." Maladho tried to find where the voice was coming from and finally recognized Officer Klusseh, standing out in his tribal attire.

The chief looked surprised. "Klusseh, you know him?"

"Yes, he's a doctor at Simão Mendes Hospital," Klusseh explained. Maladho's heart raced, hope flickering like a candle in the wind. Still, he couldn't shake the fear that clung to him, knowing well that his fate was on a knife's edge, teetering between life and death.

The villagers whispered and cast wary glances his way, their faces a complex tapestry of doubt and hostility. Maladho felt their stares sharp against his skin, a silent verdict yet to be pronounced. Time stretched on, each moment a lifetime, until at last, the village elders came to a conclusion. To Maladho's relief, they decided to let him go.

Officer Klusseh approached him, each step measured and deliberate, his attire marking him as a figure of authority and reverence within the tribe.

Maladho's eyes widened in surprise, his heart beating a mix of relief and worry. "Officer Klusseh! You're here?" he blurted out.

"Just following my faith. You, on the other hand, seem to be chasing shadows about children gone missing," Officer Klusseh responded, his words shrouded in mystery.

Maladho fell silent, digesting the accusation. Officer Klusseh's knowledge hinted at deeper truths, sending a shiver through Maladho.

"I've seen your quest, Dr. Maladho. Remember our talk? You brushed it off, and look where it got you," Officer Klusseh cautioned him, his tone serious.

Regret and thankfulness swirled within Maladho. He had indeed been headstrong, and it was Officer Klusseh's intervention that spared him greater danger. "Thank you, Officer, for your help. I was wrong to ignore your advice. But perhaps it's my destiny to face this challenge," Maladho confessed, emotion lacing his words.

Officer Klusseh gave Maladho a look that was a mix of sympathy and scorn. "Good luck, Doctor. Just remember, when you're moving in the shadows, be mindful. Darkness doesn't mean you're invisible. In the shadows, even the wind whispers secrets."

Guided by some of the villagers, Maladho made his way to the city's edge. He felt the heavy gaze of doubt and mistrust from those he left behind. The realization hit him hard. Uncovering truths was a far-fetched dream where the very people meant to enforce the law were entangled in its web. Officer Klusseh, tied to the tribe's secrets, wouldn't be the ally Maladho had hoped for in shining a light on hidden crimes. With this harsh lesson, Maladho committed to treading more cautiously, aware now that the night's veil hid more than just the unseen; it harbored untold stories and perils.

Maladho's determination to uncover the truth about the missing children continued despite the danger and criticism he faced. He turned to social media to spread awareness about the case, creating a popular blog called "Embrace Their Humanity, Not Myths" that shed light on the issue. The blog addressed how the government and the system as a whole disregarded children with disabilities. Maladho attacked leaders for their lack of commitment to the cause of disabled children. He pointed out the lack of policies. His attacks were direct. He received death threats from people who didn't like what he was saying.

One day, Maladho's chief summoned him to his office. The hospital CEO had a stern expression as he looked at the blog page in front of him. "Dr. Maladho, we have talked about this before. It would be best if you stopped," he said firmly.

Maladho was not about to give up. "But these are

important issues that need to be addressed. Nobody else is doing anything about it," he argued.

His chief sighed. "I understand your passion, but there are people at the top who don't want this information to be made public. Please consider your safety, our reputation, and the consequences."

Maladho left the office feeling frustrated and betrayed. Yet another person in a position of authority so easily corrupted. As he drove home, his phone rang. It was his mother, sounding anxious and scared.

"Maladho, you promised to stop," she said sternly. "I've been getting threatening calls about your blog. Please, be careful."

"I'm just writing my opinions, Mom. I'm not doing anything wrong."

But his mother was not convinced. "They want you to stop, Maladho. Please, think about your safety." The worry in her voice gave him pause.

He knew he was taking a risk but also knew he couldn't stop now. Too many people were relying on him. Maladho tried to reassure her, but it was too late to turn back now that he had gained a following from concerned readers worldwide. As he hung up the phone, he felt a sense of determination wash over him. He had to keep fighting for what was right, no matter the cost.

Despite having plenty of readers and personnel interested in his cause, Maladho struggled to provide solid evidence to support his theory. The debate surrounding the issue grew more heated daily, with experts failing to address the central idea. People defended cultural and traditional ideas, accusing Maladho of demonizing and poisoning their society. Some individuals knew the truth but were too afraid to speak out.

In the unfolding story, the debate around Maladho's controversial message took a sharp turn toward the political arena. It wasn't just a matter of differing opinions anymore; it had morphed into a battle line, with Maladho's supporters openly accusing the government of turning a blind eye to the truth. Perhaps the intensity of their arguments was fueled by the ticking clock of the upcoming elections. After all, in the heat of electoral battles, every point scored could tilt the scales. And in this charged atmosphere, the opposition found a powerful weapon and an unlikely ally in Maladho's proposition. They seized it eagerly, using it to cast a harsh light on the government's failures, especially highlighting the grim reality faced by the most vulnerable: the children living in deplorable social conditions. This was no longer just a debate; it had become a rallying cry for change, echoing through the streets and into the hearts of the townsfolk.

As usual, Maladho arrived at the hospital on a pleasant morning and parked his car. Walking toward the entrance, he noticed an older man standing before him. He assumed the man was either there for treatment or visiting a patient. But as he passed, the older man started following him.

"Maladho. Maladho, I need to talk to you," the old man said, catching up to him.

Maladho turned around, trying to recall where he had seen the man's face before. "Yes, how may I help you?" he asked, trying to be polite.

The older man walked closer, his eyes scanning Maladho's face. "I am here to help you. You need my help. I am the only one who can provide you with what you want," the old man said confidently.

Maladho looked puzzled. "What kind of help are you talking about?" he asked.

The older man's face grew serious. "I have the key to your secret. Don't you recognize me, naughty boy?"

The nickname shocked him. Maladho's face was filled with fear as he looked at the older man more closely. Only one person used to call him that name, but he was dead. "Who are you?" Maladho asked shakily.

"The person you least expect. I am your grandpa, Karamoko." The older man replied.

Maladho took a step backward, keeping "Karamoko" in front of him. He made it to the office doors, then turned and ran inside, past everybody at the reception, and entered his office, closing the door. He grabbed his phone from his pocket and dialed his mother. "Hello . . . hello, Mom. They are here again," he said frantically.

"Who, Maladho?"

"Mom, the dark spirits. This time it embodied Grandpa. Do you remember the last time it came as my father and almost killed me in the accident? Please, Mom, help me!" he pleaded.

"Wait there, I am coming. Don't move from your office! I am on my way."

People started knocking on his door. The behavior wasn't like him. "Maladho open the door. What is going on?" they demanded.

"Go away, go. They are here," Maladho said, and he barricaded himself in his office.

The receptionist called for backup because she was frightened. The hospital CEO arrived and unlocked the door with the spare key. They found Maladho sitting in a corner weeping like a toddler and shaking. "He is here. Please don't let him in," Maladho sobbed.

"Who, Maladho?" The CEO asked, confused.

Maladho stood up, fear and confusion in his eyes. He

walked to the window, scanning the parking lot. The old man seemed to have disappeared.

The scene at the hospital was chaotic and terrifying, with everyone stunned and confused by Maladho's behavior. They gave him some pills, and soon he calmed down. His mother arrived with Ossanti, her face filled with desperation and fear, and he was later released to go home and rest.

"Son, what did you see?" Fenda asked.

"Grandpa Karamoko. He said he could help," Maladho said.

"Are you serious?" Fear filled her eyes.

"Yes, Mom. It was him, despite being older now."

"Spirits like this kind of stage. They like posing when there is a threat. That's why we are trying to distance you from the scenario," Ossanti explained. Before leaving his home, he prepared a protective amulet for Maladho to wear around his neck, and Fenda stayed with him through the night, along with N'damesse. The entire ordeal had left everyone feeling tormented.

The following day, Maladho got ready to go to work. His mother was still sleeping, as she had barely slept the night before, while N'damesse was sitting in the living room. "Baby, where are you going?" she asked.

"I am going to work," Maladho replied.

"But you are not fit to work. You are still recovering from yesterday," she protested.

"Yes, but that was yesterday," Maladho replied as he opened the door to his garage. "M'bemba, open the gate, please."

N'damesse rushed to wake Maladho's mother. They both ran outside, but Maladho had already left, leaving a trail of dust mixed with car exhaust smoke.

When Maladho arrived at his office, everyone looked at

him strangely. The scene from the previous day was still fresh in their minds, and he could feel their fear. He looked around, feeling like he was going out of his mind. He knew how it felt. He was summoned to the CEO's office and made his way there, climbing the stairs with trepidation. Looking back at the fence, he saw the same old man standing at the other side of the building and looking at him. He continued walking down the hall, afraid. He knocked on the door.

"Enter," the CEO's voice boomed. "Sit down, please, Dr. Maladho," he said, when Maladho had stepped inside. "Do you want coffee or something to drink?"

Maladho shook his head, his mind still reeling from everything. He sat nervously in the office, waiting to hear what he knew was coming.

"Sorry, Maladho, but I am worried about what happened yesterday. I understand you because once something like this happened to me," the CEO said, concern etched on his face. "It was a similar situation, but I stopped right on time when everybody pleaded with me. But as for you, things are different. I remember asking you to stop. I spoke to your mother. She told me you don't listen." He sighed and took a sip of his coffee. Maladho shifted uncomfortably in his seat, knowing what was coming next.

"What I witnessed yesterday was serious. Therefore, I am granting you two weeks of break until you pull yourself together and sort things out. Don't worry. You will be paid." Maladho opened his mouth to protest, but the CEO cut him off. "Dr. Maladho, it is an order. Go home and rest. Another thing, leave that blog alone. It harms our reputation, and the big guys don't like it."

Maladho got up, feeling defeated, and left the office without saying anything. He walked through the hospital corridors in a daze, his mind consumed by what had happened to him. As he made his way to the parking lot, he saw a note on his passenger seat. "I am your only hope," it read. He looked around but saw no one.

Maladho was miles away in his thoughts, barely noticing the world around him. As he hopped into his car, his mind was still wandering in a maze of daydreams. Without realizing, he nearly bumped into the car right in front of him. A quick stomp on the brakes sent a jarring halt through his car, causing a loud symphony of honks from the traffic behind. Maladho sat frozen, his gaze locked on an old man walking by.

Suddenly, a tap on the window snapped him back. A worried face peered in, the driver from behind him, asking, "Hey, you alright?"

Maladho barely registered the words, lost in his trance. After a moment, he gave his head a good shake, like he was trying to wake up from a deep sleep. Blinking away his daze, he managed a sheepish, "I am sorry. I am fine," and waved the concerned driver off. With his heart still drumming in his chest, he steered his car away, a storm of questions brewing in his mind.

By the time he pulled into his driveway, a headache was tapping at his temples. Maladho sat in the parked car, the engine quiet now, replaying the day's odd turn of events. Something wasn't right, and he couldn't put his finger on it. With a deep breath, he decided it wasn't time to head inside just yet. Instead, he restarted the car, determination fueling his actions.

He needed answers, and he was going to find them, no matter what. Maladho's heart pounded like a drumbeat as he zipped along the dusty paths to the Ossanti shrine. The trip through Antula's winding roads felt like a journey to a magical place. Finally, he arrived at the shrine of Ossanti.

The moment Maladho stepped out of his car, he felt Ossanti's sharp eyes on him, watching his every move like a hawk until he reached the door.

Crossing the threshold of the shrine, Maladho was welcomed by a cloud of light smoke, swirling with the scents of herbs and ointments. It was a strong smell, but it had a strange power to soothe his nerves and fill his heart with peace. Sitting down next to Ossanti, a wave of safety washed over him. It was as if he'd just put on a warm, protective cloak, safe from any harm.

"Did you see it again?" Ossanti's voice rumbled like distant thunder.

Maladho nodded, his eyes wide. "Yes, I did."

Ossanti leaned in, his wise eyes sparkling. "What did he tell you this time?"

Handing over a wrinkled note, Maladho watched as Ossanti peered at it closely. Ossanti even sniffed it, then surprisingly, he licked it, as if tasting the truth hidden within its folds. "It seems real, but . . ." His voice faded into a thoughtful hum, his fingers tapping together. After a moment, Ossanti looked up, his face serious. "The battle is unavoidable," he declared.

Just then, a crow cawed loudly from the top of a kapok tree, breaking the silence. The tree's silk threads drifted down, casting a snowy veil over the scene, as if nature itself was listening and marking the moment with its own sign.

Without saying a word, Ossanti stood up and walked over to an old goat-skin bag. He rummaged inside for a moment before pulling out a tiny, clear bottle filled with a mysterious dark liquid. "Take this," he said, offering the bottle to Maladho.

He turned the bottle over in his hands, eyeing the liquid with a mix of wonder and worry. "What's this for, Uncle?"

Ossanti's eyes twinkled with a hint of mystery. "You'll need to use it," he said, his voice dropping to a whisper. "The next time you see him, sprinkle this over him. If he's just a man, nothing will happen. But if he's a shadow made of evil, he'll vanish into thin air. Remember, do exactly as I say."

After their conversation, Maladho stepped out of the shrine, his head buzzing with a thousand thoughts. Clutching the bottle tight, he felt the weight of his mission. He had to be brave and follow Ossanti's strange instructions to the letter. It was the only way to uncover the truth behind the eerie figure that had been shadowing his steps.

After waiting anxiously for days to test the magic potion given to him by Ossanti, Maladho decided to check his blog instead. As he scrolled through the comments, he felt a surge of courage and serenity, knowing that his words resonated with people worldwide. His former classmates from Brazil and even random strangers were offering tips and support for his cause. Encouraged by the positive feedback, Maladho returned to writing articles, exposing the government's lack of action in investigating the missing children's case.

However, his outspokenness didn't sit well with the government, and one morning, his unwavering dedication to the truth landed him in trouble. Without warning, police officers stormed his home and arrested him, blindfolding him before whisking him away to an unknown location.

Despite his mother, girlfriend, family members, and close friends' frantic search for him, Maladho remained missing for seventy-two hours. His followers and supporters flooded social media, denouncing his kidnapping and demanding release. The police department eventually admitted to arresting him for his behavior, but this only fueled anger among his supporters.

The streets of Bissau erupted into chaos as Maladho's

supporters clashed with the police, determined to fight for their hero's freedom. It was a ferocious battle, with both sides showing no mercy. However, in the end, the courage and determination of Maladho's supporters emerged victorious, and he was finally released. Though he was battered and bruised, Maladho knew that his voice had been heard, and he vowed to continue fighting for justice and speaking out against the government's atrocities.

Maladho had been released, but not without conditions. He had to present himself to the court every three days, and his passport was confiscated. Outside, the crowd was overwhelming, chanting for his freedom. The legal burden against Maladho intensified with each passing day. The pressure had become too great for the police to ignore, and they had no choice but to turn him over to the justice system. The prosecutors wasted no time in filing charges against him, accusing him of defying the authorities, spreading false information to incite social unrest, and baselessly accusing traditional authorities and doctors of nonexistent crimes.

Maladho was charged with multiple crimes, and as a result, he lost his medical license and his job. The authorities believed he was not fit to perform his profession. Maladho knew that to avoid a heavy sentence, he needed to produce solid evidence to support his claims that children with disabilities were being systematically thrown into rivers and lakes because of superstitions. He was confident he could find the evidence if they provided him with the means.

With this in mind, he was sitting in front of his house on a hot afternoon when a person approached him. He was so engrossed in his phone that he didn't notice the stranger at first. When he looked up, he saw the older man who looked like Karamoko. "What are you doing here? Go away. You aren't even real!" he yelled.

"Trust me. I want to help you. I am the only one who can help you," the man said from outside.

Maladho didn't believe him. He rushed inside and grabbed the bottle of magic potion from Ossanti. M'bemba had gone out. He was alone. Maladho panicked and didn't know what to do, but plucking up his courage, he decided to confront the old man. When he came out, he saw the old man still standing there. "Tell me you're not real," Maladho said.

Karamoko chuckled. "Indeed, I am real. Just calm down. I am not here to harm you, naughty boy. You are my blood."

Maladho was hesitant to trust him. He looked around for someone to help him confirm that Karamoko was real and not just a shadow trying to fool him. The stakes were high, and he couldn't afford to make any mistakes. "How did you know this was my place?" Maladho asked, his voice laced with suspicion.

Karamoko let out a tired sigh, his frail frame seeming to shrink further into his ragged clothes. "Let's talk about it later. We have important things to discuss now."

Maladho tossed the contents of the bottle onto the man, who just looked down at the liquid covering his body, as if he expected this test. When nothing happened, there was relief, but Maladho rubbed his forehead in frustration. "I thought you were dead."

"Everybody thinks the same. But I am alive—against my will, though," Karamoko replied, his eyes filled with a hint of sadness.

"You know I no longer trust you, even if you are the real Grandpa Karamoko!"

Karamoko shrugged, "I know it, but at least invite me inside. We can't talk about this issue in the open like this," he said, his voice unwavering.

Maladho reluctantly agreed to take him inside, but only on the patio. As Karamoko sat down, Maladho couldn't help but notice his long white beard, red fatigued eyes, and decaying shoes filled with dirt. He wore pants that dragged on the ground and a long black gown with colored characters, making him look like an old sage.

Despite his old and poor appearance, Karamoko still had that firm and commanding voice that Maladho remembered from the past. "I am sorry, Maladho. I know everything was my fault. I regret every bit of all this confusion I caused. I wish it were different." He paused, thoughtfully. "Look at you. I missed the most important part of my family life."

Maladho was still angry. "Forget about the family thing. After what you did, you then disappeared all these years while the tribe was suffering. How could you come up with these vague excuses? Did you see my mother?"

"No. Please, I do not want to meet her now. I am not ready. Your mother will never forgive me. I want to help you," Karamoko replied with a hint of sadness.

"Help me how? You keep repeating that."

"I know where you can find the shreds of evidence about the serpent kids. But please, promise to forgive me," Karamoko pleaded.

"Forgive you? After the incident with Kamboda, after trying to get us killed, leaving us all these years struggling, and ruining Kopiro!?"

"Maladho, you are right! That is why I am here, to fix what can be fixed. But you have to give me the chance to do so," Karamoko said, his voice steady and firm.

"Alright, then prove you deserve to be given a chance," Maladho said, his voice still filled with skepticism.

"We have to go to Kopiro, you and I."

"No. I am not going anywhere alone with you. We need a

larger escort. I don't know whether you are the real Karamoko," Maladho said.

Karamoko chuckled and again insisted that they should go alone. His insistence made Maladho suspicious. "Enough! Get up and get out. I don't need you here. Don't you dare come back. If you do, you'll regret it," Maladho burst out, flinging the gate wide open as Karamoko made his exit, the gate slamming shut with a resounding clang behind him.

Maladho was still muttering under his breath when the gate creaked open again. Startled, he jumped back. "Oh, M'bemba, you nearly gave me a heart attack," he gasped, catching sight of the gatekeeper stepping in.

M'bemba's eyebrows shot up in confusion. "What's happening, Dr. Maladho?" he asked, concerned.

"That old man who just stormed out . . . forget it." Maladho waved it off, his frustration simmering down.

"Old man?" M'bemba pressed, clearly puzzled.

"Yes, didn't you see him?" Maladho's eyes searched M'bemba's face for some sign of recognition.

"No, Doctor. I didn't see anyone. Are you sure you're okay?" Worry creased his forehead.

Standing there, Maladho's certainty wavered. Had he been so wrapped up in his own anger that he imagined the confrontation? Or worse, was he arguing with phantoms? The moment hung heavy with confusion, leaving Maladho to question his own senses.

CHAPTER TWENTY-THREE

THE TEMPTATION

Maladho was seated at the table, his gaze lost in the void. The accusations looming over him felt like a heavy cloud, making it hard to breathe. The possibility of death loomed large if the verdict came back guilty. Deep down, he realized the urgency of building a solid defense, and he knew he had to start laying the groundwork for it without delay. The gravity of his situation pressed down on him, making each moment feel more critical than the last.

While Maladho was absorbed in his worries, N'damesse brought him a bowl of cassava leaf soup, its steam curling up into the air. "Maladho, you've hardly eaten anything. I made this soup just for you," she said, her voice filled with worry. Her brows were furrowed, and her eyes showed deep care as she offered him the bowl, hoping to comfort him with the familiar, hearty flavors.

Maladho managed a weak smile, trying to mask his turmoil. "I've eaten. I'm just not very hungry," he said, though his voice lacked conviction.

N'damesse didn't buy Maladho's attempt to brush off his lack of appetite. She got closer to him, speaking in a gentle, hopeful tone. "Maladho, my love, there's no need to fret. We've got each other's backs. I've got an idea. You know

Professor Nankassa? He's not only super smart but also the top lawyer here, and he was a good friend of my dad's. He's our best bet to make it through this mess. I'm learning a lot from him. I'm doing my internship at his office." she added.

As the sun dipped below the horizon, Maladho and N'damesse found themselves at Nankassa's doorstep, hearts full of hope. Everyone in town dreamed of having Nankassa, the most sought-after lawyer, fight for them. They eagerly unfolded Maladho's story, watching Nankassa's face for signs of encouragement. But as they spoke, a shadow of doubt crossed the lawyer's face. His thick black hair matched the neatly aligned mustache that connected seamlessly to his sideburns. Deep lines marked his face, and as he removed his reading glasses, his eyes were filled with worry. His dark complexion seemed to glow.

"It's a great honor to be considered for your case," Nankassa began, weighing his words carefully. "But I must confess, your situation is tangled in complexities that might stretch beyond my reach."

Maladho and N'damesse shared a stunned glance. "What do you mean?" N'damesse's voice quivered, barely hiding her shock.

Nankassa paused, as if searching for the right words. "It's not about my willingness to help. Your case is layered with challenges. There's more at play than meets the eye."

"And what might that be?" N'damesse couldn't hide her growing impatience.

Taking a deep breath, Nankassa ventured further. "My personal beliefs and superstitions play a role in my decisions. Sometimes, defending certain cases is believed to bring bad luck to the lawyer . . ." He trailed off.

N'damesse couldn't believe her ears. "Are you actually saying you won't help us because you're scared of a curse?

Do you think those kids we're trying to help are evil spirits?" Her voice was a mix of surprise and frustration.

Nankassa didn't respond, his silence heavy in the air. N'damesse's voice softened, filled with desperation. "Professor, my dad would've moved mountains for me, and he considered you his closest ally. We're really counting on you."

Yet, even with N'damesse's eyes glistening with tears, Nankassa stood firm in his decision not to take the case. Walking away from his office, Maladho and N'damesse felt a cold wave of isolation. It was as if the world had turned its back on them.

They embarked on a relentless quest throughout the city, their determination unwavering as they searched for a lawyer willing to stand in Maladho's defense. With each passing day, the gravity of their situation pressed down harder, reminding them of the stakes at hand. They were well aware that navigating the legal system was a minefield in which they couldn't afford a misstep. In the midst of this storm, Fenda and Ossanti became their anchors, channeling hope and strength through their spiritual practices. They reached out to the gods and ancestors, their prayers a constant murmur in the background, weaving a tapestry of faith and resilience.

Over dinner, amidst the clinking of dishes and the low hum of evening settling in, N'damesse's eyes lit up with sudden inspiration. "Baby, I think I can do it," she declared, her voice brimming with newfound determination.

Maladho paused, his fork midway to his mouth, and looked at her, perplexed. "What do you mean?"

"I can defend you in court," N'damesse stated boldly.

Maladho's initial reaction was a mix of concern and disbelief. He sighed, setting his fork down. "That doesn't sound like a good idea. You're still in school, and you don't have a law license. We should keep looking for a qualified lawyer."

N'damesse, however, wasn't ready to back down. "But I've been looking into it," she countered, her resolve clear. "There are special conditions under which I can represent you. Plus, I'm already an intern and I'm in my final year. I know I can do this."

Despite her enthusiasm, Maladho remained unconvinced. "I appreciate your courage, but it's risky. We should focus on finding someone with the right experience," he argued.

N'damesse's smile didn't falter, even in the face of skepticism. "Don't worry, I'll continue our search for a lawyer. But just so you know, I have the potential to surpass my father."

Maladho looked at her, one eyebrow arched in mild skepticism. "Your dad was an exceptional lawyer, N'damesse, but you're not him."

At his words, a spark of determination flared in N'damesse. "I'm well aware I'm not my father, Maladho. But that doesn't mean I can't handle this. All I'm asking for is a chance."

Maladho, however, couldn't hide his concern. "I'm sorry, it's just too risky. No seasoned attorney would stake their reputation on a law student without any real courtroom experience."

Yet, N'damesse's resolve was as strong as ever. "I'll find a way to make this work, Maladho. Just wait and see," she said, her confidence unwavering.

As the sun peeked over the horizon, N'damesse was already on her way out the door, determined to find some help. She reached Professor Nankassa's office just as the day was beginning to warm up. Inside, she found the professor surrounded by the cozy comforts of morning: a steaming cup of coffee sat on his desk, sending up little wisps of steam that mingled with the gentle tunes from the radio beside him. He was flipping through the morning paper, lost in the world of headlines and stories. When he looked up and saw N'damesse, his face lit up with a welcoming smile, and he called out a cheerful greeting to her.

It was a scene straight out of a calm, pleasant morning, making N'damesse feel right at home. "Good morning, Professor. I hope you had a good night's sleep," she greeted him warmly.

"Indeed, I slept wonderfully," Professor Nankassa replied with a chuckle. "My wife brews these amazing herbal teas. They're like magic—send you straight to dreamland, and you wake up as fresh as a youngster!" He laughed softly, a twinkle in his eye as he took another sip of his coffee, then glanced back at his newspaper. His laughter filled the room with a sense of warmth and comfort, making N'damesse smile at the thought of such a simple yet profound family secret.

N'damesse made her way confidently into the room, clutching a folder close to her heart. "Excuse me, Professor Nankassa, could we chat for a bit?" she inquired, hopeful.

Professor Nankassa paused, setting his coffee cup down gently. The steam danced up around his face, weaving the comforting scent of coffee through the air. "Absolutely, N'damesse. What do you need to discuss?" he responded, his voice welcoming as he motioned toward a chair for her to take a seat. His open demeanor and the inviting gesture made the space feel safe and ready for conversation.

N'damesse pulled out a chair and settled in front of him, her determination clear. "I've been thinking about how to help Maladho," she started, her voice steady. "Since you're not able to take his case, I was wondering if I could step in and defend him."

The professor lifted an eyebrow in surprise. "And how do you plan to do that? You're not a licensed attorney."

Taking a deep breath to bolster her courage, N'damesse explained. "I discovered that with the support of a licensed attorney, I might be able to represent him myself."

A gentle chuckle escaped the professor as he shook his head, not unkindly. "I admire your spirit, but that's like diving into a river swarming with crocodiles, hoping to make it to the other side unscathed. The legal system here . . . it's complex, unforgiving. When's the last time you saw someone challenge it and succeed, especially against powerful people?"

N'damesse shook her head, feeling the weight of the challenge ahead of her.

"Exactly. You'd be going against the tide. So why do you want to fight a battle you're not ready for?" he said. After a brief silence, he continued, "Rushing into battle without a plan or strategy is not bravery. It's foolishness." Professor Nankassa took another sip of his coffee, contemplating the situation. "Defending Maladho in this situation is like fighting a pride of lions with bare hands. They will mercilessly tear you apart."

N'damesse felt a pang of fear in her chest, but she refused to give up. "Please, Professor. I have a feeling that I can win this case. I need your help, and I trust you because you were my father's best friend."

"I understand your feelings, but don't let your emotions cloud your judgment. I know you love him, but your intuition might lead to disaster. These people don't like confrontation. Please reconsider your decision," he advised.

"Thank you, Professor. I understand your concern," N'damesse said, her voice betraying her lack of conviction.

Nodding with understanding, the professor's gaze softened, reflecting a mix of respect and concern. "You are N'damesse Kubali, the daughter of Amikumas Kubali, one of the most respected lawyers we've ever had," he acknowledged, his voice carrying a hint of admiration. "But sometimes, the bravest thing is to wait for the perfect time to act."

She nodded, absorbing his words. "Thank you, Professor. I get it now."

With a warm smile, the professor leaned forward, making his decision clear. "Because of your determination and your father's legacy, I'll take on Maladho's case myself. We'll craft a careful strategy, aiming for the best outcome possible— whether that's forgiveness or minimizing the consequences. Let's buckle down, we have our work cut out for us, and time is of the essence," he said, energized by the challenge ahead.

Their conversation marked the beginning of a new chapter, one filled with hope and the promise of a hard-fought battle for justice. N'damesse nodded and got up, returning to her cubicle. She agreed to his advice, but deep down, she wasn't entirely convinced.

Just a few days later, N'damesse felt the urgency to seek out the professor once more. "Good morning, Professor Nankassa. I hope I'm not disturbing you," she said, managing a small smile despite her worries.

Professor Nankassa glanced up from the papers sprawled across his desk and gestured toward a chair, welcoming her. "Of course not. What's on your mind?" he inquired, noting the concern in her voice.

Taking a deep breath, N'damesse dove straight into her fears. "I'm really sorry to trouble you again, Professor, but something happened that's got me worried about Maladho. Last night, we had a black police truck parked outside our place, just watching. They stayed there the whole night," she explained, the tension evident in her voice as she recalled the unsettling vigil.

Professor Nankassa's concern deepened as he listened. "When did this begin?" he asked, his voice reflecting his worry.

"Just last night," she said, squeezing her eyes shut for a moment, as if hoping to block out the memory.

"They're trying to scare you," the professor concluded, his voice heavy with concern. "This is exactly the kind of pressure I warned you about. While I'm prepared to defend Maladho, the safest route might be to plead guilty for a lesser sentence."

Hearing this, N'damesse felt as if she were swallowing stones. The idea of admitting defeat without a struggle was unbearable. "Professor, I can't accept that," she responded with a determination that surprised even her. "I have faith in our case. We shouldn't back down so easily." After a brief pause, gathering her thoughts and courage, she added, "You've generously offered your help, and I'm grateful. But I really believe we have a chance to win. I don't want to surrender without giving our all." Her voice was steady, a testament to her unwavering belief in their cause.

The professor couldn't help but shake his head, a mixture of disbelief and concern coloring his tone. "N'damesse, your stubbornness is crossing into recklessness. You're not just risking your own safety, but your family's as well. If you won't consider a plea, I fear for my family's safety as well. I will need to step down from the case. I get the drive to win, but sometimes, stepping back is the wiser choice," he cautioned, his voice laden with seriousness.

N'damesse's frustration was palpable. Her hands balled into tight fists at her sides. "I understand this isn't your fight, but backing down isn't an option for me. I refuse to be bullied into submission. We have to stand our ground," she asserted, her voice ringing with conviction.

With a heavy sigh, the professor leaned back, the weight of the moment settling on his shoulders. "Alright. I'll try to find someone else willing to support your case. But I'm making no promises," he conceded with a note of reluctance.

A wave of relief briefly lightened N'damesse's burden. "Thank you, Professor. Your support means everything," she expressed her gratitude, her heart a little lighter.

As she stood to leave, the professor's gaze lingered on her retreating figure, torn between admiration for her courage and a deep-seated fear for her safety. Shaking his head, he turned back to his work.

As the day leaned into evening, the sun dipped closer to the horizon, painting the sky with strokes of orange and gold. The day's heat began to retreat, chased away by a refreshing breeze that danced through the trees and whisked dust off the ground. N'damesse was soaking up these moments, surrounded by her friends on the school patio, their laughter and chatter creating a lively soundtrack to the peaceful setting.

Out of nowhere, her phone interrupted the moment, its ring slicing through the air. "Hey, N'damesse, where are you?" It was Professor Nankassa on the line, his voice bringing a rush of uncertainty—was this good news or bad?

"I'm still at school. We were hammering out a project in the library, but now we're just catching our breath outside," she explained, a note of surprise in her voice.

"Would you mind stopping by my place on your way back?" he asked, his request hanging in the air.

"Of course, Professor," N'damesse agreed, curiosity tickling her thoughts as she hung up. She hurriedly gathered her things, politely turning down Jenabu's offer to walk home together.

As she made her way to Professor Nankassa's house, the reactions of people she passed on the street were hard to ignore. Friendly hellos mixed with sharp, judgmental stares. The whispers and rumors about Maladho had spread far and wide, painting him in an unfortunate light. And N'damesse, loyal and steadfast in her love for him, found herself caught in the crossfire of public opinion. Many believed she was out of her mind for standing by Maladho, not understanding the depth of her conviction or the strength of her commitment to him. Finally, she managed to flag down a taxi, and as the driver sped off, thick black smoke trailed behind them, mingling with the sharp smell of diesel that filled the air.

As N'damesse arrived in Alto Bandim, the affluent neighborhood where high-ranking government officials and wealthy individuals resided, she couldn't help but marvel at the stunning sea views surrounding the area. Professor Nankassa's impressive mansion, designed with the touch of the divine, was nestled amidst a lush garden of palm trees, colorful flowers, and various other plants.

The gatekeeper opened the heavy gate for her, and N'damesse strolled in, feeling like she was walking into heaven. The air was filled with the sweet fragrance of blooming flowers, and she could hear the cheerful chirping of birds perched atop the palm trees. Finally, she spotted Professor Nankassa sitting by his private pool, gazing at the picturesque seascape. The distant ships and boats scattered across the harbor only added to the idyllic scene before them.

When Professor Nankassa spotted N'damesse walking in, he sprang up from his seat and guided her inside. The living room was beautifully arranged, and she couldn't help but notice the sparkling curtains, pristine, porcelain-white sofa, and rich carpets that looked like they were from the Far East. The dining room was equally impressive, decked out as if a grand house party was in the works to celebrate something significant.

"Please, take a seat. I apologize for not informing you earlier to come over. It wasn't planned. I had to rush to the airport, and you know how crazy the traffic at Chappa can get," Professor Nankassa said, flashing a light smile.

"No problem, Professor. It's always a pleasure to visit your home. Where is Dona Nampili? I'd like to say hello," N'damesse inquired, noticing the absence of Professor Nankassa's wife.

"That's actually why I was at the airport. Dona Nampili had to travel to Portugal for medical treatment. It's truly unfortunate that our own government can't provide adequate healthcare facilities. It seems like for any serious health issue, seeking treatment abroad is the only option," he shared with a mix of frustration and resignation in his voice.

"I'm sorry to hear that she's unwell. I hope she feels better soon," N'damesse offered sympathetically, watching as Nankassa graciously served her a drink and some food. Despite the casual chatter and relaxed attitude of Nankassa, she was practically on the edge of her seat, her mind racing with anticipation as he walked around the house, fidgeting with various items. Finally, he settled down, and N'damesse leaned forward, ready to hear what he had to say.

"I won't keep you in suspense any longer, my dear N'damesse Kubali," Nankassa said, pouring himself a drink.

"I've been watching you for years and concluded that you're a true force to be reckoned with. You have your father's intelligence, bravery, and resilience, and I believe that you could be an incredible lawyer."

N'damesse's heart swelled with pride as she listened to her mentor speak. She could hardly believe what she was hearing.

"Which is why," Professor Nankassa continued, "I've decided to back you in your fight against Maladho's case. I'll sign the papers to be your backing attorney."

N'damesse's eyes filled with tears of joy and gratitude. She was so overwhelmed that she almost spilled her drink as she trembled with excitement. "Thank you so much, Professor," she said, her voice shaking. "I can't express how much this means to me."

They raised their cups in a toast, and N'damesse felt she was on top of the world. She knew that with Professor Nankassa's backing, she had a real chance at winning this case and bringing justice to Maladho. They spent the evening enjoying drinks, food, and conversation. She felt relaxed knowing she had achieved what she wanted. Her professor now understood her capabilities.

As the evening wore on and the sky grew darker, N'damesse realized it was time for her to head home. "Professor, I hate to interrupt our conversation, but it's getting late, and I should be going," she said.

"Oh, don't worry about that. Let's stay a little longer, and my driver can take you back when you're ready," Nankassa replied, his voice slurring a little. "Or why don't you sleep over tonight?"

"Thanks, Professor, but I need to go. I have some stuff to do back home, and nobody knew I was coming over," N'damesse said, her words skipping a little as she spoke.

Nankassa stood up and turned up the volume of the music, saying, "Alright, let me call the driver. He will take you. I wish you could stay because you are great at keeping someone company. Give me a hug before you go."

Feeling apprehensive due to his drunken attitude, N'damesse leaned in for a hug. He was forceful, pulling her in tightly. She tried to push him away, but he refused to let go. His hands began roaming inappropriately and he forcibly kissed her. Continually fighting against him, they fell onto the sofa, with the professor's mouth between her breasts.

Feeling violated, N'damesse used her strength and pushed him away. "Professor, what do you think you're doing?" she yelled.

"Come on. No one is here but you and me," he said, his words slurring. "There's something about you I like. Please, just tonight. I promise I can give you whatever you want."

N'damesse was appalled. "Are you sick or just drunk? I am like a daughter to you. How dare you? You think you can you try to force yourself on me? Never do that again," she said as she stood up and grabbed her bag. She went to the door and tugged, but it didn't give. It was locked. "Open the door. Otherwise, I am going to scream," she threatened.

Nankassa sobered up quickly, realizing she was serious. Not wanting to jeopardize his career and good name, he opened the door.

N'damesse exited hurriedly, and the professor was left stranded, standing speechless at the door. He learned that not all women are prey, and some stand their ground even if they are disadvantaged. She stepped out into the night, and her heart pounded with fear and apprehension.

The darkness was impenetrable, like a heavy cloak draped over everything, suffocating her senses. Her mind wandered, but a deep anger simmered inside her, fierce and unrelenting like a wounded lion.

As she approached the road, hoping for a ride home, no car passed. The sea's edge was even more ominous, the dark margins a foreboding sight. The sound of wild creatures defied the calmness of the sea, creating a haunting melody. Frogs chirped, dogs barked, and other creatures joined in the chorus. The night seemed to swallow up the sky, devouring the stars and enveloping everything in an eerie blanket of darkness.

N'damesse felt a shiver run down her spine, and she quickened her pace. She had to get to the central avenue to hail a taxi. Her blood boiled with fury, and her heart raced, battling against her brain on what to do next. Should she publicly shame Professor Nankassa or do something even crazier? The night seemed to hold the answers to her questions, but it also held secrets and dangers that she couldn't even begin to fathom.

As she walked through the door at home, Maladho saw something was wrong. There was a bitter expression on her face that she tried to hide with a forced smile. He couldn't help but ask, "Baby, what's going on?"

"Nothing, I'm just tired. School is taking a toll on me," she replied, avoiding his gaze.

Maladho was unconvinced and asked again, "Are you sure you're fine?"

N'damesse shrugged and replied, "Why? I'm fine, love."

But she wasn't fine. She didn't even sit in the living room as usual. Instead, she went straight to the bathroom to take a shower. Standing under the water, she couldn't hold back her tears. She cried to cleanse her heart and mind of the stress and emotions weighing her down.

After the shower, she went straight to bed, her heart

heavy with unspoken anger and fury.

That night, N'damesse was so consumed by anger and frustration that she completely forgot about the case and everything else. Her sole focus was to start another battle with the man she had once admired: her professor. She woke up early the following day and left for the office, determined to confront him. However, she was greeted with an empty table and a lonely, quiet office when she arrived. The scent of Professor Nankassa's coffee and cologne still lingered in the air, along with the stacks of paperwork that cluttered his desk.

N'damesse waited for hours, but Nankassa never showed up. She tried calling his phone, but there was no answer. Her frustration mounted, and she became more determined than ever to confront him. What had happened between them was shocking and deeply insulting to her, and she was not going to let it go unaddressed.

Two days had passed, and N'damesse stood at the side of the school sidewalk, waiting for passing traffic to cross the street. Suddenly, a familiar voice broke her concentration. "N'damesse!"

When she turned, she saw Professor Nankassa with a remorseful face looking at her. "What do you want?" she said angrily.

"Please, calm down. I am here to talk with you. Please, give me a chance to explain."

N'damesse smirked. "You know, I have been looking for you because I need an explanation of your actions from that night."

"I know, and I am sorry. Please, can we talk privately?" Nankassa requested.

They walked to the school garden and sat on a distant bench near the clock tower. "I apologize for what happened.

It was unintentional, and I was drunk. I have been under so much stress it has caused me some emotional disorder. Please forgive me. I felt so bad about what I had done. All I wanted was to vanish right away because you are like a daughter to me, and I can't fail you again as I did that night," Nankassa said shamefully.

N'damesse stared at him for a moment, considering his words. Finally, she spoke. "I do not forgive you. You need to earn it. And if you ever try something like that again, I'll make sure everyone knows about it and take legal action against you," she warned.

"I understand. And I will earn it. Forgiveness is divine, as our gods say. But you should know I was not lying about your skills as a lawyer. I guarantee I will back you up without any bounds," he said.

CHAPTER TWENTY-FOUR

THE CONVICTION

On the day of the trial, emotions ran high throughout the country. Radio stations abandoned their usual programming and dedicated airtime to discussing the trial instead. The bustling streets of Bissau were heavily congested with traffic, and police officers staffed intersections. Authorities were on high alert for any signs of civil unrest. Barricades were set up around the courthouse, and tensions peaked as supporters of Maladho and those who opposed him nearly clashed on opposite sides of the barriers. The resounding demonstrations of the protestors could be heard from afar.

As Maladho appeared in court, the atmosphere was tense and solemn. The room was filled with a hushed murmur as people whispered to each other about the case. The judge sat sternly at his bench, and the lawyers took their places, ready for the proceedings to begin.

Maladho himself looked nervous and uneasy as he stood before the court. He shifted his weight from foot to foot, fidgeting with his clothes and avoiding eye contact with those around him. The seriousness of the situation was palpable, and it was clear that everyone in the room was aware of the gravity of the charges against him. Despite the tension in the air, there was also a sense of curiosity and anticipation.

People craned their necks to get a better look at Maladho and whispered to each other about the case details. It was a moment of high drama and emotion, with the fate of an individual hanging in the balance.

As Maladho's defense lawyer and girlfriend, N'damesse was visibly anxious in court. She sat with her back straight, her hands clasped tightly in her lap, and her eyes fixed on Maladho as he stood before the judge. N'damesse's face was etched with worry, and she chewed on her bottom lip nervously as the trial began. She knew that the odds were stacked against them, and the lack of evidence to support Maladho's claims was a major concern. Despite her anxiety, N'damesse was determined to put up a strong defense for Maladho. She listened intently to the prosecution's arguments, taking notes and mentally preparing her rebuttal. She knew she needed to stay focused and composed, even as her emotions threatened to overwhelm her.

Throughout the trial, N'damesse's anxiety grew, and she could feel her heart pounding. She spoke forcefully in defense of Maladho, but her voice always had a sense of unease and apprehension. The stakes were high, and the trial outcome would profoundly impact both Maladho's life and their future together.

The courtroom fell silent as the judge's voice boomed, calling for order. "We gather here to examine the serious accusations against Mr. Maladho. He stands charged with levying false accusations against practitioners of traditional religion, alleging they perform ritualistic child sacrifices. Furthermore, he is accused of inciting public disorder and making unfounded allegations against both traditional religion and the government." With a stern look, the judge then turned to the prosecution. "The prosecution may now present its opening statement." The air in the room tensed, everyone bracing for the unfolding legal battle.

The prosecutor stood, confidence in their stance. "Thank you, Your Honor. Ladies and gentlemen of the jury, today we address the actions of Mr. Maladho, whose serious and baseless accusations have not only stirred public unrest but also smeared the honor of a revered religious community. Our evidence will clearly demonstrate that Mr. Maladho's allegations lack any foundation and that his reckless behavior has indeed fueled public disorder. We aim to establish, beyond a shadow of a doubt, the harm caused by these unfounded claims." The courtroom absorbed every word, the gravity of the situation palpable in the air as the prosecution laid out its case.

The judge turned to Maladho as he addressed the courtroom. "The defense is now invited to present its opening statement." The room's attention shifted, anticipation building for the defense's response to the charges laid against Maladho.

N'damesse rose, her voice steady but infused with a palpable sense of urgency. "Thank you, Your Honor. Ladies and gentlemen of the jury, we stand before you to discuss Mr. Maladho, a man driven by concern for his community's safety, especially its children. We intend to bring forward evidence that substantiates his claims, including testimonies from those who have witnessed these issues firsthand and scientific evidence that cannot be ignored. Our defense hinges on the belief that Mr. Maladho was not only exercising his right to free speech but also acting out of a necessity to safeguard the most vulnerable among us. His actions were never about causing chaos but about initiating crucial conversations for protection and change." Her words were measured and clear.

The judge nodded at N'damesse and turned his attention to the prosecution, gesturing for them to proceed. "The prosecution may now call their first witness to the stand." His words set the courtroom in motion, everyone's focus shifting in anticipation of the testimony to come.

The prosecutor's voice was clear and authoritative as they introduced their first witness. "Thank you, Your Honor. The prosecution would like to call Mr. Jambakatan, a respected elder and practitioner of traditional religion, to the stand."

Mr. Jambakatan approached, his presence commanding respect. After being sworn in, he settled into the witness stand, ready to share his testimony.

The prosecutor began, "Mr. Jambakatan, could you please share with the court your role within the traditional religious community and how Mr. Maladho's accusations have affected you and your community?"

Mr. Jambakatan nodded, his voice steady and filled with a mix of pride and pain. "For over four decades, I have dedicated myself to the practices of our traditional religion. The allegations Mr. Maladho has made against us have been deeply wounding. To suggest that our spiritual practices involves harming children or any act of violence is entirely false. Such statements have not only caused anguish within our community but have also sown seeds of discord and misunderstanding far beyond it."

When it was N'damesse's turn for cross-examination, she began, "Mr. Jambakatan, we understand that you are a respected member of the traditional religious community. However, can you confidently say that every single practitioner of traditional religion has adhered to the same principles and practices you have followed throughout your forty years?"

Mr. Jambakatan frowned. "I cannot speak for every individual, but I can say that the core teachings of our religion do not condone any form of violence or harm, especially toward children."

The trial continued in this fashion, with both sides examining the prosecution's witnesses. Professor Nankassa sat in the courtroom, visibly nervous. His hands trembled as he clutched his legal pad, and beads of sweat formed on his furrowed brow. He kept shifting in his seat, unable to find a comfortable position, and his eyes darted back and forth between the judge, the jury, and N'damesse. As she questioned witnesses and presented evidence, his anxiety seemed to increase. He occasionally whispered something into her ear, but his voice was shaky, betraying his uncertainty. When the judge demonstrated a clear bias against Mr. Maladho and the defense's case, Professor Nankassa's face turned pale, and he swallowed hard, struggling to maintain his composure.

During recess, Professor Nankassa paced back and forth in the hallway, wringing his hands and mumbling. His pessimism about the case's outcome was evident to everyone around him. He appeared lost in thought, trying to come up with a new strategy or angle to help strengthen the defense's case, but his furrowed brow and distant gaze made it clear that he was struggling to find a way to overcome the evident bias in the courtroom.

After the fifth day, on Friday evening, Professor Nankassa called N'damesse into his office. "I know you are brave and doing well so far," he said. "But it is time to stop playing the hero in this case. Let's convince Maladho to accept the plea."

N'damesse's eyes flashed with determination as she replied, "No, Professor. I refuse to back down. I will see this case through to the end, no matter the consequences."

Professor Nankassa sighed and lightly slapped the table. "Are you out of your mind?!" He yelled. Looking at her, he implored, "Please, reconsider. The odds are against us, and I fear the worst for Maladho. For all of us. You are dreaming of something unreal. Drop the case. You aren't going to make it."

"This is my case, Professor. You are just backing me up. Let me finish it, then judge me at the end. I am not a coward," N'damesse sneered, but there were tears in her eyes.

Nankassa winced at the insult but nodded, and she left. Feeling desperate, he called Fenda to see if she could forcibly convince N'damesse, claiming she was risking Maladho's life by fighting to the bitter end.

Fenda and Ossanti rushed to Maladho's house. Fenda burst through the door, her voice trembling with fury. "N'damesse! You listen to me! Professor Nankassa told me about your reckless plan, putting my son's life on the line! I won't stand for it!"

As Fenda's words filled the room, Maladho intervened, shouting, "Mom! Mom, please stop!"

Fenda, still seething, retorted, "Why don't you tell her to stop first?"

N'damesse remained quiet, her expression stoic.

Maladho asked, "What's going on here?"

"Professor Nankassa told me he advised her to have you plead guilty, and she refused!"

Maladho tried to appease his mother, saying, "Mom, we were discussing it. Please, calm down."

Ossanti stepped in to soothe Fenda. She retreated to the other side of the room, her breaths coming in short, sharp pants as she sat.

N'damesse took a deep breath and spoke to Fenda gently,

soothingly. "Mom, I understand your concern, and you have every right to be worried as a mother. I care deeply for Maladho and would never do anything to hurt him. The situation seems dire, but let's play our last card. Perhaps the spirits of Kopirondin will bless us and guide us to a favorable outcome."

Fenda held her head in her hands, looking down. "It's too late, my child. I can't bear to bring more suffering to this family," she whispered.

Maladho intervened, pleading with his mother. "Mom, today is Friday. Let's give N'damesse two more days to think about it before we return to court."

The room grew quiet, the tension slowly dissolving as everyone contemplated their next move, hoping for a resolution to bring peace to the family.

With time running out before Monday, a decision had to be made over the weekend. N'damesse informed Maladho that she required some solitude to think, and during the weekend, she decided to distance herself. Early Saturday morning, she entered her late father's office. She carefully dusted the table and chair before sitting in the very spot where her father used to sit. Her eyes scanned the room, taking in her father's awards that still hung on the wall and a framed picture resting on the table's edge, protected by glass. Another photograph of her father's graduation hung prominently on the wall behind her. The room remained untouched, a shrine to his memory. Spider webs had woven themselves around some artifacts as if they were standing guard.

"Dad, I know you can see me right now, and I feel your presence. I'm sorry if I'm making the wrong decision, but I have to fight," N'damesse spoke, her voice cracking with emotion. She sniffled, chuckled softly, and continued. "I remember how you always told me never to give up or back down because of fear. You said that cowardice doesn't run in our blood. Those words made me the strong, confident woman I am today, even though you've joined our ancestors. Now, as I face this challenge, I need your help to emerge victorious, to conquer my enemies, and to prove to the world that I am the daughter of a warrior, the daughter of the finest lawyer this country has ever known—a man who never tasted defeat."

N'damesse's voice swelled with determination and echoed throughout the room. Overcome with emotion, she collapsed onto the table, weeping like a child, her tears streaming down its surface. After sitting there for hours, gathering strength from the memories of her father, she quietly left the room, ready to face the challenges ahead.

On Monday, the courthouse was teeming with people. The outside patio was packed with journalists, curious onlookers, and supporters from both sides, holding banners and signs amidst tight security. News outlets had speculated that Monday might be the day the verdict would be announced, attracting even more people to the court. Inside the courtroom, there wasn't a single empty seat. The air was thick and humid, with murmurs echoing through the hall, reminiscent of a buzzing beehive.

N'damesse sat next to Maladho, with Professor Nankassa on her right side. The judge called for silence. "Defense, are you ready to call witnesses or is your client accepting the plea bargain?"

N'damesse cleared her throat and made a surprising announcement. "After consulting with my client and reviewing the plea proposal, my client has decided to refuse the plea bargain."

The courtroom erupted in disbelief. A cacophony of

voices filled the room as people began to talk and argue. Some were elated, while others were visibly shocked. Nankassa held his forehead, looking down and shaking his head disappointedly. On the other side, Fenda nearly fainted. The judge had to intervene to restore order. He struck the gavel several times, calling for silence. It took some time for the room to settle down as the tension had reached a fever pitch.

N'damesse continued, "Your Honor, my client believes that crimes against innocent children and young adults have been committed and continue to occur daily, yet we still pretend as though nothing is happening."

"Objection," interjected the prosecution.

"Let her finish," the judge instructed.

"Thank you, Your Honor. A few witnesses here are prepared to testify and provide undeniable evidence supporting my client's claims."

People began looking around, and the prosecution scoffed. "Unbelievable. Your Honor is entertaining this nonsense again to waste our time with manipulated individuals providing false testimony."

"Silence!" the judge commanded, and indicated N'damesse should continue.

"Your Honor, I call my first witness to testify." The door opened, and everyone turned to see who it was. A woman entered, walking as if she was levitating. At first, it wasn't easy to recognize her. It was Tombom. She was still beautiful, her face carrying an air of melancholy. It seemed she had never truly overcome the disappearance of Kamboda. Tombom's eyes caught Fenda's, and the two exchanged a nostalgic look. Their thoughts wandered to the past in Kopiro. Surely the events three decades ago never faded away from their minds.

Tombom gave a chilling testimony, leaving many in the courtroom on the verge of tears. Her emotional account of her son's disappearance almost seemed too much to bear. Even the judge, who tried to remain composed and impartial, could not hide his overwhelming feeling of pity. His attempts to camouflage his emotions were unsuccessful, and his sadness was evident to those in the courtroom.

After Tombom's testimony, N'damesse called upon another witness to provide further evidence. The judge, visibly moved by Tombom's emotional account, nodded for the witness to proceed. The defense team was attentive and hopeful, eager to present as much evidence as possible to help their client's case. On the other hand, the prosecution team appeared less confident, perhaps even nervous, as they watched the witness take the stand.

As the second witness was called, the door slowly opened, making everyone in the courtroom nervous and apprehensive. All eyes were fixed on the unknown man as he walked in, moving slowly as if afraid of stepping on the ground. His entire head was wrapped in a cloth-like turban, and he was dressed in a white gown. Each step caused the wooden floorboards to creak. He took the stand, and the room fell silent, waiting for him to speak.

People in the courtroom began whispering to each other, asking in low tones who he was. The judge asked the witness to state his name. The man slowly unwrapped his turban and removed his disguise, revealing his face.

"My name is Karamoko Kumo, and I am the leader of Kopironkos—the grandfather of the defendant Maladho N'Gayou. The great, great, great-grandson of Kopirondin Kumo. I stand here today to tell the truth and wash away my sins so I can go and rest with my ancestors," Karamoko declared, his voice echoing through the hall.

Maladho was sure he was dreaming. The crowd erupted into a frenzied uproar, and Fenda collapsed, struggling to catch her breath. Security guards were quickly summoned to quell the confusion, but the tension in the air remained palpable. The audience held their breath as Karamoko began to speak once again. Maladho listened intently, knowing that what Karamoko was about to reveal could change the course of the trial.

N'damesse began her questioning. "Mr. Karamoko, to what extent are the rituals practiced among jalangs?"

"Some jalangs refuse. Not all accept. But my grandchild Maladho here is right," Karamoko began. "I have participated in many rituals where innocent children were sacrificed, including my grandchild, Kamboda."

Gasps and murmurs erupted throughout the courtroom, and the judge demanded clarification. "Are you saying you have participated in those rituals?" he asked incredulously.

Karamoko did not hesitate. "Yes, Your Honor. I did," he declared. "And not only that, I can lead you to where these rituals were performed."

N'damesse asked, "Where can we find the ritual site?"

Karamoko handed her a crumpled piece of paper marked with strange lines and dots. "This is the map," he said solemnly. "The map that will lead you to the truth."

The courtroom was silent, stunned by Karamoko's confession. Maladho looked on in disbelief, realizing that the man he had respected and admired all his life was capable of such atrocities.

"Objection, Your Honor. We all know Karamoko died a long time ago. This man is an impostor trying to deceive us," the prosecution argued.

N'damesse quickly countered, "Have you ever seen Karamoko's dead body?"

The judge intervened, "Silence," he ordered. Turning to Karamoko, the judge questioned, "How do we know you are the real Karamoko?"

Karamoko removed his ID and a ring that only the chiefs carried, handing them to the judge. The judge asked the experts to scan the items, and Karamoko was ordered to sit and wait.

N'damesse called several other witnesses, including parents who had lost their children in the same ritual but were forced to remain in silence or face consequences. The testimonies were chilling, and the courtroom was filled with emotion and tension.

Afterward, the judge suspended the hearing until the next day, leaving everyone on edge. As they filed out of the courtroom, N'damesse caught up with Maladho.

"Maladho, what do you think?" N'damesse asked.

"I don't know," Maladho replied. "I want to believe it's him, but I also know that people can fake IDs and rings."

N'damesse nodded thoughtfully. "We'll just have to wait and see what the experts say."

Soon, news of the case spread rapidly, capturing widespread interest. National and international human rights organizations called for justice and a fair trial. By morning, Bissau was inundated with numerous media outlets and human rights organizations. Police were forced to close the street leading to the courthouse. A passionate crowd marched toward the courthouse, chanting, "Embrace their humanity, not myths!" and "Where are they?" and "They deserve to live!" in support of Maladho.

The following day, the hearing resumed. In the humid courtroom, three ceiling fans circulated air sluggishly. After confirming Karamoko's identity through the gathered evidence, the judge proceeded with the trial. Karamoko was instructed not to reveal the locations of the rituals to avoid compromising the ongoing investigation.

In the courtroom, N'damesse turned to Karamoko and requested his testimony regarding the ritual performed.

N'damesse said, "Karamoko, I would like you to provide the court with a detailed account of the rite you and the other elders conducted. Please explain the events of that night, including the reasons behind the ritual, and describe the steps taken during the process."

Karamoko took a deep breath and began to recount the events, sharing the information that would later become crucial to the trial's outcome. Several elders arrived at Karamoko's compound in secret on the night in question. They kept their actions hidden, as the main shrine did not condone such rituals.

First, the elders brought Kamboda to Karamoko's toilet, washing him with herbs and adorning his body with white ash. They then dressed him in a red gown before leading him to the river. Upon arriving at the Koff Label River, they entered a secret site believed to be the residence of spirits. Kamboda was laid down, and rice dough and eggs were placed around him. As the chief, Karamoko recited a prayer: "We are here to bear witness, O gods of other gods, ancestors, and spirits of Koff Label. We are your servants. Without you, we cannot find the path to success. Please guide us in our search for the truth and ensure we do not fail our forefathers."

As Karamoko prayed, the others threw liquid and chanted, waving lanterns. Karamoko continued, "Please let us know. If this child is one of us, let him witness the sunrise in the land of humans. If he is not, let him return to the land of spirits." As soon as he finished, they all left without looking back.

The elders believed that if Kamboda were human, he would remain at the site until the following morning. However, if he were a spirit, he would vanish and enter the river. The following day, Kamboda was nowhere to be found; he had disappeared. No one knew precisely what had occurred, but the Koff Label River was the last to "witness" Kamboda. The river serves as a silent testament to the actions taken against him. If only the river could speak, it would reveal the events that transpired that fateful night.

Karamoko then disclosed something chilling. "Most of the time, when we went back to the river to see if the child was alive, we found their body and would bury them in a secret place. Sometimes we didn't find the body. Only the river may know what happened next."

People started sobbing in the courtroom.

Karamoko took a deep breath and turned to face Tombom, seated next to Fenda. His eyes filled with sincere remorse, and his voice trembled with emotion. "Tombom, I stand before you today, humbled and deeply sorry for the years of hatred and disdain I directed toward you. My heart aches when I think about the pain and suffering I have caused you." Karamoko's whole body trembled with the weight of his apology. He paused momentarily, allowing the weight of his words to sink in. "For years, I let my prejudice cloud my judgment, and I never wanted Bakar to marry you simply because of your heritage. I now understand that love knows no boundaries, and I regret my narrow-mindedness."

Karamoko's voice cracked as he continued, "I also feel profound sorrow for the unspeakable act of taking Kamboda, my grandchild, away from you when he was just a child. I foolishly believed he was a spirit, not a human being, and subjected him to a ritual that no innocent soul should ever endure. I will never be able to fully express my regret for that and other terrible mistakes."

He glanced at Fenda, then back at Tombom. "I am genuinely sorry, and I ask for your forgiveness." He turned to the courtroom at large. "Even in this room, there are some who have taken part. For example, him, and him, and him." Karamoko indicated several respected elders. "They know what I am talking about because we made a pact." Some of the elders looked down, avoiding Karamoko's gaze.

"Objection, Your Honor! He is now attempting to fabricate evidence by implicating innocent and respected individuals. We all know that these people are community leaders and loyal priests," the prosecution argued. The courtroom erupted in chatter as people glanced back and forth between Karamoko and the elders.

"Order! Silence!" the judge struck the gavel.

Before the judge could speak further, some of those Karamoko had pointed to raised their hands. One said, "He is right. I, too, have participated in the ritual several times." Among them, Officer Klusseh also stood, admitting his involvement.

The courtroom went into an uproar. Nobody had expected such a revelation! This stunning admission dealt a final blow to the case. N'damesse looked around the courtroom and nodded. Maladho could scarcely believe it, as these individuals were supposed to be role models in the community.

N'damesse stood before the courtroom the next day, her face reflecting a mixture of triumph and solemnity. As she prepared to deliver her closing statement, she took a deep breath. "Ladies and gentlemen, today marks a turning point in our society's history. The truth has been revealed, and justice has emerged victorious. Throughout this case, Maladho's unwavering determination and courage have exposed a deeply rooted and hidden evil plaguing our community. I am honored to have represented Maladho in his fight for justice, but our work is far from over. The heartbreaking discoveries made during this investigation have shaken us all. Our collective responsibility is to ensure that such heinous acts are never repeated. We must acknowledge our society's failures and work together to build a brighter future for all, regardless of their abilities or perceived spiritual affiliations.

"As we leave this courtroom, let us carry the lessons we have learned and the memory of those innocent lives lost. Their tragic stories inspire us to create a more compassionate, just, and inclusive society. We owe it to them and to future generations to make a change. Thank you for your attention and your commitment to justice. Together, we have made a difference."

The discoveries made at various sites were both shocking and heartbreaking. Numerous skeletons and bodies were found, primarily children cast into the river or secretly buried in hidden graveyards. Children with disabilities, believed to be spirits, were discarded as rotten tomatoes. These findings ignited social outrage, confirming that Maladho had always been right. The news spread, prompting neighboring countries to authorize investigations as well. Many individuals were ultimately imprisoned, and the revelations sent shockwaves through the government, resulting in the dismissal of numerous members.

Maladho was declared innocent on all counts and acquitted on the final day in court. The judge also ordered the restoration of his license. Jubilation swept through the courtroom, and the atmosphere buzzed with excitement and relief. The truth had been unveiled, thanks to the courage and determination of N'damesse, who fought tirelessly to defend Maladho. As she looked around the room, her eyes fell on Professor Nankassa, who was beaming with happiness and hugging those who had gathered in support.

As the judge announced Maladho's acquittal, Fenda couldn't help but beam with pride and gratitude toward who would likely become her future daughter-in-law. The young woman had shown immense strength and dedication as Maladho's defense lawyer, proving her unwavering love and commitment as his girlfriend. Fenda felt a rush of emotions as she saw N'damesse's eyes glisten with tears of joy and relief. She thought about the moments when she had doubted N'damesse's capabilities, and now, she regretted those thoughts more than ever. Fenda realized how fiercely N'damesse had fought for Maladho and in doing so, had solidified her place in their family's heart.

Karamoko had a request before being sent to jail, and the judge agreed to honor it. He walked slowly to where Maladho was standing. He removed his ring and placed it in Maladho's hand. "Here, you are the new king of Kopironkos. It had been prophesied a long time ago. Lead our people, make us dream again, be brave again, and clean the mess and pain I left behind." Then Karamoko walked away, escorted by security. Fenda looked at her father and cried.

CHAPTER TWENTY-FIVE

THE CORONATION

N'damesse got into a cab, opening the window, feeling a sense of liberation as the breeze blew against her face. "Could you please turn up the radio?" she asked the driver. As she listened, a journalist enthusiastically narrated the story of the case she had just been involved in. They spoke of the state-mandated seven days of mourning for the victims and the importance of giving them proper burials to ensure their eternal rest. The journalist's final statement moved everyone to tears. "These children deserved to live, and yet their lives were taken from them—the most precious thing one can have. Now, we owe them an apology. Let's bury them so they can finally rest in peace."

N'damesse felt immense pride in being part of the fight for justice. It reminded her of another reason she loved Maladho. He had chosen a different path from most. He had earned his degree and secured his dream job but still looked after those in need. Maladho truly honored his word and valued his friendships.

The mass burial ceremonies took place across the country. People gathered together, honoring and burying the children with dignity according to their tribes and beliefs. That day was designated as "Special Children's Day," and the state enacted "Kamboda's Law." This law made it illegal to discriminate against special needs children, with violators facing a life sentence in prison without parole.

Before the mass burial, speeches from various personalities were broadcast across multiple mediums worldwide. Maladho delivered an exceptional remark: "Ladies and gentlemen, esteemed guests, and fellow citizens, I stand before you as a leader and a concerned member of our society. I want to address a deeply rooted misconception in our community—the belief that children with disabilities are spirits. This belief has led to many innocent children's unjust treatment and abandonment. We must recognize the medical and scientific reality behind their disabilities.

"Disabilities in children can arise from several circumstances, including genetics, complications during pregnancy or birth, early childhood infections, accidents, or exposure to harmful substances. Some disabilities are present from birth, while others develop later. The reasons can range from inherited conditions to environmental factors. Regardless of the cause, each child's needs and abilities can vary significantly, with some requiring minimal support and others needing more comprehensive assistance for daily activities.

"It is essential to understand that children with a disability are not spirits or lesser beings. They are human beings deserving of love, care, and equal opportunities. Our responsibility as a society is to break the chains of ignorance and offer support and understanding to these children and their families. We must educate ourselves and others about the various disabilities that affect children. This awareness will help us break the cycle of discrimination and mistreatment of these innocent souls. We must embrace these children, understand their unique challenges, and create an inclusive society that values every individual.

"Today, I call upon all of you to join me in spreading awareness about disabilities that affect our children. Let us work together to create a world where all children, regardless of their abilities, are celebrated and allowed to thrive. Remember, they are extraordinary human beings who deserve our love, support, and understanding. Let us stand together as a united community to ensure that no child is left behind and everyone is treated with the respect and dignity they deserve."

On that significant day, Maladho symbolically performed two burial rituals: one for the babies of his late friend Nené-Funé, as he had promised her, and one for his beloved cousin, Kamboda. This act served as a testament to his unwavering commitment to the memories of those who were lost and the promises he made.

After the ceremony, Maladho felt exhausted and went to bed early. He found himself immersed in a vivid dream. Kamboda and a group of people, all dressed in white, came to his house, each holding an object resembling a luminous egg as if it contained a light within. Kamboda handed one to Maladho, saying, "Thank you for saving us. We were trapped for years, and your bravery and kind heart set us free."

As Maladho looked to the side, he saw a horseman clad in white and instantly recognized his guardian angel. The man on the white horse removed his mask, revealing himself as Demba. "Father," Maladho exclaimed, embracing him. "Why did you leave us so early?" he asked.

"Son, I had a mission. Our ancestors had called me to perform a very important task," his father replied. "Now it's time to rest, but I'll always be beside you. You are now the king of the Kopironkos, and I am so proud of you. I never doubted you, my son. Remember always to use your wisdom and compassion to protect your people." After those heartfelt words, they said their goodbyes. Maladho's father and Kamboda waved as they floated into the air.

Maladho's dream illuminated a question that had lingered in his mind for years, ever since his father's sudden departure from this world. He had always pondered whether his father's death was the work of the good janfaa or the bad janfaa, entities he believed influenced the outcomes of human lives. This dream, vivid and revealing, seemed to offer an answer to the decades-old mystery that had haunted him, providing a sense of closure or perhaps opening new doors to understanding the forces that shape our destinies.

Maladho woke abruptly. It was three in the morning. He got up and stepped out onto his veranda, where he witnessed a mesmerizing sight in the sky. Beautiful, colorful lights and shining particles, like stars, ascended heavenward. N'damesse joined him and leaned against his back, wrapping her arms around him. Together, they gazed at the mystical spectacle.

In the morning, it was the talk of the town. Various specialists offered their opinions, but they all agreed on one thing: the children's souls were finally free and now rested alongside their ancestors. The same captivating display occurred over several days. In the days following the burial ceremonies, another phenomenon occurred. River Koff Label filled with water again, and everything around Kopiro began to flourish.

Maladho was invited to speak on behalf of children with disabilities in various countries, including at the United Nations General Assembly in New York. He warned the world of the risks faced by children with disabilities in general. He emphasized that everyone must be held accountable for providing them with better living conditions and protection.

Since these events, Maladho's life had become very busy, leaving little time to enjoy his family as he had before. On the other hand, he knew it was time to prepare, as he would soon be responsible for Kopironko's crown. However, before that could happen, there were specific procedures to follow. The primary requirement was that he needed to get married.

The night was calm, with a full moon hanging high in the sky. Fenda sat next to Tombom. After many years, they were finally united. "I know it's been a long time since we escaped from Koyang. I always wanted to know what happened after we left," Fenda asked.

Tombom hesitated. "Chaos and confusion," she finally said. She adjusted her position, gathering her legs. "It still flickers through my mind, sometimes making me shiver, knowing it could have been the end. But Kopirondin had us under her protection. Just after you rode the bike and a few minutes after I reached home, Bakar was looking for me. He thought I was with another man. We almost fought because he was upset. I managed to calm him down and told him it was time to worry about his sister and nephew. Before I could tell him what had happened, we heard Fambondin screeching in the sky. Everything went silent. I knew what was going on, but some felt lost. I wanted to tell your brother what had happened, but at the same time, I was afraid. The next day, when I realized they hadn't caught you, I felt relieved. I cried a lot that day. I prayed a lot, I told myself I could have run away and done the same to save my Kamboda.

"Two days later, I decided to tell your brother what

happened. He went looking for you everywhere, but he couldn't find you. Things started becoming difficult and frightening in Kopiro and its surroundings until we had to flee one day. The devastation that followed was horrific. A massive fire engulfed Kopiro, creating a scene of terror and destruction we had never seen before. Then, in its fury, Koff Label flooded everything in Kopiro and the surrounding areas. Bakar and I left to live far away from everything, leaving Kopiro confused and uncertain. It was as if things were waiting for us to depart.

"Bakar kept his identity hidden during all that time. He found out he was bewitched and unable to have kids. We sought help everywhere until he was cured. We now have two kids, a boy and a girl."

Fenda interrupted her. "Oh? I have another niece and nephew!"

"Yes, you do. Your brother never stopped talking about you. He blames himself for not protecting you."

"Really? I thought he didn't love me. What happened to him?"

"He is home with the family. He was the one who first heard about Maladho in the news. He told me to come because he felt like he had betrayed you."

"No, he didn't, and he couldn't have done anything. My father was to blame."

Kopironkos, excited about the announcement of their new king, gathered in Kopiro. New houses were built in just a few weeks, and the town began to thrive. Radio and other forms of communication broadcasted news about the rebirth of Kopiro, and it was both fantastic and surreal for the people who had returned home. The elders decided the king's wedding should occur in Kopiro before his coronation. They began constructing the venue, and the main shrine, Gaika-Tchurki, was decorated in the style of old times but with the spirit of a new era.

With only a few weeks remaining before the official request to N'damesse's family, preparations for the wedding were well underway. Fenda had sworn that Maladho's wedding would go down in history and be told in storybooks. Indeed, it was something extraordinary. The crowd in Kopiro was incredible. The ceremony started a week earlier, with music and a colorful landscape adorning the venue, Kopiro revived in a way no one expected. Just a few months earlier, it had been a ghost town; now, it had become a place everyone wanted to visit.

On Wednesday night, almost everyone was in Kopiro to witness the wedding of the future king of Kopironkos. Festivities took place, and they danced and enjoyed themselves until morning the next day. They were officially married on Thursday, with people screaming and cheering them on.

Maladho held N'damesse. "I am glad we did it, and I hope we will live this happy life forever."

N'damesse kissed him. "Yes, baby, I'm happy too. I wish my father were here to witness this wonderful day. I know you feel the same."

Maladho smiled and pulled her close.

Now, the coronation had to take place as soon as possible. As it happened, there were many rites and ceremonies to validate Maladho's coronation. One of the requirements was that Karamoko, as the former king and Kopironko's supreme chief, must attend. Karamoko was granted temporary freedom to attend and validate the coronation.

The new chief, Maladho N'Gayou, King of Kopironkos, dedicated the day to children like Kamboda, who were unjustly abandoned. Later, a special court was established to bring the accused to trial, among them were politicians and those in traditional power. The commission brought everyone to testify. Karamoko eventually took his own life, joining Jaigol in the world of the dead, and was buried in Kopiro.

N'damesse opened her law firm, which became famous and reliable. And she and Maladho had their first child, an adorable girl named Kamboda. They opened a center for children with disabilities, naming it The Kamboda Center, breaking the taboo and saving angels from predators.

GLOSSARY

Antula: a neighborhood in north Bissau

Baaba (Fulani/Mandinka): father, can be shortened to "Ba"

Baloba (Crioulo): shrine

Bandim: neighborhood in Bissau

Banta (Fulani/Mandinka): a place where community matters were traditionally discussed and resolved

Bissau: capital city of Guinea-Bissau

Bôdi (Fulani): serpent or snake

Boé: a settlement in the southeastern Gabu region of Guinea-Bissau

Buruntuma: a village in the Gabu region of northeastern Guinea-Bissau

Cantauda: a sacred village in the region of Bafata

Crioulo: combination of Portuguese and local African languages, it is the main language of Guinea-Bissau

Djambakus (Crioulo): healer and diviner who works with magic or is connected with spirits

Dunani: a village in the Gabu region

Éwuu (Fulani): vague expression with no true meaning, similar to a noise made in surprise or exasperation

Fambodin: the masquerade spirit believed to have special powers that protect the community, especially children during initiation ceremonies

Fenkato: mischievous spirits of low rank that play tricks on people in the villages.

Gabu: the largest city in eastern Guinea-Bissau and capital of the Gabu region

Gossi-Gerte (Fulani): peanut rice porridge

Gossordu (Fulani): chewing stick used to clean teeth

Griot: a traditional West African storyteller, historian, musician, and oral poet who plays a vital role in preserving the history, culture, and values of the community

Guyankos (Fulani): fictional tribe of thieves

Harmattan: a season in West Africa between the end of November and the middle of March, characterized by the dry and dusty northeasterly trade wind, which blows from the Sahara into the Gulf of Guinea

Jalang (Fulani/Mandinka): shrine

Jali (Mandinka): a hereditary caste of musicians, storytellers, and singers who (historically) are part of the Mande people of West Africa

Jambadong (Mandinka): feast at the start and end of Koyang with a traditional folk dance deeply linked to the entire Mandingo culture and found in several regions. It was a true display of strength among men.

Jamboo (Fulani): recipe consisting of cassava leaves, potatoes, and other vegetables mixed with peanuts and palm oil, sometimes including meat or fish

Janfaa (Fulani/Mandinka): betrayal

Jargas (Fulani): village guardians

Jatigui (Fulani): friend

Jarnakoli: a children's game

Jinni/Jinn: in Arabian and Muslim mythology, intelligent spirits of lower rank than angels who can appear in human and animal forms and possess humans

Jugudul: a village located near the source of the Mansôa River in central Guinea-Bissau.

Juju: in West African spirituality, refers to objects, amulets, or charms believed to have magical powers, which are often used in rituals and are believed to bring good luck, protection, or other supernatural benefits. The term is sometimes used to refer to the spiritual power itself.

Kamboda: benevolent deity of fertility and miracles

Kandonga: a motor vehicle in Guinea-Bissau that provides intercity collective transportation

Kankelifa: a village in the Gabu region of northeastern Guinea-Bissau

Kankurang: spirit that provides order and justice and is considered a protector against evil

Kapok tree: *Ceiba pentandra*, a giant tree in the rainforests

Kinkeliba: sacred West African plant used in tea and herbal medicine; considered to heal illnesses.

Koff Label River: fictional river in Kopiro land

Kola nut: the fruit of the kola tree (genus *Cola*), indigenous to West Africa and of high sociocultural importance to many African peoples; offered for birth, naming, and funerary ceremonies, as respect to visitors, in conflict resolution, and symbolizing reconciliation or friendship.

Kopiro: fictional village of the Kopironkos

Kopironkos: members of the fictional Kopironko tribe

Kora (Mandinka): a traditional West African stringed instrument with a long hardwood neck and twenty-one strings, made from a large calabash cut in half and covered with cow skin

Kotoo (Fulani/Mandinka): elder brother, a term used to show respect

Kurikoo (Fulani/Mandinka): a ceremony where the initiated boys go for laundry in the bush or river

Koyang: rite of passage

Lenkerin: fictional village in Sama Yerondin

Lumo: a designated day in Guinea-Bissau when local markets are set up for trading goods and services; often crucial social and economic events

Mana: formerly a province of the Kaabu Empire (1537–1867), now an area in eastern Guinea-Bissau

Mandinka: a West African people spread across parts of Guinea, Ivory Coast, Mali, Senegal, The Gambia, and Guinea-Bissau

Manicomio (Italian): mental asylum or psychiatric hospital

Mansôa: town located near the source of the Mansôa River in the Oio region of central Guinea-Bissau

N'naa (Mandinka): mother

N'Ghamanó (Mandinka): person who traditionally performs circumcisions

Nyantchos: the influential ruling classes of the former Kaabu Empire (1537–1867)

N'yu (Crioulo): sir

Our wife: a phrase to reflect the idea that marriage extends to include the entire family, commonly used by the man's family. In Africa, the concept of family encompasses not only the immediate family members but also the broader community.

Pitche: a town in the Gabu region east of Guinea-Bissau

Pukala (Fulani): pervert

Queen Kopirondin Kumo: fictional mythological warrior queen ancestor of the Kopironkos

Sama Yerondin: a province of the former Kaabu Empire (1537–1867), now an area in Guinea-Bissau

Sanaku (Sanankuya): a social term used in many West African societies, similar to English terms like cousinage, joking relationship, or joking cousins

Sumbia: traditional hat worn in Guinea-Bissau

Taba tree: native to Africa, scientifically called *Cola cordifolia* or *Mandingo cola*

Tambakoumba: *Neocarya macrophylla*, commonly called the gingerbread plum, a flowering tree native to West Africa with edible fruit

Tanaa (Fulani/Mandinka): forbidden

Tonso (Fulani): bat

Torri (Fulani): a meal similar to fufu

Toubabou (Mandinka): White people

Wolloto: a village in the Gabu region

Woy (Fulani): an expressed whimper

Woudou (Fulani): belly button

Yoo (Fulani): to express something positive

AFTERWORD

Serpent Boy is fiction. Its plot and characters are invented. However, they have been inspired by "The Ritual of Return," a practice rooted in ancient traditions and beliefs among various ethnic groups in Guinea-Bissau. Children with physical impairments are often viewed as burdens, most of the time even identified as evil spirits believed to bring harm to humans.

This "Ritual of Return" consists of the child being carried and left at the sea or river when the tide is ebbing, as the serpent is believed to return to its habitat during this time. According to tradition, they are considered human if the child remains there until sunrise. If they vanish with the tide, they are believed to be a spirit taken by the waves. Each ritual varies depending on the tribe to which the individual belongs.

While the horrific practice has long been illegal in some areas of the culture and within some small communities, it still continues. Despite being punishable by law today, these harmful practices persist. Guinea-Bissau guarantees children's rights under Title II of the Constitution of the Republic and criminalizes actions that endanger children's lives, such as infanticide under Article 110. However, there are still instances in urban and rural areas where such practices continue clandestinely.

I first learned about this issue when I was a teenager. I

remember having a neighbor with this condition, and people often said the boy was a snake or serpent. I always wondered how that could be possible! I used to hear horrifying stories about physically impaired individuals being seen as dangerous spirits, cursed, and so on. These children would suddenly disappear, unnoticed by many because the entire ordeal was kept secret within the communities.

In the late 1980s, my half-brother was born in our house. He was an adorable boy facing similar challenges. People in the village began gossiping about it. However, I knew these rumors were false because nothing unusual happened in our compound; everything seemed normal. Thankfully, my parents protected him, and he has grown healthy and thriving.

I have finally written the book that has been brewing in my mind since my early years, delayed by circumstances beyond my control. It is a work born from a deep conviction that we must illuminate ignorance wherever it lurks. I believe the essence of existence lies in extending compassion, love, and empathy to others.

Our lives should serve as positive messages, beacons of hope that inspire and uplift those around us. In my culture, there's a saying that "one hand doesn't clap." It emphasizes the need for collective effort to support those facing difficulties. I aspire to be a part of this collective, lending a helping hand to others in need.

I hope that this book will help catalyze change, rallying people to combat the heinous practice not only in Guinea-Bissau or Africa but worldwide, where individuals with physical impairments are unjustly burdened.

ACKNOWLEDGMENTS

My heartfelt thanks goes to:

My father, Aladji Samba Camara, whose courage, hard work, resilience, and compassion shaped me into the man I am today. Your legacy continues to guide and inspire me.

My mother, Mariama Queita, whose nurturing spirit and encouragement fueled my desire to learn. Although she did not have the chance to attend school, she instilled in me the value of education and the aspiration to achieve greatness. I wish she were here to witness this moment.

My stepmothers: Alarba Sila, Binta Niabaly, Duto Camara, and Taibo Camara.

My siblings and extended family members, whose support has been a constant source of strength.

My cherished children: Alfa Camara, Suely Mariama Delgado Camara, and Marlay Suleimane Balde Camara. You are my greatest joy.

My uncles and their families for their support during my schooling: Uncle Joncon Dibane in Gabu, late Uncle Thierno Baio in Bafata, and Uncle Mamadou Uri Diallo in Bissau.

My cousin, Breymen Beth, a brilliant brother, who is always there for me. Thank you for helping me with my website for this book.

My teachers, whose guidance has shaped my journey. Your belief in my potential and your sacrifices have paved the way for my achievements. This book is a testament to your impact on my life. Thank you from the depths of my heart.

Howard Grossman who gave Serpent Boy a face by designing its cover.

Kyle Marie McMahon, my editor, who did a great job polishing my manuscript.

Soncata Press, who believed that Serpent Boy was a story that must be told.

ABOUT THE AUTHOR

Suleimane Camara, driven by a fervent commitment to social justice and a keen sense of empathy, felt compelled to write Serpent Boy as a platform to challenge societal norms and shed light on the struggles of marginalized individuals. Drawing inspiration from real-world injustices, Camara's writing reflects a deep understanding of the human spirit's resilience and an unwavering dedication to fostering societal transformation through storytelling.

Milton Keynes UK
Ingram Content Group UK Ltd.
UKHW041850230924
448765UK00017B/276/J